BEFORE
the
AFTER

AN ERIN SOLOMON MYSTERY

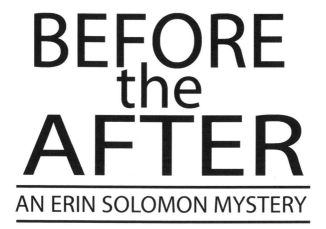

BEFORE
the
AFTER

AN ERIN SOLOMON MYSTERY

JEN BLOOD

Adian Press
Maine

Adian Press
934 River Rd. #1
Cushing, Maine 04563
www.adianpress.com

Publisher: Adian Press
Cover Design: damonza.com
Author's Photograph: Amy Wilton Photography

For Brandi
Peaceful warrior,
and sister of my dreams.

PART I
INTO THE BLACK

PROLOGUE

FOOTSTEPS.

Behind her, somewhere close, Kat hears boots pounding on the frozen ground. Sharp, icy pellets of sleet sting her cheeks as she crouches in the brush, heart thundering.

They're coming for her—there's nowhere else to hide. No way to protect herself anymore.

No way to protect any of them.

There's a ravine on the far side of the island; Kat remembers seeing it before. She runs for that, through groves of dying pine trees and over slick island trails, the ground blurring at her feet. Voices behind call to her, order her to stop, but she drives herself further. She has a bottle clutched in one hand, a knife in the other.

If she's going to die, it sure as hell won't be on their terms.

She thinks of Erin, suddenly: At Adam's funeral, her pale face blank, her hand clutched in Diggs'. Mother and daughter barely spoke that day... Like it was Kat's fault, somehow, that the Payson Church burned and Adam was weak and then, in the end, faked his own death and vanished without a word to his only daughter.

As if Kat could somehow change that reality, for either husband or child.

As if she could ever change a damn thing.

By the time she reaches the ravine, Kat can't hear anyone on the path behind her. Can't hear anything, really, beyond the pounding in her ears and the racing of her blood. The island is dark, the air cold and wet, but somehow in that mess she finds a path among rocks and the thin layer of slush now coating the ground. Head down, focused on every step, she makes it to the bottom.

And there, exactly as she'd feared, she finds them. Curled in close, silent and rotting and ended, they huddle together: Women and children she knew. A man she'd met years before.

"Kat! Come on out—you can't hide from this," the woman calls from somewhere close. "It's time to stop running."

Kat grinds her teeth and fights back fear and nausea and a marrow-deep weariness she's been denying too long.

She lays down among the others, her head down, holding tight to the bottle…

And she waits.

1

TWO MOSTLY EMPTY PLATES sat on the coffee table in my mother's house in Littlehope, Maine, set aside in favor of my laptop and a notebook filled with illegible notes. Tonight the house was unoccupied, since Kat and Maya—my mother and her girlfriend, respectively—were doing some kind of puffin-related project on an island up the coast. If puffins had been a passion of my mother's in the past, she'd never shared it with me. Now, however, she was braving a late-season snowstorm to catalogue the damn things. Which meant that for the past few days, I'd had the dubious pleasure of returning to my hometown to keep the home fires burning in Kat's absence.

Not that it was all bad, mind you.

At the moment, I was settled on the couch with Daniel Diggins, aka Diggs: rogue reporter, longtime best friend, and…well, we were working on the third thing. He sat just behind me looking over my shoulder, his breath distractingly warm on my neck. My mutt, Einstein, lay on the floor with his chin on his paws, not remotely impressed with the seating arrangement.

"This makes no sense," I said, nodding toward the computer screen. "I've done everything I can think of, and nothing's working. What idiot decided to make encryption so freaking effective?"

It had been two weeks since Diggs had nearly been barbecued in a barely averted apocalypse in western Kentucky. Since then, most of our spare time had been devoted to trying to decrypt a memory card he had literally pried from someone's cold, dead hand, just before the Smithfield College auditorium went up in flames.

So far, the whole decryption thing wasn't going that well.

Diggs rested his chin on my shoulder, his hand sliding up my side as he studied the screen.

"What did Jesse say?"

I tried to focus on the question, rather than the fact that Diggs' hand had come to rest just under my breast, his body distractingly warm behind me. With tremendous restraint, I removed said hand, set it back on his own leg, and scooted to the edge of the couch to retrieve my notes.

Jesse was a high school buddy of Diggs' who'd moved back to the area a few years before. Once just as much a degenerate as the rest of Diggs' old gang, now he was a semi-respectable family man...who happened to be a computer whiz consulting with the government on some of the most cutting-edge technologies in modern surveillance and national security.

"Honestly?" I said. "He said like three things I understood, followed by forty-five minutes when I just smiled and nodded and tried not to look like an idiot."

"I told you—you should have let me come."

"Because your manly brain would be able to sort through all that techno-babble, whereas my lesser, pea-sized woman's brain can barely handle anything more elaborate than a meatloaf recipe?"

"More or less," he agreed. He kissed my neck; I elbowed him in the stomach. "Ow. Jesus—it was a joke, woman. First off, I would never trust you with a recipe of any kind, meatloaf or otherwise. And secondly: the only reason I might have been more effective is that I would have actually taken notes."

"I took notes," I said, picking up my battered notebook as proof.

Diggs took it from me, giving up on seduction for the moment. "The only thing I can even read here is 'Hackers' in capital letters and…I'll give you the benefit of the doubt and say that's a very bad rendering of the Washington Monument."

"It's the Eiffel Tower."

"That's what they all say."

He tossed the notebook back on the coffee table. "We could just bring the card to Jesse—that would be a hell of a lot easier than explaining some hypothetical code that he never gets to see."

"Are you nuts? He's got a wife and two gorgeous kids— no way am I dragging him into this thing. We've got enough blood on our hands as it is. No. There has to be a way to do this on our own."

He sighed. "Fine. You know, if I'd realized this was why you were inviting me, I might not have been so eager to come over."

Einstein hopped up from his spot at our feet and loped into the other room, ears and tail up. Since Stein is forever chasing beasties invisible to the human eye and ear, I ignored him.

"What did you think I was inviting you over for?" I kept my eyes on the screen, very determinedly ignoring Diggs' hand as it slid up my thigh.

"I know what I was hoping for. Your mom's not home… We have the place all to ourselves. I bet if we put our heads together, we could think of some way to pass the time."

"What are we, fifteen?" I asked. "If I was planning on

seducing you, I would have chosen something a little sexier than my mother's house and my best flannel pj's."

"Works for me." He lowered his head to that spot between my neck and shoulder that tends to obliterate all reason for me.

"We're grown ups, Diggs," I said. It came out a little more Marilyn Monroe than I'd intended. I took a breath. "If we wanted a house to ourselves, we could go to yours—or my place in Portland, for that matter—anytime."

"And why haven't we done that, again?"

At the moment, that reason eluded me. Since getting back from Kentucky, Diggs and I had been in kind of a holding pattern, for very good reasons. He was still recovering from that whole nearly-being-blown-up thing, for one. Then there was the fact that I'd just broken up with someone else. And, finally, Diggs and I had made the mutual decision that we were going to venture into the treacherous world of dating slowly, with eyes wide open.

All of which was a lot easier to keep in mind during the light of day with a few miles between us, when Diggs' clever fingers weren't creeping up my inner thigh. He pulled me back toward him, his legs spread so I was cradled between them.

This time, I didn't push him away. "You should put the computer away. You work too hard," he whispered, his breath hot on my neck. His teeth scraped my earlobe before he began to work his way down.

I tried to suppress a low moan, but gave up when his hands got in on the act. He found the hem of my t-shirt, the feel of his callused palms on my cool skin ultimately my undoing. When he puts his mind to it, Diggs is one persuasive son of a bitch.

I twisted backward to meet him, my eyes sinking shut when his lips met mine. Diggs lay back, pulling me on top of him in a single, fluid move. His hands moved under my shirt, up my back, his usually bright blue eyes now dark with desire.

Diggs is a powerful man: six feet tall, a lifelong athlete who spent his youth playing hard and living fast. At forty, he's slowed down a little, but there's still something slightly dangerous about him—some reckless passion that takes my breath away, forever keeps me guessing. I felt that power, that passion, as his hands spanned my back and pulled me closer.

"You said in Kentucky that you were going to sweep me off my feet," I said breathlessly, my forehead tipped to his.

"I thought that's what I was doing." There was a trace of the devil in his smile. When I rolled my eyes, he got marginally more serious. "I'm sweeping you off your feet when we go out this weekend. Tonight, we're working."

"I'm pretty sure there's only one profession where what we're doing right now qualifies as work."

His hands shifted to my hips and he gave me a lazy, seductive grin as he arched up, hard and hot against me. My breath hitched. Rational thought faded to gray. "You're right," he said. "We should probably stop."

Friggin' tease.

"Not so fast, slick." I leaned back down and kissed him again, harder this time, my tongue moving against his before we broke apart and he pushed my shirt up over my head.

That was about the time Einstein came tearing back into the room, a growl rumbling in his throat. The growl escalated to high-pitched barking as he bolted back into the kitchen.

"Should we check that out?" Diggs asked unhappily. His mouth was already moving with definite purpose along my neck, down to my collarbone.

"Mmm," I murmured, though more in response to the

feel of his knuckles moving over the sheer fabric of my bra than in answer to his question. Einstein kept barking. I closed my eyes and pretended he didn't.

Diggs stopped working his magic. "I think we should check it out."

"That's a terrible idea," I said. I moved back, though, since there were worse things in the world than Diggs and I being interrupted before we got our groove on. We had experienced almost all those 'worse things' over the course of the past year; I wasn't taking any chances.

Diggs and I got up, his blond hair mussed and his torn jeans noticeably tighter. I wasn't feeling all that put together myself, but my annoyance gave way to anxiety the longer Stein kept up the racket.

"You have your gun?" Diggs asked.

"Just a second." I pulled my t-shirt back on, then went to an antique writer's desk against the far wall, unlocked it, and yanked the top drawer open so hard I nearly pulled it off its runners. Inside was the Ruger LCR Diggs had purchased for me, despite my protests.

When I had it loaded and in hand, Diggs nodded. "Good. Now, go on upstairs and call Chris. I'll grab Einstein and meet you there."

"I'm not calling the sheriff until I know there's actually something out there," I said. Diggs frowned. I ignored him and crept toward the kitchen, where Stein was still barking. His nails clicked on the linoleum as he paced beside a picture window looking out on my mother's backyard.

It was just past midnight on a Thursday night in April, but at the moment the only thing I could see outside was snow. Because this was Maine, and in Maine you can't actually count on spring until you're well into summer, at which point you wake up and realize you've been gypped out of the whole damn season yet again.

While the snow was annoying, however, I didn't consider it life threatening.

Einstein and Diggs weren't so easily convinced. Stein pushed past me and continued to stare outside, all fifty pounds of scruffy white fur and terrier tenacity coiled tight. He'd finally canned the barking and returned to a continual menacing growl. Diggs stood beside me at the window, his own gun in hand.

I was just about to tell him we were being idiots when a shadow moved along the perimeter outside my mother's garden shed, low to the ground and moving slowly. My heart rumbaed halfway up my throat. Einstein started barking again. I grabbed his collar and dragged him away from the window, back toward the living room.

I dimly registered the fact that Diggs had his phone out. "Get Einstein and go to the bedroom," he said again, in that this-isn't-a-debate voice he only seems driven to when I'm around.

"Only if you come with me," I said.

A garbage can clattered out back. Einstein tore away from me, headed straight back to the window. I heard glass shatter outside.

I didn't actually lose bladder control entirely, but we were on shaky ground for a few seconds.

Diggs was dialing the sheriff when the intruders finally stepped into the light and revealed themselves.

All three were fat, masked, and clearly looking for trouble.

"Diggs," I said. He was on the line with Sheriff Finnegan, so I had to repeat his name a couple of times before he came back to me. "Call him off," I said once he had. "We've got three masked bandits here, but I don't think they're armed."

He stared at me blankly, phone still in hand.

"Raccoons, Diggs," I said, feeling every inch the idiot

I knew I was. My hands were shaking—not exactly what you're hoping for from someone locked and loaded. "I'm fine. Look: It's just a trio of varmints getting into the trash."

"We should get Chris out here anyway. Just in case."

"Just in case what? The coons start rioting? Diggs—come on."

He looked out the window as though to confirm my story, and nodded before he returned to the phone. "I think we've got it under control, Chris. Sorry to wake you."

After he'd hung up, he returned to my side. "You okay?" He looked shaken, all the light and humor I'd seen earlier gone.

"It was just raccoons, Diggs," I reminded him. "I think we'll all survive."

He didn't look so sure. He double checked to make sure the back door was locked, and turned off the outside light while I got Einstein back in hand.

"I won't feel safe until everyone behind whatever you've stumbled onto in the past year is behind bars. Or better yet, wiped off the planet."

Diggs is a reporter, not a warrior—those aren't the kind of declarations he makes lightly. I took his hand and pulled him back toward the living room.

"You want to catch these guys? Then stop distracting me, and help me figure out this fucking encryption."

An hour later, the house was still. Diggs snored softly on the couch while I sat on the floor in front of the coffee table, eyes burning, and stared at the computer screen.

During our consult, Diggs' pal Jesse had steered me toward a few decryption programs created by friends of his in the business. So far, I had tried almost all of them without success. Einstein lay with his head in my lap, fuzzy belly in the air, while I continued to torture myself.

This memory card was all we had—a card that may or may not hold the key to an alleged mass suicide nearly twenty-five years ago; to the motivation and people behind the near-apocalypse in Kentucky; to a serial killer who had nearly claimed Diggs and me as victims last summer. Otherwise, I had nothing to show for the past year of work—a year that had almost killed Diggs and me multiple times over. A year when I'd learned that my father's supposed suicide the summer of 2000 was staged and he was alive… A year when my whole life, in essence, had been turned upside down.

There had to be something on this card that could explain why.

I rubbed my eyes, took a deep breath, and returned to the computer. Diggs shifted behind me, his hand settling on my shoulder.

"You should get some sleep," he mumbled. "Start fresh tomorrow."

"I just want to try one more thing. You can go on home if you want, though." Absently, I hit a couple of keys on the computer, then gave the okay for the program to run.

"I can stay," Diggs said. "I'll sleep on the couch."

"You don't need to do that."

He sat up, stretched, and began massaging the knots from my shoulders. "I know I don't. I'd feel better, though."

"So you can save me from anymore wildlife gone rogue?"

As if on cue, Einstein righted himself and sat up, ears perked. Diggs and I both ignored him when he raced to the kitchen this time.

"Maybe," Diggs said. "Or maybe—shit." His hands stilled. "Erin."

I'd been focused on the incredible things Diggs was doing to my tensed muscles, but at his tone I looked up. "What?"

"It's working."

For a split second, I wasn't sure what he meant. Then, I looked at the computer.

What had been a screen scrolling miles of meaningless symbols suddenly transformed, replaced by line after line of data—mostly alphanumeric entries, about twenty characters long. I still didn't know what they stood for, but they were at least legible.

"Do they mean anything to you?" Diggs asked, nodding toward the numbers.

I looked at the first entry: 40N85W3062210511115DM. "Not really, but it looks a hell of a lot easier to break than what we were dealing with before."

Einstein raced back into the living room, barking furiously at Diggs and me.

"Tommy's down the well again," Diggs said. "I hate to break it to you, ace, but I think your dog needs sedation. Or intensive therapy."

"He's just oversensitive since Kentucky. Can you blame him? Stein—seriously, chill. We're all right." I returned my attention to the computer screen. "What do you think this means?" I asked Diggs.

Before he could answer, my cell phone rang. It was after one a.m. The number came up as Private Caller.

Nothing good comes from calls after midnight, in my experience.

One look at Diggs told me he was thinking the same thing. Einstein gave up on rallying the troops and raced back to the kitchen.

I answered the phone. "Hello?"

"Get out of the house."

If the words themselves hadn't scared the bejeezus out of me, the voice did the trick. Fear climbed my spine and rattled my heart.

"What? Who is this?"

"You know who it is. Damn it, Erin, get out of the house. Now."

Diggs looked at me curiously. "Mitch Cameron," I mouthed to him. He was on his feet in an instant, looking just as unnerved as I felt. For more than twenty years, Mitch Cameron had shown up in all the wrong places at the worst possible times in my life. I happened to know for a fact that he was a murderer several times over… And yet, more than once, he'd been Diggs' and my saving grace.

"What's happening?" I asked Cameron.

"I don't have time to explain," he said. "But you're in danger. The evidence your mother has been holding over my people was just destroyed—there's no more leverage. Jenny is coming for you."

"Where the hell are we supposed to go?" I demanded.

"I'll contact you; just don't go to the police. That's the first place Jenny will check—and they won't slow her down, if that's where you are. Lie low until you hear from me. I need to try and find your mother before they—" There was the distinctive pop of rapid gunfire on the other end of the line.

"Cameron?"

The phone went dead. Before I could even contemplate that, I heard glass shatter on the second floor. The house alarm blared as the lights went out. Fear seized me like a fist. There was no time to hesitate—no time to think.

"We have to get out of here," I said to Diggs. "Grab the laptop and your gun; I'll get Einstein."

He didn't ask questions, just closed the computer and shoved it into my backpack. Einstein cowered beside me, all bravado long gone.

"Through the garage," Diggs shouted over the alarm. He pulled me toward the door, Stein on my heels. Less than ten seconds after we'd heard the glass break, we bolted through the side door into the attached garage, where I hoped like hell someone wasn't waiting for us to make exactly that move.

The garage was empty.

I shoved Einstein into the back of my Jetta, manhandled him into a doggy seatbelt I'd gotten for slightly less dramatic scenarios, and got in the front as I mashed my hand down on the garage door opener. Diggs jumped into the passenger's side and slammed the door.

Inside the house, there was a *whoosh* like all the air had been sucked from the building. I slammed my foot down on the accelerator without waiting for the garage door to come up all the way, bracing myself for the impact when the top of the car hit the bottom of the door. The sound of metal on metal screamed through the night. Einstein yelped, cowering behind us. I was barely clear of the garage door when an explosion rocked the house, propelling the Jetta into the street and almost into the neighbor's yard before I regained control. A second explosion followed. The windows of my mother's house blew out.

The second I was in control of the car again, I was blinded by the glare of high beams.

"Shit—Erin!" Diggs shouted.

"I see it, I see it." I put the car in gear and hit the gas, veering out of the way as a black SUV sped past, narrowly missing us. I could just make out a woman's face on the way by, her hair pulled back and pure murder in the set of her jaw. Jenny Burkett: the bitch who'd left Diggs for dead just before the final countdown in Kentucky.

"It's her," I said. "Cameron was right."

Diggs already had his phone out. "Head for the sheriff's station. We can regroup there—give them a description and let them handle this."

"Cameron said we can't go to the police," I said. "We need to hide until he calls back."

"And you're listening to him? You've had nightmares about the man since you were ten years old... Now you think it's a good idea to start taking his advice?"

"Diggs, just—please. We need to get in touch with Kat. The puffin thing is through the college up in Bar Harbor—you should be able to reach someone if you contact them."

I sped down Littlehope's main stretch. Behind us, Kat's house was now a fireball in the rearview mirror. Littlehope's volunteer fire department was already mobilizing at their station on Main Street, but I didn't dare to stop. I knew from experience that Jenny and her people—whoever those people were—didn't give a rat's ass about collateral damage. They wouldn't blink at the idea of taking out all of Littlehope at this point, if it meant they could get rid of Diggs and me.

I drove past Diggs' father's church and Kat's medical clinic, Bennett's Bar and Lobster Shanty, the turnoff to Edie Woolrich's residential home... The pavement was greasy on Route 97, the two-lane stretch of rutted, twisting road that leads from Littlehope to coastal Route 1. Diggs white-knuckled the car's Oh Shit handle while I clutched the steering wheel. He craned his neck to see behind us, looking for any sign of Jenny.

It didn't take long.

"Someone's coming up fast behind us," he said.

"Can you tell if it's her?"

"At that speed? I'm thinking it's a pretty good bet."

We were still ten miles from Route 1, with nothing to prevent Jenny from running us off the road into oblivion. I eased off the accelerator. Made the conscious decision to avoid tapping the brake.

"What are you doing?" Diggs asked.

"Just trust me," I ground out. The SUV got closer. And

closer. Ahead of us, the road dipped and curved, a barely discernible turnoff just ahead on our right.

"Erin—" Diggs warned.

I didn't listen. At the last possible second, I turned the wheel hard to the right. The car slid, losing purchase on the slick pavement. I willed myself not to panic. Jenny sped past, continuing along 97. I was too focused on recovering from the slide to see whether she turned around to come at us again.

Einstein whimpered in the backseat while I prayed silently that we could stay upright. Time froze in a haze of fast-moving trees and the terrifying, weightless feeling of a car out of control.

Somehow, miraculously, I recovered from the skid. Another endless second or two later, we were back on the road. I took a fraction of a second to get my breath and my bearings. We were on Cross Road, a series of picturesque twists and turns that's beautiful in the light of day. By night at sixty miles an hour in a snowstorm, it's not nearly as idyllic.

I pressed my foot back down on the accelerator.

"She's back again," Diggs said, a few minutes later.

"Damn it."

"You're doing great. Just keep going—we'll make it."

"Have you reached the college?" I asked. "You have to keep trying them—we have to get to Kat."

"She's on Raven's Ledge, right? Out near Mount Desert?"

I checked the rearview, noting the high beams bearing down on us. "Yeah," I agreed. "I think she said there's a boat that goes out from Bar Harbor."

"Jamie Flint's business is out there. You want me to call her?"

Jamie Flint made her living training some of the best search and rescue dogs in the country. Last summer, she and those rescue dogs were responsible for tracking down Diggs and me during our debacle with a serial killer in Northern Maine. I hesitated.

"Sol?" Diggs pressed.

"I'm thinking." Behind us, those high beams were getting closer by the second.

"This isn't like bringing a civilian in on it," he insisted. "Jamie's good. She knows what she's doing, and she's got muscle behind her. We can't do this alone—if we've learned anything in the past year, it should be that."

Up ahead as we came around a hairpin curve, blue and red lights flashed on the side of the road. I saw the glow of the SUV's brake lights in my rearview, and slowed down myself. A pickup had turned over on the shoulder along one of those picturesque twists and turns we were currently navigating, the top of the cab smashed and the wheels still spinning.

I barely waited until we were clear of the emergency crew before I hit the accelerator again.

"Go ahead," I said to Diggs, after a long few seconds of thought. "Call Jamie. See if she can get us out to that island."

"There's another call I think we should make," Diggs said.

"I'm not calling Juarez."

"We need someone on our side here, Sol."

"Not him," I said evenly. "I told you: call Jamie. I'm not calling my ex-boyfriend in the middle of the night to save our asses."

"Goddamn it, Erin—"

"No."

I knew he was frustrated, but at the moment I didn't much care. I stayed quiet, focused on the road ahead. Finally, he punched in Jamie's number. I kept driving.

I managed to get some distance from Jenny by rocketing along a series of side streets once we hit the town of Thomaston. She was back again by the time I turned onto Old County, a country road that serves as a less-traveled shortcut for locals determined to avoid Route 1 at the height of tourist season in midcoast Maine. Diggs snapped his phone shut.

"Jamie will meet us at the Bar Harbor ferry terminal," he said. "She'll have a boat and a crew."

"Just like that?"

"Just like that. She's apparently got some interests out on the island herself… If there's trouble, she wants to stop it before it gets out of hand."

I sped up along a twisting stretch of road where metal guardrails and cement walls hemmed us in. Rockland, Maine, is home to some of the deepest quarries in the world, thanks to a once-booming market for the limestone found there. The deepest of those quarries run along Old County Road— vast, watery graves where people have killed themselves and one another for decades. Diggs' brother had died in one such quarry, when they were just kids. Now, Diggs hung onto the dashboard with both hands as the guardrail loomed closer.

"Erin—"

"Just hang on," I said through clenched teeth.

We made it over the narrowest of bridges, along another stretch of open road, and then I hung another fast right with no warning. A stone wall loomed large at the corner, but I kept my head and managed to avoid it.

Behind us, Jenny wasn't so lucky. I heard a crash and the blare of a car horn. I didn't waste time celebrating.

"Nice driving," Diggs said beside me.

My stomach churned. "Thanks. This reporting thing's getting a little stale… I'm thinking NASCAR would make a nice second career."

He leaned back in his seat, exhaling slowly. "You're a natural. Just do me a favor and leave Stein and me in the stands, would you?"

To bring that point home, Einstein puked in the backseat.

I knew exactly how he felt.

On Main Street, Rockland, all the lights in town were out. The only vehicle in sight was a plow truck, yellow lights casting shadows on old brick buildings and trendy shop windows. We had lost Jenny, but I didn't plan on waiting for her to catch up to us again. Cameron still hadn't called back. Since it had sounded like high noon at the OK Corral when he hung up, I wasn't holding my breath until we heard from him again.

I took a left down a little side alley off the main drag, and stopped in a dark parking lot that stood empty except for a hulking green dumpster and a very well-used pickup truck. Einstein perked up, his tail wagging hesitantly now that we were back in familiar territory.

"I assume you have a plan," Diggs said.

We were in the employee parking lot behind the Loyal Biscuit, Einstein's favorite local hangout. I nodded toward the pickup beside the dumpster.

"That's Mel's truck," I said. "They use it for local deliveries… We can take that."

"Seriously? I don't think that's a great idea." Mel is one of the gang at the Biscuit: a pint-sized pirate who's run Diggs up and down more than once for some story or other he's reported over the years. She's cute as hell, tough as nails, and Maine to the core. Diggs is alternately turned on by her or terrified of her—though he'll only admit to the turned-on thing.

"Who would you rather face: a slightly-pissed-off

Melody, or Jenny and her psychotic syndicate?"

Diggs frowned. "Hang on—let me think about that one."

"Suck it up, Diggins. Unless you have a better idea, this is our only option."

I scrawled a mostly illegible note in my notebook promising my firstborn if we wrecked the truck, and stuck it on the dashboard of my car. Meanwhile, Diggs took Einstein for a quick pee on the nearest brush pile. Mel's key was strategically placed in one of those magnetic Hide-A-Key deals under the wheel well. I snagged that, unlocked the pickup, and transferred our stuff. Five minutes later, Diggs, Einstein, and I were crowded into the cab of the pickup. This time, Diggs was behind the wheel.

"Just remember," I said as he pulled back onto Main Street, "it's your ass on the line if you break this thing."

Diggs grimaced, but he didn't ease up on the accelerator. He headed north while I prayed to some nameless deity that Kat was still out there somewhere. Preferably alive, with all of her limbs. If we could reach her safely, I swore to the heavens that I would change my ways: clean up my language, save the planet, help little old ladies cross the street.

Whatever it took, I just needed all of us to survive this.

2

THREE ROCKY HOURS LATER, Diggs and I pulled in at the Bar Harbor-Yarmouth ferry terminal. It was just past five o'clock in the morning. The storm had let up, but it wasn't exactly a night I'd choose for island hopping. We still hadn't heard from Cameron.

Jamie was waiting inside the ferry terminal, her blonde hair pulled back and hidden beneath a purple ski cap. Jamie is one of those women who looks good no matter what: no sleep, no make-up, zombie apocalypse, whatever… She's tall and slim and vaguely southern, and if I didn't like her so much, I would definitely hate her. A German shepherd and a white pit bull lay peacefully in crates in the waiting area, while a woman with a Smurf-blue crew-cut slept stretched across three plastic chairs. Otherwise, the place was deserted, the lights low.

Jamie greeted Diggs and me with a perfunctory nod, saving a more effusive greeting for Einstein. The dog gets all the love.

"I wasn't sure how much you had a chance to pack," Jamie said. "I brought clothes if you need them."

Diggs was fine, but I'd left Littlehope in flannel pj bottoms and a Night Ranger t-shirt. I took the stack of clothes Jamie offered, then excused myself and headed for the bathroom with Einstein trotting beside me.

By the time I got back, Diggs and Jamie were deep in conversation off in the corner. Together, they were an Arian's wet dream: tall, blond, blue-eyed... I'm smaller, with red hair, green eyes, and a predisposition for pig-headedness. I'm not a leper, don't get me wrong, but there are a few things I'd change given the opportunity. Jamie, on the other hand, has no visible flaws. Diggs said something, and Jamie laughed like he was the funniest thing since Gallagher.

Einstein bumped against me impatiently, waiting for me to make a move. A lean, well-muscled teenage boy guided the shepherd and the pit bull toward the loading ramp, which of course made Stein that much more impatient.

"I know, buddy. We can make friends later."

I took one more look at Diggs and Jamie laughing it up, stuffed down the green-eyed demon rising in my chest, and strode toward them.

"Nice look," Diggs said when I reached them.

I was wearing Jamie's bright red ski pants, rolled half a dozen times since she's about a foot taller than me, and a neon green jacket. If stealth was needed on this mission, we were all in trouble. I shot Diggs a withering glare and focused on Jamie.

"Have you been able to reach anyone out on the island yet?"

"Not yet, but that's not unusual considering the weather. The team at the station did check in with the college yesterday, though. They didn't report any problems."

"Well, that's something. So, when do we leave?"

"I'll let Diggs fill you in," she said. "There are a couple of things I need to take care of."

I nodded and watched in silence as she walked away, headed straight for the teenage boy. She waited until the dogs were loaded and he was back on shore, then pulled him aside.

"What's that all about?" I asked Diggs.

"She was planning on bringing Bear out with us—I told her it might be smarter to leave him behind this time. It's one thing risking her team's life, but there's no way I want her kid out there with us."

"Smart." I did a double-take, looking at the two of them together. "Hang on; that's her son? She can't be much older than I am."

"She's not," Diggs agreed. "She had him when she was pretty young—sixteen, maybe seventeen, I think. It was quite the scandal back in the day."

"Huh. Interesting." I filed that away as something that might have relevance in the future but clearly had none now, and focused on the issue at hand. "So, what were you two talking about over here? It looked like you were getting pretty cozy."

He waggled his eyebrows at me. "Jealous?"

"You wish." I ignored the rising heat in my cheeks. "I'm just trying to make sure you're not giving away state secrets while I'm out of the room."

"Nope—no state secrets. I was just filling her in on what we can expect out there. Jamie has a couple of guys who'll be coming out with us."

He nodded toward two very well-built black men helping to load the boat. One was about 5'8", the other towering above him at well over six feet. Based on the way the taller one was standing, arms crossed over his chest, his face completely blank, I was guessing they weren't just for show.

"That's good," I said. "You think we'll need them? I mean, maybe Jenny doesn't know where Kat is yet."

"It's possible."

"But not likely."

"I don't know. I just know that right now we've got a shit storm brewing, and I'm glad to have whoever we can get on our side." He hesitated. "She's also given the Coast Guard the heads up about where we're going—" I bristled, but he held up his hand to keep me quiet until he could finish. "She didn't use your name… Just told them where she was going to be, and when, so if there's trouble they know where to find us."

I grudgingly agreed that probably wasn't the worst idea on the planet. Before I could say anything more on the subject, however, a tall, dark, well-groomed god of a man swept into the ferry terminal, jaw clenched and shoulders tense. I clamped my mouth shut and stared at him. Diggs turned, following my gaze. I didn't miss the flicker of apprehension that crossed his face.

"Shit," he said softly at sight of Jack Juarez.

"You called him?" I demanded. "After I specifically asked you not to—"

"Yes," he said, his own voice tight. "I did. Whatever reasons you have for keeping him out of this, I care more about keeping you alive. I called him early this morning. I didn't know he'd fly out here, though."

Jack Juarez is an FBI agent. He's also my ex-boyfriend, as of about two and a half weeks before, when he dumped me because he was convinced I had "feelings" for Diggs. And Diggs had "feelings" for me. And while, yes, he may have been onto something there, that was all the more reason why I didn't want him thrown into the middle of the madness all over again. Especially when I still wasn't totally clear what this madness was. I shook my head, piping mad, and left Diggs in the dust while I strode off to confront the Fed.

Juarez looked like he knew exactly what was coming when I reached him, his dark eyes reflecting a quick hint of worry before he recovered.

"I know what you're going to say…" he said.

"Oh? That's good, because I hadn't figured it out yet. What the hell are you doing here?"

Diggs reached us a second later. He and Juarez shared a quick, manly nod hello. They both looked at me like I was a bomb about to go off.

"You shouldn't have come," I said.

"I figured you'd see it that way," he said, unperturbed. "But I was concerned—especially after some of the things you told me last night," he said to Diggs. My blood pressure edged upward. Diggs gave Juarez a quick Shut-the-fuck-up-I-haven't-told-her-anything-yet look, and Juarez clamped his mouth shut.

"And what did he tell you, exactly?" I asked.

Jamie got in on the action before he could answer, giving Juarez a warm hug hello while I stood there seething.

"Can I talk to you for a minute?" I asked Diggs, turning my back on the others. Before he could refuse, I grabbed his arm and pulled him into a side room where the vending machines lived. A nautical map was tacked to the opposite wall. I stared at the coordinates and lines and symbols for a second while I tried to calm down.

"Are you going to talk?" Diggs finally prompted.

"What did you tell him?" I demanded.

"I'm not apologizing for this," he said. He wasn't that calm himself. "We need some help here—I'm done trying to do this alone. Before, our silence was Cameron's condition: If we stopped digging, if we didn't tell anyone about him or Jenny Burkett or any of the countless friggin' secrets we've uncovered in the past year, he would let us live. But Cameron said it himself last night: the leverage Kat had is gone. They blew up her house, and they nearly did it with both of us in it. They have a vested interest in seeing you dead now,

Solomon. I'm not sitting idly by to watch that happen when there are resources we could be using."

"But if Cameron finds out you gave his name to the Feds, how do you think he's going to react to that? How do you think the people he's working for will react?"

"I don't know—they can't try to kill us anymore than they already are, can they?" He lowered his voice, taking a step toward me. "Look, you need to trust me. We're in this together, and I'm doing everything in my power to make sure we come out of it the same way."

I bristled, anger, fear, and adrenaline riding over me like a razor's edge. "This is my family's life at stake, not yours, so don't tell me how I should deal with it. No one said you have to stay. It's my fight—I never asked you to go to war with me."

"Maybe you've forgotten, but I was the guy in the passenger's seat beside you when your mother's house went up in flames last night," he shot back, his voice rising. "I watched dozens of people die two weeks ago—people I knew; people I'd been trying to save, for Christ's sake. I was right there when a lunatic looped a belt around your neck last summer and slowly tried to strangle you. I've watched this thing play out for the past year from the front lines, so don't tell me this isn't my fucking fight, too."

"Right now, you have the chance to walk away," I said, refusing to back down. The references to all his near-misses in the past year thanks to me didn't help things. If anything, they just freaked me out more. Reason went out the window, replaced with cold, calculating fury. "Maybe you should take that chance. I don't have that luxury. I know Kat isn't much, but she's all I've got."

He didn't say anything for a second. I could practically see his brain working, pulling him back to some kind of reason. "She's not all you have," he said, quieter now. "The sooner you get that through your thick skull, the better off we'll all be."

He took a deep breath. When he spoke again, it was with that cool Diggins logic that has been driving me nuts since I was a teenager, way back when Diggs was my mentor at the local paper. Back when life made some semblance of sense.

"Now," he said with maddening calm, "we'll be heading out in a few minutes, so I'm going over there to talk to Juarez. You can stay here and stew, or you can come with me and find out what he knows. Your choice."

"I don't stew."

"No, actually," he agreed after a minute. Sensing weakness, he took a step closer. "You don't. Your bursts of temper are more flash-in-the-pan, everybody-take-cover rages. Ninety-eight percent of the time, it's sexy as hell."

"And the other two percent?"

He leveled an even gaze at me. "Not so sexy."

Diggs isn't an easy man to stay mad at. I bit my lip and took a step in his direction, meeting him halfway. "I do trust you," I said after a minute. "I'd just rather keep Juarez out of things right now."

"Well… tough shit. He's in it now, and he's proven more than once that he can be discreet. He has resources and he has firepower. I'm not apologizing for this. If it means the difference between you surviving or getting killed, I'm okay with pulling your superhero ex-boyfriend into the mix."

I narrowed my eyes at him. "That's very evolved of you."

"Well, you know me." He pulled me to him. I resisted, but not that much. When we were toe to toe, he locked his hands at the small of my back to keep me close. "I'm an evolved kind of guy."

"You once punched a man because he said he liked my t-shirt. You're one of the least evolved men I know."

"I'm a work in progress." He leaned down and kissed me lightly. "Also? You were seventeen when I punched that idiot…and it wasn't because he said he liked your shirt."

Jamie cleared her throat from the doorway. "If you two have pulled it together, we're boarding. Unless you have more surprise guests on the roster."

"No," Diggs said. "I think this should do it."

We went back to the waiting area to find Juarez leaning against the wall, arms crossed over his chest. For the first time, I noticed the shadows under his eyes. Juarez is just this side of superhuman; he almost never shows those pesky frailties the rest of us are burdened with. The fact that all of this was wearing on him, too, was ultimately what got to me.

"Sorry I went a little nuts back there," I said.

"A little?" he said, straightening.

"She's queen of the understatement, our Solomon," Diggs said.

"Screw you both. I'm apologizing, all right? I know you're trying to help—I just didn't expect you."

"No problem," Juarez said after a second or two, still keeping his distance. "I know it's been a rough night. I'm sorry I caught you by surprise."

"You know, I won't spontaneously combust if you two want to hug it out," Diggs said.

I shot him a wilting glare, which he happily ignored. Juarez pulled me into his arms for a quick, utterly awkward hug before he pulled back.

"Happy now?" I asked Diggs.

"Ecstatic." He clapped Juarez on the back. We may have been uncomfortable, but Diggs didn't seem bothered in the least. "Now, what the hell are you doing here?"

"There are some things I want to go over with you," Juarez said. "I didn't want to do it over the phone."

"Such as?" I asked.

"We'll talk on the boat," he said.

"Good plan," Jamie interjected. "It'll take a good hour to an hour and a half to get out there. You'll have plenty of time on the high seas to catch up."

Juarez didn't look thrilled at the thought. I wasn't dancing on the rooftops over it myself.

●

At six o'clock that morning, we boarded the Hurricane—a big old commuter boat with more power than a ferry and considerably less seating. It had a kickass GPS, a dead fish smell, and no crew to speak of—apart from Jamie's blue-haired pal, who was piloting the thing. Diggs, Juarez, and I took a paint-chipped bench off to the side, Einstein winding his leash around my legs like a friggin' sea serpent.

Monty and Carl—Jamie's security detail—sat across from us. According to Jamie, they were both former military, now inexplicably doing private security in the backwoods of Maine. They weren't the kind of guys eager to answer a lot of questions, but my keen reporter's nose told me there was one hell of a story there. Common sense convinced me now wasn't the time to pursue it.

As soon as the boat took off, Diggs indicated the hatch leading below deck with a nod. "This might be a good time to get up to speed?"

Juarez nodded, following us down the stairs to a narrow cabin with two bunks and a worn wooden chest. Diggs and I parked on one of the bunks; Juarez chose the chest. With the hatch closed and the roar of the diesel engine to ensure no one would overhear, Juarez dove in.

"Do you have any idea why Jenny Burkett would be in

Maine right now?"

I shot what I hoped was an appropriately withering glare at Diggs, not sure how much he had told Juarez the night before. Based on his reaction, I was guessing he hadn't mentioned Jenny.

"How do you know about that?" he asked.

Juarez pulled his phone from his jacket pocket and scrolled through several photos until he found what he was looking for. "Does she look familiar?" he asked.

It wasn't a flattering picture—grainy and black and white, clearly a screen capture from a traffic cam. Jenny Burkett smiled into the lens like she knew perfectly well she'd been caught on film.

"Where did you get that?" I asked.

"After everything in Kentucky, I've been keeping tabs on her," Juarez said. "It hasn't been easy, but yesterday she showed up on a couple of traffic cameras in Portland. When Diggs called, it set off some alarms."

"So you decided to come to Maine in the middle of the night to tell us?" I pressed.

He hesitated. For the first time, I got the sense that he wasn't telling us the whole story. "I have some connections," he said. "I was worried, which meant I wasn't above using those connections to book a flight so I could get to you quickly."

I could tell Diggs wasn't satisfied with that answer. Neither was I. Juarez plowed ahead before either of us could ask any follow-ups, though.

"Listen," he began seriously, "the Bureau has been… monitoring you, a little. You made some purchases recently; used some websites—"

"I'm sorry—*what*?" I demanded. Any semblance of calm I might have been feeling vanished in an instant. "How the hell do you know what purchases I've made or what websites

I've visited?"

"Calm down," he said evenly, his gaze never wavering from mine. Diggs stayed quiet, but I could feel the sudden tension radiating from him. Neither of us are big fans of the Patriot Act. "I told you: the Bureau has been monitoring you. You downloaded nine sophisticated decryption programs in the past week. You also spent some time with an NSA consultant named Jesse—"

"Stop," I said. My voice shook. "What the hell do you want? What's going on, Jack?"

"If you are working on something—Some kind of memory card or computer chip or... some piece of information that has to do with Mitch Cameron, your father, or J. Enterprises, then I need to know that."

It took a few seconds before I answered, the quiver in my voice replaced with overt anger. "There was a memory card Diggs got from one of the victims in the university explosion in Kentucky," I said. "The card was encrypted. I've been trying to break that encryption."

"And where is that card now?" Juarez asked, intractable. "Have you gotten anything from it?"

"No," I lied. "And it was destroyed in the explosion. We don't have anything now." I didn't look at either of the guys, focused instead on the floorboards. As liars go, I may not be the best on the planet. "The card was with everything else when the house went up in flames. We couldn't save it."

He studied me for a second before turning his attention to Diggs. "That's true? You gave the memory card to Erin, and now it's gone? You have no copies."

When I didn't intervene, Diggs nodded. "Yeah, it's true," he agreed smoothly. Diggs has it all over me in the lying department. "I gave the card to her. We didn't think it would be safe to try and copy it."

Juarez didn't say anything, but I knew he didn't believe

us. It hurt to see the betrayal in his eyes, but there was something under that—a hint of determination, maybe even anger, that made me think Diggs and I weren't the only ones holding back. He scrubbed his hand along his jaw, looking frustrated as hell—not a look I associate with Jack Juarez, usually the most Zen man on the block.

"So, we know… what, exactly?" he asked me. "Your father's sister was raped and murdered in 1970, and from there he went underground. Before that, he was apparently childhood friends with this Mitch Cameron, who went on to join U.S. Army Special Forces and was reported dead in 1975 in Saigon. Then, your father reappears in…" he looked at me expectantly.

"1978," I supplied.

"Right," he said. "Your father reappears as Adam Solomon in 1978, when he joins the Payson Church of Tomorrow. And then, in 1990, you say you saw Cameron on Payson Isle the day the church burned to the ground."

I nodded. "That's it in a nutshell. Ten years later, Dad faked his own death and vanished again."

"But we know now that Adam Solomon is still alive," Diggs said. "And both he and Kat have something—some piece of information—over these people, which up to this point has been keeping Erin alive."

"But Kat's always refused to tell me what that something is," I said. "Believe me, I've tried to get her to talk."

"All the same, based on the explosion at your place tonight, I'd say no one's killing themselves to keep you breathing anymore," Diggs said. "So, here's what I've come to in all this: We know what Adam Solomon was doing until 1970. We know what he was doing—for the most part—after 1978. If we can figure out what happened in those eight years in between, I'm willing to bet that will go a long way toward unraveling this whole mess."

"Have you made any progress on that so far?" Juarez asked.

"Dad covered his tracks well," I admitted. "So far, we haven't had much luck."

"I'll get on it—see what I can find," Juarez said.

"You need to be careful," I said. "Cameron's been clear from the start: we're not supposed to look into this. Anyone who has so far—with the exception of Diggs and me—has turned up dead."

"I'll be discreet," Juarez agreed. "You just focus on staying alive. When we get out to the island, maybe I can get some information from Kat."

"Yeah. Good luck with that," I said.

"And you're sure you have no idea what was on that memory card," he said. "And you have no copies."

"Positive," I agreed. This time, I looked him in the eye. Maybe I was better at this lying thing than I'd thought.

By this time, we were forty-five minutes into the trek, far out to sea. The bad weather and the fact that we were below deck meant we felt every swell, every rock and roll. Diggs has spent the better part of his life in shitty boats on shittier seas in the quest for the perfect wave, and I might as well have been born with fins, but Juarez wasn't looking so good. Once we'd finished our briefing, he excused himself and went up for some fresh air. I stayed with Diggs, staring after the Fed.

"What the hell was that about?" I demanded when he was gone. "They've been monitoring my purchases? Checking the websites I'm looking at? What are we onto here?"

"He's lying about just deciding to come out here on his own, too," Diggs noted. I noticed that he didn't seem quite so keen on his buddy Juarez now that we knew what he'd been up to since we had seen him last. "There's no way he arranged a trip like this without his boss knowing. Ten to one, they're the ones who sent him."

"So, we're agreed we say nothing about having the memory card. I don't know what's going on, but right now I don't trust him—or anyone—with that information."

"Agreed," Diggs said.

"Which means we need to keep a close eye on this." I pulled my laptop from the backpack we'd been dragging with us since Littlehope and powered it up. We argued briefly about the wisdom of using it with Juarez just above deck, but I could tell that Diggs' heart wasn't in it. It was clear that he wanted to know what the hell was going on just as much as I did.

I opened the decrypted document I'd saved the night before. Two neat columns of alphanumeric entries filled the screen. Now that we had a few minutes of down time, I made more of an effort to decipher what I was seeing, focusing on the first entry in the list: 40N85W 3062210511115DM. Going down the line, every number began with the same format: two numbers followed by a letter—usually N—and another two digits followed by either W or E. I paused close to the bottom of the first column.

"Do you have a map?" I asked.

"Not in my back pocket, no."

"The first numbers on here—these are coordinates." My blood was humming now, something slowly clicking into place. Once I realized what that something was, I couldn't decide whether it was good or bad. "This number, here," I said, stabbing an entry halfway down the page with my index finger. "These are the coordinates for the island we're headed out to."

"Wait…" Diggs shook his head in confusion. "What? How do you know that?"

"There was a nautical chart back at the ferry terminal.

The coordinates of the island were up in the corner—these are the coordinates: 44 North, 68 West. 44N68W. Diggs, why the hell would the coordinates for an island where my mother is counting exotic birds for no earthly reason anyone can think of, be on an encrypted memory card you took from a dead guy in Kentucky?"

"Are you sure those are the same coordinates?"

"Positive. I don't have a clue what the rest of the numbers mean, but these are definitely locations. And one of them is the island we're headed for now."

Diggs looked as unsettled as I felt. "We should print these out when we get to the island. I don't know how safe it is having the file on the laptop at this point."

"Especially if Uncle Sam is monitoring my activity." I continued staring at the numbers. Eventually, they began to swim in front of my eyes. I stifled a yawn. "We need to figure out where the rest of the coordinates are. I don't suppose they have Wifi on this boat."

"I think that's a safe assumption, yeah." When I yawned again, he took the laptop from me, powered it down, and snapped it shut before I'd even managed a worthy protest.

"What are you doing?"

"Saving you from yourself. Or saving *us* from yourself. We have at least an hour before we hit the island... Plenty of time for a power nap."

"I'm all right—we should be using this time to go over those numbers. What do you think they mean?"

"Solomon—"

"I'm not tired."

"Give me a break, would you? I'm exhausted. Just humor me." He stowed the laptop in my bag, lay down on the bunk, and pulled me down with him. If he wasn't such a comfortable pillow, I would have put up more of a fight. Instead, I settled in with my head on his shoulder, my hand resting on his stomach.

"How many entries would you say are on there?" I asked.

"I don't know. Sixty, maybe seventy."

"And they all start with coordinates, followed by a series of maybe fifteen numbers and two letters. What do you think the numbers mean?"

"I don't know."

"Maybe they're a code," I mused. "Substitute the numbers for letters, or… pass codes, maybe. There could be safes in each of those locations, and the numbers are the combination or… something."

He turned onto his side to face me. "Close your eyes."

I didn't. Instead, I gnawed on my lower lip and considered our future, for the first time surrendering to the possibility that things might be slightly out of control. The thought sent a surge of fear through me. "Do you think they've already gotten to Kat and Maya?"

Diggs looked at me seriously, pushing the hair back from my forehead. "I don't know," he said. I was grateful he didn't hand me some bullshit line about everything being all right. We both knew by then that things don't always go that way. "The fact that Jenny was on the mainland when Cameron called, though… If he was still looking for your mom, then maybe Jenny was, too."

"What do you think Juarez is hiding?"

"Erin," he said. He touched his lips to mine. "For the love of god, just close your eyes."

This time, I did. A few seconds of silence passed before I spoke again.

"Thank you," I said.

"Don't mention it, ace. It's what I'm here for."

I ran my hand along his side, cuddling in a little bit closer. For a guy who hadn't slept or bathed and had nearly been blown up just a few hours ago, he smelled surprisingly good. When I nipped his neck, I could feel his heart speed up.

"You're supposed to be sleeping," he said.

"I told you: I'm not tired."

"Well, you should be."

I kissed along his jaw line, up toward his ear, remembering things I thought I'd forgotten about him in the years since we'd done this last: the taste of his skin, the feel of his body; the things he whispered and the way he whispered them. I nipped his earlobe and he growled, low in his throat, before he wrapped his hand around the back of my neck and pulled me to him. The kiss was hard, just this side of rough, his lips moving over mine with an urgency that left me breathless. When he moved back, my heart was pounding and his eyes were dark.

"Go to sleep," he said, a little breathless himself.

I raised my eyebrows at him and propped myself up on my elbow. "You want me to sleep after that kiss? Are you nuts?"

"Probably," he muttered. He pulled me back down and wrapped his arms around me. "But I'm not fooling around with you in the belly of a boat while your mother's missing and your armed ex-boyfriend is just above us. A man has to draw the line somewhere."

"Fine." Despite everything, I felt the tiniest knife edge of fatigue cut through the adrenaline that had been fueling me for hours. I closed my eyes when his hand fell to the back of my head, stroking my hair. "I'll try to sleep, for your sake."

"That's what I love about you, ace. That generous spirit."

He pressed a kiss to my temple. Against all odds, I slept.

An hour later, we docked at a small landing on Raven's Ledge. The island wasn't any different from any other Maine island I'd visited over the years, as far as I could tell:

evergreens, granite, and a whole lot of water. My nap had left me blurry and dazed and not especially refreshed by the time we docked at eight a.m. The cold weather and spitting snow didn't help matters any.

Once we'd gotten the dogs and the crew off the boat and onto solid ground, Jamie led us up a narrow, snow-covered path into the woods. The trees closed in around us. I kept Einstein on leash, but he wasn't exactly chomping at the bit to get away from me. The past year had left both of us more than a little gun shy.

I tried to focus on the path ahead of me instead of the months behind, and kept walking.

The Raven's Ledge research station was a two-story log cabin perched on the edge of a granite cliff. Solar panels lined the roof, with a shaky-looking crow's nest at the top of the building. By the time we got there, about half an hour after docking, the snow was lighter and the sun was making an honest effort to push through the clouds.

Jamie slowed down at the top of the path and waited for us to catch up. There was a picnic table in front of the station, with an empty bottle of root beer and a half-filled ashtray on it. When we were all together again, about twenty yards from the front door, Jamie stopped.

"Since we haven't been able to raise anyone on the radio yet, we'll go in first," she said, indicating Juarez, Monty, and Carl. "Cheyenne will stay with you two. Nobody wander off, and don't move until you get the all-clear from us."

I didn't argue. Cheyenne—the blue-haired boat captain—and her pit bull, Casper, joined us as Juarez went to the door. He went in first, Jamie and her dog on his heels while Monty and Carl brought up the rear. The door slammed behind them. I stared after them, wishing for x-ray vision or psychic powers or anything that might speed up the agony of waiting to find out what the hell was going on behind that door.

For a few tense minutes, no one said anything. Cheyenne managed what I assumed was supposed to be a reassuring smile, but mostly she looked as freaked out as Diggs and me. She was younger than I'd thought when I first met her— early- to mid-twenties, maybe 5'6", with a body built for power, not grace. She focused on Casper and Einstein, clearly more comfortable with them than her human companions.

When Jamie reappeared about ten minutes later, I couldn't hold back a sigh of relief.

"You can come on in," she called. "It's clear."

Clear, and empty.

The research station wasn't so different from your average, run-of-the-mill hunting lodge, but instead of deer heads and stuffed fish, the walls were decorated with nautical charts and drawings of island birds. It opened on a spacious Great Room with cathedral ceiling and fireplace, a breakfast bar separating it from the kitchen. A stairwell just off the kitchen led to the second floor, a loft and another fireplace visible from the Great Room.

"It's a nice set-up," Diggs said.

"The Nature Conservancy paid for renovations to the Melquist place," Cheyenne said. "Which is how we convinced the family to let us build here. We set the family up with a windmill to help power things… It's been a very friendly, mutually beneficial set up."

"Cheyenne's been volunteering with the project from the beginning," Jamie said. "Trying to butter the family up in the hopes that they'll let us move the business out here."

"The dog business," I said, surprised. "You think they'd go for something like that?"

"Probably not," Jamie said. "But our lease is up in a few months, and the owner's being a dick about negotiations on a new contract. I'd like to just go… A place like this would be ideal. No issues with zoning or noise, no worry about the dogs getting loose and eating the neighbors."

"Do they usually get loose and eat the neighbors?" Juarez asked. He sounded worried.

"Only on full moons," she assured him. I liked the little spark of mischief in her eye—and more, the fact that Juarez looked like he wasn't sure if she was kidding.

"Is it unusual that no one's here right now?" Diggs interrupted, pulling us back to the point.

The look on Cheyenne's face was all I needed to know that it was beyond unusual. Someone should have been there to meet us at the door; hell, someone should have been waiting at the dock for us. Rather than saying that, though, she shrugged.

"Hard to tell. They might be out checking one of the nests or doing some observation on the north shore."

No one said anything to that, but I clenched and unclenched my fists and gnawed at my bottom lip, trying to calm myself. There had been some deep, stupidly optimistic part of me that had been hoping we'd find Kat and Maya here at the station, Kat blissfully ignoring my phone calls while the two of them took pictures of puffins and chased seagulls. The fact that the place was deserted was feeding demons I'd been trying like hell to keep at bay since this whole thing started.

Cheyenne continued with a grand tour of the station, leading us upstairs. At the top of the stairs, there was a closed door to our left and a full bath directly in front of us. Farther down the hall on the right were the loft and two more closed doors. Cheyenne stopped at the farthest one, labeled STAFF ONLY in giant gold letters.

"This is where the magic happens," she said as she opened the door.

I stopped at the threshold to take it in. It was a bigger

room than I'd expected, with one wall comprised of floor to ceiling windows that looked out on the ocean below. A set of rickety spiral stairs led up to the crow's nest I'd seen when we first arrived. Shelves lining the wall were filled with island specimens: crabs and urchins, flowers and herbs, stones and soil.

Otherwise, though, there was no sign of a living soul.

After the lab, Cheyenne let us check out the other rooms: two bedrooms on the second floor, and a larger bedroom below with a private bath and two sets of bunk beds.

"Bedrooms on the second floor are for staff," she explained when we were on the ground level again. "But when we have volunteers or research groups around, they stay here."

Which meant this was where Kat and Maya were staying. The room was efficient but impersonal, decorated only with framed photos of the research station during the building stages. All the bunks were made, the blankets smooth enough to bounce a quarter on.

Except for one.

A backpack lay open beside the bottom bunk closest to the door. The blankets were thrown back. A pair of gold earrings lay on the night table beside an empty glass and a half-empty bottle of Jack Daniels.

I saw Diggs watching me, but looked away quickly while I reminded myself to keep breathing. I knelt and pawed through the pack, my heart beating harder. It sped up that much more when I found a soiled lab coat with *Dr. Katherine Everett* stitched in the upper right corner. Half a dozen little bottles of booze, some open and some not, lay at the bottom of the bag.

I put everything back, folding Kat's lab coat carefully, and then made the bed. My hands were shaking.

Kat was a heavy drinker back in the day—and not in a

life-of-the-party kind of way. She was a mean, messy drunk, and more often than not I paid through the nose for it. As far as I knew, though, my mother had been sober for over a decade.

If she'd fallen off the wagon, she'd fallen hard. Kat doesn't do anything halfway.

By the time I'd finished compulsively straightening Kat's bunk, I'd pulled myself together. I turned around and looked at Jamie, ignoring Diggs for the moment. "We should start looking for them."

Jamie shot Diggs a *What now?* look, clearly not thrilled with our findings.

"If Kat and the students aren't here, what's next?" I pressed.

"I'd like to go talk to the Melquists, actually," Jamie said.

I thought of the coordinates we'd found on our magic memory card of indecipherable numbers. This island was part of those numbers… And the Melquists were at the heart of this island.

"What can you tell me about them?" I asked.

She looked surprised. "The Melquists? Nothing, really… They're pretty harmless, as far as I know. Jonas Melquist—the father—is the only one I've really dealt with. You can ask Cheyenne… I think she's talked to them more. They're very religious. Not crazy about technology, but nice enough. It's a large family, about half a dozen kids, but they keep to themselves for the most part. Not a lot of interaction with the outside world."

"How far are they from here?" Diggs asked.

"Other side of the island," Jamie said. "It's a half-hour, forty-five minute walk at the most. I'll just take the guys with me, and we'll have a quick chat with Jonas. You two can wait here until we have a better idea what's going on."

"Listen, I'd really like to tag along," I said. "I don't want to sit on my hands here. I can't. I'll stay outside while you talk to them. I won't get in the way, I promise."

Jamie looked skeptical, at best.

"We won't interfere with whatever you need to do," Diggs said. "But if you do find Kat, it might be good to have us along. She can be... difficult, sometimes. Erin can keep her calm."

He was seriously overselling any influence I might have on my mother, but I appreciated the effort. I could tell by the way Jamie tilted her head, eyes narrowed, that she knew damned well that she was being manipulated. She had the grace to let it slide. Or maybe she was just too tired to care.

"I need your word that you won't interfere while I figure out what's going on," she said.

"You have it," I said. "It's not a problem. I—" I stopped, glancing at Diggs. "We'll wait for you to call the shots."

"All right, then. We'll meet out front in ten."

I nodded, and Jamie left us alone. As soon as she was gone, I turned my back on Diggs and started pilfering through Kat's stuff again.

"We'll find her," Diggs said. "She'll be all right."

I sat on the edge of the bunk, nodding. Diggs sat down beside me, a few inches away. Just like that, I felt things shift between us—like the Grand Canyon had sprung up in the course of half an hour. I tried to think of something to say, but all I could focus on was that backpack of booze at my feet and the thought that Kat and Maya were out there somewhere. Jenny was after them. Their house had burned to ashes on my watch, and my gut was telling me that we hadn't hit bottom yet.

Shit was happening, and it was happening fast.

"We should get going," I said finally. "I don't want to make Jamie wait."

I got up and headed for the door. Diggs didn't try to give

me a pep talk; he didn't wait for me to spill my guts or tell him all the ways I was freaking out. Instead, he slipped his hand into mine as I was heading out the door, and squeezed my fingers a little too hard. I looked back at him. He gave me one of those knockout smiles he does so well, shy and earnest and slightly dazzling.

"We'll get through this," he said. I nodded, trying to keep a handle on things.

"I know," I said.

He settled his hand at the small of my back as we walked out, and I hoped like hell that we found Kat intact and reasonably coherent so we could get off this rock and back on solid ground.

3

APRIL MEANS MUD IN MAINE. Unless you're on an island, of course—in which case, April means mud and ice. And snow, apparently. And a bone-deep, damp chill that's impossible to shake.

Or maybe that's just me.

Raven's Ledge was no different, with the exception of the creepy log cabin research station and the fact that my mother had apparently fallen off the wagon here after a decade of sobriety.

Diggs and I trudged after Jamie and her crew along a path through dark, damp woods, Einstein by my side. Diggs was quiet. I was, too—busy fighting with Kat in my head, over everything from J. Enterprises to Mitch Cameron to why the hell she'd flushed her ten years' sober chip down the toilet in favor of her old buddy Jack Daniels.

The arguments fizzled once we reached the Melquist house, partly because it turned out I couldn't even win a fight with Kat when it was only in my head; partly because the Melquist house was, in a word, terrifying.

That's primarily because whoever had purchased Raven's Ledge way back when had apparently made it his personal mission to build the creepiest house humanly possible. Think Scooby Doo meets Bela Lugosi: A three-story, Victorian monolith complete with circular towers and shuttered windows, looking out over a stark granite cliff high above the ocean. My skin was already crawling, and we hadn't even set foot inside.

True to my word, I stood back while Jamie and Juarez approached the front door. Diggs stood beside me. We hadn't touched since we'd left the station. I knew that was my fault, but at the moment I couldn't seem to do anything about it. The bottles of booze in Kat's bag, combined with the solitude and isolation of this place and the fact that Kat's house was now ashes…

I wasn't feeling that huggable, just then.

Though it killed me to admit it, I felt the absence of Diggs' steadying hand a lot more deeply than I cared to admit.

Since I'm useless when it comes to mysteries of the human heart, I chose to focus on our surroundings instead. Quiet, creepy, and colder than a witch's intimate bits pretty much summed it up. No one answered when Juarez knocked on the door, and there didn't seem to be anyone around. Phantom, Jamie's German shepherd, whined unhappily. Einstein echoed the sentiment. I didn't whimper personally, but it was certainly implied.

"Maybe we should go in," I suggested.

"Not without probable cause we shouldn't," Jamie said. "These people value their privacy. I won't violate that without reason."

"The students at the research station are gone," I argued. "Vanished without a trace. My mother is gone. Maya is gone. And we know for a fact that someone is after Kat, because they blew up her house last night. With me in it, incidentally. And it all seems to lead to this island… Which is owned by these people. Who, it seems, have also vanished. How is that not probable cause?"

She looked at Juarez. It hit me just then that she'd been doing that a lot since he'd arrived—deferring to the G-man, when I doubted there were many people in the world that Jamie Flint ever deferred to. I waited for a twinge of petty jealousy to needle at me, and was relieved to find none. If any woman looked twice at Diggs, I was ready to throw them to wolves; someone new liked Juarez, and I was ready to throw him a party.

The Fed thought things over for a few seconds before he went forward himself, one hand on the gun at his side, and knocked again.

Still no answer.

The door wasn't locked when Juarez tried the knob.

"Wait out here," he said to the rest of us. "Give us a minute."

He and Jamie went in with Phantom, leaving everyone else to sweat it out on the front lawn. I waited for screams or gunshots, bracing myself for something to blow up again. Nothing happened. When Juarez and Jamie reappeared a few minutes later, though, they didn't look happy about what they'd found.

"What's in there?" I asked, taking the two steps up to the porch in a single bound.

"There's no sign of anyone," Jamie said.

"I'd like to check it out," I said. She looked at me doubtfully, but I didn't back down. Something about this house spoke to me, calling back a childhood that seemed more mystery than memory these days. I couldn't shake the feeling that there was something in there I needed to see.

We went around in circles for a while before Jamie finally came around, thanks in no small part to Juarez pleading my case. Juarez was fast proving to be the best ex-boyfriend ever.

Inside, the house was exactly as you'd expect a creepy old Victorian mansion to be: antique furnishings, dark drapes, weird religious paintings. Diggs and I walked the corridor together while Jamie and Juarez Holmes-and-Watson'd it up on their own. Diggs glanced at a stairwell with a mahogany banister, then at me, eyebrows raised. I nodded. He went up first, Einstein and me close behind.

There were five bedrooms lining the hall on the second floor, all with at least a couple of twin beds. The wallpaper was old but well-maintained, as was the antique furniture. Each bed was neatly made. Jesus pictures hung on the walls, along with several framed Bible verses embroidered in deep red thread.

It was the most powerful déjà vu I'd ever experienced, being in that place. The architecture may have been different, and maybe there were a few cosmetic variations, but other than that I may as well have been standing in the Payson boarding home. I stopped in the doorway to the last bedroom on the left and stared at a set of bunk beds. Girls' names—Jeanine and Nancy—were written on faded construction paper at the foot of each bed.

Jeanine had the top bunk. The letters were precise, printed with desperate care; Nancy's name was written in an impatient scrawl I could barely read.

You're not supposed to go outside the lines. Isaac won't put it up if you scribble.

I almost turned at the words, as though they'd come from somewhere other than inside my own head. A child's voice, all but forgotten, floated back to me. Along with it came an image, as clear as if she was standing in front of me: Allie Tate. My best friend, as a kid growing up on Payson Isle.

Don't make him angry or he won't let us live in the house anymore. He'll send us away to the woods. It's not safe there.

He wouldn't do that, I remembered myself insisting. *Isaac won't hurt us.*

I tried to stay with the memory, tried to remember what Allie's reaction to my words had been. Had she agreed? And why would Isaac send us to the woods, anyway? The thought made my chest tighten and something stick in my throat. Allie was pale and thin, with brown hair and thick glasses. She had walked with a limp. I tried to remember what had happened to her, but found myself coming up blank.

Had I ever known?

"Well, there's nothing any more or any less creepy in the other rooms," Diggs said as he came into the bedroom, startling me out of my reverie. "You find anything in here?"

I pushed past the memory of Allie Tate and shook my head. "No. Let's get out of here."

I started to follow him to the door when something hanging on a hook beside the bottom bunk caught my eye. Half-hidden by pillows, I'd missed it before. When I pushed the pillows aside, my mouth went dry.

"Sol? You coming?" Diggs asked from the door.

I wet my lips. Shook my head. My hand floated an inch above a marionette hanging beside the girls' bunks. It was an angel, its white gown dirty and the china-blue eyes faded. The wings were made of real feathers, half of them gone and the rest dingy and ragged.

"Sol?"

I took a step back and nodded to the doll. "What does that look like to you?"

His eyes widened. "One of those creepy-ass marionettes Isaac Payson used to make, to give to the kids in his church?"

"That's my guess," I agreed. My voice was shaky. My knees weren't holding up that well, either. "I mean… I don't know what else it could be."

"You think it actually came from Isaac Payson?"

"I don't know. It's possible, I guess—it's definitely not new."

"Maybe it's a replica." He came over and stood beside me, both of us gazing at the doll like it was about to come to life and steal our souls. Which, honestly, wouldn't have been that surprising. If there was ever a time for it, this was it.

"Why would anyone make a replica of something like that?" I asked.

"We're talking about an entire extended family that's holed themselves up on a remote island and vanished without a trace. Whys and wherefores aren't exactly in abundance," he said.

"Fair point."

"Either way, I'm sure there's a rational explanation."

He was right; there was no reason to freak out. Just because this house felt exactly like a boarding home where thirty-four members of a fundamentalist church were murdered in cold blood didn't mean there was any real connection. For one thing, this wasn't a church—this was a family.

And Isaac Payson, the leader of the Payson Church, had been dead for over twenty years, burned to death along with the rest of his congregation. There were any number of ways that this girl, this Nancy, could have gotten her hands on a doll that looked exactly like the ones given only to children born into the Payson Church… and none of them involved Isaac rising from the grave and handing the doll to her.

"Okay, so what's next?" Diggs asked. He took the marionette from me and hung it back where it belonged. "Kat obviously isn't hiding under the beds here, right? I heard Jamie say she'll try to get the Coast Guard over here now. Clearly, something isn't right."

"Cameron didn't want us to bring the police into this," I said automatically.

"I don't give a rat's ass what Cameron wanted. We're not equipped to handle this… Not alone. Besides, it's Jamie's call."

"Yeah—I know," I said. The place was getting to me, Diggs' voice suddenly hard to make out above the rushing in my own ears. I shook my head, trying to clear it. "You're right. I don't like this… It's probably a good idea to get someone out here."

When he didn't say anything, I looked up. He was studying me, concern clear in his eyes.

"What?" I asked.

"You're agreeing with me. Are you feeling okay?"

"I'm fine."

"You don't look fine—you look like you've just seen a ghost. And not the friendly kind. We'll figure this out, Sol. Everything will be all right."

He didn't look like he believed that anymore than I did, but I appreciated the effort.

Downstairs, a door slammed. I heard footsteps in the hall below us, s and the distant sound of conversation.

"Can you come here a second?" Jamie called up from below. Her voice sounded strained, a pitch higher than usual.

I exchanged a silent look with Diggs. "Now what?" he asked me. Since I didn't have a clue, I didn't answer. He followed me out of the bedroom, down the hall, and back down the stairs.

"Where are you?" Diggs called at the bottom.

"Kitchen," Jamie answered.

We followed her voice down the hallway, to a bright room with custom-made kitchen cabinets and polished countertops. Like the rest of the place, there was no sign of any member of the household.

No sign, that is, but a piece of paper sitting on the table, weighed down at the center by a smooth, rounded stone.

Jamie looked shaken. Juarez was beside her; he didn't look any better.

Our time has come, the note began, in a flowing, precise script.

"What is this?" Diggs asked.

"A suicide note, we think," Jamie said. "It goes on for the whole page. It doesn't say anything about where they might be, though."

Juarez rubbed his hand over his forehead, looking dark and grim. I thought of the Payson Church, Reverend Barnel and his followers in Justice, Kentucky... And now this entire family, with a note that, as far as I could tell, didn't make an ounce of sense.

"What do we do now?" I asked.

"Seal the place off," Juarez said immediately. "This is a crime scene—whether they're here or not. Or at least it's a potential one. No one comes in or out again. You called the Coast Guard?" he asked Jamie.

"I will as soon as we're back at the research station," she said. "I don't know how fast they can get out here, though. Not in this weather."

"What about Kat and Maya?" I asked. "And the students who are supposed to be manning the station?"

"We'll figure that out when we get back there," Jamie said. "Right now, let's lock this place up so I can go talk to the cops. We can figure out our next move once I know how they want us to handle things."

Half an hour later, we left the house the way we'd found it. In case this was all some horrible misunderstanding, Jamie left a note on the front door asking someone to contact her at the research station as soon as possible. We'd found no sign of foul play in the house... other than the note, of course, which was as foul as it got, as far as I was concerned.

The team regrouped when we got back to the station, gathering in the dining room for an impromptu meeting while Jamie went up and tried to reach the Coast Guard on the satellite phone in the lab. The note at the Melquist house had left everyone shaken. The fact that Kat, Maya, and the students manning the research station appeared to have fallen off the face of the earth wasn't doing much for morale, either.

About fifteen minutes after Jamie had gone upstairs to call in the troops, she reappeared at the dining room entryway. She didn't look happy.

"There's a call for you, Erin—a Maya Pearce. That's your mother's partner, isn't it?"

The team had been gathered at the table speculating about the shit storm brewing around us, while the canine members of our team whined and paced. This latest development didn't bode well; I barely managed a coherent "Excuse me" before I left the pack and trailed behind Jamie.

The satellite phone was in a corner of the lab, at a sturdy old desk looking out over the water. Jamie led me there, then left me with the distant, disembodied voice of my mother's lover in my ear.

"Is she all right?" Maya asked without preamble.

Somewhere deep down, I'd been hoping all this time that maybe there had been a mistake. Maybe the backpack with all the liquor didn't belong to Kat after all; maybe she and Maya were still on the mainland, bickering about work schedules and interior decorating choices. It took me a second to get back on track once that bubble had burst.

"I don't know if she's all right," I finally answered. "We can't find her. We can't find anyone. Where the hell are you?"

"Syracuse," she said. There was a slight time delay between us. Maya was already far enough away, but with the delay it felt like she was on another planet. She might as well have been. "There was a conference... I didn't want to go, but your mother insisted."

"Why would she do that? I thought this puffin deal was your project together."

"What gave you that idea? The island was all her... She seemed excited about it, so I agreed. But then, later..." She broke off. After a second or two, I heard her clear her throat.

"Maya?"

"We split up, Erin. I'm sorry... I wanted to tell you, but Kat wanted to wait."

"What do you mean, you split up?" I demanded. "I saw Kat three days ago and she said you were picking out paint for the living room. She didn't say anything about you two breaking up. What the hell happened?"

"It just... things changed. It happens. I'm sorry."

"You mean Kat changed. That's it, right? How long has she been drinking?"

More silence. I stared out the giant windows at the endless blue expanse of water below. This couldn't be happening.

"It's not just the drinking," Maya said.

"How long?" I pressed.

"About a month," she finally admitted. "It started before you left for Kentucky."

"You could have told me."

"Kat didn't want you to know. The drinking was just a symptom, Erin. She's been harder to reach, for a couple of months now. Darker. She kept pushing me away... Finally, I didn't have the strength to fight her on it anymore."

I resisted the urge to throw the phone at the wall—which, I was sure, would be frowned on by the establishment.

"Do you want me to come?" Maya asked. "I could get a flight out there... I can leave as early as tonight, if you think it would help."

I shook my head, but I couldn't get my voice to work.

"I didn't want to leave, Erin—I hope you know that. I just... I didn't know what else to do. I thought maybe if we had some time apart..."

"I know," I said when I found my voice again. "It's not

your fault. I know she's not easy." It felt like some kind of betrayal saying that now. Like I should be defending Kat, who'd been nothing but jagged edges for as long as I had known her.

"Will you call me when you find her?" Maya asked. "I'm sure she'll be okay, but just… let me know, all right? And you know you can always call me, Erin. If you ever need anything, you know where to find me."

"I know," I said numbly. I hung up the phone and sat. The ball of dread in my stomach had grown toenails and hair—like those tumors you read about in medical journals, these unidentifiable masses of cells and viscera growing rampant.

I stood when Jamie knocked on the door. "If you need another minute…"

I looked around, suddenly nauseous, and beat feet for the exit. "No, it's all right. I'm done here."

I left the lab and stood in the hallway for a few seconds, getting my thoughts together. Kat was on this island somewhere—she had to be. She was here, and she was alone. I had no idea whether she was alive or dead; I didn't even know if she wanted to be found. But that didn't matter…. I was all she had. Whether she liked it or not, I was all Kat had ever had, really. And I'd be damned if I was abandoning her now.

4
DIGGS

JUAREZ CAME DOWN shortly after Solomon left to talk to Maya. I was in the kitchen making coffee, trying not to think about the suicide note or the way Sol was slowly shrinking into herself or all the ways this trek to Raven's Ledge would likely end badly.

Juarez sat on a stool at the breakfast bar, nodding when I indicated the coffeepot.

"Erin's still talking to Maya?" I asked.

"Doesn't sound like it's going well," he said.

Great. It didn't take a genius to know that if Maya was calling while Kat's backpack was here—containing her soiled lab coat and a tidy supply of booze—then the honeymoon was over between the two women.

While Solomon was on the phone, Cheyenne and the guys continued looking for any sign of Kat and the students in the immediate vicinity. Juarez and I talked around that for a few minutes, not really saying much of anything, before I decided I was tired of dancing.

"So… You want to level with me and tell me why you really decided to brave plane, train, and fishing boat to get here? And don't hand me anymore bullshit about being worried about Erin. I know you're worried. This is a little excessive, though."

I pushed a mug of coffee toward him and took one for myself, pulling up a seat on the other side of the bar. He let me hang for a minute as he stirred creamer into his mug. Finally, he gave in.

"I am worried. I have been for a while now. But you're right—that's not the only reason I'm here." He hesitated. "Have you heard of Howard Rhodes?"

I knew the name. It didn't sit well with me. "Howard Rhodes, Deputy Director of Homeland Security? Yeah, I've heard of him. What's his interest in this?"

"J. Enterprises."

Sweat trickled down the back of my neck. The station, up until now downright chilly, seemed about forty degrees warmer. Solomon and I had heard of J. Enterprises for the first time a couple of weeks ago, but I still wasn't completely clear on their significance. All I knew at this point was that they had something to do with Erin's father, Mitch Cameron, and the drama we had all watched unfold in western Kentucky with a fundamentalist preacher by the name of Jesup Barnel.

"You were already looking into J. Enterprises before I called last night?" I asked.

"I started after the case in Kentucky," he admitted. "When Jenny showed up last night and you told me about the connection with this Mitch Cameron, I had no choice but to go to Rhodes... I'm sorry, Diggs. I work for the FBI—I have certain responsibilities when I think something relates to an ongoing investigation with the Bureau."

He was right, of course. It rankled, but it had been a stupid assumption from the start that he would risk his career—and possibly our lives—by keeping his mouth shut, just because I'd asked nicely.

"Erin's already on the FBI's radar," Juarez continued. "You both are, which is why they've been monitoring you. Rhodes' first inclination was to send me out this way at word of the explosion—I didn't have to request the assignment. In case you haven't noticed, very bad things tend to happen wherever you two go. Rhodes thinks Erin may be involved."

"With this J. Enterprises?" I said. He nodded briefly. "So, what the hell are they? What is this company Solomon's supposedly in bed with? Because I've gotta tell you, so far we haven't been able to find out a damn thing about them."

"I'm not sure, either," Juarez admitted. "I've been digging, but all I come up with is another dummy company behind another shell corporation, more tax shelters and phony names. I've had my assistant trying to track them down, but she's had no luck yet."

A shadow crossed his face, the faintest flicker of something in his eyes. Something tightened in my gut. Despite what he'd said, I still wasn't completely sure what Juarez's motives might be, or even why he was here with us. One thing was suddenly, infinitely clear, though: He was lying now.

I pretended I hadn't noticed. "So, how much trouble are Solomon and I in, exactly? Should we be worried?"

Any trace of subterfuge vanished in an instant. He looked me in the eye, his frank concern almost as unnerving as his lies a moment before. "I don't know how far this extends or even what it's all about, but part of the reason I jumped on this assignment was because someone needs to make Erin understand how serious this is."

"They can't honestly think she has anything to do with this. How many times has she almost died in the past year? If she's engineering this whole thing, she's the worst fucking terrorist the world's ever seen."

Jamie poked her head into the room before he could answer. We both shut up so abruptly that she cast a suspicious eye at us. "I talked to the Coast Guard and the cops… With the weather, no one can get out here until tomorrow morning. Which means if Erin's mother and the students are still alive, we need to find them on our own—and soon. Temperatures are supposed to drop overnight."

"They expect us to stay out here until then?" I asked. "Did you mention the suicide note? Or the fact that everyone on the island has vanished into thin air?"

"Gee, I must have forgotten that part." She stepped into the room with a weary roll of her eyes. "Yeah, Diggs, they know. Their recommendation is that we get out of here now, while we still can."

"Meaning we could make it back to the mainland if we left now?" Juarez said.

"There's a window, if we leave in the next half-hour or so," she said. "Seas are already at three to five feet, and they're predicting four to seven or higher by this afternoon." She hesitated, lowering her voice. "I almost think it would be worth the effort, though. Erin's looking a little rough as it is… Considering what we may well find out here, I don't know if this is the best place for her."

"She won't leave until we've found Kat," I said. "Regardless of whether the rest of us stay or go. I can guarantee that."

"She'll listen to you," Juarez said. "If you tell her about the storm…"

I quirked an eyebrow. "Seriously? You dated the woman—you really think anyone has any sway when she's like this? Short of tranquilizer darts and a strait jacket, there's no way you're getting her on the boat without her mother."

"And even with the darts and the jacket, I'm not going peacefully," Solomon said as she rounded the corner, inserting herself into both room and conversation. She faced off against Jamie, arms crossed. "Diggs is right: I'm not leaving until I find Kat. You guys can go if you want to.

I'm not leaving her out here."

"We have no idea what we've stumbled onto here," Jamie said. "This isn't what I expected when I agreed to bring you out here. We have no clue what's happened to Kat or the research students; an entire family could be dead. I'm sorry. My gut is telling me that whatever this is, it isn't good. We could be in real danger out here."

"I know that," Erin said. I expected her to argue, since in the past Solomon has been known to take threats to life and limb with a grain of salt. Instead, she bit her lip and took a second to consider the dilemma. "When is the Coast Guard coming?" she asked.

"They should be here by o-six-hundred tomorrow morning," Jamie said.

"And in the meantime we have you, Cheyenne, Juarez, two armed former soldiers, and Diggs and me—both of whom are trained to use a gun, licensed to carry one, and currently armed. What else can we do to make this as safe as possible for everyone?"

There was nothing snide in the question—she was genuinely asking. It was a reminder of just how much she had changed over the past year. When Solomon strong-armed me into our trek into the northern Maine woods last August, she'd given barely a thought to my safety or her own. Now, it seemed she was at least willing to consider the fact that none of us were invincible.

Jamie considered the question. She scratched her forehead, clearly torn. She and Juarez shared a glance before the Fed intervened.

"If we're not going back, then the smart choice—the responsible one—would be for the civilians out here to hole up until the authorities arrive," he said. "I could work with Carl and Monty to search for Kat."

"First off," Jamie interrupted. "Carl and Monty are just

as civilian as I am. Secondly, you're not gonna find a damned thing without the dogs—not in this weather. And no one handles the dogs but Cheyenne and me."

"Look, we have snow and free-falling temperatures in the forecast," Solomon said. "And my mother is out there somewhere, possibly hurt. Probably drunk. She…" She shook her head, her jaw set. "You want the truth? You can try to keep me in here—it won't work. Short of shooting me or tying me down, I'm not waiting on the sidelines. I'm sorry, but the second your back is turned I'll be out that door. We can fight about that inevitability, or you can accept it and come up with another plan. One that involves me being out there with you, searching for Kat. Please."

There was another hushed conversation between Jamie and Juarez, followed by three more minutes going around in circles before the decision was finally made: we would set out together, and we would remain together. As long as we could safely manage it, we would search the island. At the first sign of danger, however, we would come back to the research station and wait for help to arrive.

And that was that. As we were heading out, I tugged Solomon back with a hand on her arm. The others went on without us. I didn't like the shine to her eyes—a combination of fear, fatigue, and sadness that was becoming all too familiar.

"What the hell, Diggs—"

"Settle down," I said, once the others were out of earshot. "When Kat's safely back here, we need to talk. We were right about Juarez… He's definitely hiding something."

"You're sure?"

"Positive."

She gnawed on her lip, considering for a long few seconds before she shook her head. "I can't think about that until we have Kat back. Let's focus on one disaster at a time."

Four hours later, we were still focused on the same disaster, with little progress.

"We'll knock off for lunch soon," Jamie said. She led the charge, the rest of us fanned out while we waited for the dogs to catch a scent. A miserable wet snow drove down, and the entire search party—both human and canine—was soaked and frozen.

"I don't need to stop," Solomon said. "Maybe I could just keep going, and I'll meet up with you guys after you've eaten."

The sun had never broken through the clouds, though by now it was midday. I couldn't feel my fingers or my toes, the temperature hovering at around freezing for most of the day. I was cold and tired and scared as hell, and at the moment all I wanted was to head back to the mainland.

Juarez was the kind of man who would stay with Solomon in the freezing cold and driving snow, I knew. No matter how long it took to find her mother, he would keep going. Even though her mother was probably dead—or at the very least, incapacitated and drunk off her ass. I'm not Juarez. I was dead on my feet, and Solomon's teeth were actually, physically chattering, for Christ's sake. Einstein's tongue lolled, his head down as he plodded along beside Erin.

"You might not need to stop," I said, nodding toward the mutt, "but I don't think Stein's on the same page."

She looked guilty instantly, which of course had been the point. Solomon thinks of that damned dog's welfare above everyone else's, including mine. I wasn't above exploiting that weakness for her—and my—benefit.

"Maybe you could take him back to the station," she said.

"Forget it," Jamie said, before I could say the same. "We

had an agreement. You'll come back to the station with the rest of us, refuel, and then we'll head back out again to finish up with the rest of the island."

Solomon didn't argue. That alone spoke volumes about her level of exhaustion.

At the station, the pantry was stocked with homemade bread and massive cans of Spam, tuna fish, and chicken noodle soup. I found a small jar of natural peanut butter and some slightly furry grape jelly and contented myself with PB&J, setting toasted tuna and a bowl of soup in front of Solomon. Then, the team sat down at the over-long picnic table in the dining room and talked strategy. Solomon, Cheyenne, and I sat on one side of the table, Monty and Carl across from us. Jamie and Juarez sat on either end, as though presiding over the meal.

"We've already gone over the whole damn north shore," Monty said. He was the shorter of the two men, powerfully built, with a southern accent and the voice of a master orator. A master orator with a filthy sense of humor—which meant Solomon, of course, loved him. "If anybody's on the other side of the island, the dogs should've caught the scent by now. What the hell good're they doing otherwise? Jesus, they're like a virgin trying to find the clit, these dogs."

"The wind and snow are throwing them off," Jamie said. "But it won't be much longer—you're right, there are only so many places to search on an island this size."

"The missing family makes me nervous," Carl said. Carl was from Nigeria, his accent so thick it was hard to understand much of what he said. That worked out all right, though, since he rarely spoke. His skin was a dark, rich ebony, his face marked with tribal scars. "One missing woman is one thing. A dozen men, women, and children, though... If they were alive, we would have found them by now."

"Is the storm supposed to get worse before morning?" Juarez asked.

"The snow should stop by midnight," Jamie said. "With the cold front coming in, though, whatever's falling now will freeze overnight. The whole island will be a solid sheet of ice by morning."

Sobered, I noticed Solomon's eye drift toward the clock. She fed a hunk of her sandwich to Einstein when she thought no one was looking, then left the last couple of bites uneaten. Less than ten minutes after we'd sat down, she was on her feet again.

"I'm just going to get freshened up," she said. "When are we heading back out?"

Jamie turned to look at the clock on the wall behind her. It was two-thirty, the wind still howling and the snow falling in earnest now. "I'd like to be back out by three. I'll rotate Phantom out for the afternoon—she's getting tired. We'll leave her with Einstein."

Solomon started to object, but one look at the mutt's bedraggled white coat shut her up. "Fine."

"And Beth—one of the students staying here—is about your size," Jamie continued, still focused on Solomon. "You should go up and see if you can find a change of clothes."

"I don't need to—"

"Maybe not," Jamie interrupted. "But it'll make this afternoon easier on you if you're dry, wearing clothes that actually fit. There's a bureau in the bunk room with some stuff in it."

When Solomon was gone, Jamie and Carl cleared away the dishes. Cheyenne took off to tend the dogs, while Monty went outside for a smoke break. Juarez and I remained. He sat back in his chair and stretched, his eyes drifting shut. It occurred to me for the first time that he hadn't gotten any sleep last night, either.

"Listen, I'm sorry about this," I said. "Being around her like this has to be awkward."

"Not as awkward as I thought," he said. "I'm not here to play the martyr, I'm here to do a job. I've said it before: Erin was never mine. Not really. She's where she should be… that's a good thing. I don't have a problem with that."

"Especially not when there's a long tall blonde who's already got you on speed dial," I said.

He glanced around discreetly to make sure Jamie was safely out of hearing range, shooting a withering glare at me. "That's not true—we're just friends. She's… I don't even think she likes guys."

"She does," I said shortly. "One in particular."

"I'm so not talking to you about this right now," he said. "You're as bad as Erin, for crying out loud. We've got some real problems here—let's try to focus on that, huh? Kat's missing, her house is ashes, and an entire family has apparently committed revolutionary suicide for reasons no one seems to understand."

"So, in other words, things are dire—in case I hadn't gotten that before."

"It's not a joke," he insisted, tension rising. "I know they've been bad before, but this feels bigger. And I'm not sure how well Erin will take whatever comes next. Maybe you haven't noticed, but she's not eating—"

"I noticed," I said, cutting him off. The air between us got cooler. "I've got it covered."

He looked doubtful. Annoyance scraped ragged fingernails just below my skin. In the next room, I heard the water running. Under it, Carl and Jamie argued over who would do the dishes. Someone turned on the radio; Marvin Gaye started up, soulful and low. Something Juarez had said stuck in my brain, just registering.

"What did you say the Melquists committed?" I asked.

He looked at me blankly. "You used a term: 'revolutionary suicide.' Why would you call it that?"

"I didn't. I mean, I didn't come up with it. That's what they called it in the note we found at the Melquist house. I thought you and Erin saw it."

"We were a little preoccupied—I didn't read the whole thing."

"I just thought the phrasing was strange," he said. "That's why it stuck with me: 'This isn't suicide. It's revolutionary suicide.'"

I forced myself to get up slowly, the words reverberating in my brain. Solomon was still upstairs, probably changing. Possibly pulling herself together; possibly falling apart. There was still a plate on the table with a couple of sandwich halves that hadn't been cleared away. I grabbed them both along with a bottle of water and started for the stairs.

"I'm just going to talk to Solomon for a few minutes. We'll be down in time to leave at three."

I was already halfway out of the room by then, but paused to hear his reply. "Is everything all right?" He watched me warily.

"Yeah, it's fine. Sorry, I just…" I held up the sandwiches. "She needs to eat, right? We'll be down shortly." And then, because Juarez still looked concerned and vaguely confused, I nodded toward the kitchen. "You should go in there. Help clean up. I'm sure there's a long tall blonde who'd welcome the extra hand."

"Keep pushing, pal," Juarez said with an unexpected gleam, "and I might just rethink being so gracious about letting Erin go. You don't need to distract me—it's obvious something's up. Just promise me one thing?"

I hesitated before nodding.

"Let me know if you think you're in over your head, please. I'll help any way I can," he said seriously.

"I will. I just..." I stopped, not sure how to continue.

"I know. You don't have to apologize. Just go—take care of her. I'll stay here and help the long tall blonde," he said with a bashful grin. "It's a tough job, but someone has to do it."

●

When I reached the upstairs bedroom, I found Solomon seated at the edge of the bed, staring at the floor. She had on a sports bra and underwear, but hadn't gotten any farther than that. Her shapely legs were pale and goose pimpled, a sweatshirt draped over her lap. Solomon and I have seen each other in all stages of undress over the years; modesty is a lost concept. I strode into the room, my adrenaline running high.

"Get dressed. I need to talk to you."

"It's creepy wearing someone else's clothes."

"You'll survive."

"I appreciate your concern." She paused. Her eyes narrowed at sight of the sandwiches. "What are those?"

I walked across the room, set the sandwiches on the nightstand, and took the sweatshirt from Solomon's lap. "Lift your arms."

She didn't move, trying to decide whether this was worth a fight. Finally, she did as I asked. I pulled the sweatshirt over her head. It was roomy, but fit better than anything she'd been in up to that point. I pulled it down to her waist, my hand grazing her bare thigh. Before she could recover, I grabbed one of the sandwich halves and put it in her hand.

"Now, eat this."

"I'm not hungry."

Einstein's fuzzy face lit up. He ambled toward her, lured

by the promise of more free tuna salad.

"Keep your distance, dog," I said, my own temper rising. "Come on, Erin. For Christ's sake—eat the damned sandwich, or I'll tie you to the friggin' bed and feed it to you."

"I don't want the damned sandwich, for crying out loud. And while you in full alpha is kind of a turn-on, it doesn't make me any hungrier."

There was a brief standoff, while she sat there with the sandwich in hand and her temper rising fast.

"Okay, why don't we try blackmail, then?" I paused, waiting until I knew I had her attention. "Eat half the sandwich, or I won't tell you the major breakthrough I just had about your father, the Paysons, and a possible link to the Melquist family and Barnel's Kentucky flock."

That got her. She narrowed her eyes at me. "You're lying."

"We'll see. Half a sandwich, ace. A small price to pay for a little information."

She took a bite, nearly gagged, and choked it down. I handed her the bottle of water. She took a slug, set it down with unnecessary roughness, and looked at me. "I'm listening."

"You don't want to put some pants on first?"

"Diggins," she threatened.

I handed the rest of the unfinished sandwich half back to her without a word, and watched until she finished it off. Once we were done talking, there was no way in hell I'd get her to eat another bite. When the sandwich was gone, she drained her water bottle, crossed her arms over her chest, and sat back down. Still without any pants, of course.

I went over and closed the bedroom door, then returned. Solomon watched me uneasily. "Juarez told me what the Melquists' note said—the one they found at the house," I began. That was all it took to get her attention. "He couldn't remember all of it, but one phrase stuck with him." I repeated it, word for word as Juarez had said it to me: "This isn't suicide. It's revolutionary suicide."

Solomon paled instantly.

"You recognize it, don't you?" I asked.

"Barnel said something like it, in the videotape he sent to the FBI." She got up and went to the dresser, where a pair of cargo pants were folded neatly. She pulled them on without comment, then continued. "And I think Isaac Payson used almost the exact words during a conversation I remember him having with my dad when I was a kid." She held her hand up, stopping me before I could speak. "But those weren't the only times I've heard the phrase."

I already knew what she was talking about. I mentally replayed an audio recording I'd heard years before, when I was researching a story on mind control. Beneath the words, music played and children screamed as a madman proselytized to a mass of dying believers.

We didn't commit suicide. We committed an act of revolutionary suicide protesting the conditions of an inhumane world.

"Jonestown," she said. "Jim Jones used the term in the death tapes authorities found while they were sifting through the bodies."

Jonestown. The single event has become a landmark in American history, a kind of dark touchstone. People remember the assassination of JFK, the day the Towers went down… and a revolutionary preacher from Indiana who convinced over nine hundred followers to die with him in a remote jungle in Guyana.

"It could be coincidence," I said. "Or maybe these religious leaders—Payson, Barnel, maybe even this Melquist guy—were admirers of Jim Jones."

"Did Jesup T. Barnel strike you as the kind of man who'd

follow a self-proclaimed communist preaching civic reform and racial equality?" she asked. "Especially after that man went nuts, relocated his followers to the wilds of South America, and killed them all?"

"You have a point there." I hesitated, trying to come up with a rational explanation. I'd been trying for a while now, but Juarez's words had set something in motion in my head. I looked at Solomon. "When did you say your father joined the Payson Church?"

"1978," she said without hesitation.

"When in '78?"

"Around Christmas, I think."

"And when was Jonestown?"

"November 18, 1978." I could tell from the look in her eye: Neither of us had missed the correlation in the timing.

"And we still have no idea where your father was between 1970, when his sister was murdered, and the day he met up with Isaac to join the Payson Church in '78."

She shook her head. A few seconds of silence passed. "Please say something," she finally prompted.

I'd been doing research—looking up facts and figures, doing random Internet searches, during the endless six months that winter when Solomon had insisted we not see each other. I started calling up those facts now, hoping that Sol's logic would shine through and she'd reassure me that this was all nonsense. Conspiracy theory crap, all of it.

"Do you know where Jim Jones was from?" I asked.

She waited a few seconds, no doubt running through the same information I had amassed on the subject: The People's Temple, founded by Jim Jones in the 1950s in Indianapolis, before Jones moved the entire operation to California in the '60s. By the time he'd settled in San Francisco in the early '70s, he had massive support from politicians, celebrities, and a loyal and ever-expanding congregation. He—or his church, at least—was worth millions.

Solomon frowned, her forehead furrowed. "Do *you* know where Jim Jones was from?"

"I did a search on your father's hometown, since it's come up more than once in this investigation. I mean, it all seemed to start there: Mitch Cameron is from there, your dad… Not to mention psycho killer Max Richards. All roads seem to lead back to Lynn."

"And Jim Jones…?"

"Grew up in a shack in Lynn, Indiana."

"He would have been gone before my father was born, though," she argued. "Jones started preaching in Indianapolis, right? I doubt he had any ties to Lynn by the time my father was born in '55. And Dad's family didn't even move to Lynn until he was older."

She fell silent again, working through something.

"Noel Hammond…" she began. Noel was a former Bridgeport detective who'd been murdered in Littlehope the previous spring, when Solomon's investigation was just getting off the ground.

"What about him?"

"That scrapbook I found at his place before he died… I didn't get much chance to check it out before Kat commandeered the whole thing and refused to give it back. But I saw enough to know there were two recurring themes in that book: The fire on Payson Isle, and the 1978 mass suicide at Jonestown. At the time, I'd assumed Noel was just learning more about cult suicide as a general topic, in order to better understand what happened with the Payson Church."

She didn't need to finish that thought—I knew exactly where she was headed: What if he wasn't doing research at all? What if there was a tangible tie-in between Solomon's father and Jonestown?

I started to say something, but was interrupted by a knock on the door.

"We leave in five, if you two are still in," Jamie called.

"We keep this to ourselves," I whispered to Solomon. "If there really is a connection here, everyone who's made that connection so far is dead. We keep our mouths shut, and we take things slow."

She nodded silently.

"We'll be right there," I called to Jamie.

I listened to Jamie's footsteps recede down the hall. Solomon hadn't moved. She wasn't touching me, sitting carefully apart. I let her have her space, lost in the implications of our theory myself. Had her father been a follower of Jim Jones and the People's Temple? And if so, what the hell did that have to do with everything that was happening now, thirty-five years after Jones' congregation killed themselves and Jones put a bullet in his own skull?

I slipped my hand into Solomon's. It was cold. "We can't say a word. Whatever this means..."

She nodded, not looking at me. "I know. We trust no one."

5
DIGGS

JAMIE AND JUAREZ were already outside, the rest of the team waiting at the door by the time Solomon and I rejoined them.

"That was fast," Monty said. He insinuated himself between Solomon and me, helping her into her jacket before he draped a well-muscled arm around her shoulders. "You know if I was in his place, I would've kept you up there all day, baby girl."

"I couldn't take it," she returned, fluttering her eyelashes at him. "You're too much man for me, Monty."

"Oh, I'll go nice and slow, baby. By the time we get done—"

"Jesus, Monty," I interrupted. "At least wait until I'm in the other room before you start putting the moves on my girl, huh?" It came out with more intensity than I'd intended. Solomon looked at me in surprise. Monty removed his arm from her shoulders, chastened.

"I didn't mean anything by it, man. Just havin' some fun."

"I know—sorry. I just… I think I'm a little on edge."

As we were walking out, Solomon slipped her hand into

mine and held me back. She looked up at me intently. "You all right?"

"Yeah," I said, embarrassed. "Just... you know. Tired. And I've never been wild about watching you be manhandled by other guys."

"Because that happens so often."

"It happens more often than I'd like," I said.

"What did I tell you? Least evolved man I know."

Before she could get away, I pulled her in and kissed her, hard and fast. "You love it," I murmured when we parted. She looked a little dazed, but she didn't argue.

Back in the driving snow and freezing ocean air, things got serious again fast. Everyone looked determined; no one looked optimistic. There were only a few places left on the island Kat could possibly be. If she'd ended up in any one of them, she probably hadn't done so in good health.

Solomon trudged through the slush with her head down. The wind had risen to a dull roar and darkness was falling fast when the pit bull stopped suddenly, head up, and sounded off with two sharp barks. Before I could ask questions, the dog was leading Jamie and the rest of us on a mad race through the underbrush. There was a dip in the rocky terrain, then another hill. At the top, Jamie, Cheyenne, and the dog came to an abrupt halt. Juarez reached them first, Solomon and me straggling behind. Carl and Monty brought up the rear, doing their part to ensure we weren't murdered by nightfall.

Juarez held up a hand for us to slow down, but his gaze was fixed on whatever was ahead. I pushed sweat and snow from my eyes and continued forward.

"Hang on," Jamie called, her voice strained.

"What is it?" Solomon said. She didn't slow down.

Juarez looked at me, then at Solomon, the look an

unmistakable plea for me to do something. I grabbed Solomon by both arms and held on, pulling her backward.

"Wait," I said. "Let them do this."

She shook her head. "I need to see—"

I didn't let go. No one moved on the hillside. Carl and Monty finally reached us, breathing hard. For once, Monty didn't have a quip. They strode past us without a word and half-skidded, half-climbed up the greasy hillside to join the others.

"What the hell is it?" Sol shouted to them. I watched as she forced herself back to calm, or at least the pretense of it. "Please, Diggs," she said. "I'm all right."

"Jamie?" I called up.

She turned. Even from a distance, even in the driving snow, there was no mistaking the look on her face: Horror, through and through.

"Let her go," Jamie said.

I did, reluctantly. Sol ran up the hill and I kept pace beside her, catching her when she slipped in the slush and went down hard on one knee. At the top, we both stopped at what appeared to be a manmade ravine, maybe fifteen feet across and ten feet deep. The bottom was filled with about a foot of slushy snow and hunks of rock.

It wasn't the slush or the rocks that nearly brought me to my knees.

At the bottom, a dozen or more bodies lay half-buried in the snow. Men; women; a little girl, maybe seven years old, holding tight to an infant whose face was blue with the cold, eyes shut as though in sleep.

I fought to stay calm, searching the faces. The bodies were huddled together, as though seeking warmth or comfort in the moments before death. I thought of the Payson Church, suddenly: whole families burned to death, trapped within the walls of a place that was supposed to be their sanctuary.

Jonestown. Jesup Barnel's manic eyes as he stood at the podium just over two weeks ago, addressing an auditorium filled with people prepared to die.

Revolutionary suicide.

Ultimately, the Payson deaths hadn't had anything to do with suicide.

And the Melquists? Did these people really, willingly head out in a snowstorm, crawl into a pit, and sit there waiting to freeze to death? And if so, why? Jim Jones claimed suicide was the only option for his congregation—that if he and his followers didn't kill themselves, the U.S. government would come for them. Take their children.

Why would this family choose to die?

Solomon stood beside me. She started the treacherous descent into the pit alone, ignoring Jamie's order to stop.

"I can't tell who's in there," she said, looking back over her shoulder. The dead were bundled in parkas and hats, bodies slumped together. The cold had staved off the most obvious signs of decay, so it was hard to tell how long they had been there. Based on the amount of undisturbed snow covering the scene, however, it had been at least a day.

There would be no survivors.

I forced myself to look at the dead again, still searching. I paused at sight of a slight figure almost swallowed by a deep red parka. In the glove-clad hand was a bottle of Jack Daniels whiskey. The woman wore stylish black boots and blue jeans that were drenched and frozen stiff. Her face was hidden by the parka hood, but that didn't matter.

I knew exactly who it was.

"Solomon," I said, my voice hoarse. She hadn't seen yet. She looked back at me, a question in her eyes. "Stop," I said quietly. "Please."

"I just need to check them—just to make sure she's not here."

"Let them do that. Come back up with me."

She read the look in my eyes. I watched fear, then sorrow, cross her face. When she went back to looking, it was with a desperation that hadn't been there before. I didn't try to stop her again. It wasn't like she could make things worse.

It wasn't like she could do anything at all.

I stood by and watched as she plowed headfirst into the sea of corpses, useless as she checked the pulses of the bodies surrounding her mother. Otherwise, she was careful not to disturb the dead—we knew protocol well enough. Crime scenes had become a part of daily life for both of us by then.

She paused for a second before she reached Kat, suddenly calm. The sight of blood makes me weak, but Solomon always seems to take it in stride. She just sets out to fix what's broken. And then, to record what can't be fixed.

And she stays so eerily calm, in the face of it all.

"Erin!" Jamie called down to her.

Solomon held up her hand, signaling the other woman to wait. She stepped over an old man, slumped on the ground with his legs stretched out and his mouth slack, his face half-submerged in slush. There was a little boy in his arms, maybe three years old. The boy had been crying when he died.

My stomach lurched, bile rising in my throat.

When Solomon reached the woman in the red parka, she crouched.

Pushed the hood back.

Dark black hair tinged with grey; green eyes closed. Despite everything else she may have been, Solomon's mother was always a beautiful woman. Death hadn't changed that. I took a step forward, ready to brave the worst if it meant pulling Solomon out of this now. I waited for a look of despair, any dawning realization of what we'd found. Instead, Solomon looked over her shoulder at me with a wild light in her eyes.

"She's alive."

"What?"

"Help me get her out of here," she shouted, coming to life herself. "She's breathing!"

She'd snapped—clearly. There was no way in hell anyone was alive here.

"Solomon, this place... They're all dead—"

"She hasn't been here as long as the others," she insisted. She knelt, checking for a pulse. "She couldn't have been. And there's staining around some of the victims' mouths, but I'm not seeing any here. I'd guess poisoning... but I don't think she was. Pulse is weak, but steady." Solomon ran her hands over her mother's body, checking for injuries. "Hypothermia is the biggest concern right now. We need to get her out of here."

She continued an ongoing, one-sided dialogue while Jamie unpacked a portable stretcher from her bag of tricks, and she and Juarez headed into the pit. Kat's skin was ice cold. There was a deep gash on the left side of her forehead, the blood clotted. We loaded her as carefully as possible onto the stretcher. Solomon took a thermometer from Jamie's kit and crouched beside her mother, sticking the instrument in Kat's ear. Her face flashed clear relief when she read the result.

"Ninety-six," she said to Jamie. "We just have to make sure it doesn't drop any farther, but she's not hypothermic."

With that tiny bit of good news, we coordinated our efforts and maneuvered the stretcher through and over the fallen bodies around us until we were back on even ground.

Monty and Carl were still staring into the abyss when we came out, both men silent. Monty's usual light expression had gone dark. "What do we do about the others?" he asked, looking at Juarez. The Fed ran a hand over his face, looking as exhausted as I'd ever seen him.

"The police can process the scene tomorrow. Right now, we need to get inside. We can ride out the rest of the storm at the station. There's nothing more we can do here."

Carl remained silent. Monty scratched his head. "It doesn't seem right, leaving them out here. The kids…" His voice broke.

"I know," Juarez said. "But right now we need to focus on keeping the rest of us alive. It's the best we can do."

Despite his words, I noticed that Juarez lingered when the rest of the group walked away, carrying Kat on the stretcher between us. I looked back over my shoulder. The agent knelt at the edge of the pit, head bowed. He crossed himself, wiped his eyes, and stood before anyone else had even noticed he was gone.

The trek back to the research station was quiet. Kat remained unconscious, bundled in a warming blanket while Solomon fussed over her the whole trip back. Despite the fact that we'd found her mother alive, the memory of the bodies we'd left behind kept the mood dark. It was all too raw, too horrifying, to do anything but move on in silence.

When we got back to the station, Jamie and Cheyenne took Casper in to tend to icy paws and hungry mutt bellies while Juarez and I hauled Kat down the hall to the community bunk room, Solomon on our heels directing traffic.

We transferred Kat to one of the bunks. Twice during the trek, she'd started to come around—babbling nonsense, thrashing on the stretcher. Now, I watched as her eyelids fluttered and her hands clenched into fists. The others left Solomon alone while she concentrated on warming her mother, but I stayed behind. It still made no sense to me how the woman had ended up in a pit of corpses without being one of those corpses herself. Something wasn't right here.

Sol pulled up a chair next to her mother's bed. I took one of the neighboring bunks. I watched as she silently cleaned her mother's head wound, her head bowed like she was doing penance. Maybe she was.

"Can I do anything?" I asked.

She shook her head without looking up. "I've got it. You can go if you want. Get yourself something to eat."

"I'm all right. How long do you think she'll be out?"

"I don't know for sure. Her temp's rising at a good rate, and she's responsive to light and sound—I don't think it will be long. For all I know, she's only under now because of the booze. She smells like a distillery."

"The thing about whiskey warming core body temperature isn't true, right?" I asked. "Otherwise, we could say Jack Daniels actually saved her."

"No. Jack Daniels definitely didn't save her," she said shortly. She put ointment on the gash and carefully bandaged it, brushing Kat's hair away from her face. It made me think of the girl Solomon had been when we'd first met almost two decades ago: all blazing eyes and unbreakable spirit, her chin perpetually held high.

"You want me to get you something from the kitchen?" I asked.

"I'll get something later." She leaned back in her chair on a slow exhale, running her hand through her hair. "Did they lock all the doors? I wonder if there's a way we can barricade the windows."

"You're afraid Jenny will come for her?"

She looked at me for the first time, her eyes shadowed. "I'm afraid she'll come for all of us."

So was I.

"Do you have any idea what Kat would have been doing

in that pit?" I asked. "They were obviously already been dead when she went in."

"Yeah, definitely. It doesn't look like she went down there to try and help anyone."

I scratched my chin. "I have a theory."

"That she was hiding among the dead?" Solomon guessed. My surprise must have shown, because she shrugged. "It doesn't make much sense otherwise, does it? A pit full of dead bodies, apparently poisoned at least a day ago… And still no sign of those two students who were manning the research station. I think someone was out here looking for Kat. Maybe the pit was the only place she could think to hide, where the bad guys wouldn't come looking."

What the hell had happened out here in the past twenty-four hours?

Solomon got up and retrieved a piece of paper with two columns of numbers printed on it, then sat down beside me.

"It's the contents of the memory card—there's a printer in the lab. I took a couple of minutes and got everything printed out," she explained. She took out a pen and scrawled 'Raven's Ledge' beside the entry with the island's coordinates. The numbers following those coordinates remained a mystery, though.

"What do you think they are?" she asked.

I had no more idea now than I had before. "No clue," I admitted.

The room was chilly, the light just fading outside. It was five o'clock. My stomach rumbled. I wasn't sure I had enough energy to propel myself into the kitchen for food before I passed out.

"What are you thinking?" I asked.

The only time Solomon is reluctant to say what's on her mind is when she knows I won't like it. A few seconds of silence passed before she gave in.

"When the cops get here tomorrow, there's no way they're letting us near the Melquist place again."

I didn't disagree—partly because she was right; partly because it wouldn't have done any good if I had.

"So, maybe if we can get Jack to come with us, we could go back? There are a couple of things I'd like to check out before we leave here, and I have no idea when I'll have the chance again."

"We should go before dark, if we're going," I said. She raised her eyebrows. I managed a half-hearted grin. "You were expecting a fight?"

"Hell, yeah, I was expecting a fight. This is us we're talking about. I'm not sure what to do if you're just going to start agreeing with me all the time."

"I don't think you have to worry your pretty little head about that anytime soon, ace. Juarez and I already talked about this, though. It makes sense to go back now, before cops are crawling all over the scene. We'll go with you. The others can stay here to keep an eye on Kat."

She tipped her head at me, eyebrows raised in bemusement. "You know, somehow I thought the fact that Jack and I dated, broke up, and you and I started... whatever we're doing, less than twenty-four hours later, might have strained your bromance."

"Nope. The love affair lives on." I hesitated, not sure whether we were still on even ground. When her focus returned to Kat, I figured we were all right. "But I'm serious about the nightfall thing—if we're doing this, we should do it now."

"Yeah, okay." She waved her hand at me in the same gesture she'd use to shoo a pesky housefly. "I've got it, Diggs. Just give me a second."

I'd no more than crossed the room, just a foot or so from the door, when Kat groaned. I turned as her eyes opened.

"Kat," Solomon said. "You're all right. Just relax."

"Why am I here?" Kat asked, her voice pure gravel. Usually the quintessential ice queen, right now it was impossible to miss her panic. She struggled to sit up.

"It's okay," Sol said. She scooted her chair closer to the bed, but made no move to touch her mother. "You're fine, Kat. We found you in time."

The other woman's eyes rounded. She sat up, moving farther from Solomon. "Why the hell are you here? What did you do?"

"I didn't do anything. We found you in—with…" Sol trailed off, flustered. "We found you in time, Kat. You're safe now."

"No." Kat shook her head, the fear replaced with fury in the blink of an eye. "Damn it, Erin. You weren't supposed to be here. No one is supposed to be here."

She started to get out of bed. Solomon pushed her back, hands at her shoulders, but Kat slapped her away. I stepped in before a fist fight broke out.

"Easy, Kat—you need to stay put, just for now." I was even more reluctant to touch her than Solomon. Thankfully, it seemed my voice was enough. She eased back, her cheeks flushed. "We have everything under control," I said.

"The hell you do. You're idiots—both of you. How long have you been here?"

"We came over on a boat this morning," Solomon said. "We were looking for you."

"Well, you found me." She fingered the cut on her head gingerly. "What's my temp?"

"Ninety-six point nine, last I checked," Solomon said.

Kat nodded her approval. "So, no hypothermia. Frostbite?"

"No."

"Have you heard anything from Maya?" Kat asked. For

the first time, I saw a flicker of vulnerability.

"I talked to her on the phone," Solomon said. "She's okay. Worried about you, but safe."

"Good," Kat said absently, obviously still disoriented. She searched the room, scanning every corner. Being a recovering addict myself, I recognized the look in her eye before she said anything. "Where did you put my bag?"

"It's—" I started.

"I threw it out," Solomon cut me off, her jaw suddenly rigid. Unaware she was even doing it, she mirrored her mother's pose: arms crossed over her chest, chin up. I got a chilling glimpse into my future.

"Well, bravo," Kat muttered. "You tossing half a dozen little bottles of whiskey will definitely get me to hop back on the wagon."

Despite her bravado, it was impossible to miss the tremor in Kat's hands or the light sheen of sweat on her forehead— neither of which had much to do with her injuries, I was willing to bet.

I didn't say anything, but Erin caught the look on my face. Her eyes hardened. "She's fine," she bit out. "Will you give us a minute?"

It wasn't a request, I knew. Kat glared at me like this was all somehow my fault. As if I had any control whatsoever over her daughter.

"Do you want Jack and me to go out to the house without you?" I asked.

"No—I won't be long. Just give me a minute."

Against my better judgment, I left.

In the other room, Carl and Monty played cards at the table while Juarez stirred a mammoth pot of pasta boiling on the stovetop.

"Where's Jamie?" I asked.

"Checking over the dogs with Cheyenne. Did Kat wake up?"

"Yeah. I think we were better off when she was unconscious."

Monty looked up from his hand. "Maybe she'll liven things up. We've got another twelve, thirteen hours before the Coast Guard gets out here. I could use a little excitement."

"I'm all right with a quiet night," Carl said. "Too many dead bodies today... It would be nice to survive until morning. That's all I hope for, right now."

"I'm with you," I agreed.

I leaned over Juarez's pot of boiling water and lowered my voice, waiting until the guys had resumed their game before I spoke.

"You still up for a walk?"

"We better make it soon," Juarez said. "I don't want to be running around out here in the dead of night. And I don't know how safe it is leaving everyone else unattended."

"Agreed. Solomon's on the same page—she won't be much longer."

"Is Kat all right?"

"She's not happy."

His lips quirked up slightly. "Is she ever?" He had a point there. He nodded toward the table. "Have a seat, dinner's up. Nothing too fancy—"

Before he could finish, there was a crash down the hallway, followed by a string of very colorful profanity. Juarez started toward the bedroom, but I held up my hand.

"Hang back—I've got it."

Another crash followed, then the sound of breaking glass. I hurried down the hall and pushed the door open without knocking.

Kat was on her feet, her face flaming red. A side table had been overturned. Her bag was now open on the bed.

Solomon stood on the other side of the room, chest heaving. She held tight to one of the travel-sized liquor bottles. Blood dripped down the fingers of her right hand. Three jagged scratches were carved into her cheek. Two other bottles were shattered on the floor between her and her mother.

"I've got this," Solomon said tightly. She didn't even look at me. "I'll be out in a few minutes."

"If it's all the same to you, I think I'll stick around this time."

I gently pried the bottle from her fingers. Kat pillaged through her bag until she came out with the half-empty bottle of whiskey that had been on her nightstand when Solomon and I first arrived. Eyes locked on her daughter's, Kat opened the bottle and took a long slug.

I didn't try to intervene. Neither did Solomon.

When she was done, Kat sat down heavily on the bed, a marionette whose strings had been cut. Solomon remained where she was, back against the wall.

"Now that you've had your medicine," Sol said, her voice laced with venom, "maybe you wouldn't mind answering some questions."

"I'm tired."

"I don't care." Solomon's chin came up. "You're well enough to fight to the death over a freaking drink, you're well enough to talk." Her gaze flickered to me, waiting for me to stop her.

Instead, I pulled a chair up next to the one already beside Kat's bed. I nodded to the other one. "Have a seat, Sol."

Kat scooted to the other side of the bed, back against the wall, arms crossed over her chest. Solomon's fear was palpable the closer she got to her mother. I thought again of the years I'd known her as a kid: All those times she'd come into the paper with a black eye or split lip; the brooding silence that invariably accompanied them. I hadn't seen that girl in a long, long time.

She sat, her gaze steady on Kat's. "Did you know the Melquists?" she asked.

Kat's eyes fell to Solomon's hand. "You're bleeding."

"I'm fine."

Kat got up abruptly—so abruptly, in fact, that Solomon flinched. I may have done the same. She brushed past us and disappeared into the adjoining washroom. When she closed the door, Sol's eyes sank shut. I squeezed her knee.

"You okay?"

"I'm an idiot. I should've just let her have the stuff—it was stupid."

"Never a good idea to get between a drunk and their next drink," I agreed. "Still… it's no excuse for what she did." Water ran in the other room. I ran a finger over the scratches on her cheek, my own anger rising. "She did a number on you this time."

She pulled away. "I've had worse. I'm fine."

Maybe two minutes trickled by before the bathroom door opened again. Kat emerged with a damp washcloth and a first aid kit. She sat down on the edge of the bed and guided Solomon's hand to her lap. I got the feeling this had been a ritual between mother and daughter, years before—Kat's way of trying to heal the wounds she'd inflicted. She may have done all right with the physical ones, but it dawned on me then—maybe for the first time—just how deep the psychic scars ran for Solomon. A band-aid and some antiseptic would never do the trick there.

Kat wiped the blood away with a deft hand. An odd mix of frustration, resentment, and shame radiated from her. When she finally looked up, she avoided Solomon entirely. Instead, she focused on me. There was no trace of confusion, no sign of weakness, in her rock steady green eyes.

"You love her, right? You love my daughter."

"Jesus, Kat—" Solomon said, mortified.

"Yes," I interrupted. It might have been a hard thing to admit once upon a time. Now, it was the one certainty I knew wouldn't change—not with time or distance or any one of a thousand disasters the universe might set in my path. "I do."

Solomon wouldn't look at me.

"Good," Kat said with a brusque nod, as though my answer had been a foregone conclusion. "If you love her, you'll get her to run."

"What?" Solomon said. "We're not running."

"I'm not talking to you," Kat said, though not unkindly. She never shifted her gaze from mine. "If you really care about her, you'll convince her to get the hell out of here. You'll leave the country, find some beach somewhere, and stay there. Stop digging. Now. They're done playing—you'll both be dead before the week's out if you don't get her out of here."

I didn't say anything, but Kat seemed satisfied that she had done what she could. She returned her focus to Solomon's hand, cleaning the last of the wound before she retrieved some ointment from her bag.

"Ask your questions," she instructed her daughter.

"What?" Solomon asked.

"You have questions, right?" Kat said impatiently. "What do you want to know?"

"The Melquists," Solomon said, after a second of uncertainty. "You knew them."

Kat nodded.

"What happened to them? How did they die? And why? What the hell happened out here?"

"You want to choose one of those questions, for now?" Kat said. "I'm not exactly in peak storytelling form here."

Solomon didn't relent. Kat scratched her neck, nodding thoughtfully. "Right. Of course you don't. Jonah Melquist knew your father. The information that's been keeping you safe, all this time?"

"It was hidden here," I guessed.

"Jonah had it," Kat agreed. "Jenny found out."

"And then the whole family up and killed themselves?" Solomon asked. "I feel like there are some key points you're skipping."

Kat applied a bandage to the back of Solomon's hand, smoothing it down with a kind of tenderness I'd only seen her use when she was working. Medicine allowed for softness; life did not. When she was through, Kat looked her in the eye again. "Jonah killed his family. The alternative was to let Jenny and her people have them. It wasn't an alternative he was willing to live with." Her eyes clouded. "I tried to stop it. I was too late."

A few seconds passed in silence before Solomon got herself back together enough to move on. "The man named Mitch Cameron—you know who he is?" she asked.

"We've met," Kat said dryly. Solomon pulled her hand back. When Kat tried to clean the scratches on her cheek, she pulled away.

"I'm fine, leave it," Solomon said. Her voice was steady now, her eyes cool. "Dad ran away from home when he was fifteen. He didn't show up again until December of 1978, when he joined the Paysons. Why then? Where was he before that?"

Kat didn't answer this time. Sol continued, undeterred.

"Noel Hammond's scrapbook—the one you stole from me. It had a bunch of articles from the Payson fire."

"I never said I stole that," Kat said immediately. Solomon glared at her, which I could understand. Kat Everett was enough to push the pope himself to matricide.

"Fine," I interrupted, before things devolved once more. "The scrapbook *someone* stole."

"What about it?" Kat said eventually.

"It was filled with two things: One was the Payson fire," Solomon said, then hesitated. "The other was Jonestown."

Kat stood abruptly. She started toward the door, but Solomon blocked her path before she could go anywhere. I remained seated, tensed to my toenails.

"Everything that's gone wrong in your life?" Kat said, her voice hushed. She turned to face Solomon, shutting me out. "These people are behind it. Let it go. Your father tried to run; he tried to hide. Jonah Melquist—one of the men lying in that pit back there? He tried to hide. They couldn't. You don't get away from people like this. Not when you know as much as your father does. He saw the worst of it— knows every secret. It's been a death sentence from the day he walked away from the Brigade. When you're part of the Project, you don't just leave. No one just leaves these people."

"The Brigade?" Solomon said. It wasn't what I expected her to follow up on. I stayed quiet, curious despite myself. "Do you mean the Red Brigade?" She looked at me briefly, explaining. "That was the name of Jim Jones' security detail."

"Erin—" Kat began.

"No—you said you'd give me answers. Did Isaac Payson and Dad know each other before they joined the Payson Church? Was it because they were both part of Jones' church? Both members of the Red Brigade?"

Not surprisingly, Kat shook her head. "If I tell you more, you're as good as dead. Or did you miss the pit of bodies we just left behind? A war is coming—these people have been building up to it for a long, long time. If you get in their way…"

"I'm already in their way!" Solomon shouted. "They blew up your house, Kat. Jenny would have killed Diggs and me if she'd caught us… Her people are coming for us. At least tell me what the hell they want me for."

"They don't want you—they never have!" Kat shouted back. "They just want you to keep quiet. How is that so hard to get through your head, for Christ's sake? Just keep quiet. Leave it alone."

"If we leave this alone, they're just going to keep killing," I said. I got up from my chair and joined Solomon— defending her because I knew she'd never defend herself. "Erin tried to let it go," I said. "She didn't go near this thing all winter, because she was trying to save my life. That didn't stop these people from engineering an apocalyptic nightmare in Kentucky."

"Look: we know there's a link to Jonestown, all right?" Solomon said. "You said you met Dad in December of 1978. You told me he was hurt—that you nursed him back to health. What happened to him?"

Kat went to the table and unscrewed the cap from her whiskey bottle, took a slug, and set it back down. Then, she exhaled slowly and leveled a cool glare at Solomon and me.

"Isaac Payson met your father in San Francisco in the early '70s, not long after your dad's sister was murdered. Your father had gone out west to find Jones—Isaac was already a member of the People's Temple at that point."

"Why was Dad looking for Jim Jones?"

Kat hesitated, but only for a second. "His parents— your grandparents—knew him when he used to preach in Indiana. He had family in Lynn, so they all knew each other from the start."

"Dad was part of the People's Temple, then?" Solomon asked. Her voice was strained. "Was he in Guyana the day everyone killed themselves? Was he at Jonestown?"

Kat's eyes slid to the door, as though she thought someone might be listening in. Not an unreasonable assumption, considering recent events. She didn't answer.

"Was the Payson Church some extension of the People's Temple?" Solomon pressed. "Or did Isaac break off from Jones to start his own church? And what does Mitch Cameron have to do with any of it?" She took a step closer, forgetting in her fervor just how dangerous that could be. Instead of breaking, however, Kat returned to her bunk. She stared at the floor, her mouth shut and her jaw hard.

"I'm done. I've already given you enough information to guarantee they'll gun you both down. As soon as we get off this rock, I'm disappearing. I hope to hell you do the same."

She closed her mouth again and crossed her arms over her chest, pulling a book from her bag.

I knew there was no way in hell she was saying anything more.

6
SOLOMON

IT WAS ALMOST SIX-THIRTY by the time we walked through the Melquists' front door again, shooting Diggs' and Juarez's plan to keep to daylight hours straight to hell. The temperature had dropped a good twenty degrees, but the snow had almost stopped and the winds had died down. Between exhaustion, the events of the past twenty-four hours, and Kat's revelations, the voices that had only been whispering at the start of the day were deafening by the time I crossed the Melquists' threshold.

For thine is the power and the glory…

She can't stay here, Katherine…

Isaac will be angry. He'll send us into the woods.

And then, suddenly, a voice I'd never imagined had anything to do with this: *We didn't commit suicide…*

The memory of Jones' voice alone was enough to stop me cold.

"Solomon?" I heard Diggs say behind me. I couldn't make my vision level out enough to turn. I felt his hand on my shoulder, anchoring me. "Hey—talk, please, or I'm carrying you out of here now."

"Sorry. Yeah, I'm here. The bedrooms… I want to check

the bedrooms again."

I went on ahead, Diggs and Juarez trailing behind. We were all armed. On top of the guns and ammo, we had a radio with us and strict orders to check in with the research station every ten minutes. I wasn't stupid enough to think any of this ensured our safety, but it was at least an honest effort.

"Have you noticed that you two spend an awful lot of time in creepy abandoned houses?" Juarez asked when we reached the second floor.

"Too much Scooby Doo as a kid," Diggs said to him. "And if I remember right, you've been in most of the same houses lately."

"A trend I wouldn't mind breaking. You know, I was never a fan of that show. The van never seemed that safe… or sanitary. And the dog…"

"Careful," Diggs said, nodding in my direction. "Bad mouthing the dog is never a good idea around this one."

"So I've learned."

I left them to their banter, bypassing the first several bedrooms off the long hallway. When I finally stopped, it was at the last bedroom on the left. Both Diggs and Juarez had fallen silent.

I stood in the doorway. With the light failing, the creep factor in Jeanine and Nancy's room had grown exponentially.

"What are we looking for?" Diggs asked. He was closer than I'd expected. I started, my heart tripping faster.

A child's voice echoed the words, twenty-five years past. *What are we looking for, Erin? We're not supposed to be here. If Isaac catches us…*

If Isaac catches us, what?

There are rules that we must follow, Erin, I remembered my father saying. *Isaac has them for a reason. This is the safest place for us right now. Someday, maybe I can take you away.*

Maybe we can go somewhere far from here—somewhere that no one can find us.

"Erin," Diggs said, pulling me up from the depths of those lost memories so fast it felt like I'd get the bends. His hand was on my shoulder. I shook him off, desperate to get the memory back.

My father had wanted to leave Payson Isle. Why was it so hard to remember that shit, when the good times we spent together with the Payson Church had been front and center in my brain for decades?

"Wait," I said impatiently. "Just give me a minute."

I went inside the bedroom, but mentally I was still chasing that conversation. Where had my father and I been? The garden on Payson Isle, I was pretty sure. Or in the greenhouse. It was the day after I'd watched Isaac whip Dad in front of the entire congregation. The whole thing was too elusive now, though—like a dream already receding into my subconscious.

I took a breath and finally let the memory go. There would be time later. For now, I had other things to worry about.

"Are you back?" Diggs asked. Juarez watched me warily.

"I am," I confirmed. "Sorry."

"Good. So remind me why we're in this particular bedroom?"

"The name tags. You saw them at the end of the beds?" Diggs nodded. "They're all written in the same handwriting, except for one." I indicated the scrawled name at the end of Nancy's bed. "It sets her apart, but she clearly didn't care. Plus, she was the one with the marionette hidden beside her bunk."

"So you're saying little Nancy was a rebel?" Diggs asked.

Was. Men, women, and children, lying at the bottom of a pit like last week's trash… One of those kids would have been Nancy. The thought made me sick.

"I'm not sure how Nancy can help us now," Juarez said.

"I'm not, either," I conceded. "But if anyone was marching to their own drummer out here, it was this kid. Maybe she wasn't following quite so blindly as everyone else."

There was a small bureau against the wall, beside a window that looked out over the ocean. On top of the bureau was a well-worn Bible and an old music box with an angel on top. I opened the top drawer of the bureau and riffled through plain white underwear and plain white socks. So far, everything looked pretty innocuous.

"What did you expect to find?" Diggs asked.

I shook my head, continuing to look. *We're not supposed to snoop,* I heard Allie say. *If we hear Isaac coming, I'm running away. You'll get in trouble, and I won't even care.*

I finished going through the bureau and moved on to a narrow closet, the door swollen closed. It took some effort before it finally budged. Hanging inside, I found miss-sized, ankle-length dresses with high necks and long sleeves. There hadn't been a dress code in the Payson Church; I wore dungarees and overalls, sported shorts and skinned knees every summer.

This wasn't the same.

And yet, it *felt* the same.

I pushed the dresses aside and ran my hand along the wall, going by feel alone.

"Solomon," Diggs said. The way he said it made me think he'd been trying to get my attention for a while. Outside, the sun had set. The room was all shadows, lit by an old lantern and Juarez's flashlight.

"Yeah?" I said.

"If you could give us some idea what we're looking for, maybe Jack and I can help."

"I'll know it when I find it."

You're not supposed to be so nosy—God doesn't like a snoop. You can't just go anywhere and do whatever you want, Allie said, her voice carrying through the years. *If Isaac finds us, he'll put us in the woods.*

Why would he put us in the woods?

I stepped farther into the closet, half-expecting the back wall to open up to Narnia.

"What the hell are we doing here, Sol?" Diggs asked, an edge to his voice now.

"I *was* this kid," I said. I gave up and left the closet. "The one always breaking the rules. Everyone else might have made their bed a certain way and eaten all their peas every night, but this one's different. And if she kept something…"

"Something like what, though?" Juarez asked.

"I don't know. Something." I looked at her bed again— covers mussed, pillows askew, blue-eyed angel hanging on the bedpost. I thought of the bunk beds at the research station.

Suddenly, I scooted in and lay down on Nancy's bunk.

"So much for preserving the crime scene," Juarez said dryly. I ignored him.

There, secured under the wire springs of the bunk above me was a sketch pad. I pulled it out, sat up on the bed, and began thumbing through.

It turned out that Nancy had been quite the little artist. Most of the sketches were still lifes of the island: spruce trees and granite cliffs, foaming ocean and soaring sea birds. I paused at the sketch of a girl with long hair and wide eyes, her mouth serious. A self-portrait? What had she been thinking, when she made the trek out to that pit with her family? Did she have a sketch pad with her then? Had she known she was about to die?

I pushed aside the image of Nancy and her family as I'd

seen them last, dead and abandoned, and flipped through the rest of the pages.

About three-quarters of the way through the sketch pad, the tone of the drawings changed. The shading was darker, the shadows more ominous. In one, a cross stood at the top of a cliff overlooking the ocean. In another, a blue-eyed angel emerged from the sea, water streaming from her wings. A chain was clenched tight in the angel's teeth. At the end of the chain was a pocket watch with a broken face, what looked like blood seeping from its cracks.

The angel watches over you, Erin… but she also watches you. Isaac Payson's voice came back to me, his face close to mine as he laid a blue-eyed angel in my lap. I was four, maybe five years old, but I was well aware what that meant. This was my angel.

Time doesn't exist for the Lord, Isaac had told me. *There's no escaping the eyes of the Almighty. It doesn't matter how old you are, where you are or what you've done… The angels are always watching.*

The bed dipped beside me as Diggs sat. Juarez stood in the doorway, looking miserable and out of place. He wasn't paying attention to us, though, his gaze fixed somewhere off to my right instead. I followed his line of sight. His eyes were locked on Nancy's angel marionette, now hanging from the bedpost in full view.

Something roiling and dark burned in my chest.

I turned to the next drawing.

And nearly dropped the sketch pad.

The picture was a sketch of Christ on the cross. Behind him, a thousand warriors stood in flames, their eyes black with terror and pain. Diggs took one look at the drawing and took the pad from me, closing it quickly.

"We should go," he said.

"What are the drawings?" Juarez asked.

"Nothing," I lied. Badly, I might add. "Just random kid stuff. Unicorns, rainbows. The usual."

Diggs looked at me, trying to figure out why the hell I wasn't telling Juarez what we'd just seen: An exact replica of one of Isaac Payson's paintings, once hanging above the hearth at the Payson boarding home.

Juarez didn't believe me. I saw his eyes slide to the marionette beside the bed again, and my thoughts catapulted back to Payson Isle. Or, more specifically, to a day in Littlehope when Juarez and I had been investigating Payson Isle, last spring.

I stood abruptly and pulled Diggs with me. "I think we're about done here. But do you mind taking the radio down and checking in with Jamie?" I said to Diggs. "Let her know it'll be another few minutes, and then we'll head back."

He knew I was up to something, but he didn't argue. Instead, he looked at Juarez, then back at me, and nodded. "Yeah, sure—no problem. I'll be right back."

"That's all right," I said. "We'll meet you down there. Just give us a minute."

He agreed after another second of hesitation, but there was no doubt that he had some concerns. I didn't blame him—I had some concerns of my own.

Juarez and I didn't speak until I heard Diggs' steps on the floor below.

"You're remembering, aren't you?" he asked me.

I felt that same niggling unease I'd felt earlier, back in the boat on the way over. Almost unconsciously, I took a step back. There was a draft coming in from the window, ice cold on the back of my neck. I didn't answer his question, choosing to ask one of my own instead.

"The blue-eyed angel—the one I found in your things, back last year in Littlehope. Where did you get that?"

A flicker of surprise touched his dark eyes before he chased it away. "Matt," he said. "I just assumed the doll had been Zion's—that maybe Rebecca had given it to him for safe keeping after the boy died."

Matt Perkins had been kind of a surrogate uncle to Juarez when he was growing up. Over the course of our investigation last spring, we'd ultimately learned that Matt's devotion to Juarez—an orphan from Florida Matt had literally picked up off the street—was intricately tied to the man's link to the mass murder of the Payson Church. I had assumed the same thing about Juarez's connection to the angel I'd found while going through his things last spring: that Matt had passed it on to him, just one more way that Juarez replaced Zion in the old man's mind. Suddenly, I wasn't quite so sure.

"You told me once that you don't remember anything before you woke up in the hospital at thirteen," I said. "Everything before that was a blank slate. None of those memories have come back, still?"

"Not really, no." He hesitated. "What does it feel like for you, remembering the Payson Church? Not the memories you had before, but the flashes you're getting now. Do they seem real? Are they whole?"

"How do you know about that?"

"Diggs told me you started having them when we were in Kentucky. He was worried—*is* worried. Answer me, please," he said, urgent now. "Are the memories whole, or just pieces?"

"They're just flashes: pieces of conversations, images that are just now coming into focus."

"Do you recognize everyone in those flashes?"

It was too specific a question not to have some significance—something that was resonating with him, but he wasn't ready to share yet.

"When did you watch Scooby Doo?" I asked. Juarez

looked baffled at the sudden change of topic. "You said earlier that you never liked Scooby Doo," I explained. "But it seems weird that you would watch something like that as a teenager—especially considering that the years you do remember, you were basically raised in a convent with a bunch of nuns. Maybe I have outdated ideas about Catholicism, but I'm pretty sure the church isn't wild about the Scooby gang."

"I don't know when I watched," he said after a moment. "There are things that I know: songs I like, shows I've watched, places I've been, but I don't know where the knowledge or those experiences came from. My life is like one endless déjà vu."

"And Scooby Doo is part of that."

He smiled dryly, his eyes distant. "Yes. Scooby Doo is part of that." I waited for him to elaborate, but he fell silent. There was something there, though—something behind his eyes, a truth he wasn't willing to reveal, that chilled me. I wasn't used to being shaken by Jack Juarez.

I didn't much care for it, either.

"What aren't you telling me, Jack? Diggs says you two talked about J. Enterprises, but he doesn't think you're telling us everything you know."

Five seconds ticked by, endless in the silence. Just when I was sure he was about to speak, Diggs shouted up to us. We both jumped. I took the time to pull myself together as Diggs ran up the stairs. A second later, he was at the door.

"We need to get back—no one's answering my call at the station."

There was no argument, no discussion; we raced for the stairs without another word. Our footsteps echoed through the still house. Shadows lurked in every corner as I sprinted down the hallway, thinking of all the ghosts these tragedies had left behind. I'm not really the superstitious kind, but with this much blood, I figured there were bound to be some restless spirits on the island tonight. I just hoped none of us were about to join them.

An instant before I reached the front door downstairs, Juarez caught up to me. He grabbed the doorknob before I could, practically knocking me out of the way.

"What the hell are you doing?" I demanded.

"Potentially keeping you from racing straight into an ambush."

"If they're in trouble at the research station—" I began.

"Then us getting killed on the way there won't help," Diggs said. He joined Juarez, both of them barring me the door now. They were really taking this whole bromance thing too far these days.

I forced myself to take a breath. "Okay. Then what do you propose?"

"Slow and easy," Juarez said. "I'll go out first and check the perimeter. When I'm sure it's clear, we'll head back."

I started to argue, but Diggs stopped me with a look. Reluctantly, I had to admit they had a point: Any lunatic could be outside that door waiting for us.

Juarez drew his gun. A blast of cold air hit us when he opened the door. He braced himself, went into a crouch, and crept into the night. Diggs kept the door open a crack after he'd gone. We watched until Juarez was completely swallowed by the darkness.

"What was that about upstairs?" Diggs whispered when we were alone. "That sketch—we've seen that before."

"You really think now is the time to talk about it?" I asked.

"You have something better to do?"

Neither of us are the most patient people in the world; waiting in silence was unlikely. He had a point.

"Okay… yeah, we've seen the sketch before—out on Payson Isle."

"And why are we not letting Juarez in on that, exactly?"

"I don't know It's just a feeling I can't shake. He's tied up in this somehow— you said it yourself. He knows more than he's saying."

Diggs stood behind me at the door, his breath warm on my neck, his hand on my hip. There was no sign of Juarez. No sound but the waves pounding the shore far below.

"You don't think he's behind the attempts on your life, though," Diggs said. "I mean—I agree, the guy is holding something back. But this is Jack Juarez we're talking about. He would never hurt you. And when we found the Melquists…"

"I know," I said with a shake of my head. "Relax—I'm not trying to besmirch your boyfriend's honor."

"Besmirch?"

I elbowed him in the stomach. "You know what I mean. Look, it's not like I'm saying Jack is secretly in cahoots with Jenny Burkett or something. Or even Cameron, for that matter. But something's up with him."

"Agreed," Diggs said. He peered past me, out the door and into the darkness. "Where the hell did he go? Have you heard anything?"

"Other than you yammering in my ear? Not so much, no."

Between the darkness and the fact that he was standing behind me, I couldn't actually see him roll his eyes, but I felt it. He moved in, his fingers gliding along my hip to pull me closer.

"I do a lot of things, Solomon, but I've never yammered in my life."

The way he whispered the words in my ear started a little fire in my belly, which quickly spread lower when his lips brushed my earlobe. Count on Diggs to turn a life-or-death situation into an opportunity to cop a feel.

"You ready to go?" Juarez asked. He appeared from nowhere, nearly sending me into orbit.

"Jesus, Jack. I know stealth is important right now, but you couldn't give a little warning?"

"Just trying to keep you two on your toes. There's no sign of anyone out here, but we should go. I still haven't been able to raise the others on the radio."

Any thought of inner fires fizzled. Diggs and I got into formation behind Juarez. Diggs drew his Glock, but the idea of trying to navigate the island in the dark holding a loaded Ruger in my trembling paw was too much for me.

"But you have it with you, don't you?" Diggs said when I protested.

"The only person I would end up shooting is one of you lunkheads," I hissed back. "You really want that?"

"It's all right," Juarez interrupted. "Two guns are plenty if we're sticking together. Now, let's move."

We moved.

The combination of plummeting temperatures and a day of fresh slush and wet snow on the ground was deadly; it was like hiking over an ice rink. In the dark. With guns. The air was so cold it seared my lungs every time I took a deep breath. I put my scarf over my mouth and nose, and concentrated on staying on my feet.

I kept waiting for a sign of someone behind us: a branch snapping; footsteps or falling rocks or Jack's scream just before his throat was cut. What the hell had I been thinking? Why would we leave Kat unprotected? Sure, she was a pain in the ass—she was still my mother. I wanted answers, true, but was it worth getting her killed in the process? Was it worth getting any of us killed?

Halfway back to the station, I slipped and fell, hard. When I landed, my weight fell on the wrist Will Rainer had broken the summer before—the wrist that had taken three surgeries to repair. The wrist that still wasn't one hundred percent, even with a pin in it. Pain shot up my arm. I bit my lip to keep from screaming.

When I looked up, I saw a figure in black lurking behind the trees. I shook my head, disoriented by the pain. The figure stepped closer, moving toward me. By the light of the moon and a snow-covered island, I caught a glimpse of a man: tall, lean, a black watch cap on his head. All I could make out of his face was the beginnings of a beard and kind, concerned eyes. It had been fifteen years since I'd seen him last, but I knew him in an instant.

"Dad?"

He turned and ran. I felt Diggs' hands at my side an instant later, pulling me to my feet.

"You okay?"

"Yeah," I said. "I'm fine." The pain in my wrist was still enough to make throwing up a very real possibility, but I pushed past that. I had other concerns at the moment—namely, why the hell my father might be here.

"We can slow down," Juarez said, joining us. "We're almost there."

"No," I whispered. "I'm fine. Let's keep going."

I took off at a run again, more focused than before on the icy path at my feet. My father had gone in the same direction, bound for the research station. I heard Diggs and Juarez say something—no doubt cursing my name—before they took off after me again.

We stopped short at the edge of the woods, fifty yards from the station. There had been no sign of my father since I'd spotted him when I fell. Already, I was starting to question what I'd seen.

I had prepared myself for the worst when we got back—a raging fire, maybe a few bodies strewn on the ground. Instead, we watched from the woods as someone sat on top of the picnic table in front of the house, smoking a cigarette. Cheyenne, I thought. She had the dogs with her, the three of them idly snuffling the snow before Einstein caught my scent and came running. Phantom and Casper lagged behind. Cheyenne looked up.

"Hello?" she called, her voice wavering.

"Can we go ahead?" I asked Juarez.

"Hang on." He went out first, greeting the dogs only briefly before he continued on—searching the night, gun drawn. I dropped to my knees to greet Einstein. All the while, I kept waiting for someone to come; for a shadow to emerge from the darkness and open fire. My father was no more than a memory now, as ineffectual as a ghost. We had real things to worry about.

Juarez reached Cheyenne without incident. I heard them talking, too low to make out the words. A few seconds later, he waved us over with an "All clear!" that echoed in the stillness.

I straightened. Diggs and I loped over to the picnic table while Einstein and the other dogs circled, back to snuffling the grounds.

"What the hell happened?" I asked as soon as Cheyenne was within hearing range. "Why didn't anyone answer the radio for the last check-ins?"

"Sorry," she said roughly. Her eyes were wet. I realized she must have been out here crying. "I forgot. I just—I can't get those kids' bodies out of my head. Every time I close my eyes, I see that little girl with the baby. I just needed some fresh air."

"But everyone's fine in there?" I pressed. "No one's hurt?"

She wiped her eyes with the back of her hand, clearly mortified at having been found this way. "Yeah. Everyone's fine. Your mother was still asleep when I checked on her last.

Jamie and the guys are playing cards."

I took a deep breath and let it out in a disgruntled huff. "You scared the shit out of us. You couldn't have let someone else take over the control room before you decided to—"

"Let it go, Sol," Diggs said. "Everything's fine. That's what's important. Now, why don't we go inside, check on your mom, and see if we can get some sleep before the troops show up tomorrow."

I got the message: stop being a bitch and let the chick having a nervous breakdown off the hook. Move on.

In this instance, I knew he was right. I patted Cheyenne's shoulder awkwardly. The adrenaline had run its course. Now, all I felt was weak-kneed and rung out. "Sorry—it's fine. I know this hasn't been an easy day for anyone."

"I've had better," she agreed. She finished off her cigarette and stubbed the butt out in the ashtray. "See, this is why I like dogs. They may fight every once in a while, but at least they're predictable. People are nuts."

I couldn't disagree.

Once she'd pulled herself together, we all filed back into the station. Despite Cheyenne's assurances that everything was fine, I half-expected another disaster to greet us at the door. I wasn't sorry to be wrong.

"There she is," Monty said when I came in. He barely looked up as he dealt a fresh hand of cards. "I was wondering where you got off to, baby girl. Thought we'd need to send the cavalry out."

"Nope," I said. "We're fine. Any excitement here?"

"We tried to talk the girls into a little strip poker," Monty said. "Jamie here ain't no fun, though. Says she into candy, not co—"

"We can deal you in if you want," Jamie interrupted, shooting a glare at my pal. Monty just grinned at her, unfazed.

"Let me check on Kat first," I said. "Then I may take you up on that. Especially if there's chocolate involved."

"She was sleeping when I looked in on her last," Carl said. "Forgive me for saying, but your mother is much easier to handle when she is unconscious."

"You're preaching to the choir," I assured him. I told Diggs I could handle this mission on my own, left everyone else to their cards, and shuffled off to the back bedroom.

The first thing I noticed when I went into the bunk room was the fact that Kat wasn't in it.

A millisecond of panic followed before I realized her bag was also gone.

The panic turned to blind terror. It's hard to keep things in perspective after a year of dead and half-dead bodies turning up at every turn.

About half a second before a coronary dropped me where I stood, the toilet flushed in the next room.

The bathroom door opened, and Kat emerged. Her hair was wet. She'd changed into a fresh pair of jeans and a deep burgundy sweater—cashmere, no doubt.

"Going somewhere?" I asked, forcing my heart out of my throat.

"No," she said smoothly. If she was surprised to see me, it didn't show. "But in case you've forgotten, I spent the better part of today under a pile of dead bodies. There's not enough soap in the world to get that stink off, but I thought I should at least give it the old college try."

I tried to take her bag from her, nodding toward the bed. "Have a seat. I just want to check your temperature and take a look at your head."

"I'm fine, Erin." She didn't relinquish her bag, but she did sit. "I'm a doctor, remember? I know how to diagnose mild hypothermia."

"What's your temp?"

"Ninety-eight point two. I told you: I'm fine."

"How'd you get the gash in your forehead?" I asked. I crouched so I was eye level with her, checking her pupils.

"I don't remember," she lied. "The whole morning is a blur."

"Were you with the students who were staying here before you ran?"

"I was. I don't know what happened to them—I told you, I don't remember anything."

Right. "Well, it's nice to see you've gotten over that insane bout of honesty you were suffering from earlier."

Her pulse was steady. Heart rate good. She wasn't happy that I was touching her, but she didn't try to scratch my eyes out, which was an improvement.

When I stepped away, she grabbed my wrist. I swallowed a scream of pain and pulled away. "Ow! Jesus, Kat. What the hell are you doing?"

"There's swelling there—what happened? You know you're supposed to be careful."

"I'm fine."

She rolled her eyes at me. Since I knew exactly what was coming, I sat down, shut up, and let her do her thing. She ran her fingers over my wrist: palpating here and there, checking the radial pulse, making sure everything was where it belonged. I can say a lot of things about my mother—and do—but I've never questioned her expertise when it comes to medicine.

I took the opportunity to study her in a rare moment when she wasn't on the defensive. Her hair had been a deep, deep black when I was growing up, but now I noticed a few streaks of gray. My mother had me when she was young— barely eighteen, which meant she was only in her early fifties now. When I was in high school, she had been in her prime:

the hottest woman in town, and the fieriest. She ran the town medical clinic, drank like a fish, and slept with every man who'd have her in the tri-county area. In between, she raised me. Or, we raised each other. Sort of.

I thought of the man I'd seen in the woods—or the man I had thought I'd seen. It had to have been my imagination. The father who had been playing dead for over a decade wouldn't just show up on this island of the damned, out of nowhere. Whether it had been wishful thinking or I was just genuinely losing my marbles, I was sure now that my father wasn't on Raven's Ledge. He couldn't be.

At least, I was pretty sure he couldn't be.

I never knew my parents when they were together. Kat took off not long after I was born, and she didn't come back until I was nine. I still can't imagine the two of them together, though: my father, a quiet man who tended the church garden and mostly kept to himself, and my mother—a hurricane, a wrecking ball, a woman too prickly to let anyone too close.

My father had done better than most, though.

"Do you know where Dad is now?" I asked while she wrapped my wrist.

She stopped what she was doing for just an instant before she continued, without looking up.

"No idea."

"Have you seen him lately?"

"Define lately." Still without looking up.

"Lately, lately," I said. "The past month, let's say." Or today.

"Can't say that I have." When she looked at, there was something stormy and dark brewing behind her green eyes. She dropped my hand into my lap and backed away from me. "You should ice that. Take some ibuprofen tonight, and keep it immobilized as much as you can. You should see Dr.

Hardy when you get back to the mainland, too. Wouldn't hurt to get some fresh x-rays. I think it's fine, but you did a lot of damage this year. You need to be more careful."

"I will. Thank you."

She shrugged. "It's what I do."

An uncomfortable silence fell.

"You should call Maya," I said. "I told her I'd let her know you're okay. Maybe you could do it for me."

Those dark and stormy eyes got that much stormier. "I don't think so."

"She wants to get back together, you know. I could tell."

"It wouldn't work out. Anyway, I'm leaving town after this—taking my own advice. I don't want her coming after me." She looked at me meaningfully. "I don't want *anyone* coming after me."

"You don't have to do that," I said, more vehemently than I'd meant to. "We can beat these people—"

"No, Erin, we can't beat these people," she said wearily. "I'm through trying… I'm leaving. And I want you and Diggs to do the same. Start a new life. And don't try to find me. Don't try to contact me."

"Kat."

"Listen to me, damn it," she spit out, her mood turning on a dime. "I know what we are to each other. I've never been a mother to you. When you were growing up, the best I could claim was roommate. But I know you: you get sentimental. You'll try to make us into something we've never been. Don't make that mistake with me."

"For Christ's sake, Kat," I bristled. "I know we've had our problems—"

She moved forward so fast I flinched, grabbing my arm with one hand as she lifted my chin with the other. She forced my gaze to hers, holding me hard enough to leave a mark. Another one. "Don't do that. I'm not saying this to make you feel sorry for me. I'm saying it because it's a fact. I never wanted to be a mother; I never made any secret of that. Now we both have a chance for a clean slate. Don't screw that up by getting emotional."

I pulled away abruptly, my anger rising. "What the hell is wrong with you? If you would just work with me, we can get out of this."

"No, goddamn it, we can't," she roared, any trace of softness gone. She pushed me away and got to her feet. "Are you blind, or just stupid? I'm telling you: this is the only option left."

She went to her bag, pulled out the last of the whiskey, and took a long pull. When she looked at me again, her gaze was cool. Detached. Oh, how I hated that look. "You might not want that clean slate, but I've earned it by now. I've spent the better part of my life trying to protect your father and you from these people. I'm done. You can do whatever you want—just don't come after me. I don't want to see you again."

For as much as a minute, it was hard to get a full breath. It's not like I wasn't used to Kat's cruelty, but it had been a while since I'd experienced it like this. I'd forgotten how deeply she could cut.

"Fine," I said. "Do whatever you want—I don't give a rat's ass. Drop off the planet for all I care. But I'm not running. I'm sorry you had to waste your life trying to keep me from getting killed, but I won't let them manipulate me that way. They've gotten away with too much as it is. I'm taking them down."

I walked to the door, my hands shaking. When I turned around, Kat was seated on the edge of the bed with the whiskey bottle in hand. Staring at the floor.

"I have no idea if you have a plan or not," I said, "but the Coast Guard will be here at daybreak. You might want to sober up and get some sleep before you drop off the grid for the rest of your life."

I left without looking back, slamming the door behind me.

7
DIGGS

IT WAS ONLY EIGHT O'CLOCK by the time we were back at the station and safely settled in the dining room. The snow had stopped, but the wind still battered the trees outside. Down the hall, I could hear Solomon and her mother—not their words, necessarily, but the volume was enough to clue us all into the content.

The card game had expanded, most everyone now gathered around the dining room table. Juarez kept getting up to check the perimeter, while Jamie bounced up every ten minutes to do something for the dogs: food, water, bathroom breaks... It was worse than having a house full of kids. Cheyenne spent most of her time staring out the window, still shaky from whatever breakdown she'd suffered while we were gone.

Carl and Monty were the only ones who seemed unaffected by the horror show around us. Carl apparently took his card playing very seriously: we were only playing with M&Ms, but he considered every call and every raise like it was high stakes. Monty, on the other hand, kept up a running commentary—designed, I suspected, primarily to drive Carl nuts. It didn't appear to be working.

"Diggs? You in or what?" Monty asked.

I started, realizing suddenly that I'd been staring sightlessly at my cards for the past several minutes. The shouting was getting louder down the hall, which meant intervention might be required soon. Just before I took action, a door slammed. Everyone at the table jumped, including me. No intervention necessary, then.

"Uh—yeah, I'm in." I tossed a couple of M&Ms into the pot.

Monty got up and headed for the fridge. "Anyone want another beer?"

"We should probably lay off for the rest of the night," Jamie said. Juarez flashed a grateful smile her way. They'd talked about this, then. "If someone makes a move on us, the last thing we need is something to slow down reaction time. Everyone needs to be sober and ready to act."

The protest I'd expected didn't come. Instead, Monty nodded unhappily and contented himself with a Diet Coke.

Between the generator and the wind and the card game, the research station was not a quiet place. I strained to hear over the noise—which was laughable, really. Like anyone coming after us would make a sound before they attacked. I glanced at the doorway, willing Solomon to walk through it.

It took a good ten minutes, but eventually she did. She collapsed into a chair beside me and laid her head wearily on the table.

"So… clearly that went well," Jamie said dryly. She slid a bag of miniature candy bars to Solomon, who smiled gratefully as she raised her head. With all the things I've done with, and to, Solomon over the years—many of which I've been told by others are pretty damned memorable—the woman has never looked at me with quite the devotion a chocolate bar inspires.

Erin tore into the bag before she answered, going straight

for the first mini Snickers she found. "You could say that," she said between bites. "Mothers... Can't live with 'em; can't legally set them loose on an ice floe anymore."

"I don't know," Carl said, completely taking me by surprise. "A jury might look the other way if they met your mother."

"I know she's not the easiest person," Solomon said uncomfortably, her mouth full of chocolate nougat. "Intimacy, trust—whatever. She's got... issues."

"That's white speak for saying your mama's a stone cold bitch," Monty explained to Carl, loudly enough for the rest of us to overhear. At Solomon's look, he lowered his eyes apologetically. "No offense."

An awkward silence ensued. Solomon stared at the table, brow furrowed, rubbing at a scratch in the wood with the thumb of her left hand. I noticed for the first time that her right wrist was wrapped.

"She's not a bitch," she finally said. She still wouldn't look at anyone. I put my hand over hers, if only to stop her before she rubbed a hole clear through the table. "That's not what I said. It's not what I meant."

"You should never listen to Monty," Carl said. He offered a quiet smile when Solomon met his gaze. "He was raised by wolverines. The man has no manners."

"He's right," Monty said miserably. "You can't listen to me, I ain't got no filter. Just seems like after you been killing yourself all day to dig her ass out of this mess she's in, maybe she could be a little nicer. That's it."

Solomon shrugged, but when she looked up the frown was gone. While it hadn't been replaced with an actual smile, she did look marginally friendlier. "It's all right. I'm sure she's been called worse. Anyway..." She looked at Jamie, almost visibly pulling herself out of her funk. "We've had enough drama today, right? Is it too late to deal me in? If we're stuck here for the night, I might as well win a little chocolate while we wait."

For the next hour, we found a kind of mad joy in the simple fact that we were still alive on an island of the dead. The doors were all locked, the windows barricaded. Monty provided a running, off-color commentary while Carl schooled all our asses in five-card draw.

By nine-thirty, the joy had worn off. In its place was a raw weariness that had everyone in the room—including Erin—fading fast.

Juarez looked at his watch for the hundredth time, then back at Erin again. Her eyelids were drooping, and she could barely hold her head up. He looked at me, his meaning clear: put the girl to bed already. That same raw annoyance I'd felt earlier rode my spine again. I liked Juarez, no question, but the man really needed to stop trying to take care of my girl.

Cheyenne had plied everyone with hot chocolate half an hour before, then begged off saying she needed to check on the dogs and get to bed. I pushed the lukewarm cocoa around in my mug. Carl stood, swaying with exhaustion.

"If you'll excuse me, I don't think I can keep my eyes open any longer. I'm going to bed."

Monty sat with his head on the table, snoring softly. Carl rapped him on the head with his knuckles. "Come on, Sleeping Beauty. Bed."

"I'm just going to take one more look around," Juarez said, getting up himself. Even Jamie's eyes were at half mast by now. She nodded and rose with him.

"I'm pretty friggin' knackered myself. I'll see you guys in the morning."

"Knackered?" Juarez said quietly, the words for Jamie alone. "I don't think I've ever met a Georgia girl who used the word knackered."

"That's Georgia *woman*, Agent Juarez," she said, bumping

him lightly with her hip. He followed her out of the room, the pair still bantering. Maybe a little good would come out of this nightmare after all.

When Solomon and I were alone, I got up. She remained seated, looking dazed.

"You need sleep," I said.

"Someone should stay up. In case anything happens—we need somebody to keep an eye out."

"We've got it covered."

"You're staying up?" she asked.

"I've got a shift later. Don't worry about it."

She still wasn't making any move to get up, so I pulled her to her feet with my hands at her elbows. She swayed, looking up at me blearily.

"You haven't gotten any more sleep than I have," she said. "I can get up with you."

"Fine."

She frowned. "You won't wake me when it's time. I know you."

"You're right. But I'm not gonna fight with you about it right now." I pushed the hair back from her face, gently tracing the scratches Kat had left. "You've had enough fighting today."

She flinched, her cheeks heating. "I'm okay. She's just… you know. Kat."

"You don't have to defend her to me. I know who she is."

"I'm surprised you haven't run for the hills by now," she said with a brittle laugh. The intimacy vanished, replaced by tension and that thin shell Solomon tries to wear like armor. It works for Kat; it never has for her daughter. "I wouldn't blame you. Talk about baggage."

She tried to pull back, but I kept one arm wrapped around her. With the other, I tipped her chin up so she looked me in the eye. "You really want to start comparing baggage, kid? Because I've got three ex-wives and a sponsor who'll be happy to weigh in."

I expected some kind of comeback—this is Solomon we're talking about, after all. Solomon always has a comeback. Instead, her eyes drifted shut. She rested the top of her head against my chest, which is one of Erin's favorite, weird half-embraces. Her body sagged in my arms.

"All right, come on. Bedtime." She groaned, but otherwise didn't move. "Hey." I jostled her slightly. She managed to lean back and look at me. Her pupils were so big they left only a sliver of green around them. A shiver of panic started at the base of my spine.

"Solomon? Hey, Erin," I said more loudly. I hit her cheek lightly, and was rewarded with a very definite glower.

"Ow. What the hell was that for?" There was a detectable slur in the words.

"Did you take something?"

I thought of the others: Monty and Carl, half-asleep through the last hand of cards. Jamie, barely able to drag herself out of her chair. Juarez, leaning heavily against the doorframe when he agreed to take the first watch.

Shit.

Solomon leaned against me again, body slack. Head lolling.

Why wasn't I affected?

"Erin, I need you to wake up for me. Come on, ace. Up and at 'em." I forced her to walk beside me, pointing her toward the kitchen so we could get some water. Behind me, I heard footsteps. Someone was approaching the dining room. My heart raced, my palms slick with sweat.

"Erin. Come on—I think someone drugged you."

"They'll be out for a few hours—that's it. Nothing serious," I heard Kat say from behind me. When I turned, she was standing in the doorway, fully dressed. Her backpack was over one shoulder.

"You did this?"

"I needed to clear the way to leave," she said simply. "Your friend Cheyenne was happy to help, once she understood her options."

Solomon roused herself, just barely. Kat nodded toward her, then looked at me. "You should let her sit. It's just a mild sedative, but Erin's never done well with drugs."

I slid her as carefully as I could into a chair. She'd gone borderline boneless on me, sliding low in the seat.

"Why isn't it affecting me?" I asked.

"I don't dose recovering addicts," she said simply. "Especially not one who's dating my daughter. Give me a little credit. Besides, I knew I could make you see the light."

"The way you made Cheyenne see the light?" I asked. "Maybe you should explain it. I think I'm missing a crucial piece of the argument."

I heard the side door open. Casper and Phantom barked in the next room, where Jamie had them crated for the night. Einstein yipped wildly at my feet, racing for the nearest exit.

"You left us vulnerable here," I said, my voice rising. "How do you not get that? People died out here today— or do you really not care about that?" I went for my gun. Where the hell was Juarez? Monty and Carl might be down for the count, but Jack hadn't seemed completely out of it. Not like the others.

Einstein raced back to me after his jaunt down the hall, barking the whole way. He spun in a circle, dove back toward the hallway, and returned. I hit the safety on my Glock and nodded Kat out of the way. Measured footsteps approached. I turned toward them with my gun up. The panic I'd been fighting from the moment I looked in Erin's eyes officially took over when Mitch Cameron appeared in the doorway, his gun up and pointed at my head.

"Put that down, please," he said, nodding to my Glock. I heard someone pounding deeper in the house—banging against a door, while the dogs continued to bark bloody murder.

"You first," I said.

"Please." He looked at me like I'd just insulted him. "We know who's getting off a shot first, don't we? Put it down, Diggs. I have no interest in doing any harm here."

I lowered the gun, flicking the safety back on.

Solomon wiped her eyes as she fought the drugs. "Cameron?" she said.

"We need to be quick about this," Cameron said to Kat, ignoring Solomon and me completely. "There's been a change of plan."

"What do you mean?" Kat asked.

"Jenny. We couldn't get enough distance—she'll be here soon." He strode toward me so suddenly I was tempted to take a step back. He slapped an envelope in my hand. "There's a silver Camry waiting for you on the mainland, with everything you and Erin will need. I want you to wait forty-five minutes, then go."

"We're not going anywhere," Solomon said.

Kat shook her head, tension burning through her. "Jesus—for once in your life, use a little common sense."

"We don't have time to fight about this," Cameron said urgently. "I'll get Kat away from here—you take Erin. I will find you both as soon as it's safe, and I'll explain everything then. But right now, you need to get out of here."

"But—"

"NOW!" Cameron roared. In our limited interactions, he'd always been all about control: calm, measured. Now, he strode toward Solomon like a man possessed. I reached for my gun again. "You think I'm fucking around here? They're coming for you. The gloves are off; there's no reason left to keep you alive. Now—get dressed, and get moving."

Solomon started with another barrage of questions, but all it took was a glare from me and she quieted. If there were options, I wasn't seeing them. Cameron took Kat's arm.

"You have what you need?" he asked.

She indicated the pack on her back. "Don't need much."

"Good girl," he said. There was a surprising hint of softness in the way he said it. "Now—we're headed to the other side of the island; I've got a plane waiting. I'll take care of Jenny. There's a good GPS in the Hurricane—the boat you brought over here. You use that, and get back to shore as fast as you can."

"And leave everyone else here?" I asked.

"The Coast Guard will be here by morning," he said without missing a beat. "You know that. You think you can handle this?"

I looked at Solomon, still looking wobbly at the table. I nodded silently. Cameron studied me for a second, as though trying to decide whether or not to speak. Kat shifted impatiently.

"I know you both want answers, but I can't give them to you right now. I'll get them to you in time. Right now, my only priority is keeping Kat and Erin safe before this whole thing goes to hell. You believe that?"

Either he was the best actor on the planet, or he was speaking the truth. I chose the latter, if only for simplicity's sake. "Yeah. I believe you."

"Good." He pulled something out of his pocket and put it in my hand. A phone. "This is a burner—untraceable. You need to leave the phones you have behind, along with the laptops or ipads or whatever you usually carry. Any electronics you need will be waiting for you on the mainland, everything outfitted with the equipment you need to move under the radar. You cannot contact anyone. For now, this is just you and Erin—the rest of your world is gone. It doesn't exist. I'll reach out to you as soon as I can."

"But where the hell are we supposed to go?"

"I've got that covered, don't worry about it." He put his hand on my shoulder and looked at me squarely. "They'll kill Erin if they catch her; you need to know that. And Jenny… She hates easily, and she hates well. There's nothing in this world she loathes more than Erin. Which means your girl's death won't come easy. It won't come fast. Jenny knows how to make a body hurt in ways you can't even imagine. She's been studying it for a long time."

The words hit me in a way I didn't even know words could: a shot to my stomach followed by a surge of fear and hate so strong that, for a minute, I didn't know what to do with it. This, I thought, is why loving someone is a bad idea. It's impossible to be logical about it—to look at anything objectively. All I wanted in that moment was to take Solomon and run as fast and as far as humanly possible with her. If there was a shuttle to the moon, we would have been on it.

Cameron studied me with the beginnings of a pale smile, as though he knew his words had hit their mark. "You're a good man. I know you can do this."

I had no idea how to respond to that, so was almost grateful when Sol staggered to her feet and approached.

"My father," she began. Not a good start. "He… is he with you? Is he on the island right now?"

"Sol—" I said.

She held up her hand. Adrenaline or sheer willpower were apparently stronger than whatever Kat had given her, because she looked completely present when our eyes met. "Just a second. Please." She turned back to Cameron. The flicker of hesitation on his face was all I needed to know she was on the right track.

"We need to go, Erin," Cameron said instead of answering her. "You will get your answers. I give you my word—you'll get them. But if any of us hope to make it out of this alive, you have to let me take Kat out of here now."

There was a gunshot somewhere far off, toward the south side of the island. Cameron flinched, another crack in that usually impenetrable calm. "Shit. She's here sooner than I expected." He turned his back on Solomon, focused on Kat now. "Let's go."

Another shot sounded, closer this time. To my infinite surprise, Solomon nodded. "Just take her. Keep her safe," she said, indicating her mother with a nod of her head. "We'll be all right."

"I want you out of here in forty-five minutes," Cameron repeated as he made for the door. "No more, no less. Don't tell anyone what's happening, because I can guarantee they'll be caught in the crossfire if you do. I know you don't want that."

If Solomon was expecting a heartfelt farewell from Kat, she was disappointed—her mother went through the door without so much as a backward glance. Sol stood beside me, mute, as we watched them go. Before they were out of sight, I turned to her with a single goal in my mind:

Get her the hell out of there.

"We need to do what Cameron said," he said. "I know you don't necessarily trust him—I don't, either. But right now this is the only alternative I can think of that doesn't end up with you dead. And I can't live with that."

She blinked at me, her eyes still a little foggy. A lock of hair lay loose across her forehead. I pushed it back behind her ear. She caught her lower lip between her teeth and thought for a second, maybe two.

"Okay," she said. "Until we can come up with something better... okay. We run."

PART II
THE ROAD TO NOWHERE

8
KAT

FOR YEARS, Kat blamed Maddie for the worst things in her life. Maddie Tate, her best friend since kindergarten: the first girl ever to kiss her, at six years old out behind the swings at Jefferson Elementary. The girl who gave her her first cigarette; her first drink. The girl who convinced Kat to steal her father's boat one grey winter's night when they were teenagers, so they could sneak out to Payson Isle together. *Just to see if they're really as crazy as everyone says*, Maddie told her.

And now, thirty-five years later, here she was: still paying for that stupid lapse in judgment she'd had by trusting Maddie Tate the winter they both turned seventeen.

She and Cameron had run maybe fifty yards, no more, before he stopped and produced a gun from his jacket—another gun, different from his own. Smaller, but certainly no less effective.

"What the hell is this?" Kat asked.

"You may need it. I have no idea what Jenny has in store, but it's probably not good."

The thought was sobering. An image of a tow-headed, brown-eyed little girl popped into her head. *How do you know my daddy?* Jenny had a lisp as a child. Always dressed in ribbons and bows; Daddy's little girl.

"I don't need a gun," she said. "You have one. That will do the trick. I'm a surgeon—I don't shoot people. I fix them after other idiots have shot them."

"Spare me," Cam said. "It's not like you've never used one before. Just take it."

He forced it into her hand. The steel was warm from being carried close to his body. She shoved it into her pocket without checking to see what kind it was, or even if it was loaded. Her father was a military man who lived and died by the second amendment; Kat knew her guns. If she needed to use it, she knew perfectly well how to do so.

Cameron continued on, slowed to a more cautious pace now, his own gun up and at the ready. Kat followed alongside. The island was eerily still now. She wondered if Erin and Diggs were getting ready to go. If Erin would follow Cam's directions at all, or if Diggs would have to fight her on it. She had no doubt that he would do exactly that, this time around.

"You're sending them where I told you, right?" she asked. "You got the tickets?"

"I got them," Cam agreed, glancing at her. "They're taken care of. Now let's focus on getting you out."

It was freezing, the snow stopped and the island a glistening, gleaming sheet of ice. Less than ten hours ago, she'd been lying in a pit of the dead, convinced she was about to join their ranks. And now here she was, still very much alive. She had no clue what would happen next, no idea how long she might stay that way, but for now at least she had a pulse. Her legs were still moving; her heart was still beating. And Erin was safe.

She saw a flash of her daughter's future, then—the cheesy Hollywood ending she would never admit she fantasized about: Diggs and Erin, on some godforsaken beach somewhere. Diggs tanned to a golden brown; Erin with a floppy hat and zinc oxide on her nose, bouncing a mop-topped toddler on her knee.

A branch snapped behind them on the path, pulling her back to the present. Cam stopped her with a hand on her arm, guiding her into a grove of spruce trees so thick she was nearly blinded by a branch that grazed the side of her eye. That was what she got for getting sidetracked by sentimental bullshit like Erin's blissed-out future with her cradle-robbing boyfriend.

"What was that?" she whispered.

Cam put a finger to his lips. They stayed that way for a minute, maybe two, frozen in the undergrowth. Kat was just beginning to lose feeling in her toes when she heard more branches snap not far from them. Seven breathless seconds passed—she counted each of them—before an island deer nudged its way through the foliage. It stopped to nibble at the bark on a nearby birch tree, and Kat breathed an audible sigh of relief.

About to head back into the open, she stopped when the deer's head came up. Its ears tipped forward, then back. Cam grabbed Kat's arm. Every breath came on a puff of white in the darkness. The deer's tail twitched, then flipped up. It stood in the stillness, frozen.

Somewhere too close for comfort, there was the smooth, throaty ratchet of a shotgun being cocked.

At the sound, the deer glided noiselessly back into the forest.

An instant later, Jenny took the animal's place, the shotgun raised to her shoulder. Cameron's fingers tightened around Kat's arm. Neither of them moved.

Neither of them breathed.

Jenny wore a parka with fur at the cuffs, collar, and

hood. Even bundled, it was clear that she had grown into a beautiful woman. She was younger than Erin by at least a few years—only in her early to mid-twenties, Kat thought. Still, the girl was a veritable carbon copy of her mother. Looking at the cold smile and calculating eyes that glared into the darkness, it occurred to Kat that the similarities were more than skin-deep: Cameron's wife had been a sociopath from the word go.

His daughter was following in her footsteps.

As if to confirm the theory, Jenny took aim at a spot just to Kat's right. Her finger tensed on the trigger. Kat was sure they'd been spotted. She could practically feel Cam preparing himself to step in front of the bullet. To surrender. Never, of course, to shoot. Not Jenny.

For a second, Kat considered doing it herself. She could take out the gun Cam had given her, and take the girl down. It wouldn't end anything—not really. There were plenty of others ready and willing to take Jenny's place; plenty in J's ranks anxious to hunt them down and end the threat the Solomon family presented once and for all. None of them would take this whole thing as personally as Jenny had, though.

The seconds passed.

No one moved.

If Jenny saw them, she gave no indication.

Kat's hand curled around the gun in her pocket. She wondered if Cam would stop her. Maybe he would be relieved.

How do you know my daddy?

Ribbons and bows; a gap-toothed smile. That was fifteen years ago. Kat was just getting to know Cam, then.

She let go of the gun.

"Where did you go, Daddy?" Jenny whispered the words into the night, singsong. A child's voice, from a grown woman's lips. Cameron tensed beside Kat.

A shiver ran up Kat's spine when the girl's gaze shifted. For an instant, Jenny stared directly at her father.

"Jenny!" A man shouted in the distance. The girl started, her finger still on the shotgun trigger. Kat closed her eyes and waited for her world to end.

Instead, she heard the roar of a boat motor rev to life somewhere nearby.

"I've got 'em!" the man shouted. "Come on—the boat's leaving, Jen. We've got them."

Fear ran through Kat's body like an electric current. She made a move toward the clearing, her hand once more at the gun in her pocket. They'd found Diggs and Erin. Cameron clapped a hand over her mouth and pulled her back, her back pressed to his front. He was stronger than she had expected, his grip like iron.

Jenny lowered the gun. "You sure?" she shouted back.

"Come on, damn it," the man responded. There was a rustle of brush and then he appeared beside her: a tall, broad man with an angular face and clear, uncomplicated eyes. Kat flinched. A scene on Payson Isle nearly a year before flashed through her mind: That same man, eyes cold and unaffected as he beat her. Nearly killed her. *Erin gets worse than this unless you convince her to back off,* he'd promised then.

"We lose them and this is on our heads," the man said. "Move!"

Jenny looked back into the undergrowth one more time, forehead furrowed, before she dropped the gun to her side and loped back in the other direction.

As soon as Jenny was gone, Kat scrambled away from Cameron. Her heart was racing. "What the hell is wrong with you? Diggs and Erin—"

"Won't be leaving the island for another..." he consulted his watch. "Twenty-six minutes. They're all right."

It took a minute for that to sink in. "That boat was a diversion, then," she guessed. She felt like an idiot for having doubted him. Cameron was the kind of man who would have this covered. Then, it dawned on her. "Who was driving the boat, Cam?"

He returned to the trail without looking at her. "I think you know that. Adam's been doing this a long time now… He'll be all right. But I couldn't do it alone, and I sure as hell don't have any other allies anymore."

There was the sound of another boat revving to life, this one louder—more horses, without a doubt. Cameron stood still beside Kat, waiting as his daughter ran from the island. For the first time, Kat took note of the man beside her. Usually fit and trim, Cam was looking a little ragged around the edges.

"How long have you been on the run now?" she asked him.

"Not long," he said. "J. was suspicious before, but things went to shit after Kentucky."

"Because you helped Erin," Kat guessed.

"It was a long time coming," he said with a shrug. "Things had been tense for a while. Jenny was the one who caught on in the end."

There was nothing in his face or voice to indicate that this bothered him. Maybe it didn't. She'd known Mitch Cameron for a long time now, but Kat had never really been able to read him.

"And she couldn't see your side of things?" she asked.

He barked a laugh, a soft burst of air that was barely audible in the stillness. "Jenny only sees her side of things. She doesn't let silly things like family get in the way—even with her father."

"Smart girl," Kat murmured.

Cameron had no response for that.

They traveled fast from there, low to the ground, through a thick forest that didn't slow Cam down in the least. He'd always been like that. Adam used to call him The Ghost. Kat remembered being terrified, the first few times her ex-husband mentioned him:

If he comes for us, you'll never know it. He'll be on us, and it will be over… I've seen him do it.

He was more legend than man, back in those days. She knew better now: Mitch Cameron was as human as the rest of them.

Ten minutes later, they reached a clearing at the top of the island. A little twin-engine plane waited. Both boats were out of sight. Kat waited for an explosion on the horizon or a burst of gunfire, but there was only silence now. She felt an unexpected surge of hope at the thought.

She followed Cameron into the plane.

Maybe they would make it out of this alive after all.

9
SOLOMON

WITHOUT STORMY SEAS and spitting snow to battle against, Diggs and I made the trip back to the mainland in just over an hour. When we got to the other side, the silver Camry was parked exactly where Cameron had promised it would be. Diggs slid into the driver's side before I could beat him to it, which is typical of Diggs. The man does not like to be driven.

"Check the glove compartment," he said once Einstein was settled and Diggs and I were both safely buckled in.

All three of us were wet from the boat ride, and beyond frozen from the cold. And exhausted, which seemed to be my default setting these days. I opened the glove compartment while Diggs started the car. There was a sealed yellow envelope inside.

"What have you got?" Diggs asked.

Jesus. What didn't we have? "Passports. Fake IDs." The pictures showed me with dark hair, and Diggs with a buzz cut and glasses. "There's a key card for a hotel. The note here says we should go to the hotel first. And apparently there's luggage and a laptop in the trunk of the car."

I looked at the names on the passports: Nick and

Danielle Winston. Along with the paperwork were two simple gold wedding bands in a plastic pouch. Apparently, Diggs had made an honest woman of me in this alternate universe Cameron had created.

"Where's the hotel?" Diggs asked.

I directed him back to Route 1. Within three minutes, Einstein was passed out in the backseat. Within five, we reached a series of cabins set back from the road. It was secluded and dark, three a.m. post-snowstorm quiet.

"This is it?" Diggs asked.

"Apparently. The perfect place to be murdered in our sleep."

He turned off the car. "Nice. You know, when I'm dying, I really hope you're the one by my bedside whispering words of comfort in those final moments."

"I'll do my best."

Diggs grabbed the luggage while I took Einstein for the final walk of the night. I steered clear of the woods and the road and basically everything but a small strip of grass within sight of the cabin—partly because Diggs had asked me to, and partly because bad things tend to happen when I walk Einstein at night.

Even though I'd stayed close by, Diggs still reappeared within a couple of minutes.

"I'll be right in," I said.

"I know. I just figured I'd stretch my legs."

"Sure." I noted the bulge under his jacket; Diggs was packing. He would probably always be packing, from here on out. I suspected it would be a long time before I'd be able to go for a walk without worrying about what was waiting in the shadows. "Is the place nice?"

"It's fine."

I turned to find him staring into the darkness, his shoulders tensed. I wanted to go to him; to reassure him that everything was okay. We would be all right. I didn't, though, uncertain in a way I'd never been when we were just friends. When we were just friends, I'd make some asshole, off-the-cuff remark, and he'd make some asshole off-the-cuff remark back, and that would be the end of it. Even when we were sleeping together, I could handle it because I knew what I could expect at the end of the day: Great sex, great conversation, a shoulder to cry on when the going got rough. But, ultimately, I knew not to get too attached because he would, without a doubt, be gone at the first sign of daylight.

But I didn't know how to do *this*. There was nothing witty or off-the-cuff about this. We were running away together. Assuming the fake identities of Nick and Danielle Winston, who probably traveled together and ate breakfast together and gave each other foot rubs.

I'd known Diggs for seventeen years, and not once had I touched his friggin' feet.

He glanced back at me, almost like he'd forgotten I was there. He seemed as uncertain as I was, which didn't make me feel any better. One of us should really know what the hell we were doing.

"I keep thinking of the Sanctuary—that place Will Rainier kept us," he said. "Not that this is the same. But I can't shake the feeling that we're being watched."

I hadn't even thought of that. Perfect: one more thing to worry about.

"I don't think we are, though," Diggs added, as though he'd read my mind. "Cameron has enough on his plate—I don't think he has time to listen in, necessarily."

"Maybe." The doubt was plain in my voice.

"We should go in," he said. "Figure out what comes next, according to the puppet master."

I followed him inside, neither of us touching. And all I could think, endlessly, was: *This is a mistake. It's a mistake to take him from his life, just because I can't return to mine. And this is a mistake we can't come back from, once it's made.*

●

The cabin had a tiny kitchen, living room with a sofa and TV, and a bedroom with a king-sized bed and an old, scarred dresser. Diggs had left the unopened luggage—two black suitcases, worn enough to appear well-used but hardly threadbare—by the sofa.

"Check this out," he said when I sat on the sofa, handing me a high-end leather briefcase. Inside, I found a slim, state-of-the-art laptop that couldn't have weighed more than a couple of pounds. "I think I'm going to like Cameron footing the bill," he said. "That thing must have set him back a few pesos."

"I don't think money's a big worry for Cameron." I paused. "I think he might be a robot. Do robots worry about money?"

"No more than the rest of us, I guess. Do you still have the envelope?"

I handed it to him, then laid the first suitcase on the floor and opened it. "This one is yours," I said at sight of the men's jeans, sweater, and boxers. There was a folder on top with NICK WINSTON written in bold letters. I moved to the next suitcase, curious despite myself. Diggs was looking over our passports, getting to know the couple we were about to become.

When I opened the second suitcase, my jaw dropped. "Uh… Diggs."

He looked up. "What is it?"

I nodded to the suitcase, now open. Stacked along the side, in between my clothes and the dossier for my new identity, were several neat stacks of cash.

"Holy shit. How much is in there?"

I counted while Diggs went through his own suitcase. When I was done, I noted a box of hair dye and some hair clippers that he'd set on the sofa behind us. Not a good sign.

"Fifty grand," I said. "Five thousand in small bills, the rest in hundreds."

Diggs scratched his head. "Jesus. So… he's serious about this. These people he wants us to become."

"Nick and Danielle," I said.

"Dani," he corrected me. Where I was ready to jump ship at the nearest port, Diggs suddenly looked surprisingly at ease. "Nick and Dani."

"Of course. Nick and Dani—what was I thinking?"

"It could be worse." I noticed he didn't say how, though. "He wants us back on the road tomorrow morning. There are plane tickets to Melbourne, business class out of Allentown, Pennsylvania. We leave Sunday afternoon."

Australia: Where the men are men, and the spiders are as big as Shih Tzus. Jesus.

Diggs got up from the floor and held his hand out to me. "Come on, ace. Bathroom. We've got some work to do if we're going to make this happen. Time for a makeover."

I groaned. After a moment's hesitation, I took his hand and let him pull me up. He handed me the hair dye, picked up the clippers, and pulled me along behind him.

"You really think we need to go this far?" I asked. "Because, honestly, this seems like overkill."

The bathroom had a tub/shower combo and very limited sink space. Diggs plugged in the hair clippers.

"These people have never heard the term overkill. Sorry, kid. Red's out; brunette's in. For now, anyway."

I turned on the water with a heavy sigh.

If I ever saw Kat again, she was a dead woman.

●

"There are things you need to remember, and things you need to forget. You understand?"

I sit on the ground, my knees to my chin. My father is across from me, cross-legged like a true-blue yogi. He's very serious. I nod. He opens his mouth, his eyes blue like the ocean, but nothing comes out. Somewhere far off, someone screams. I look away, trying to figure out how I know that sound. When I look back, my father is gone.

And then suddenly, in a nonsensical flash you only find in dreams and art house flicks, I am in the woods. Allie is with me. We're both running—fast, far, trying to get away from something I can't see behind us. Allie isn't limping. I want to ask her why, but I can't get my breath.

"Things to remember, things to forget," I hear my father say again.

We're almost safe. Another few feet and we'll be out of the trees and the dark, and back in the light. We'll be safe if we can get out of the woods. I don't want him to keep us in the woods.

Three more steps.

Two more.

The light is on me, I can feel the sun, when I hear Allie scream.

When I turn, she is on the ground. Bleeding. Isaac stands over her.

"You're safe, Erin," my father says. *"Just forget the dark spots, and nothing will hurt you."* I can't see him, though. I can't find him.

Isaac looks up. He's spotted me—he knows I'm here, and we weren't supposed to be. Allie is crying.

"Forget the dark spots," my father whispers.

Isaac leaves Allie on the ground, and comes for me. His eyes are angry and dark and full of something I don't want to see.

I bolted up in bed, breathing hard, damp with sweat. The cabin was still dark. Diggs slept beside me, snoring softly. *Forget the dark spots.* What the hell did that mean? I sat still for a minute, torn between trying to call up the images and trying to stuff them as far back down in my subconscious as they would go.

I didn't have that luxury anymore though, did I? Something had happened on Payson Isle when I was a kid... Those shiny, happy memories I'd clung to my entire life weren't the whole story. They couldn't be. What had Juarez asked me the night before, when we were at the Melquist house? *Are the memories whole, or just flashes?*

Just flashes—more and more of them, in a patchwork I couldn't make any sense of.

Gradually, my heart settled back to a reasonably normal rhythm. The desire to crawl out of my own skin faded. The clock by the bed said it was 5:30. Diggs and I hadn't turned in until almost four, when we'd passed out on opposite sides of the bed, like the old married couple we now were.

Now, I lay back down beside him, careful not to wake him. I'd cut his hair, shearing the golden locks I loved until all that was left was a half-inch of peach fuzz. He'd shaved his face clean for the first time in years—I couldn't remember the last time he hadn't had at least some scruff, if not a full beard. He looked younger. More innocent. A different man than the one I knew and loved and had come to rely on, despite my best efforts not to.

I slid a little closer and ran my index finger along the furrow in his forehead. He sighed, but remained asleep.

Risking everything, I leaned in and kissed his temple. Breathed in the only safe thing I had left.

Then, I got out of bed before he woke up.

There were no cars on the road when I took Einstein out for his first pee break of the day. A few seagulls flew overhead, shrieking about whatever it is seagulls shriek about at daybreak. It was cold and clear outside, a thin crust of ice coating the snowfall from the day before.

When I went back inside, I retrieved the laptop Cameron had left for us and set myself up on the sofa with Einstein. I pulled up the home page and typed 'Jonestown' into the search engine.

It wasn't like I'd never seen the material before: the articles on Jim Jones and his People's Temple; Jones' history as a religious leader and semi-respected member of society in Indiana and, later, California; his decline into paranoia and drug addiction after he'd led his followers to the jungles of South America, in a supposed attempt to get away from capitalism and corruption in the United States. I had read it all before.

Now, I looked at it with new eyes.

Forget the dark spots.

Did the dark spots in my childhood have anything to do with Jonestown?

My father had been there.

Growing up, my dad hadn't had a happy childhood—I knew that much from reading a diary my aunt had kept when they were kids, before she was killed. Dad hadn't gotten along with his parents. He'd been a rebellious kid who caused more than his share of heartache in the small Maine town where he spent his teen years. When my aunt was killed during Dad's fifteenth summer, everything must have changed for him. How could it not?

That was when he ran away.

Kat had said his family had known the Jones' family back in Indiana, so Jim Jones would have already been on his radar. Alone and traumatized, my father would have been searching for something—some reason to keep going after he'd witnessed the brutal rape and murder of his little sister.

That was in 1970.

Jones was already in California by then; the base in San Francisco would be established in the next few years.

In the other room, I heard Diggs get up. A few minutes later, the toilet flushed. The water ran. When Diggs came out, he was in boxers and a t-shirt, his feet bare. He still looked like a stranger. I checked the clock. It was just after seven a.m.

"How long have you been up?" he asked.

"An hour, maybe," I said. "Did you know there was a big dinner honoring Jim Jones in 1976? All the political heavy hitters were there: Jerry Brown and Mervyn Dymally... Walter Mondale was a fan. So was Rosalynn Carter. Hell, Harvey Milk stood in the way of a full-fledged investigation into Jonestown when people started saying things had gone bad down there."

He sat beside me, forcing Einstein to the floor. The mutt hopped down unhappily, circled, and resettled in front of me. I shifted to give Diggs more room, but he curled his hand around my ankles and pulled my feet into his lap.

"Does it say anything about the Red Brigade?" he asked.

I typed in 'Peoples Temple Red Brigade' and scanned the results. "Most of the hits are from conspiracy theorists. The gist is that the Red Brigade was a group of armed security guards... The catalyst for the mass suicide at Jonestown happened the day before, on November 17. A group of Americans known as the Concerned Relatives arrived in Guyana to interview members of the Temple and check out the facilities..."

"That group included Congressman Leo Ryan," Diggs said, clearly familiar with the details. "At which point, people started slipping him notes saying Jones had gone off the reservation and could they please get help getting back to the U.S."

"Not so much, actually," I corrected him, still reading from the screen. "By the time Ryan and his Concerned Relatives were ready to leave the next day, the Congressman said he thought reports of abuse were unfounded. He was prepared to file a favorable report when he got home. Jones still freaked out, though."

"So, the next day when Ryan and his delegation got ready to leave..." he prompted, looking at me expectantly.

"They were gunned down at the airstrip," I completed. "Supposedly by members of the Red Brigade, sent there by Jones to do whatever was necessary to keep everyone in Guyana."

I stared at the computer screen for a long time, trying to imagine all of this. It all seemed too fantastical to have actually happened: a village of nearly one thousand Americans, living in a third-world country their leader touted as the 'New Utopia.' I searched Google images for photos from Jonestown, but only came up with the shots that had become synonymous with the tragedy: layers of bodies lying face down outside a collection of huts deep in the jungle.

Diggs took the computer from me and set it aside. "You really think your father was there, then?"

"Yeah," I said after a minute's thought. "I do. And Kat didn't disagree with it... I just can't figure out why anyone is trying to shut him up now. Or why they have been, all along. Even if Dad was part of the Red Brigade, it's not like Jones' crimes aren't public knowledge at this point. Investigators uncovered the money, they knew about the sexual, physical, and emotional abuse… I mean, what the hell could my father possibly have told people?"

"I don't know. But it must be pretty friggin' damning, to justify the bloodshed we've seen."

I didn't argue. Silence fell. Diggs reached out and tugged a strand of my hair, curling it around his finger. "This isn't so bad, you know. Brunette… It could be worse."

"It looks stupid. My complexion, my freckles… Anyone will know it's not my natural color, the second they see me."

"Only if they get close. Though I could have done a better job."

"It's all right. It's not like I'm gonna run out and enroll in beauty school when this is all over, myself."

"Are you kidding?" He grinned. "You shaved my head like a pro. You'll be setting up camp in Hollywood before we know it, giving buzz cuts to the rich and famous."

"Yeah, right." I rolled my eyes, unable to completely squelch a smile. I ran my hand along the top of his head, the bristles tickling my palm. "I love your hair. I miss it already."

"It'll grow back. And yours will be red again." He took my hand in his and ran his fingers along my knuckles, looking at me thoughtfully. "We'll get through this, Sol. Life will go back to what it always was."

"Not soon, though."

"Maybe not soon," he agreed. "But it will. And in the meantime, we can deal. We've got each other, right?"

I didn't answer. It got quiet. The sun was up now. Einstein got up and paced the cabin, restless. We were far enough from the road that you couldn't hear the traffic from our little hideaway. Diggs continued to look at me, reading me in that way he does.

"You know we need to keep talking, right?" he asked. "That's the only way this will work… You can't shut me out here. If you're nervous about this, we can talk about that. Go over it." I nodded, but I wasn't sure how to respond beyond that. "*Are* you nervous?" he pressed. "I mean… I'm freaked out. You must be freaked out."

This was confession time, I knew—time for me to get vulnerable. Open up. Tell him all my darkest fears about everything we were about to face. Confess that I had my doubts about us. About him.

I wet my lips. "Nah," I lied. "I'm fine. I mean, we've got a plan, right?" I hopped up before he could call me on it, avoiding his eye. "I'll get dressed, and we can head out. We've got some miles to cover."

I could feel him watching me as I walked away, too unnerved to look back or ask questions or talk about the fact that it felt at the moment like we were about to make a catastrophic mistake. I was walking off a cliff, and I was dragging him with me.

He called after me as I slipped through the bathroom door.

I didn't answer.

10

KAT

THE TRICK TO BEING A DECOY, Cameron said, was to stay just far enough ahead of Jenny that she was sure she was on the right track, without letting her get so close that they got caught.

"It's a balancing act," he told Kat as they drove west, toward New Hampshire. "But I think we can pull it off. Right now, they're still following Adam, thinking they have Erin and Diggs on the run."

Kat nodded, but remained silent.

"You're quiet," he said. "Are you all right?"

"It's been a rough few days," she said.

At the reminder, his face turned grim. Cameron had always been thin, but now he looked gaunt. His eyes were shadowed, a tension in his spine that she'd never seen before. Most of the time, it was easy to forget that he was human. Cameron didn't seem to need food, sleep, human companionship… At least, that was the story Adam had always told. Even later, when Kat was well-acquainted with the man behind the legend, she had a hard time remembering that Cam had the same basic human needs the rest of them did.

"I thought I could get there in time—to save them," he said. "I'm sorry."

"It's not your fault," she said, thinking of the Melquist family: the little girl with the baby in her arms, all of them huddled together in that goddamn pit; of Jenny's shouts, close behind her; of lying with the bodies, heart pounding, while she waited to be found.

Sure she would be found.

"We'll get you away from them," Cameron said. He ran a long, cool fingertip over the back of her hand, his brow creased with worry. "I know it's been a long road, but we're almost to the end now."

Kat didn't know what that meant. She didn't ask, though, sure she didn't want the answer. It was better not to know, whenever Cameron and Adam were involved.

Cam drove a Mercedes Benz, a ride so smooth and so quiet that sleep was easy to come by. They listened to classical music, his choice—one that Kat was grateful for. Anything else would have been an intrusion, but this struck a good counterpoint to the scenes that had been running through her head for weeks now.

On their first trip to Payson Isle, Kat and Maddie reached the island at eight o'clock that night. There was a church service going on, held in an old barn in the middle of the woods It was December, cold as hell, and Kat knew full well that her father would murder her if they didn't get back soon. But Maddie wanted to check out the church. To be honest, Kat had been curious herself. The mass suicide at Jonestown had happened a month before… Ever since, Maddie had been obsessed with the religious community out on Payson Isle.

"I bet they have orgies," she told Kat, her eyes wide. Maddie was gorgeous, but not all that bright. Kat doubted she even knew what an orgy was. "And do loads of drugs. There's probably a pot farm right out there. Who knows what could be going on."

And so, they went to find out for themselves.

In the barn, the smell of hay and farm animals was thick in the air. The preacher was surprisingly good looking—tall and broad shouldered, with silver hair and piercing blue eyes. He didn't look like any preacher Kat had ever seen, that was for damn sure.

"We have created a world for our children, safe from temptation," the preacher was saying when they came in. "Safe from violence and prejudice. Safe from the vanity and temptation inherent in mainstream life. We serve a purpose. Our children serve a purpose."

Maddie went in before Kat could stop her. The preacher saw them, but he didn't look surprised. Didn't look worried. He gestured for them both to come inside. His smile got wider.

"Welcome. What can we do for you ladies tonight?" He didn't tell them to sit; didn't start preaching at them. Everything came to a halt, every person in the congregation focused on the newcomers.

"We were just… uh, curious," Maddie said. Maddie was tall and slender, with dark feathered hair and big dark eyes. Kat was shorter, with more curves, Irish, fish-belly white skin, and charcoal black hair. Every man who ever set eyes on Maddie fell for her. Kat could all but see it happening to the preacher, then and there.

"Well, why don't you two come in and sit? Brother Jonah, move down a bit so these ladies can join us."

A short, curly-haired man in jeans and a lumberjack flannel scooted his chair over. Maddie sat in one folding metal chair, Kat in another.

The preacher kept up his sermon for another two hours.

The difference from any other church service Kat had been at, though, was that this preacher talked *to* everyone in the congregation, instead of *at* them. He made jokes. Asked questions. When he read from the Bible, he did it in a way that made it sound real, instead of like something made up hundreds of years ago for a society that had lost its relevance eons ago.

By the end of the night, Kat still had her reservations, but Maddie had fallen for the whole act hook, line, and sinker.

Afterward, Isaac asked them both to stay a little longer. Kat hedged. Her father wouldn't be home until the next night, but if he ever found out she was there…

"I won't keep you long," Isaac Payson promised. "I'll make sure you get back to the mainland safely."

"We have to leave by midnight," Kat said.

"It won't be a problem."

He led them through the woods. There was a fresh blanket of snow on the ground, coating the trees, lighting the night. Isaac pointed out the different trails. He talked about when his family first bought the land, back in the early 1900s. He talked about the places he'd traveled, and how every one of them just made him more homesick for this place. This island.

By the time they reached a little greenhouse overlooking the ocean, Kat had almost forgotten her life on the mainland. It was like Isaac had keyed into everything she had ever considered wrong with her life: seventeen years sheltered by a domineering father, every minute of her day accounted for; every year of her future already planned.

"Here, we believe young people must be given the space to grow on their own. To develop their own interests. In the past, women your age would already be raising families," Isaac told them. "And yet, we've chosen to shelter our children today, as though they are little idiots set on the planet only to be molded into our vision of what, and whom, they should be."

Kat had graduated high school a year early, and then had taken a year off to work with her father. He already had her medical school (Johns Hopkins, the same college her father and her grandfather and her great grandfather had graduated from) picked out and a spot for her practically guaranteed.

"You want to be a doctor?" Isaac said when Kat told him about her plans for the future. He looked impressed.

"I've been working with my father since I was eight," she said.

"She's already better than half the doctors I've ever met," Maddie said. "Go ahead—ask her anything."

Isaac looked thoughtful. For a second, Kat thought she might have said too much. Maddie said she bragged sometimes, and guys didn't like that. Kat's father always told her she should never apologize for being smarter than everyone else in the room.

"We have a young man who's been injured," Isaac said. For a second, she thought this might be like the hypothetical game her father always played with her: A man comes in with hives and diarrhea, his left pupil blown. Diagnosis?

Isaac wasn't playing a game, though.

"Injured how?" Kat asked.

He didn't answer right away. "We've been praying for him. Trying to keep the wounds clean, but honestly no one here has known what to do. You may be the answer to Adam's prayers."

That was how she met Adam Solomon for the first time.

●

She and Cameron stopped at a rest area in Orleans, New York, that morning. The sun was up, the day surprisingly warm considering what they'd left behind in Maine. Still, Kat couldn't stop shaking.

"Can I get you something?" Cam asked when they'd stopped. "They have food here. Or I could maybe get you a drink, if you like…" He looked down, too embarrassed to finish the thought.

"I don't want anything," she said. It took real effort to get the words out.

"You're sick, though." This time, he managed to look her in the eye. "A drink may take the edge off…"

"It will go away," she said shortly. "I just have to wait it out, until then."

Rather than argue, he nodded toward the brick building that served as the Orleans rest station. "All right, then—suit yourself. I'm just going to use the facilities. If you change your mind, though…"

"I won't."

He smiled at her thoughtfully, his head tipped to the right. "No. I know you won't." Their gaze locked for a moment. Cameron was an odd one to figure. He was far from traditionally handsome, his face too angular, his body too lean. But there was something magnetic about the way he carried himself, the intensity of his pale blue eyes.

He looked away first, and Kat was relieved to have even that small measure of control over the situation.

"I don't want to stay long," he said. "Fifteen, twenty minutes is all we should take."

"You've been driving for hours. Why don't you let me take the wheel for a while?"

"No need—I'm fine," he said briskly. "We don't have much farther, then we can stop for a few hours. Get our bearings."

She didn't bother to argue, already knowing it would be pointless. There wasn't one among them willing to listen to reason—not Cameron, not Adam, certainly not Erin. It sure as hell wasn't Kat, but she'd at least learned to pick her battles. This wasn't one she particularly cared to fight.

Instead, she told him to go ahead. She took a second to pull herself together before she opened the door and ventured into the fresh air.

A woman walked two chocolate Labs in the exercise area—one dog grayed at the muzzle, the other barely more than a pup. The sight brought to mind Einstein as a puppy, back when Erin had first gotten him. Kat had been traveling through Boston, which usually meant she'd try to grab lunch with Erin, if she could. This time, though, there was a conference in town; every hotel room in the city booked.

Michael—Erin's husband at the time—was the one who volunteered to let Kat stay. She could tell Erin was horrified. Those sporadic lunches were painful enough. The last thing her daughter wanted, she knew, was to have her camped out overnight there.

Erin had gotten the puppy the week before. Einstein was the only survivor in his litter; the others died of Parvo virus. The mother was hit by a car. The dog was tiny, malnourished, his eyes runny.

Why would you get a dog no one thinks will even survive? Can't you do anything the normal way? You should just have him put down—end the misery for both of you.

Erin didn't even dignify the comment with a response.

She'd always been the same, though: forever bringing home half-dead strays no one else would have. Diggs was the equivalent, as far as Kat was concerned. He might clean up well, but the man screamed mutt.

That night, Kat was awakened by a commotion in the kitchen—the clattering of pans, a glass breaking. She got up and went to the kitchen door, half-expecting to hear a fight between Erin and Michael. Despite what her daughter might say to the contrary, Kat knew the marriage wasn't going well, for obvious reasons. For one thing, Michael was twenty years older than Erin. And an idiot. The fact that Erin was in love with another man didn't help matters.

Instead of a fight, however, Kat opened the door a crack to find Erin on the floor surrounded by broken glass. The puppy was in her lap—not moving. Erin wept quietly, head bowed, the phone clutched in her left hand. Kat hovered on the threshold, caught in the same dilemma she had always had where her daughter was concerned: was it better to stay, or go?

It took some effort to pull herself back to the present, but eventually Kat managed. The woman with the Labs nodded at her with a smile. Kat nodded back. She turned and walked away, trying to quell her nausea.

In the restroom, a chubby, dark-skinned little girl came in with her mother while Kat reapplied her make-up, trying in vain to look at least half-human again.

"I like your hair," the little girl said, watching Kat with her hands in her pockets. "It's nice. I like black hair. My hair's black, too."

The girl's mother smiled awkwardly. "Sorry. I've been trying to teach her about talking to strangers…"

"It's all right," Kat said. Maya would say something back to the girl: tell her she thought her hair was pretty, too. Talk to the mother about their trip; ask where they were going. Sometimes, Kat watched the way Maya interacted with the world and felt complete awe. Honest to god, actual wizardry wouldn't have been as mystifying as Maya's ability to relate; to communicate. To care.

That bone-deep ache returned. She wouldn't see Maya

again—she knew that. However this ended up, Maya was out of her life for good.

The little girl went into one of the stalls, while her mother stood outside the door. She was a stout, unattractive woman with crooked teeth and acne scars on her dark face. Twice, she looked at Kat as if she wanted to say something, then quickly looked down at the tiled floor again.

Finally, Kat gave one last look at herself in the mirror, sighed, and turned her back on the hollow-eyed ghost who stared back at her.

She was barely out the door when someone grabbed her arm. She started to struggle, then stopped at sight of Cameron's wide eyes and raised eyebrows.

"Sorry," he said. "I didn't mean to scare you. I was worried—you were in there for a while."

"Jesus, Cam. You don't want to scare me, don't sneak up behind me when there's a whole band of lunatics out to kill us all."

"Could you say that a little louder?" he whispered, ushering her toward the exit. "A few people may have missed it."

Outside, the woman with the dogs was gone. There were more cars in the parking lot than there had been. It was just past eight a.m. Cameron opened her door first, then strode to the other side to get in. One glimpse at his profile was all it took for her to know something was wrong.

"Something happened," she said as soon as he slid into the driver's seat and closed the door. "What is it? What's wrong?"

He turned to face her. "Did you talk to the FBI agent?" he demanded.

"What? You mean Juarez? No. I didn't talk to anyone—"

"Well, someone talked to him. Which means our problems just multiplied, because now the Feds are on high alert."

"What does that mean for us?"

He started the car and jammed it into reverse. "It means J. is about to panic. You think we had problems before? You haven't seen anything yet."

She fell silent, thinking suddenly of Erin at ten years old, confused and abandoned and broken... Then, her face yesterday—a mix of shock and fear and pure loathing, when Kat fought her for another bottle of whiskey. Erin, sitting on the kitchen floor in the middle of the night surrounded by broken glass, trying to bring a dying puppy back to life.

Kat leaned back in her seat and closed her eyes.

She could almost feel them getting closer. The end was coming; J. was coming.

And Kat had never been more afraid in her life.

11
SOLOMON

LISTENING TO WCLZ a few hours into our drive from Bar Harbor, we heard the first news report come in about Raven's Ledge:

Details are sketchy at this time, but police have confirmed a multiple homicide on Raven's Ledge, a private island ten miles from Mount Desert. According to sources close to the investigation, multiple victims were found in what is a suspected murder suicide on the remote island. Two college students manning the Jensen Research Station have also been found dead. Authorities have not released the names of the victims at this time.

"Where do you think the students were?" I asked.

"No idea," he said. We both fell silent.

The report went on to provide background on the Melquist family, focusing primarily on Jonah Melquist—a decorated Vietnam vet who returned to Maine in the 1980s, where he isolated himself and his growing family on Raven's Ledge.

Jonah Melquist had known my father. According to

Kat, he and Dad were at Jonestown together, both part of the Red Brigade. I thought of Kat's words the day before: *It's been a death sentence from the day he walked away from the Brigade. No one just leaves these people.* Why? What did my father know that made leaving impossible? What did he know that made killing entire families a justifiable measure, in the minds of the people intent on keeping him quiet?

My nightmare that morning came back in a flash. *Things to remember; things to forget.* What had I forgotten about my childhood? And, maybe more importantly, why was it so hard to remember now?

"You're quiet," Diggs said at one point, as we crossed from Maine into New Hampshire.

"Just thinking."

"About?"

I looked out the window. Below us, the grating on the Portsmouth Bridge hummed beneath our tires. *Things to remember; things to forget.* "I'm not sure yet," I said.

He glanced at me, that by-now-familiar crease of concern in his forehead again. "You'll let me know when you are sure, though?"

"Yeah," I said absently, still locked in my nightmare. "I'll let you know."

At eleven that morning, just as we were leaving New Hampshire, the burner phone Cameron had given us rang.

"I don't have much time," Cameron began when I answered. "Where are you?"

I checked the highway signs. "We'll be in Massachusetts in about five minutes. Where's my mother? Is she all right?"

"She's fine. What the hell did you tell Juarez?"

I didn't care for his tone, and I was already on edge. Putting it on speaker, I shot a glare at Diggs. "*I* didn't tell Juarez anything."

"Kat's house had been blown up," Diggs intervened. "You really think I was going to keep quiet after that?"

"That wasn't me, you idiot," Cameron ground out. "Do you have any idea how much worse you've made things by bringing the FBI into this?"

"As far as I knew, you were on the same team with Jenny when I decided to go to the cops," Diggs said. "I needed an ally. I chose Jack Juarez."

"Well, now you need to stay away from him and the Feds. I'll do whatever damage control I can on my end. Don't breathe a word of this to the police… Don't breathe a word of this to anyone."

"I'll cancel the press conference, then," Diggs said.

If Cameron appreciated the humor, he gave no indication. "I'll have instructions for how you can contact me when you reach Melbourne. Any goodbyes you might want to make before you disappear, loose ends you want to tie up… You need to curb that impulse."

My chest tightened. "How long are we doing this, exactly?"

"You know how long you're doing this," Cameron said evenly. "This isn't a short-term proposition."

"We never talked about this, though," I said. "You can't just expect us to pick up and leave our lives. Diggs and I are barely dating, for Christ's sake, and you want us to run away together."

"We're out of options," Cameron said. "You have exactly two choices: Do this and live, or don't, and die."

"What if I said screw you, called your bluff, and went to the police?" I said. My blood ran hotter. I didn't look at Diggs as I said the words. "What happens then?"

There was a long pause on the line. Cameron cleared his throat. "I hope you won't do that."

"And if I do?"

"If you do, Jenny will come after you, whether or not the police are watching you. You have no proof to substantiate any of your claims, no idea who is implicated in all this, and thus you are no good to the police. They might—and this is a very big might—provide some protection from Jenny, but not for long. She'll wait them out, and then she will kill you. And there won't be anything I can do."

My mouth went dry. Diggs stayed quiet, his jaw tensed as he continued driving. When I didn't say anything, Cameron continued.

"When you're safely out of the country, we'll talk as soon as I am able. In the meantime, I will get you, Diggs, and your mother out of this safely. But to make that happen, you have to meet me halfway. I'm sorry I can't give you more time to think about this, but it needs to happen now."

I glanced at Diggs, but quickly looked away when he met my eye. My palms were so damp the phone kept slipping out of my hand.

"We'll do it," Diggs said.

"Good man," Cameron said.

I remained silent. I felt like there was a cliff on one side of us, a brick wall on the other. We could take the plunge and be lost, or just slam ourselves straight into the rocks. Damned if you do…

I only tuned back into Cameron when I heard the tail end of his last statement.

"… and the dog will need to go."

"I'm sorry—what?" I said, snapping back to reality.

"J's people will be looking for a man and woman traveling with a dog. To pull this off, you need to get that dog out of there. You certainly can't leave the country with it."

"And where, exactly, do you want me to *put* the dog?" I was trying very hard not to panic. "Am I just supposed to drop him on the side of the road somewhere?"

"I can help you arrange something—"

"Meaning what?"

"Your ex-husband—"

"My ex-husband has a new girlfriend and a new dog and no interest in Einstein or me. You want me to just show up on his doorstep with my fake hair and my fake ID, and dump my dog—"

Before I completely lost my shit, Diggs took the phone off speaker and put it to his ear again. "You need to find another way," he said to Cameron.

I didn't hear what Cameron said on the other end, and was too freaked out at that point to even try to listen in. I resisted the urge to crawl into the backseat with my dog, and contented myself with reaching back to pet him, my gaze fixed on the landscape passing us by.

We were supposed to just… leave. Abandon the dog; abandon jobs and friends and family; forget about the fact that Diggs and I had hardly worked things out enough to decide we were ready to date, let alone ride off into the sunset. We weren't ready for this. I wasn't ready for this. I held onto Einstein's paw and tried to remember the lost art of deep breathing.

Two minutes later, Diggs hung up the phone. He touched my arm.

"You still in there?"

I nodded. Breathing was still a challenge, though. "I'm here."

"We'll figure something out with Einstein. Just don't worry about it right now."

I managed another nod, noting that he hadn't actually said the dog was coming with us. I leaned back in my seat, eyes still fixed on the horizon. "Right. Sure."

"We'll be all right, Sol," he said. I could feel him watching me. Try as I might, I couldn't think of anything to say that didn't sound ridiculous or borderline hysterical. Einstein was just a dog, after all. With our lives on the line, it should be an easy decision to leave him behind. And Diggs was right: We had each other.

My borderline hysteria was creeping dangerously close to overt histrionics. "I think I'll try to get some sleep," I finally managed. "Wake me when you need a break, all right?"

"Yeah. Sure. If you want to talk, though…"

"I don't—thanks. I'm fine." I closed my eyes. We drove on.

For most of the rest of the day, we traveled in virtual silence. Whoever wasn't driving read the lengthy dossiers Cameron had provided on Nick and Dani Winston. They didn't make me feel any better.

Nick and Dani weren't reporters. Instead, Nick was a professor of American and European history; Dani was an advertising copywriter. They were both from Portland, Oregon. They had no kids. No parents. Two orphaned expatriates looking to start a new life Down Under. I imagined that these characters we were playing, this imaginary couple who seemed nothing like either of us, would have bonded over their solitude. They would have clung to each other, made a family together where there had been none.

At seven that night, we reached a hotel not far from the airport in Allentown. Diggs checked us in while I took Einstein and our things upstairs, scoping out the hallways for the closest exits and most promising vending machines. The room had floral bedspreads and matching drapes and ugly maroon carpeting. A watercolor of ducks in a pond hung over a corner table and two chairs. We had to pay for the Wifi. There were rust-colored stains on the tub and a dirty handprint on the sheets.

I thought about Raven's Ledge, and the scene we'd left

there. What did Juarez think? Was he okay? And what about everyone else? When Diggs and I were boating away from the island, I kept expecting something to blow up behind us; for more casualties thanks to this war I was fighting. But there was no explosion. There was no fire. There was... nothing. We ran off into the darkness, and no one seemed any the wiser.

Maybe they thought we were dead.

I laid down on the hotel bed, staring at the ceiling while Diggs flipped through the cable channels. The color was bad—everyone on screen had a sort of greenish tint.

"We should get some food," Diggs said.

"I'm not hungry."

"Well, I am," he said, tension bleeding in. "I saw a store on the corner—I'll grab something and bring it back. Any requests?"

I shook my head. He left without another word.

It had been like that all day, every exchange terse and awkward. Einstein lay beside me on the bed, his chin resting on my stomach. Despite the snowstorm in Maine yesterday, it had been bright and sunny throughout most of the drive today. I kept asking Diggs if it might be smarter for us to drive under the cover of night, but he'd been adamant: *There are fewer cars on the road at night. That makes us more conspicuous. The more cars there are, the safer we are.*

It made sense.

We both kept a lookout for someone following us, but we'd seen no one. Half a dozen times, I thought I spotted Jenny behind us, but it was never her. That begged the question: Was Jenny out there now, still searching for Diggs and me? Or was she too busy trying to track down Cameron and my mother?

About fifteen minutes after Diggs had gone, there was a knock on the door. Einstein woofed lightly, but remained on the bed with me. Diggs let himself in without waiting for me to answer. Einstein hopped up to greet him. I stayed where I was.

Diggs sat down beside me and handed me a plastic bag of goodies.

I hauled out two plastic-wrapped subs. "You're a vegetarian. These are both turkey," I said, reading the labels.

"It was all they had. I'll take the turkey out."

I frowned. "Don't you need protein?" He looked drawn, and it seemed like he'd gotten skinnier in the past couple of days. Great—I was already killing him, and we hadn't been married a day.

"There's cheese," he said with a shrug. "I'll eat that."

"Maybe we should go out somewhere. Have an actual meal, before we go off and die of monster spider bites in the Outback."

He picked up one of the subs, unwrapped it, and handed it to me. "I don't think we should be seen in public anymore than we have to be. I was already nervous, just being at the store."

"But Jenny and her people can't be everywhere, right? I mean, let's be real here. We could be anywhere at this point. What are the chances they have a spy hanging out in Allentown, Pennsylvania?"

He picked the turkey out of his sandwich and fed it to Einstein, who wriggled ecstatically. "I don't want to risk it."

"All right, fine. But you need to find a better way of doing the vegetarian thing, then. You can't just pick the meat out of everything and call it a balanced meal." His mouth twitched. "That's funny how, exactly?" I asked.

He pushed my as-yet untouched sandwich toward me. "You're telling me I need to eat better? Seriously? You had a quarter of an Egg McMuffin for breakfast, and a couple of HoHos since then. Eat the damned sandwich. Don't worry about me."

I took a bite of the sub and grimaced. The bread was sticky-white and soggy, the lettuce limp. But Diggs was right: I wouldn't be any good if I didn't eat, and I was getting damned tired of him harping on me all the time. I took another bite, watching as he fed another turkey scrap to Einstein.

"Have you been where we're going?" I asked. "Melbourne?"

"Sure," he said. Of course. "It's beautiful. You'll love Australia."

He took the pickle I'd discarded from my sandwich and popped it in his mouth. He was wearing a pair of jeans Cameron had left for him, with a striped Oxford he wouldn't have been caught dead in otherwise. At least it was a good fit, though. Cameron had done just as well with my clothes, even managing to get the sizes right on my bras and underwear. Which was creepy in ways I didn't even want to contemplate, at the moment.

"Did you ever think about living there?" I asked. "Australia, I mean?"

"All the time. I used to think I'd like to take you there, actually... Teach you to surf." He looked at me shyly, and I felt my cheeks warm. I always get a sort of Tiger Beat, Teenage Dream thrill when Diggs looks at me that way.

"Well, I guess this is your chance," I said. "They have bugs there, though. Huge ones. And snakes. And dingoes. Rabid kangaroos and wild boars. Plus, the toilets flush backwards. I don't think they like Americans, either."

"They don't like obnoxious Americans. They'll love you." He gave me another of those heartthrob grins of his, pushing the hair out of my eyes. I didn't even appreciate it, though, too freaked out at the thought of the thirty-hour journey we would be taking tomorrow, disguised as strangers.

I forced myself to take another bite of my sandwich before I set it on the nightstand with a shudder.

"You finished?" Diggs asked, nodding to my plate.

"I can't eat anymore. Sorry."

We were so polite. Jesus. Was this who Nick and Dani Winston were? Polite to a fault, dancing around fights Diggs and I would have had in a heartbeat. They probably flossed before bed and had noiseless, missionary-position sex with the lights off. I'd barely touched Diggs since waking beside him that morning. Everything felt different.

I felt different.

Diggs stood, wrapped the last of my sandwich, and dumped it in the plastic bag along with his wrapper. It was eight o'clock. Our plane left at seven the next morning, which meant we would need to be out by five to make it to the airport and through security in time. Neither of us had gotten much in the way of rest since leaving Littlehope. We should sleep.

I was wide awake, though.

"I think I'll take a shower," Diggs said.

I nodded, relieved. Twenty minutes without having to make up inane small talk while we danced around the fact that we were running away together to start a new life, and I still didn't know for how long or, really, why.

When he shut the bathroom door behind him, I collapsed on the bed with Einstein and screamed into the pillow.

I'd barely gotten any air behind it when I heard the bathroom door open and close again.

"Okay, fuck this. We need to talk," Diggs said from behind me. His voice had gone tight, the polite distance he'd maintained all day completely gone.

I rolled over. He'd gotten as far as untucking his shirt in the bathroom, but was still dressed otherwise. "About what?"

"About whatever the hell is going on between you and me. Or whatever's going on with you."

"I don't know what you're talking about." I sat up.

"Don't give me that. I've been babbling like a friggin' idiot all day, and you smile and nod and pretend I'm getting through…"

"I'm trying to be agreeable."

"Well, knock it off," he said roughly. "Agreeable doesn't suit you. You're freaking me out."

I stood, my temper just starting to simmer. Einstein hopped off the bed and headed for the other room, sensing trouble. "What do you want me to say, exactly?"

"I don't know. How about starting with what you're thinking right now? Or better yet, go completely nuts and tell me what you're feeling. Tell me you're scared, or pissed off, or dancing on the inside at the prospect of moving your whole life to the South Pacific. Just tell me *something*, for Christ's sake."

"You're telling me you're not scared?" I countered.

"I already told you I am!" he shouted. "Stop turning this around on me—we're talking about you." He advanced on me, his jaw tight. I stood my ground, fighting the very real urge to deck him. "You're terrified. Why can't you just admit that? It's not a problem for me: I'm fucking petrified."

It was strangely liberating to hear him say it out loud. "Of what?" I asked cautiously.

"Everything. These sons of bitches catching you; you worrying yourself into the ground; them finding Kat, and you spending the rest of your life blaming yourself…"

He stopped, studying me. We were just a few inches apart now, anger propelling both of us. "You don't care about that, though, do you? You getting hurt. Dying. Hell, half the time I think you're *trying* to kill yourself with this whole thing. It's sure as hell not what you're really afraid of, anyway."

"And what am I really afraid of?" I asked. I held my chin high, working hard to appear impassive. I failed, by at least six miles.

"You not being able to save Kat. Never finding your father." He took a step closer, so that only an inch or so separated us. I could feel his heat, his body, solid and warm and very, very near. "Me leaving."

"You're saying I shouldn't be afraid these assholes will kill my mother?" I demanded. "I shouldn't be concerned that I might never see my father again, after I just found out he was still alive?"

"No—I'm not saying that. I'm saying you should admit to it. Jesus, Solomon, *talk* to me. Don't tiptoe around me like we don't know each other—like I can't see every lie you feed me before you even spot them yourself. We're in this together."

"Stop saying that!" I finally exploded. I pushed him away, both hands on his chest, and strode across the room. "We're not in this together. *I'm* in this. *I'm* tied to this. You can leave anytime; you can walk away. You could always walk away. And usually did."

He shook his head in disbelief, running his hands over his newly shorn scalp. "We're still on this? For Christ's sake, Solomon, what do you want me to do to prove I'm in this for the long haul? I'm not the same guy I was when we were together before—"

"A few years may have passed, but we've done this dance before. We get close, I start to think we're going one way, and then the second we sleep together..."

He laughed—a quick bark of disgust, glaring at me. "You think I'm just here because we haven't screwed in eight years? That I'm just blinded by a monstrous case of blue balls? You honestly believe that?"

I hesitated, shaking with suppressed rage and this

sudden release of everything I'd been holding in for… well, ever, apparently. Diggs pulled me closer with a hand at my back, his gaze heated. Hurt flickered in his eyes before it was replaced with a kind of dangerous resolve.

"Diggs—"

"What?" he said. He wrapped one hand around the nape of my neck, the other still at my back, pulling me closer still.

"What are you doing?"

"You think I'll be gone in the morning if we do this—right?" I pulled out of his grasp and stepped away. He followed. I took another step back, then stopped when I felt the wall at my back. "Can you think of something else I can do to prove to you I'm not going anywhere, once that bell is wrung?" he asked.

He'd blocked me in, my back pressed to the wall, his body tantalizingly close to mine, but he made no move to touch me. He wouldn't, I knew: this was up to me. My body was on fire, a deep-seated ache in my southern hemisphere as all the fear and frustration and fury of the past few days rose to the surface.

This time, I was the one who closed the distance between us. I fisted my hands in the front of his shirt and pulled him to me, leaning up at the same time. When our lips met, there was nothing soft about it—nothing forgiving, nothing remotely friendly. I kissed him so hard my teeth rattled, his hands at my sides as he pulled me closer. I was burning, melting, desperate to toss everything else aside and just feel something that wasn't about fear or sorrow or the end of the world as we knew it.

When he pulled back and our eyes met, I answered his question before he could ask. "I'm sure. I'm positive." He hesitated. This was the test, wasn't it? If we did this, would I wake up tomorrow to find he'd walked out the door and vanished from my life for good?

Suddenly, I didn't give a rat's ass about tomorrow.

"Diggs, just… please," I said.

He pulled me in then, slanting his mouth to mine. The kiss was urgent, furious, infused with the fear that was rocking both of us. Diggs' tongue teased the seam of my lips and I opened willingly, gasping when he found the hem of my shirt and I felt cool hands on my bare skin.

My knuckles grazed his side, my fingers creeping toward the button of his jeans. Just as I reached it, brushing the trail of hair along the flat of his stomach, his hand closed over mine. He brought my arm up over my head and pinned my wrist there, our eyes locked. "Don't rush this," he whispered. "We've got time. I'm not going anywhere, Sol."

I swallowed hard, caught in those eyes, aching and hot and filled with some need I couldn't even name anymore.

Diggs pushed my shirt up—past my too-white stomach and the swell of my breasts, over my head, the knuckles of his other hand caressing every inch of newly-exposed flesh. I arched into his touch, breathless now that we'd started.

The hotel room was cool. Next door, I could hear someone's TV: garbled electronic voices that I could make no sense of. Diggs pushed my bra strap down and kissed my shoulder and my neck and beyond, scraping his teeth along the ridge of my collarbone. When I reached out to touch him this time he didn't stop me. I set to work on his Oxford and nearly gave up. I was tempted to do the romance novel thing and just rip the damn thing open, but Nick and Dani didn't have enough clothes to just start tearing them off willy-nilly.

Diggs stopped what he was doing. He pulled back, a flash of very welcome amusement in his eyes. "Problems?"

"Your stupid shirt has too many buttons."

He pushed my hands away and stepped back, eyes on mine, as he finished the job I'd started. When he shrugged the shirt off and let it drop to the floor, going maddeningly slowly, my mouth went dry. Diggs has broad shoulders and a rugged chest and Celtic tattoos on both of his well-muscled arms.

Diggs is gorgeous.

My knees liquefied.

Before they buckled completely, Diggs was there to catch me. His mouth found mine, softer now, sweeter, and I felt his fingers at the front of my jeans, fumbling in a distinctly non-Diggsian way for just a second before he pulled himself together and managed to unbutton the top button. He slid the zipper down, while I ran my hands over his arms and the strong muscles of his back, his neck, smoothing my fingers over the soft bristles of his too-short hair as he pushed my jeans down over my hips. He knelt in front of me, his head bowed, trailing butterfly kisses down my belly as his hand slid higher up my thigh.

And then, just at the point when I was on the verge of completely forgetting the fact that we were about to move to Australia so we wouldn't be killed by the psychotic survivors of one of the biggest mass murders in U.S. history; just when my underpants had pooled at my feet and Diggs' teeth grazed my hip…

The phone rang.

Diggs groaned.

It wasn't a happy groan.

"Don't answer it," he said.

It rang again. I rested my hand on his shoulder and tipped my head back against the wall, aching and still on fire. "I have to—it's Cameron. Something could have happened."

"Right. I know." He straightened, his knuckles brushing up my side and over my breast, his eyes still dark. "We're not done, though," he said, and kissed my forehead.

I pulled my underwear back on while he fetched the

phone from the other room, answering with a terse, "Yeah." He sounded exactly like a man who'd just stopped having sex to answer the phone. Subtle.

I picked his shirt up off the floor and put it on. Einstein peered around the corner at me, checking to see if the danger had passed.

"You're safe, buddy," I said. "Nobody's having any fun anymore." Sexual frustration at an all-time high, I let out a long deep breath and pulled myself together. When I heard the TV come on in the next room, I figured Diggs and I probably weren't going to pick up where we'd left off anytime soon. I scratched Einstein's ears and padded after him.

Diggs stood in front of the TV with the phone at his ear, bare chested, his jeans slung low on his hips. It took a concerted effort to refocus, but the peroxide-blonde newscaster gave me a shove in the right direction once her words registered.

"…Authorities are asking for any information leading to the arrest of Daniel Diggins and Erin Solomon—two journalists currently wanted for questioning in connection with multiple bombings in Maine and Kentucky in the past month. Police say the couple should be considered armed and dangerous…"

Diggs muted the TV. I stood there with my mouth hanging open, staring at the screen as two very unflattering photos of Diggs and me appeared.

"As you can see, things have gotten a bit more complicated," I heard Cameron say. Diggs had put him on speakerphone.

"A bit?" I said. My voice went up at least three octaves. "Um… yeah, I'd say they are definitely a bit more complicated. Jesus, Cameron, how did this happen?"

"J," he said shortly. "They have connections in law enforcement at every level you can imagine. Which is why I need you to do exactly as I say from here on out."

"Because we haven't been doing that up 'til now?" Diggs demanded. "What the hell is going on here, Cameron? What do they think this will accomplish?"

"It discredits you, for one thing," Cameron said. "This is their preemptive strike, until they know for certain just how much information you have. Now if you try to go to the media, you're already the bad guys."

"And since they have people on the inside, if we are arrested it's likely someone will get to us before we're able to prove our side of the story," I guessed.

Diggs shook his head in frustration, rubbing the knots from his neck as he walked away. "All right, so what the hell do we do now? It's not like we can swim to Australia, but I'm assuming our flight out of the country is no longer an option."

"Not necessarily," Cameron said. "This is why I picked a smaller airport for you—the security isn't as tight. You've changed your appearance…"

I let Diggs continue the conversation, went to the window, and pushed the ugly drapes to the side. It was only a little past nine o'clock on a Saturday night, people still checking into the hotel. Cars sped past on the highway out front. A cluster of college-aged guys walked in the front entrance. A man in suit and tie walked out. Headlights illuminated his path as a car drove up behind him—gray, nondescript, but I'd seen enough vehicles like it to know exactly what it was. My heart stuttered.

"Diggs," I said. He was still arguing with Cameron, but came to immediately at my tone. He stood behind me, pulling me closer as his lips brushed the top of my head.

"What've you got?" he asked.

I nodded toward the car. The man in the suit and tie had gone around to the passenger's side. "What does that look like to you?"

"What's happening?" Cameron asked.

"Unmarked cop car," Diggs said grimly, confirming what I'd thought. Less than a minute later, two police cruisers pulled into the parking lot.

"Shit," I said softly.

"Don't panic," Cameron said. "This may not have anything to do with you."

"Or it could have everything to do with us," I said. Despite his advice, I was panicking quite nicely, thank you very much.

"Did you do what I said: only one of you checked in? Didn't use your new IDs. Just paid in cash. You've kept the dog under wraps?"

"Yeah," Diggs agreed. "It's not the kind of hotel where they ask questions. I didn't say anything to them about the dog. Erin dyed her hair last night, and I've got a buzz cut and no stubble… We did everything you said."

Two more police cars pulled in.

"They're surrounding the place," I said to Cameron. "Four police cruisers now and an unmarked police car on top of that. One of the cops from the unmarked was in the hotel talking to the front desk."

There was silence on the other end.

"Cameron?" Diggs prompted.

"Hang on," he snapped. "I'm thinking."

"Screw that," I said. "There's no time to think—they're coming. Now. We need to get out of here."

"You're right," Cameron said, much to my surprise. "But you need to be smart about this. Right now, you can't afford to make mistakes because you're scared. Here's what you're going to do."

Ten minutes later, I walked out the front exit of the hotel. Alone.

I reached the door at roughly the same time that one of the multitude of cops now swarming the place did.

Stay calm. Keep moving. Don't panic. I repeated the mantra in a continuous loop in my head, trying to appear casual.

The cop was dark-haired and trim, her uniform neatly pressed. A rookie. She opened the door and held it for me.

"Evening, ma'am," she said.

"Evening, officer." I gave her a neutral smile and silently thanked the gods that Cameron had had the foresight to make me leave without Diggs and the dog.

In the parking lot, a stocky man in a trench coat and glasses stood beside a big, beat-up old blue car, talking on his cell phone. I walked past without acknowledging him, my sights set on our car.

Five more steps, and I was home free.

"Hey!" It was a voice behind me—male. The guy in the coat.

I kept walking.

I took out my keys and hit the button to unlock the door.

Behind me, I heard footsteps. My heart sped up. *Stay calm. Stay calm. Stay calm.*

I reached for the car door handle.

"Hey—excuse me, ma'am." A hand stopped me, solid on my shoulder. I whirled. "Sorry," Trench Coat said when I faced him. He looked embarrassed. "I didn't mean to startle you. It's just, you dropped this."

He handed me a bag of peanut M&Ms that must have fallen out of my purse.

"Oh—thank you. Wouldn't want to go off without those."

"Never leave home without them myself," he said with a cheerful grin. He nodded toward the squadron of cop cars now surrounding the place. "It's crazy, huh? Any idea what this is all about?"

"No," I said, too fast. I forced myself to take a breath and look him in the eye. "Not really... Maybe drugs?"

"Maybe," he agreed. "This country's going to hell. Used to be, this was a safe town to live in. Now you never know who's gonna wind up in our little corner of the world."

"Right," I said. Was it my imagination, or was that comment directed at me? I took the candy, and waited for him to figure it out—to realize who he was talking to: Public Enemy number one. Or at least the top ten.

Instead, he just turned with an affable smile and walked away.

When I got in the car, I was nauseous.

Being a fugitive was not going to work well for me.

I started the car, popped a handful of M&Ms, and drove slowly out of the parking lot. The cop I'd met at the entrance was just coming out of the hotel when I drove past. We locked eyes for a second.

Had she recognized me?

I checked the rearview mirror with my heart racing, sure I'd see lights behind me.

There were none.

12
KAT

"WHAT THE HELL IS GOING ON?" Kat demanded. She stared at the TV screen, unable to get her head around what she was seeing. "How did this happen?"

"I told you," Cameron snapped. "Jenny. The Project. I should have seen it coming."

He set the phone down and strode to the window to look out over the parking lot. They were in North Carolina, in a five-star hotel just outside Asheville. The staff knew Cameron on sight—though they knew him as Alex Beaumont, apparently. Their suite was on the top floor, and it was gorgeous. Any thoughts about the extravagant setting had been forgotten as soon as Cameron turned on the news, however.

"So, what do we do now?" Kat asked.

"Exactly what I just did," Cam said. "Erin has been warned—she and Diggs know what to do from here. I'm handling it."

"Yeah," she scoffed. "The same way you and your people handle everything. Tell me, is that what J told you when you first signed on? That they were handling things?"

He stood, his eyes flashing with an ire she rarely saw in

him. Cameron didn't really get angry, in her experience.

Cameron didn't really get much of anything.

"First of all, I never *signed on* with J. It was out of my hands from the day we met—just like it was out of your husband's hands. It was never our choice, all right? I'm doing the best I can to make things right; to keep you and your daughter safe. Which would be a hell of a lot easier if either of you listened to a word anyone said."

"I've been listening from the day you set the fire on Payson Isle. Erin isn't my fault—she doesn't listen to anyone."

"Yeah, well… it's going to get her killed one of these days. That damn dog…"

Kat flashed on that image again: Erin on the floor of her Cambridge kitchen, a bedraggled pup lifeless on her lap. How long had Kat stood in the doorway, frozen, trying to decide whether to go in, to try and help, or just to return to the living room and pretend she hadn't seen? It seemed like she'd spent most of Erin's life that way—forever on the sidelines, trying to decide what her role was.

It had been that way from the very beginning—from the day she'd brought Erin, kicking and screaming, into this world.

I never wanted to be a mother. That's what she'd said, wasn't it? Back on Raven's Ledge, that's what she had told Erin. It was the truth; it was reality. From the day she'd realized she was pregnant, she had known bringing a kid into the world was not a wise decision. Not for her—not for them. And sure as hell not on Payson Isle, with Isaac Payson watching their every move. Erin deserved better than the hand she'd been dealt: a father who could barely keep his head above water most days, and a cold bitch of a mother who would rather be doing just about anything but staying at home raising a willful little carbon copy of herself.

"She won't give Einstein up," Kat said, pulling herself

back to the present. "Once she gets attached to someone, she doesn't let them go. She's in it—she won't abandon him."

"Well, she's probably going to get all three of them killed, then."

The thought shook her. Kat went to the window and looked out over the neatly manicured grounds: swimming pool, tennis courts, walking paths populated by neatly manicured, lily-white guests. Despite the warmth of the room, she was still cold. Her hands still shook, though she knew that had nothing to do with temperature—either internal or external.

"Will you answer a question for me?" she said, without looking at Cameron.

"Depends on what it is."

She smiled faintly. Typical. "Why are you so bent on keeping us safe? It's not your concern—it's never been your concern." She turned her back on the world outside, focused on Cameron again. "When you went out to Payson Isle almost twenty-five years ago, you sure as hell weren't thinking of our safety when you struck the match and murdered more than thirty people. When did that change?"

Something broken and buried deep flickered in Cameron's eyes. He turned his back on her and went straight to the minibar across the room. Kat watched as he stooped to survey the contents, pausing at a bottle of scotch before he opened the refrigerator instead.

"Do you want anything?" he asked.

Her mouth watered and her stomach burned. Hell, yes, she wanted something. "No."

He retrieved a can of ginger ale and some nuts, returned to the sofa, and sat.

"Why do you care what happens to Erin and me?" Kat persisted.

Cam pulled the tab on the ginger ale, setting the nuts

on the coffee table in front of him. He sat at the edge of the couch with his elbows on his knees, and he didn't look at her. "I don't know why I care," he said finally. He took a long drink and set the can down on a wooden coaster with the hotel's logo carved into it. "But I do. If I can get you away from them... if I can keep you safe, and I can bring them down in the process, then that's what I need to do."

"But why? Jesus, Cam, it's a simple enough question. What changed for you? I know Adam's story, but what happened to you that you suddenly went from being J's number one killing machine, to its number one enemy?"

"Why the hell does it matter?" he demanded. "Motives don't matter—it's what you do that counts, not the why or the how. Not what you feel while you're doing it. You've spent most of your life saving people—healing them. How often do they ask why you do it? It's the action that counts, not the whys and wherefores that led up to it."

She held up her hands in surrender, shaking her head. "Fine. Forget I asked."

"Gladly."

After she'd taken a couple of turns around the suite, pacing the floor, she came over and sat beside him on the couch. The décor had been a surprise to her. Somehow, she'd always thought that anywhere Cameron hung his hat would be sterile, industrial feeling, but this place was soothing greens and blues, fountains and wind chimes; more health spa than hideaway for a serial-killing assassin.

"So... what comes next?" she asked after a minute.

Ignoring her, he picked up a hotel telephone on the end table and hit 0. "Iris? Yes, it's Alex. Can you have the kitchen send something up? The linguine will be fine—two plates, please. And the lava cake, if it's available... Excellent. Thank you."

After he'd hung up the receiver, he returned his attention

to Kat. "Next? We eat—both of us. You need fuel if you're going to make it, especially while you're trying to kick the alcohol out of your system. Then, we sleep. You can take the bedroom."

"That's all right—I'll sleep out here. You've been driving nonstop... you should take the bed."

"It would be wasted on me; I don't really sleep. I'll be up and down all night. This way, you'll be able to get some rest and I won't disturb you."

"And, coincidentally, I won't have access to the minibar or the exit."

"The minibar is your decision, not mine," he said evenly. "And leaving isn't in your best interest, so I'm not concerned about the exit. You're not stupid."

She smiled faintly. There was a foot or so of space between her and Cameron, the space oddly intimate. Did Adam know this was the situation? That the man he'd been running from for so many years, the man he'd loathed all that time, would bring her here? She tried to imagine her former husband setting this up, being all right with it, but all she could think of were those years when she'd known him; all the stories he told... *He's a monster. He kills without a second thought—without remorse. It doesn't matter who. It doesn't matter how. I know I've hurt people, Katie. But this man does more than hurt—he destroys lives.*

Cam looked at her for a second, his sharp eyes catching hers as if he knew what she was thinking. It wouldn't surprise her, really, with him.

"Do you think they'll be all right?" she asked. "Diggs and Erin?"

"I don't know. I hope so... They're smart, when they're not being complete idiots. And Adam..."

She looked up at the name. Met his eye. "Adam...?" she prompted.

There was a knock at the door. Cameron got up without answering her question. She sat back and watched as he smiled with seeming warmth when he greeted a pretty, doe-eyed girl who'd brought their dinner up.

He destroys lives.

If this was the man who destroyed lives, who was Adam, she wondered? The man forever on the edge, the man so haunted by the ghosts of his past that he barely seemed rooted in reality most of the time… The man who ran away, time after time.

What was his role in all of this now?

13
DIGGS

CAMERON'S ORDERS WERE TO LEAVE Allentown and drive to a rest stop on the Ohio/Pennsylvania border. When we asked what we were supposed to be waiting for, he told us we'd know when it happened. Solomon and I aren't really the type to let shit lie, though, so his response didn't go over that well. Sadly, Cameron didn't give a rat's ass. His final instructions to us:

Drive within five miles of the speed limit at all times, keep the damn dog out of sight, and wait.

Lacking other options, that's exactly what we did.

Solomon drove, mostly because I was too tired to put up a decent fight. After watching her pass cars without signaling and completely ignore those nifty white lines meant to keep us in one lane, I finally gave up and closed my eyes.

"Have you thought anymore about the numbers on the memory card?" I asked.

"Recently? No—not really." I felt the car jerk to the right, and opened one eye to see her sliding into the left lane without signaling—cutting directly in front of an eighteen wheeler. I gripped the seat, pumped an imaginary brake with my foot, and closed my eyes again. "I saw the truck," she said.

"I'm sure you did. But maybe next time you could actually do something more than just see it. Maybe you could give the driver a little warning, or—I don't know—stay the hell out of the way."

"You're such a baby," she said. I felt her hand on my leg. My breathing eased incrementally. No matter how badly timed Cameron's phone call may have been, I was glad that I'd pushed things in the hotel room. Despite everything, it felt like Solomon and I were on our way back to even footing again.

"So… those numbers," she prompted. "What do you think?"

I pulled the printed page from her bag and used my penlight to go over the contents. The numbers made no more sense now than they had before. I glanced at Solomon, driving with one hand on the wheel and the other on my knee, eyes intent on the road. I had lied earlier: I didn't like the brown hair. It wasn't bad—Solomon's beautiful, and it doesn't really matter whether she's a redhead or a brunette or bald as a cue ball. She'll always be beautiful. But it didn't look like her, the same way I didn't look like me. It was… unsettling, to say the least, to take on these new identities and new looks and new credit histories, with no clue how long the act would continue.

I kept telling myself that all that really mattered ultimately was that we got clear of this; that we got the hell out of the country safely. Strangely enough, the thought of Solomon and me sharing some shack on a beach in Australia didn't bother me. It was the idea that we might not make it there—that *she* might not make it there… That thought left me shaking and weak-kneed.

"Any brilliant ideas?" she asked. I looked up, only just realizing that she was still talking about the numbers.

"Uh—no, not really. Just what we said before: pass

codes, ID numbers, numerical code..."

"Maybe," she said doubtfully. "So, all we really know at this point is the whole longitude/latitude thing at the beginning of each entry."

"Right," I agreed. "A few of these I already know off the top of my head."

She shot me a look. "The amount of useless information in that brain of yours really does boggle me."

"My prowess with an atlas drives the ladies wild."

"I'm pretty sure that's not what's doing it for them. But, please, continue."

"The first one—40 degrees North, 84 degrees West... I'm pretty sure that's somewhere in the Midwest. I wouldn't be surprised if that's Lynn, Indiana. The rest vary: Texas, California, New England... they're basically all over the map. Literally."

I continued running through the rest of the numbers, but after a few minutes, I folded the page and put it away again. It would keep; I wasn't sure if the conversation I knew I needed to have with Solomon would, though.

"So..." I began. She glanced at me, then back at the road. Just one word, and I could already sense her tensing up.

"Yeah?" she returned.

"Back in Maine, at the cabin. When we were sleeping?" She nodded. I wet my lips, flashing back to the scene. Solomon, small and rigid in the bed, hands clenched, deep in sleep. "You were talking... Dreaming about something."

She pulled her hand from my knee and returned it to the wheel. "Was I?"

"You were. It sounded intense. You said a couple of days ago that you've been remembering more about Payson Isle. Were you dreaming about that?"

She bit her lip, a wrinkle returning to her brow. A truck

blew past us going maybe ninety. Solomon looked up with a frown, but made no comment.

"I'm not sure what it was about," she said after a while. "I don't remember that much… I've tried. And what I do remember doesn't make a lot of sense."

"When you asked to talk to Juarez alone, out on the island…"

No response. We were in the center lane, a sedan pacing us on the right while the occasional car whizzed by on the left. It was eleven o'clock, Saturday night traffic out in full force. When Solomon finally answered me, her response lacked the defensive bite I'd expected.

"I think he's connected, somehow," she said. "He asked me what I remember from growing up with the Payson Church. He's always been curious about that… But now, I get the feeling that maybe he's remembering, too. Like maybe these memories I can't seem to call up aren't buried just because I was traumatized by some horrible secret that happened out there when I was a kid."

For years, the thought of Solomon growing up in that church made my stomach knot. Hearing her actually voice it now brought the old fear rushing back—the certainty that her childhood couldn't possibly have been as innocuous as she claimed. How long had I been imagining what happened on that island, while she insisted it had all been Kumbaya and home baked bread every night? As though I was an idiot for thinking anything darker might have happened out there.

"So… do you think something happened on Payson Isle?" I asked. "To you, I mean?"

She hesitated, her lower lip caught between her teeth. "I don't know. I still don't think my dad would have let anyone do anything to me…" She swallowed hard, eyes still on the road. "But I think maybe I saw some things."

When she didn't say anything more, I reached across the seat and ran my hand through her hair. She leaned into my touch, eyes still on the road. "What kind of things?"

"I'm not sure. Nothing I see makes any sense right now. Or else it makes sense when I'm dreaming, but it just… goes away, when I wake up."

"Maybe if you talk it through, though… What do you remember? Even if it doesn't make sense: what images stay with you?"

A long moment of silence followed that, then her lips tightened and her forehead furrowed as if she was in pain. She pulled away from my hand, shaking her head. "I can't, I'm sorry. I don't remember."

That fact alone made me uneasy, unnerving me all the more because I could tell she was genuinely trying like hell to get at this, somehow.

"Don't push it," I said. "Maybe you're trying too hard. Just… if it comes back, it comes back. If it doesn't, that's okay, too."

"Yes sir, Zen Master Diggins."

"I'm trying to be supportive here. The New Age me."

"Just be you," she said, her hand drifting to my knee again. "Everything is changing enough as it is… I don't think I can take it if you're suddenly enlightened and laidback."

"So I should just continue being the same pushy jerk I always was, then?"

"It worked for you back in Allentown tonight, didn't it?" Her hand slid higher up my thigh. I'd forgotten just how much Solomon loves being in the driver's seat—something it would clearly be in my best interest to remember in the future.

I caught her hand just before it reached dangerous territory, and set it firmly back on the steering wheel before she got us both killed. "Actually, it *almost* worked for me in

Allentown. Let's not start something we can't finish when we're speeding down the highway at seventy miles an hour. I don't think I can take that kind of disappointment again."

"Tell me about it," she grumbled. After a second or two she turned toward me again, studying me for a flash of an instant. A slow grin appeared, the tiniest spark returning to her eye. "So, how crazy is this making you, huh? Being at my mercy while I've got the wheel?"

I affected a yawn and stretched in my seat. "Are you kidding? This is great. Einstein and I are liberated men—we have no problem being chauffeured around the countryside by a beautiful woman. Right, Stein?"

I looked in the dark backseat, where I could just make out the mutt's outline. He thumped his tail a couple of times when I pet his head, but otherwise didn't move. I made a conscious effort not to think of my conversation with Cameron earlier: *Eventually, you've got to convince her to leave that goddamn dog behind.* I wasn't looking forward to that moment, but I knew it was coming.

"You're such a liar," Solomon said. "Stein might be liberated. You, on the other hand…."

"I'm completely liberated," I argued, pulling myself back from the depths. "I'll be the first one to vote a woman into the White House, and you know it. I believe in equal wages, women on the battlefield, women in the board room. I love seeing a good woman on top." I glanced at her. She rolled her eyes, squelching a smile. "I just like being in the driver's seat. It wouldn't matter whether I was riding with you or Mario Andretti. I want to be behind the wheel."

"Well, you're gonna have to get over it, sweet pea. Because I like driving, too."

"Sweet pea?" I grinned. "All that power's clearly gone to your head, baby doll. It's kind of a turn on." I reached across the console and swept the back of my hand up her thigh.

And promptly froze.

Every other thought flew out of my head when I caught the flash of lights behind us. An instant later, a cruiser's siren kicked in.

"Shit," Solomon said. I pulled back, convinced there was a conspiracy. Every damn time I got a little turned on around the woman, the sky fell. Erin's hand remained steady at the wheel. Her speed didn't falter.

"Slow down," I said. "He might not be coming after you."

"I know that," she said sharply. "You want to drive?"

At the moment, I wanted to drive more than I wanted my left nut, but I kept my mouth shut. Solomon put the blinker on and slid into the right lane, slowing incrementally. The siren got louder, the lights closer.

"Do I stop?" she asked.

"We don't have much choice."

"Right. Shit." She pulled off to the shoulder, continuing to slow. Einstein got up when we hit the rumble strip, whining anxiously. I opened the glove box and got out the paperwork for the car—registration and proof of insurance, both under Nick Winston's name. Solomon slowed to a stop, her knuckles white on the wheel.

Two seconds later, the cruiser sped past us.

After it was gone, it took a full minute before Solomon got going again. I rubbed my damp palms on my jeans and tried to ignore the taste of bile rising in my throat. Based on the look on her face, Solomon wasn't faring any better.

"Why don't you take the next exit," I said. "We should probably refuel, anyway."

She put the blinker on and got us back on the road without a word, hands still clenched tight.

We drove on in silence.

The next rest area was in Rockton—eighty miles from

Cameron's meeting spot in Harrisburg. Solomon pulled up at the pump. I got out without a word. She did the same.

"I can—" I started, indicating the gas pump.

"That would be great—I'm just going to walk Stein."

I started to object, Cameron's warning about keeping the dog out of sight fresh in my mind, but stopped at the look in her eye. Solomon is as tough as they come, but at the moment she was dangerously close to unraveling. I nodded.

"Yeah—okay. Just stay close."

"I will," she said. As she was walking past to get the dog, I caught her by the elbow. "Hey… We're going to be all right, you know. I promise you—we'll be okay."

She laughed, the sound still wrought with tension. "You keep saying that. I can't tell whether you really believe it, or you just hope I'll buy it if you say the words enough."

I put an arm around her. She leaned up to kiss me. I knew she was just going for a reassuring peck, trying to convince me she wasn't about to break. Before she could go anywhere, I caught her by the waist and held her there, my mouth moving over hers with the heat still warming my blood since the hotel room. When she pulled back, I held her face in my hands.

"We will make it through this. And as soon as we can stop for more than five minutes, I plan on finishing what we started in Allentown. And then we're sleeping for twenty-four hours straight."

She leaned her head on my chest. "I don't know which of those sound better right now."

"I can't believe I'm saying this, but… right now, I'm not sure of that myself. Now, go on—walk the mutt. I'll find you when I'm done here."

Stein hopped out of the back happily and Solomon clipped the leash to his collar. I swatted Sol's ass as they walked away. She turned, rolling her eyes at me.

"Watch it, slick."

"Oh, believe me—I am."

That earned another eye roll, but I noticed an extra switch to her step as she walked away.

It was almost midnight. Neither of us had slept well in days. We couldn't keep going like this—I knew that. Eventually, something had to give; I just hoped Cameron understood that. Whatever he had planned in Harrisburg, I hoped to hell it involved more than two hours of sleep and another meal of shitty convenience store sandwiches.

"Nice looking girl," someone said behind me. I started. I hadn't even noticed the car that had rolled up at the next pump, the driver standing behind a column as he gassed up an old blue Cutlass. He stepped into my view: a husky guy, maybe 5'6", wearing a trench coat and wire-rimmed glasses.

"Uh—yeah," I said. "She is." The gas seemed to be moving at a trickle.

"You two been together long?" he asked. "I'm assuming you're married, of course—got a nice, comfortable way about you."

I forced myself to stay calm. This didn't have to mean something. He could just be a bored, lonely businessman striking up a conversation.

"We've been married a couple of years," I said, thinking of the fake world Cameron had built for us.

The man's eyes never left mine. Beneath the friendly façade, I sensed something darker. More intense. "Well— you're a good looking couple. Nice dog, too. You from around here?"

I nodded toward our license plate, more uneasy by the second. "Oregon. Just in the area on vacation."

Solomon had disappeared with the dog. I focused on the task at hand: Finish filling the goddamn tank and get the hell out.

"Where'd you go on vacation?" the man asked. "Seems like kind of a long way to drive, all the way out east here."

I'd meant to fill the tank, but there was no way I would make it that long. I stopped with barely twenty bucks in. Solomon was still nowhere to be seen.

"I should go," I said.

"Sure. Sure." He nodded. "Don't want to let the little woman get too far without you. No telling what kind of trouble she could get into."

The words were delivered with his eyes still locked on mine, the pretense suddenly gone. He knew—I was sure of it. I grabbed the receipt from the pump and slid into the driver's seat, forcing myself not to look back as I drove away.

Solomon was sitting under a tree with the dog beside her, staring into the night when I found her. She stood when I pulled up, returning to the car without a word.

"All set?" I asked.

"Yeah. Just needed a little fresh air."

"Good."

She and Stein got in. I pulled away from the station at a fast clip, forcing myself to stay calm.

Traffic had slowed for the night, with only a few cars on the road now—which made it easy to spot someone tailing us. Try as I might, though, I saw no one. If Trench Coat had suspicions about who we were, he wasn't following up on it yet.

In the passenger's seat now, Solomon fell almost immediately into a listless sleep. Whatever was about to happen, I just hoped it happened soon. We were both too close to the edge to keep this up for long.

We reached the Harrisburg rest area at two o'clock that morning. Cameron hadn't called again, so we had no real option other than to sit tight and wait like he'd ordered.

I reclined my seat back as far as it would go, and slept for the next four hours—an exhausted, dreamless sleep—with Solomon's hand in mine.

I think I would have gone right on sleeping through the next day, had I not woken when Sol got out to walk the dog at just after six a.m. My neck was cramped and my spine felt like it had been ripped out and put back in backwards, but otherwise it was great to be alive. The sun rose over the rest station, washing the sky out to a pale pink. The air was refreshingly cool when Solomon opened the door.

"Sorry," she said. "I didn't mean to wake you."

I got out of the car and stretched, my back popping in the process. "It's not a problem. If I slept any longer in there, I think you'd need the Jaws of Life to pry me out."

"I was just going to take Stein for a walk. Up for a stroll?"

"You sure you want the company?"

She slid her hand into mine, giving me a sly smile. "What's the matter, Diggs—starting to doubt your charm?"

"I haven't showered, I haven't slept, and I haven't had a decent meal in days… So, yeah. The old Diggins magic may be suffering."

"I can live with that," she said. She leaned up and kissed me. "I'm not feeling all that magical myself, at the moment."

We let Einstein lead us to the edge of the woods, my arm around Solomon's shoulders. There were a couple of cars in the parking lot, but at the moment no people were in sight. The grass was covered with dew, birds singing in the trees. It may have been winter when we left Maine, but we'd migrated to full spring the farther west we traveled. We found a picnic table and settled while Einstein christened every bush, Erin's head tipped to my shoulder.

"How long do you think we should wait for whatever it is Cameron has planned for us?" she asked. I'd been wondering the same thing.

"I'm not sure. I don't like how exposed we are here. Eventually, we'll need to move on."

"Yeah," she scoffed. "Because it's that easy. There's a nationwide manhunt on for us. Who knew fugitives had it so bad."

"When this is over, we should start an outreach group," I said. "An underground railroad for hoodlums."

"You're in charge of writing the grants for that one," she said. "You're exactly the man to convince the government to fund a network harboring—"

She stopped abruptly.

I looked at her, following her gaze when she didn't continue. On a hillside with the rising sun at his back, a man stood watching us. Solomon let go of my hand. The man took a step toward us. He was tall and lean, his gray hair dusted with strands of copper.

Solomon got up from the table. Einstein headed for the stranger with no detectable malice, tail wagging.

He took another step. Solomon remained frozen until he was within a few feet of us, then took a shaky step forward herself.

"Dad?" she said, her voice suddenly not her own. All at once, I was looking at the girl she'd been—the terrified child who'd lost her father too young.

Adam Solomon took another step toward us, his smile even in that moment haunted and hesitant. "Hello, honey."

14
KAT

IT WAS A LISTLESS NIGHT—which Kat had expected. The bed was huge and the mattress plush, the room quiet except for a fountain in the corner and the hushed voices on the television in the next room. Frankly, she would have preferred a little noise. A little chaos wouldn't have been unwelcome, even. Over the years, Kat had found that the places she slept best were invariably the ones where she shouldn't be sleeping at all: hospital break rooms, classes, movie theaters. The silence out on Payson Isle had nearly driven her mad.

Eventually, when the thoughts and memories and worries got to be too much, she surrendered and turned on the bedside lamp. It was midnight; Diggs and Erin were probably still on the road. Unless they'd been caught—which was a distinct possibility. Kat got up and went to the sliding glass door that opened onto the balcony. Below, a few people still splashed around in the hotel pool, their shouts nothing more than a murmur through the plate glass.

She wondered what Cameron was watching. Maya always insisted they couldn't have a TV in their bedroom at home, which meant most nights Kat ended up on the couch.

Maya quoted study after study to her on the disruptions electronics and blue light and white noise caused to the sleep cycle. Kat didn't care what the studies said: The fact was, the only time she slept well at home was when the TV was on and she was too dead tired to do anything but lie there and let the meaningless noise wash over her.

Gingerly, she pushed her bedroom door open. Cam was stretched out on the couch with a blanket carelessly tossed over his legs. The light from the television cast eerie shadows on the walls. Someone shrieked in the pool below. Kat tensed, waiting until she heard laughter to confirm that everyone was alive and well. The laughter faded quickly; her tension remained.

"Couldn't sleep?" Cameron asked without moving. She hadn't even known he was awake.

"I told you—I'm not much for it, usually." She closed the bedroom door behind her and went to the couch. Some former child star whose name she couldn't recall was all grown up now, and currently selling an exercise system on deep cable. Cam sat up, nodding to the end of the couch. He shifted to make room for her.

"Have a seat."

She did, taking part of the blanket from him. "Nothing else on?" she asked, nodding at the television.

"A couple of old movies. It's easier to fall asleep to these, though."

"I like the cooking shows better," she said. "The ones with the gadgets. I think I have every one ever made."

"I bet I've got you beat," he said, almost shyly. "The Magic Bullet; Chop Magic; RoboStir; Chop Wizard; Slice-O-Matic…"

"Do you even cook?"

He actually laughed, shaking his head. "No—not at all. But my kitchen's stocked, if I ever want to try."

"Maya banned me from the phone at night. She said if I bought one more useless piece of shit, she was staging an intervention."

"Susan used to throw mine away as soon as they came," he said. "I was convinced the mailman was stealing them. Jenny always loved them, though. Whenever one actually made it to me, we'd do a demo—try it out, then grade it to see if it was as good as the infomercial."

He looked like he was a thousand miles away. Kat had only met his wife twice, when Cameron brought his family on a vacation to Maine in the '90s. That was nearly five years after Cameron had first introduced himself to Kat. Meeting Susan and Jenny, seeing their happy little family—all while knowing exactly who and what Cameron was—had left her unsettled. Angry, though she could never say exactly why.

"I never really thought of you and Susan having a house," she admitted. "Not one with an actual address and a mailman and a flock of pink flamingoes in the front yard."

"What did you think?" he asked, eying her curiously. "We just slept under rocks?"

"Not you… but Susan, maybe. I figured you had a Fortress of Solitude somewhere. Where is it?"

"The Keys," he said after a minute. "So, we actually did have flamingoes in the front yard, sometimes. Real ones."

"Did you have a regular job, ever? Or did you just work for J?"

"Does Special Forces count as a regular job?"

"Not in any way, shape, or form."

He smiled faintly. "Well, then. No. I always worked for the Project. When I was younger, though, I used to daydream about other things."

"Such as?"

"Nothing important," he said with a shrug. "A bookstore, maybe. Or a record shop. Just a quiet little hole in the wall somewhere… It would be a nice way to retire." He wet his lips, that faraway look in his eye again. "I thought maybe if Jenny ever settled down, had kids… It would be nice, for them. They could come in after school sometimes, maybe help out."

She had no idea how to respond—especially since Jenny was a card-carrying psychopath now. Cameron ran his hand through his thinning hair, clearly embarrassed.

"It's not as though I thought it would actually happen—especially as Jenny got older, and…" He stopped abruptly. "They were just daydreams."

"Nothing wrong with that. We all have them."

"Do we?" He was teasing her, she realized. She hadn't even imagined he was capable of it. "What was yours, then? What did you daydream about when no one was looking?"

An ancient fantasy rose, blurry and surreal, from the days when she still believed in fantasies: Adam leaving that goddamn island. The two of them taking off for Europe, where he raised Erin and she became chief pediatric surgeon at one of the better hospitals in Vienna or Paris.

"I don't know," she said with a shrug. "Nothing specific, really. I knew I'd never be Mrs. Brady, but I figured if Adam was willing to give it a shot, I could at least bring home the bacon while he played housewife."

"While you protected him from the big bad world, you mean?"

She paused, studying him for a moment. "While I protected him from you, actually."

Hurt flashed in his eyes, but he didn't look away. "You shouldn't have to protect anyone. You're not invulnerable—you shouldn't be forced to pretend you are. You should have someone strong enough to take care of you."

"I don't need anyone to take care of me," she said. And immediately thought of Maya. *Why can't you just let me in? Let me carry things once in a while.*

"I don't think that's true," he said. "I think you wish it was. But I think you realized a long time ago that you're not as strong as you pretend."

She tilted her chin up, her chest tight. They faced off, gazes locked. Silence prevailed, light and shadow playing along the walls, flickering across Cameron's face. Outside, she heard laughter, low conversation.

And then, something else.

Something scratching, the grate of metal against glass. *Scritch. Scritch. Scritch.*

Cameron heard it at the same time. He held his index finger to his lips, gesturing her to stay quiet. The scratching got louder. Tension changed to overt alarm in the space of a second. An instant later, he was on his feet.

"Get down," he said. Before she could comply, Cam shoved her to the floor—none too gently, either. "Stay there," he whispered.

He left her crouched between the wall and an arm of the sofa, peering out as he went toward her bedroom. His gun was already in hand, which made her wonder where the hell he kept it when he slept—or didn't sleep, as the case may be. The hotel suite was dark except for the flickering light of the television, now muted and onto the next infomercial.

"Cam?" she whispered.

He held his hand up to keep her quiet. She couldn't hear the grating sound she'd heard before, but she knew he was headed in the right direction—it had definitely come from her bedroom. She thought of the balcony and the sliding glass doors with dread.

Cameron moved as silently as a shadow. His hand fell to the doorknob, ready to push the bedroom door open, gun raised. An instant before he made his move, the front door of the suite burst open. In the dim light cast by the television, Kat saw the same tall, thick-bodied man they'd seen on Raven's Ledge push his way inside. He led with a sawed-off, double-barrel shotgun. Cameron pivoted, aimed, and fired in the space of less than a second, catching the man in the side. Before he could fire again, a second figure sprang from the bedroom, her own gun raised.

Jenny.

The girl flipped on the light switch. Light flooded the room. Kat blinked in the sudden glare, adrenaline flooding her veins.

Jenny's partner stood tall, apparently none the worse for Cameron's attack. Cam stood there in his t-shirt and pajama bottoms, his own gun still raised. Jenny barely glanced in her friend's direction.

"Okay, Lee?"

"Just grazed," the man said. Jenny looked at Cameron, anger touching her face for an instant before that eerie calm descended once more.

"Put down the gun, Dad," Jenny said. "We're going on a little trip."

Kat held her breath, still crouched behind the sofa—waiting to see what he would do. Trying to figure out what the hell *she* would do, if it came down to it. Jenny took a step toward her. She didn't even bother to look at Cameron. Kat wondered at the girl's faith in her father, that she would turn her back on his gun without a moment's hesitation.

"Get up," Jenny ordered.

Kat remained where she was, biding her time, until Jenny was close enough to grab her arm. Before she could yank Kat to her feet, Kat reared up fast, focused on the gun. She caught Jenny off guard when she brought her left hand down, hard, on the girl's wrist. She was dimly aware of Cameron as he sprang into action at the other end of the room. Otherwise, her focus remained on Jenny, and the crash of the pistol as it hit the floor.

Jenny didn't make a sound. Her foot came up, catching Kat in the ribs as she dove for the gun. Kat kept moving, ignoring the pain, the thought of cold steel and a powerful, burning hatred propelling her forward.

Her fingers closed around the grip just as Jenny caught her, Kat down on the ground with her belly on the hardwood floor. Jenny grabbed her by the hair and pulled hard, sitting astride her like a damned cowgirl. But Kat had the gun—she *had* it. She twisted her body, moving fast and hard, working the safety on the Glock the way her father had taught her years ago. Somehow, she managed to flip to her back, Jenny still on her. Kat leveled the gun at the girl's face, now flushed, her eyes wild.

"Get the hell off me," Kat ground out.

Jenny made no move. Kat scrambled backward herself, her hands steady, gun still pointed at Cameron's daughter.

"Put down the gun," a voice behind her said. Lee's voice. Kat didn't even look, eyes still trained on Jenny.

"You put it down, or I'll kill her," Kat said.

"Put the gun down now," Lee said again. "You're not leaving here if you don't lay it down."

"Katherine," Cameron said. Jenny's eyes darkened. The girl kept her chin up, nostrils flared as she struggled for breath.

"Drop your gun, or I'll drop her," Kat said evenly. "We're getting out of here, and we're sure as hell not going with you."

"Katherine!" Cam said again, more firmly this time. At the sheer command in his voice, she finally turned.

And stared directly into the wrong end of Jenny's partner's shotgun. Two other men had come in during the struggle, unbeknownst to her. All were armed. Most were focused on her. Cameron stood against the wall with blood dripping from his nose and lip, staining his clean white t-shirt.

Kat lowered her gun.

15
SOLOMON

IF EVER THERE WAS a worthy-movie moment, this should have been it. The man I'd thought was dead for over a decade, the man who had meant home to me for the first ten years of my life, was walking toward me. He wasn't a ghost; he wasn't a dream…

He was my father.

And he was here.

But instead of racing across an open field to leap into his arms, I just stood there. Mouth opening and closing with no words, like a friggin' land-locked salmon. Diggs' hand was at the small of my back. He looked as shocked as I was. My father took another step toward us.

"You'd be Diggs," Dad said, hand extended. Diggs met him halfway. They shook hands.

"Mr. Solomon," he said. "It's a pleasure to meet you."

"And you," my father agreed. It was official: I was losing my mind. "Though I'm sorry to meet you under these circumstances."

"They could be better," Diggs agreed. And then, he fell silent. As did the rest of us. Finally, my father cleared his throat.

"Diggs, would you mind giving us a minute?"

Diggs stood his ground, hands dug into his pockets. He looked at me, waiting for my word. I nodded.

"Uh—yeah, it's okay. I'll be all right."

"I'll just get cleaned up, then," he said reluctantly. "But if you need anything, I won't be far."

"Thanks."

A wave of panic washed over me as he walked away. That left my father and me, standing there. I had no idea what to say. No idea what to do. I remained rooted to the spot, mute. Eventually, my father closed the distance between us, while I just stood there staring at him stupidly. Einstein sat down beside me and looked at us both expectantly.

"I know this is a shock," he began.

"Yeah," was the best I could manage. Dad nodded toward the picnic table.

"Will you sit with me? We can't stay here long—Cameron has everything arranged, but we don't have a lot of time."

I sat down. My father took the seat beside me, turning his body so he could look at me. He looked the same. Not the way he'd looked after the Payson fire, when he'd been so broken, so lost…. but the way I remembered him when I was growing up. Older, sure, but his presence remained the same: solid; steady. He reached out and ran his hand along my cheek gently.

"You grew up," he said.

My eyes watered, the weight building in my chest. I nodded again. "You, too," I managed. He smiled at that, and all at once it hit like me like a slab of concrete:

Things to remember, things to forget.

People won't understand the world out here, Erin. Some of the things you've seen… the things Isaac has done. People off the island won't understand. They can't know.

"Erin? Honey, I know you've been through a lot."

"You made me forget something." I stared at him, only half aware I was even speaking. "Before I left the island, you said there were things people wouldn't understand."

I'm going to help you forget, baby. Everything that's confused you about this place, everything that scared you...

"How?" I asked, my voice surprisingly even. "How did you make me forget? What out there was so bad that I shouldn't remember?"

He touched my arm. I cringed. And it hit me for the first time: Everything I believed my childhood had been was a lie. The life I thought I'd had with my father, the bond I thought we shared... I had no idea anymore how much of that was real. Somehow, he had manipulated everything I thought I knew about my past on Payson Isle.

I stood up and walked away, arms crossed over my chest, trying to hold myself together.

"What did you do in Jonestown? Why are they still after you? Why are they after Kat?"

"Honey—"

I wheeled on him. "Don't 'honey' me! I know this is supposed to be some Lifetime movie moment, but I'm running for my life. *Diggs* is running for his life—he almost died three weeks ago. Did you know? Were you there somewhere, lurking in the background the way Juarez told me you were in Black Falls?"

He stood again, an odd combination of regret and defiance in his eye. "I'm sorry you got pulled into this, Erin—I truly am. It was never my intention. When I faked my death thirteen years ago, it was to try and keep you out of that world. When I took those memories from you, I was doing it to keep you safe."

"But safe from whom? Cameron? Jenny? Max Richards? Or safe from J. Enterprises?"

He hesitated, wetting his lips. "You know I can't tell you that."

"Yes, you can—but you won't. You and Kat have been doing this since I was a kid, trying to keep me safe. Well, guess what, Dad: It's not working. I'm not safe—I don't know if I ever will be, at this point. Tell me what this is. What is J. Enterprises?"

The sun was up now, cars pulling out of the parking lot as people tried to get a jump on another day of travel. Einstein stuck close, sensing trouble. Dad turned his back on me and walked away, his hands in his pockets. For one irrational moment, I thought he might not turn back. When he finally did, it looked like he was locked in some deep, internal battle.

"Erin," he began again.

"Please." My voice broke on the word. "My whole life is fucked six ways to Sunday because of these people. Just… please, Dad."

He ran his hands through his hair, then returned and sat down beside me. "What I'm about to tell you… You can't tell anyone this, Erin. This can't be a story you pursue; you have to let this lie. You have no idea what they can do to you—to everyone you care about."

I actually had a pretty good idea, as a matter of fact, but I kept my mouth shut. "I won't say anything. You have my word."

He took a deep breath. "J. Enterprises was a front for the federal government," he said, his voice low. "It was a dummy corporation concealing an elite division of the United States military."

I couldn't have been more surprised if he'd said it was a front for Christ himself. I just stood there for a second, blinking stupidly at him. "I don't understand," I finally managed.

Before he could clarify anything, my cell phone rang. It had to be Cameron… with impeccable timing, as usual.

Much as I didn't want to take it just then, I couldn't run the risk that he wouldn't call back. I held up my index finger to ask for a minute. Dad nodded.

"It's about time," I said into the receiver. "We've been here for hours, waiting for you to tell us what the hell the next move is."

There was no response for a long few seconds. Nothing, that is, but breathing. Heavy breathing.

"Cameron?" I said uneasily.

"Erin," a woman's voice purred into the phone: Jenny. My blood turned to ice. "You have no idea how long I've waited to have this conversation."

"Where's my mother?" I demanded. "Where's Cameron?"

Dad looked up sharply. Jenny laughed. "We're all together," she said. "It's actually really sweet. Now—I have some instructions for you."

My father was still watching me with a clear question in his eyes, but I dodged him and walked away. "Let me talk to my mother," I said.

"You don't give me orders," Jenny said, her voice suddenly cold. "I'm in charge here—not you. You'll do what I say, and you'll do it when I say. Now: I need you to listen closely. I think it's time we finally meet, face to face."

"Erin?" Dad whispered. "What's going on?"

Heart in my throat and lacking any better ideas, I took a step closer to him. He leaned down so we could both listen to the phone, his cheek close to mine. He smelled the way he had when I was little—back when I believed he could do anything. Fix anything.

"What do you want?" I asked.

"What do I want?" she repeated, a lilt to her voice. "Oh… Where do I begin? How about we start with your father's head on a platter, and go from there."

I could almost feel my father flinch beside me. "Well…

I can't give you that," I said. "I don't have a clue where he is. Now—let me talk to Kat, and then we can work something out."

"Spare me, please. All that leverage your dear old mom and dad held over our heads all this time? Jonah Melquist is dead. The evidence they were keeping out on that island is gone. We found everything. Which means not one of you is in the position to bargain anymore. My orders are very simple."

"That's not actually true," I said. I forced strength into my tone. My father took a step back, away from the phone—like he didn't have it in him to listen anymore. I walked away, aware of his eyes on me. "That professor you killed in Kentucky… the one you shot just before you blew up an entire building filled with innocent people? He was working on something, wasn't he? That was the reason you guys were there in the first place—at least, that's the way Diggs and I figure it."

I was shaking, had the eerie feeling it wasn't me saying these words at all.

"What are you talking about?" Jenny asked. I had her, I could tell; she hadn't expected this.

"That professor had a memory card with some information on it," I continued. "A lot of information, actually. Diggs got it before the building went up. We have it now."

My father was watching me, dumbstruck. Jenny didn't answer for a couple of seconds, her breathing audibly faster.

"You're lying," she said.

"First entry: 40N85W3062210511115DM," I said, reciting it from memory. "Do you want more? It's a long list—this could take a while."

There was the distant sound of voices on the line, as though she was conferring with someone. It was as much as a minute later before she spoke again.

"You want to deal? Here's your deal: We'll trade your mother for that card. I'll even let you and that cute boyfriend of yours go, for it. And then all three of you can leave town, free and clear, just as soon as the information is in my hand."

"And if we don't? If Diggs and I just keep running… Or we bring that list of numbers to the first cop we find? What happens then?"

"Don't test me," Jenny said. "You want an idea of what I'll more than happily do to your mother? Take a look." A second later, an image came through. I took one look and the world spun sideways, my stomach tilting sickeningly.

I waited for my father to intervene; for him to grab the phone from me and tell this bitch exactly what he would do if she hurt Kat. He didn't do that, though. Instead, he remained silent when I showed him the photo Jenny had sent: Kat, her face bruised, dried blood crusted around her nose, holding a newspaper with today's date and headlines…

"The longer this takes, the harder this will be on her. You don't want to do that to your mommy now, do you, Erin?" Jenny crooned. I was holding the phone so tight my hand ached. "I mean… I know you two have your problems, but let's be reasonable here. I'm going to send along some coordinates and a meeting time. We'll make our trade, and that will be that. You go on your merry way."

Diggs was walking toward me, already sensing trouble—it was clear from his pace, the wrinkle in his brow. He started moving faster, gearing up to a slow jog as I continued with Jenny.

"How do I know we'll be safe? How do I know you won't kill all three of us the second I hand over the numbers?"

"Because, unlike you and your family, I actually keep my word," Jenny said, her voice hardening again. "We'll make the exchange in a public place. You leave the numbers and the memory card and a guarantee that you don't have a copy hidden away somewhere, and you can all walk away. If I find out you double crossed me, then you'll spend the rest of your life looking over your shoulder. And when I catch you—and I *will* catch you—then I'll make sure you're watching when I kill Diggs and your mother, as slowly and painfully as possible. And then, I'll kill you."

Her voice had darkened, all reason leeched out by that last sentence. It lightened a moment later, though; she was suddenly all business. Dealing with psychopaths, incidentally, is exhausting. The mood swings alone could kill you. "So… We have a deal, right? You follow my instructions—without Jack Juarez, without Willett and his band of idiots—and we can all part company happy."

"What about Cameron and my father?" I demanded.

"Cameron and your father have some things to answer for," she said. "There's no other deal here. When I catch dear old Adam, trust me when I say he won't be leaving. There's no bargaining chip big enough to get him out of here. But that's none of your concern. And neither is Cameron. Let me worry about them."

Diggs reached me then, that furrow in his brow getting deeper. Before Jenny could say anything more, I turned my back on both the men in my life and steeled myself for the next step. "Where and when?"

"See how easy that was?" Jenny asked with a laugh. "All right—good. I'll text you the details. No police. No more games. It's time to end this."

She hung up before I could ask anything more. Maybe three seconds later, a text came through:

11993 Walnut Grove Ln
Trumann, AR
15:00, Monday April 10

"Arkansas? Jesus, can't they make anything easy? How far is that?" I asked.

"I'm not sure," Diggs said. "Maybe ten, fifteen hours. You mind telling me what's going on?"

"They've got Kat," I said. No tears, no shaking voice or trembling lip. Now was definitely not the time for a psychotic break. "We need to go."

"Erin—" Dad began. He may not have been a father to me since I was nine, but I remembered the tone well.

"I'm not arguing about this," I said. I thought of Kat's words to me back on Raven's Ledge: *We were never more than roommates.*

It wasn't true. Whatever else we may have been— roommates, soldiers in arms, often overt enemies—we were still mother and daughter. I had her eyes and her stubborn streak; her sarcasm and her vitriol.

"I'm not leaving her to die," I said.

"She would never forgive me if I let you do this," Dad said. He was torn, I could tell—scared, pissed off, and ripped in two. He didn't need to be, though. The solution to this particular problem was simple.

If it meant they would let Kat go, I would do whatever Jenny asked.

"We'll be all right," I said. "We have some leverage, still. They'll let us go."

"Do I get a vote in this?" Diggs asked. "Because I'm pretty sure I'm part of the equation here."

"You don't have to come," I said. That earned a glare from him—not surprising given recent conversations.

"Spare me," he said. "Just hear me out, would you? If we're doing this, I think it's long past time we call Juarez in on it."

I thought of Dad's revelation: J. Enterprises was a

government operation. Or at least it had been, once upon a time—I had no idea what it was now. Juarez had to know that. That's what he'd been hiding. Whoever was behind the death and destruction on Payson Isle, Kentucky, and possibly Jonestown itself, had once been part of the United States government.

"They said no cops," I said, then turned to my father. "And what was that she said: Willett? Who the hell is Willett?"

"He's… It's a long story," Dad said. "But you're right. If we bring someone in, I have no doubt that they'll hurt your mother."

"How would they find out?" Diggs asked. "Jack might not be telling us everything, but he's on our side, Sol. You know that."

Suddenly, I didn't know that at all.

"You can't bring Jack Juarez in on this," Dad said. "It's too dangerous right now. Trust me: Jenny will know."

"Well, Jenny will also know if we don't show up where we're supposed to tomorrow afternoon," I said. "And maybe I'm crazy, but I don't think that will go over any better."

"You're being unreasonable" my father said. It was like no time had passed at all. How many times had he said those words to me? *You're just like your mother, Erin.* "This isn't a debate," he continued. "Your mother and I have talked about something like this happening. Your safety is our priority. It always has been."

"And so Diggs and I are just supposed to disappear, knowing that Kat is being tortured and killed? Knowing that when all is said and done, nothing's changed? These people will keep killing; Diggs and I will live the rest of our lives in fear, waiting for them to find us."

"You don't have any choice where they're concerned," Dad said. "I'm sorry, but that's the reality… The best I can do for you, the best Cameron and your mother could do, ultimately, is to help you get away."

"But why? Who the hell are these people?" I asked. And again, he hesitated. If I got stonewalled on this one more time, blood would absolutely, positively be shed. And it wouldn't be mine. "You said J. Enterprises was an elite military division." Diggs looked as shocked as I expect I had when I'd first heard the news, but I kept right on going. "What does that mean? Are they still part of the government? How long have they been around—and what the hell did Jonestown have to do with any of it? What does *any* of this have to do with the U.S. military?"

Suddenly, Diggs took my hand, pulling me away from the parking lot. "I think we should have this conversation on the move."

"What? Why?" I asked. My father was already on the alert, following Diggs' gaze.

"Last night while you were walking Stein, someone else was gassing up their car. He struck up a conversation."

"And…?"

"And he just pulled in," Diggs said, nodding toward an old blue car just pulling up to the curb. When the man stopped and got out, my stomach dropped.

"I know him," I said. Dad pushed us toward the trees. We hadn't been spotted yet—or at least I thought we hadn't. Hoped to hell we hadn't. "Back in Allentown, when I was trying to get out of there that morning. He spoke to me."

"Come on," Dad said. "We can't stay here."

"Why? Who is he?" I demanded.

"You wanted to know who Willett is? That's him: Trent Willett."

"What does he want with us? He can't be police—he would have just arrested us back in Allentown."

"He's hoping you'll lead him to me—and J."

"But who does he work for?" I persisted.

"Government—"

This was getting ridiculous. "I thought J. Enterprises was government."

Dad looked at Diggs. "Is she like this all the time?"

"Oh, you have no idea," Diggs said. "We can ask questions once we get out of here. Right now, I think we need to figure out how to lose this guy."

"He knows your car," Dad said. "We'll need to leave that behind. We can take mine."

I thought of the suitcase with the few material possessions I had left in this world.

"But our stuff…" I began.

"Cameron told you to carry the cash and IDs with you. You have that?"

Diggs nodded to a backpack slung over his shoulder. "Yeah—we've got it. But everything else…"

"We can replace everything else," Dad said.

"So, we just… what?" I asked. "Leave the car here?"

"That's right," my father agreed, like it was the most natural thing in the world. "I'm sorry, but right now this is what you can expect—a life where nothing is permanent. Nothing is certain. It's not a good way to live."

"Well, right now I don't see a lot of options," I said. "We have to get Kat. We'll give them the memory card; we can figure out the next step once I know Mom is safe."

He massaged his temples, as though he had a monster headache. Another flash came through from childhood: My father in the greenhouse, head in his hands, staring at the stone floor beneath our feet for what seemed like hours. *The world is a hard place, baby. That's why we stay here… Isaac isn't perfect, but he cares about us. He would never hurt us. But out there…*

"It'll be all right," I said, surprising myself. I've never

been much of a cheerleader. "But we can't just leave her. I won't."

"Okay," he agreed after several seconds. He wasn't exactly jumping up and down over the change in plans, though. "We'll try this. But if we do it, you have to do as I say."

With the clock running down and this new, trench-coat-clad mystery man on our heels, I agreed: I would let my father call the shots.

From there, Dad pointed out a dark blue SUV in the parking lot. We waited until Willett had gone into the rest station before we made our move—heart pounding, Einstein panting, me looking over my shoulder the whole time.

The entire operation took maybe ninety seconds. If I hadn't been so tired and wired and generally freaked out, it might have felt anticlimactic. The four of us piled into the SUV and pulled out, me in the front with Dad, Diggs and Einstein in the back. I ducked down in my seat. Diggs reached around and touched my knee.

"All right?" he whispered to me. I squeezed his hand; he squeezed back.

"No problem," I said. "Easiest getaway ever."

"You've had a few of them by now, I guess," my father said, tapping my shoulder after we'd hit the highway. "You can get up now." His SUV was a tank—one of those vehicles that takes up two parking spaces and makes the planet wheeze every time you put it in drive.

"More than I can count," I said, glancing back at Diggs. He didn't seem so assured that we were in the clear. He craned his head back to scan the traffic behind us, not even acknowledging what I'd said.

"Now—how about some answers," I prompted, once we were safely rumbling west.

"Your mother warned me about you and the third degree." I started to protest, but he held up his hand before

I got a word out. "You're right, though: It's pointless keeping the secret anymore. They're after you, whether you know these things or not. You might as well have some idea why."

Finally, someone who saw things my way.

"Okay—so, let's start with an easy one: Who is J?" I asked immediately. Diggs stopped looking backward and focused on the conversation, leaning forward in his seat.

"It isn't a who—it's a what," Dad said, after only a second of hesitation. "Project J-932—shortened to J for simplicity's sake."

"J-932," I repeated, turning it over in my head. "When did it start?"

"1936. You've heard of something called MK Ultra?"

"Of course," I said. "I mean—I have a general idea. I don't know a lot of specifics."

"MK Ultra was a controversial government-funded operation," Diggs said. Because these are the kinds of things Diggs knows. "Using human subjects, they experimented with things like mind control, ESP, and… what did they call it? 'Behavioral engineering.'" Dad nodded. "The project was officially shut down sometime in the '70s."

"That's right," my father said. "There were about one hundred and fifty subprojects that were part of MK Ultra—J-932 was just one of them. It involved four different research bases around the country: one in northern California, one in Kentucky, one in Maine… and one in Lynn, Indiana."

"And what did they do, exactly?" I asked. "What was the goal?"

"It was started by a behaviorist by the name of Dexter Mandrake. He wanted to find a way to manipulate behavior over the course of a subject's lifetime," my father said. He didn't look at me as he said it, his focus instead on the busy highway ahead. I got the sense his mind was far, far away.

"So, he targeted children who fit within certain behavioral parameters: shaky home life, no discernible support system, a predilection for… questionable morality."

"Jim Jones, then," I said as understanding dawned. "That's where Jonestown fits into this whole thing: Jones was one of Mandrake's subjects."

"One of the most successful," my father agreed. "If you can call Jonestown a success."

"And Max Richards?" I asked.

Dad nodded. "That's right. Max Richards, Cameron, Isaac Payson…"

"You?" I asked.

My father's fingers tightened on the steering wheel. "That's right. I didn't move to Lynn until later—I was seven when my father moved us out of Chicago. Your grandfather…" He hesitated.

"Was a mobster," I said, recalling the story Juarez had unearthed when I was first learning about my father's past. "He got caught by the Feds, flaked out on a deal to testify, and disappeared."

Dad smiled faintly. "Apparently I have no secrets here. Yes… My father was with the mob, so there was already some moral ambiguity. When we moved to Lynn, Mandrake zeroed in on me immediately."

I dug my fingers into my palms. "What did they do to you?"

He reached across the seat and slid his hand into mine. "It doesn't matter. What matters is that it was working… for a while, anyway."

"Until your sister was killed," Diggs said. A shadow crossed my father's face, grief coloring his blue eyes.

"Yes," he agreed with a nod. "Mandrake never bargained for that degree of violence… or if he had, he wouldn't have admitted it. What they did to my sister, though…" He shook his head, his eyes welling. "It knocked me out of the project. It knocked me out of my life. I tried to disappear… Mandrake suggested maybe I should talk to Jim Jones. Then, I would see firsthand that not everyone who came out of the project was a monster. J-932 was capable of inspiring greatness—making the world a better place."

"So you joined Jones and the People's Temple," I said.

"I was screwed up, but not so much that I didn't recognize the church's imperfections. It didn't feel… right, exactly, when I saw what Jim was doing. The way he manipulated his followers. But, by then I was under Mandrake's thumb again. Taking the drugs. Following the protocol. I saw the results we were achieving: Jim making the papers, striving for racial equality, establishing social outreach programs… Mandrake's kids were always taught that the ends justify the means."

"And Cameron?" I asked. "Where did he fit into this? Or Isaac Payson? What is the point of a project where the subjects just start killing indiscriminately?"

"That's why J-932 was ultimately shut down," Dad said. "MK Ultra was officially put out of commission in 1973, but it continued for a few years beyond that—off the books, of course. After Jonestown, though, the CIA cut all ties with Mandrake. He went underground… but he continued with his research, using private funding."

"Why the hell is he still out there?" Diggs asked. "If the government knew about this, why hasn't he been arrested? Why aren't you working with them to take him down?"

"It's not that simple," my father said. "For one thing, Mandrake died about twenty years ago—there's no 'him' to take down anymore. There's the Project, and Mandrake's successors have kept things going over the years. As for why I'm not helping the government get rid of them…" His eyes shifted toward me for a split second before they returned to the road. "You don't know what Willett is like. He's ruthless—and corrupt. Whatever happens, don't let him anywhere near you. The Project may have been bad, but it doesn't have anything on Willett and his people. At least with J, I know their end goal."

"Which is?" I asked. He glanced in the rearview mirror briefly. I thought of the memory card Diggs and I had decrypted. What the hell did it mean? "Dad?" I pressed.

"When Mandrake started, the Project was all about scientific inquiry: How much could an outside party manipulate the human mind? By the time the government cut off funding and Mandrake died and new concerns took over, that question had been answered. Under the right conditions, there are no limits to how extensive that manipulation can be. You can make people kill *en masse*; you can remove conscience, you can change belief systems, you can shift consciousness."

"If they've already done that," I said, "then what are they after now?"

"Now, they're putting those theories into practice. They have three generations of foot soldiers around the country— around the world—who were raised under Mandrake's tutelage. Now, it's a matter of activating those individuals to gain the power, the prestige, the money the higher-ups want."

I fell silent. As did Diggs. We continued driving, Einstein sitting up with his nose out the window. What did you say to something like this? It was… ridiculous. Nuts.

"You're talking about a global conspiracy," Diggs said. "An ongoing conspiracy that's been hidden for nearly eighty years, if your timeline is accurate. If this is at the root of Jonestown, Payson Isle, Raven's Ledge, and Justice, Kentucky, not to mention the women tortured and killed by Max Richards, then I'm assuming it's at the root of other mass casualty tragedies, as well."

My father nodded.

"So, these people are responsible for killing thousands of innocent victims," Diggs continued. "And you've known about it all this time. Why haven't you gone to... I don't know, *someone*? I can maybe understand avoiding the police, but why not alert the media? Tell them what you told us."

Dad didn't answer for as much as thirty seconds. I cleared my throat, the conversation weighing like lead on my shoulders.

"Because they would have killed me," I said. "That's been the deal all along, hasn't it? Since Payson Isle, when Cameron found you... He killed everyone else in that church, but he didn't go after me or Kat. J was letting you know, then: The only way we would be safe is if you kept your mouth shut."

My father reached across the console and took my hand, squeezing it fiercely. His eyes were wet, his voice choked when he spoke. "I left J-932 when I ran from Guyana in 1978, and I swore I would never go back. I wouldn't let them find me... I would never go through that again. And then I met your mother, and you were born... It felt like redemption. As though, somehow, God had looked past what happened to my sister, had seen that I hadn't chosen these things... And he'd given me you. By then, I was off the drugs Mandrake had raised me on. I was far from that world."

"And then they found you," Diggs said. "Cameron found you."

"If I were a better man, I would be able to weigh things more wisely," my father said, his hand still in mine. "I would be able to say, 'my daughter's life is not worth one hundred victims, or two hundred, or ten thousand.' But I could never do that."

"And Kat?" I asked. Because, frankly, if anyone could

flush my life down the toilet for the sake of the planet, it seemed like my mother could do it. "Kat must have known that was insane."

"Your mother isn't as hard as you think. But you're right: She didn't realize until recently just how deep this went. She didn't know about Max Richards, or the women he and Will Rainier were tracking and torturing. She didn't know about Jesup Barnel. The indiscriminate killing you've seen in the past year is new to the Project—a reflection of a new regime. Your mother thought the kind of mass deaths you're seeing now were confined to Jonestown, and that it ended there."

"Because you told her it had," I guessed. I pulled my hand back. "She had no idea what protecting me cost."

"This isn't your fault, Erin," my father said. "The people who died… There's no blood on your hands here. It's never been about you."

I thought of the family on Raven's Ledge: the little girl with the baby in her arms; the old man, half-buried in slush… If I hadn't been part of the equation, would my father have stopped this in time? Or would the higher-ups in J-932 have just done away with him years ago?

My father cleared his throat again. "This information you have—this memory card you're using as a bargaining chip to save your mother. Where is it now?"

For the first time, I felt a twinge of anxiety.

"Honey?" he said, glancing at me curiously. When he saw the look in my eye, his face fell. He forced a smile. "It's all right, Erin. You don't know me yet. Tell me what you're comfortable telling. I have to earn your trust, after all these years. I understand that."

An awkward silence descended. I fought the urge to blurt out everything Diggs and I had learned about the memory card, from the moment Diggs got it to the decryption process to the bizarre scroll of coded entries I now carried in my back pocket.

I stayed quiet.

Eventually, we moved on to other topics. I felt those walls start to crumble, all my doubts fade away. My father was back. He was different, sure, but he was still the man I had known on Payson Isle. There was an ease about talking to him that I never would have expected. It was almost shocking how simple it was to relate to him again, after all these years.

We drove on for hours like that, my father answering more questions; occasionally putting me off; occasionally tearing up, his hands gripped on the steering wheel. We made good time, more and more of the country passing us by as the day wore on. Diggs had been notably quiet for the better part of the trek—letting Dad and me have the time to get reacquainted, while he and Einstein squabbled over who took up more space in the backseat. By five o'clock that evening, we were already in Tennessee.

At a rest stop somewhere near Knoxville, my father went to use the restroom while Diggs and I stretched our legs, walking the picnic area with Einstein. A family ate at one of the picnic tables, their three kids climbing under and over the benches while the parents tried to summon the energy to care. Almost unconsciously, I redirected our path to avoid them. It had become second nature: I avoided everyone, now. Who was to say this innocuous family wasn't some plant, a bizarre Manchurian familial unit sent there to kill us all?

"How are you doing?" Diggs asked as we walked—once we were well out of earshot of everyone else, I noticed. Great: He was getting as paranoid as me now.

"Honestly? I'm a little freaked out. You?"

He nodded thoughtfully. We weren't touching—I wasn't sure whether that was my fault or his, but I wasn't sure how to remedy it, either.

"It's a lot to take in," he agreed.

"Daniel Diggins, master of understatement. Do you believe him?"

"I do… Mostly because he'd have to be completely certifiable to come up with anything this elaborate."

"Completely certifiable isn't out of the question," I said. "But I think maybe you're right. As insane as everything he's said is, it makes sense. I mean—in a very Oliver Stone kind of way, but… it sort of fits. Explains how everything is tied together, anyway: Payson Isle and Max Richards and Jesup Barnel and Raven's Ledge…"

My father walked out of the visitor's center. After ten hours with him, it still felt weird that he was just… here. No longer the lunatic I remembered after the fire at the Payson Church, but far from the quiet, understanding Father Knows Best in my childhood memories of Payson Isle. But then, I was starting to suspect that that time hadn't been as idyllic as I remembered it.

"Erin," Diggs said. I looked up to find him watching my father with an intensity that made me uneasy.

"Yeah?"

He scratched his neck and took my arm, gently ushering me onto a pretty wooded path out of my father's line of sight.

"What are you doing?" I asked.

There was a picnic table in a cleared glade not far along the path. Diggs led me there and sat down. Einstein found a patch of grass and started grazing enthusiastically—a clear sign that our life on the road wasn't doing him any favors, either. I sat in the grass beside him, taking a moment to be grateful for soft earth and no road moving beneath me for a few beautiful minutes.

"I just wanted a chance to talk to you while he's not around," Diggs said. My hackles rose, but he forged ahead anyway. "I just… I have some questions I think we need to ask ourselves here."

"Such as?"

He studied me for a second—me seated on the ground, idly picking dandelions while Diggs sat at the table with that perpetual shadow of worry on his face.

"Why is he doing this, Sol? Your father has spent the past thirty years doing everything in his power to keep you safe. Why is he suddenly giving up all his secrets? And why would he possibly deliver you to these people, when he's worked so hard to keep you out of their clutches all this time? It doesn't make any sense."

"That's not his idea, it's mine—we're trying to save Kat. It's not like I'm giving him a choice here." There was a chill to my tone that I knew Diggs didn't miss. "It doesn't matter, though, he wouldn't put her life in danger. You see the way he talks about her: I don't care what happened, he's still in love with my mother. And she's obviously still in love with him. So, maybe he sees this as the only chance for them to be done with this. For all of us to be done with it."

"So, in this fantasy you've created…" Diggs continued. His tone grated; I pulled another chunk of grass from the earth and slowly showered it back down. I wouldn't look him in the eye. "Your mom and dad are still in love. Forget the fact that Kat has been living happily with a *woman* for the past two years—we'll just put a pin in that for now. So what, exactly, do you think is about to happen here, Sol? We'll get to Arkansas, your father will deliver us to the J. project heads, they'll shake our hands and say, 'We've heard so much about you—here's a little confidentiality agreement, if you don't mind. Just sign this, take your mom, and you can be on your way?'"

"I haven't figured that part out yet," I said. "But I will. We still have the information from the memory card—that's a powerful bargaining chip. We'll handle it."

"But how?" Diggs demanded. "We're not allowed to call in the people we trust—and apparently, Cameron and your father don't trust anyone. The government, according to your dad, is worse than J-932. And the bad guys already have Cameron, so it's not like we can expect backup there."

"I told you," I snapped. "He'll figure out a plan. I'm not letting Kat die: Dad knows that. This is his only option. He'll figure it out."

"Right," Diggs said shortly. "I forgot: your father's a friggin' superhero. So what if he's stood by while thousands of innocent people have died over the years, ostensibly just to protect his little girl—"

I got up. "You don't have kids—you wouldn't understand that kind of devotion—"

"I've been in love with the same woman for fifteen years," he said, his voice dangerously low. "And there's nothing I wouldn't do—eat your shitty cooking, suffer through political debates with your mother… I'd kill or die for you, so don't tell me I don't understand devotion. Listen to yourself, damn it. Or, if you're too blinded to see it, then listen to me: This doesn't add up."

"Erin!" my father called. I looked up. Diggs glanced in the direction of his voice irritably.

"Just think about it, all right?" Diggs said.

I turned my back on him without acknowledgment. "We're here," I called back. Dad appeared from around the bend, his flannel shirt slung over his shoulder.

"I hope I'm not interrupting," he said. "But we should get back on the road. There's a place not much farther along where we can stay tonight—I think we can all use a full night's sleep and a decent meal before the meeting tomorrow."

"That would be good," I agreed. I strode on ahead with

Einstein. Dad put his arm around my shoulder. He looked back at Diggs.

"You coming, Diggs?"

There was a very long, very loaded second there when I thought he might say no. Instead, Diggs looked at me pointedly and nodded.

"Yeah—I'll be right there."

That tension followed us back to the car. Diggs took the front this time, at my father's insistence: *There's no reason you should be relegated to the back with that dog this whole drive… that's just cruel and unusual punishment.* With a multitude of reservations, I settled in the back with Einstein. It didn't take long before Diggs started in.

"Since I'm up here, I was hoping you wouldn't mind answering a couple of my questions, Mr. Solomon," Diggs said.

Here we go.

"Adam, please," my father said. "Call me Adam. And no—I don't mind at all. Just as with Erin, I'll tell you what I can."

Diggs shifted in his seat. I couldn't see his face, but I was sure that if I had, I would recognize the look there: His classic interview face. Take no prisoners; accept no pat answers; believe nothing.

"These kids that Mandrake experimented on all those years, starting with Jim Jones and whoever else was selected back then… Did they know what was happening?"

"Some did. Some didn't," my father said. "Jim was never aware of it. Cameron didn't know, at first. I always did. There were parts I even liked. Mandrake could be very flattering. He made it seem like I'd been chosen above all these other kids."

"And the ones who didn't know?" Diggs persisted. "They

just… what? Had the whole experience wiped from their memories? Never knew someone had been roaming around their psyches, crossing the wires there?"

Dad glanced into the rearview mirror at me. It looked like he was getting an idea of what he was in for. "You weren't one of the subjects, Diggs, if that's what you're worried about. I'm sure with everything that happened in Kentucky—"

"I wasn't asking about me," Diggs said pointedly. He looked back over his shoulder at me.

A shiver of dread crawled into my lower intestine and stayed there, holding court. Dad shook his head, adamant once he understood the question.

"I already told you: Erin was never part of the experiment. No one ever went near her—I always made sure her mind was her own."

That wasn't completely true, though. A jumbled flash of memories ran through my mind, sparking like fireworks: *Something to remember; something to forget… For thine is the kingdom and the glory… He'll put us in the woods again.*

Allie Tate, lying on the ground with Isaac towering over her.

Diggs was still looking at me. He could tell what I was thinking, I knew. The bastard can always tell what I'm thinking.

"What are the things you've been remembering, Sol?" Diggs asked pointedly. "All those little mishmash glimpses that make no sense?"

"I told you, Erin," Dad said. "That was necessary—I had to do that to keep you safe."

"I know that," I said. My voice sounded wooden, though.

Instead of asking more questions, I went quiet. The road unfolded. Somewhere out there, Kat was being held hostage. Maybe she was hurt; hell, she could be dead by now. But my father was here—he knew how to fix things. It was an idiotic, childish thing to believe, but he'd been the one I could rely on for the first ten years of my life. In those first ten years, I was safe. I was loved. I knew where I belonged.

I waited for Diggs to follow up with something more, but instead I felt a weighty, disappointed silence. He was waiting for me to wake up and be reasonable—I knew that.

I just wasn't sure I had it in me.

16
DIGGS

THAT NIGHT I LAY IN BED staring at the ceiling, listening to the murmur of voices in the next room. Adam had rented a cabin in the woods of western Tennessee—three bedrooms, of course. Isolated and eerie. He was tucking Solomon in next door, the two of them talking in hushed tones, punctuated occasionally by the sound of Erin's laughter.

She was a different woman, with him. And I was glad of that—really. I was thrilled to my fucking toes to see her open up like that, lighten up, suddenly transform into a woman with faith in someone other than herself. But there was still something that bugged me about the whole scene; some vicious little knife of doubt that kept pricking at the back of my brain. I closed my eyes and tried to dismiss it. Maybe I was just so used to demons around every corner, I'd started seeing them where there were none.

Maybe he really was an innocent victim of circumstance, just trying to do right by his daughter.

I closed my eyes and tried to convince myself that was the whole truth.

I was just drifting off when there was a soft knock on my bedroom door.

"Yeah?" I whispered.

Solomon opened the door a crack and peered in. We'd gone to the local Walmart and restocked our wardrobes after leaving everything behind in Harrisburg. Now, Erin wore sleep shorts and an oversized Iron Maiden T-shirt. Adam had protested the Iron Maiden thing, but I was pleased to see that Solomon hadn't gone completely spineless. So… sleep shorts and heavy metal. That's my girl.

"Are you asleep?" she whispered back.

"No. Come on in."

She slipped through the door, looking back over her shoulder, and carefully shut it behind her.

"Your father's asleep?"

She nodded and came to sit at the edge of the bed. I sat up. The bed was a twin, the room wood paneled. A bookshelf with the discarded paperbacks of previous renters lined the wall—Faust and Nancy Drew and Danielle Steele living in dangerously close quarters. I'd found a waterlogged copy of Edward Abbey's *Monkey Wrench Gang*, which now occupied the nightstand. Solomon picked it up and leafed through before I took it from her and set it back down.

"Hey," I said. "Why aren't you sleeping?"

She twisted her body so she could look at me, tucking one leg beneath her. "You were quiet tonight. And then you took off… I was a little worried."

"I just wanted to give you and Adam some time. I took a walk, checked out some trails around the cabin."

"You moved the truck."

I hesitated. This could get tricky fast. Solomon searched my face, twisting her fingers in one of the countless gestures she has when she's nervous. She'd been favoring her bad wrist ever since Raven's Ledge, though I knew she would never say anything if it was bothering her. I studied her face, trying to read her mood.

"I did, yeah," I finally said.

"And the memory card? It's not in my bag."

"I'd like to hang onto it. I'm still a little worried about your father," I admitted. The anger I expected never came. Instead, she nodded.

"I know."

"It's just… I think we need to be as smart as possible right now. If for some reason something happened tonight, I want to know that we've protected ourselves—that we have a way out of here, no matter what. Did he see?"

"No. It was dark… I told him you'd gone out for a breather, but you'd be back soon. By the time you got here, he and I were talking. I don't think he paid any attention."

"Good," I said. Her eyes were still shadowed, though. "I'm sorry. I'm sure he's a great guy… I just don't want to take any chances."

"I know. It's not that. I just…" She rolled her eyes at herself. Shrugged. "Forget it, it's nothing. I'm glad you came back, that's all."

That's when it clicked. I took a deep breath, let it out on a slow sigh, and lifted the blanket. "Come on—get in. It's cold out there."

"My father's in the next room."

I grinned. "I know."

"He could hear us."

"We're just talking, ace. We'll be quiet." Said the scorpion to the frog. Solomon didn't look fooled in the least, but she got in anyway. I pulled her close, my blood already flowing south at the warmth of her curves under my hand. She squirmed back to look at me, a knowing gleam in her eye.

"Just talking, huh?" she whispered.

"Just talking," I agreed. I slid my hand under her t-shirt and felt the warmth of her skin, the hard bones of her spine, her soft gasp when my knuckles grazed the underside of her breast. She hooked her leg over my thigh and moved in closer. Her lips found my jaw line and my ear, her body pressed to mine.

"Your father's in the next room," I reminded her.

"We'll be quiet," she parroted back.

I think she was waiting for me to argue the point. Instead, I flipped us so that she was on top and pushed the t-shirt over her head. And then, I stopped.

I love women—always have. I love their curves and their complexity, the softness of their skin, the way they taste and the way they smell, their lilt and their cadence and the delicate brush of eyelashes against their cheekbones when they sleep.

Solomon, though...

Solomon is the reason men fall in love with the species. She's also the reason they go mad, but I was setting that aside for the moment.

She sat astride me with that impish grin on her lips and the light in her eyes, and I remembered, suddenly, the highs and the lows and the reason I had hung in with her this long. I ran the knuckles of my left hand from her navel up to the swell of her breast, watching as her eyes sank shut. She caught her bottom lip between her teeth. I stroked my other hand up her thigh until I could feel her heat.

"You're sure?" I asked.

Her response was to push my boxers down past my hips—not an easy task when she was on top of me, but Solomon's nothing if not determined.

I ran my hand over the soft curve of her ass. "We have to be quiet," I whispered. She nipped my ear.

"You said that already."

When she sat up again, her eyes were darker. She rose slightly off my body and shifted until I was pressed to her entrance, my hands on her hips. I watched her throat move when she swallowed, her lip still caught between her teeth. When she lowered herself onto me, her small hands on my stomach to steady herself, her breath caught. We stayed that way for a second, not moving. She was hot, wet, tight as a fist around me. I fought for control.

"Okay?" I whispered finally.

She nodded. I pulled her hips down and rose to meet her at the same time, filling her. Her eyes sank shut again. The softness of her hitched breath set me alight. We settled into a rhythm that built quickly as the night closed in, the world shrinking to nothing but the slide of her skin against mine, her whispered breath in my ear.

When she was close, beneath me now with her legs wrapped around my hips, her body arching to meet me, I slowed again. I brushed the hair back from her face, balancing myself above her. Her eyes were closed, her fingers gripping my shoulders.

"Look at me."

She opened her eyes, deepest green in the dim light of the room. I thought of her words when she'd first come into the room—that fear she refused to admit. *I'm glad you came back.*

"I'm not going anywhere, Erin," I said, willing her to believe it.

"I know." Her voice was breathless and whiskey-coated, but the way she looked at me made me think she might, finally, have gotten the picture. I rocked into her warmth, loving the way her face changed. "Jesus, Diggs," she whispered. "Please… You're not going anywhere. I get it. Just, for the love of God…"

I grinned when she wrapped her legs tighter around my hips, arching up to take me deeper. "You sure? Because we can stop, if you want."

"I will hurt you, Diggins."

I waited until I had her full attention—and potential wrath, one of my biggest turn-ons—before I began to move again.

Afterward, when the glow had faded and we'd both snuck off to the bathroom and gotten water and done all those other unromantic things you never see in movies, we lounged on the bed together munching on grapes and potato chips. Solomon lay with her head in my lap, her eyelids getting steadily heavier. It was just past eleven o'clock. It felt like three a.m.

"I think you're right, you know," she said. She peeled the skin off a grape and popped it into her mouth—a uniquely Solomon-esque move.

"I knew you'd come 'round to my way of thinking eventually," I said, pausing for effect. "What is it I'm right about this time?"

She pulled one of my leg hairs—another uniquely Solomon-esque move.

"Ow—Jesus. Sorry... What am I right about, dearest?"

It took another two grape peelings before she'd answer. When she did, the fun was gone from her eyes.

"My father. He's hiding something—or planning something, maybe." She sat up and faced me, cross-legged, our knees touching on the bed. "He keeps asking about the memory card."

With effort, I kept my voice steady. "What's he asking?"

"Everything: Who the guy was you got it from. How we decrypted it. Who we think created it in the first place... If we've broken the code yet. He wants to see it."

"But you haven't shown him?" I asked.

"No—not yet. Do you think I should?" She shook her head. "I feel bad, not trusting him. But, honestly?" Her eyes slid from mine. "I'm not sure how safe we are with him right now. Not that he'd intentionally hurt me, but…"

"The ends justify the means," I said. The dictate by which J-932 ran their lives; the creed they had drilled into their operatives. "If he thought he was protecting you…"

"He could justify almost anything," she finished.

I set the plate aside and pulled her into my arms. "We could be wrong. It's not like we don't have reason to be paranoid, but maybe we're off this time. You're right about one thing: I don't think he would do anything to hurt you." At least, I hoped to hell she was right. I lifted her chin with my thumb and kissed her lightly. "Why don't we just hang on to that for tonight?"

"Good plan," she agreed. She kissed my neck, scraping her teeth along the sensitive skin just below my ear. "And now… we should probably get some sleep, right?"

The fact that her pert little ass was parked on my lap made that unlikely—which, I suspected, was the point. Instead of dignifying that with a response, I flipped her off my lap and onto her back. She shrieked before I clapped my hand over her mouth and covered her body with my own.

"Suddenly, I'm not that tired," I whispered.

Her eyes lit as she wrapped her legs around my hips. We began again.

If I'd known how long it would be before I would see that light in her eyes, hear her laughter and feel that spark again, I like to think I would have taken more time; reveled in that rare moment of joy. But you never know how quickly the tide can turn until you're in the midst of it. We made love and we laughed and then we slept, Solomon wrapped around me like a climbing vine…

Until the tide turned.

●

I was up at four o'clock the next morning with my heart pounding, unsure of what had woken me. Before I could make sense of anything, Solomon pushed my clothes into my arms. She was already dressed. Downstairs, Einstein barked madly.

"We have to go," she whispered. Moonlight bled in through a slit in the curtains. I pulled my boxers on and peered out the window. Two pickup trucks were driving up, headlights off.

"What the hell's going on?"

Solomon didn't answer. The night took on an otherworldly, desperate edge. I was still zipping the fly on my jeans as I followed her out the bedroom door and into the hallway. The house was dark. Einstein met us when we were halfway down the stairs, still barking. Sol ran past him to her father's bedroom door. I searched for our bag and found it on the kitchen table. It was lying open, clearly riffled through. Half the cash Cameron had left for us had spilled out, but I couldn't tell how much—if any—had been stolen. My stomach churned. Outside, I heard the trucks come to a stop. A door slammed.

"Dad!" Solomon whispered loudly.

"He's gone, Sol," I said. A second car door slammed outside. I caught Einstein and clamped my hand gently around his muzzle. "Come on, buddy—shh." Solomon raced into the other rooms, whisper-shouting for her father. I could hear men talking outside now—getting closer with every passing second.

"You sure it was them?" one of them asked. "The folks from the news?"

"Positive," another said. It was a familiar voice that

took only a moment for me to place: Trent Willett, the government spook Adam was so terrified of.

I caught Solomon by the elbow. "Your father's not here, Erin. We need to go—now."

She took one last desperate look around the room before she nodded. I handed Einstein's leash to her and we raced for the back door. I'd barely closed it behind me before I heard Willett come in the front.

"Police!" someone shouted. "We have a warrant to search the premises."

I pushed Solomon toward the path. She took off running, tearing through the woods with Einstein alongside and me close behind. The forest closed in. Instantly, I was back in Black Falls. Back running for our lives, Will Rainier set to murder us both.

There was pandemonium behind us: Cops shouting; doors slamming; sirens in the distance. I followed Solomon blindly, branches slapping at my face, tearing at my eyes. We'd gone only a few yards when Solomon hit a fork in the path. She stopped. I hesitated.

"Left," I said, after a split second.

"You're sure?"

Einstein danced at her feet, waiting for her to give him the go ahead. I nodded. "Just go."

She went.

Ten yards in, I realized my error. Up ahead, there was a flash of bright light.

"Dad?" Solomon whispered. There was no answer. Einstein growled. Sol hesitated on the path. I grabbed her arm.

"Hang on," I whispered, dread burning through me. "We're going the wrong way." There was no question—we'd circled back, now headed straight for the house. Straight for Willett. "Wait, damn it," I said. She struggled to get away.

"I think he's up ahead," Solomon insisted.

"We took a wrong turn. We need to go back."

She shook her head, about to argue the point, when I pulled her none too gently into the thick brush at the side of the path. Half a second later, a voice ahead stopped us both.

"Here! We've got 'em," a man called out. "Come out slowly, hands up," he said.

We were still half-hidden by trees, but I had a clear view of the cop who'd spotted us. He was young—no more than twenty-five. Terrified. The cold steel of his pistol shone in the moonlight. Einstein growled. Solomon held tight to his collar.

"I said, step out of that brush with your hands up," the cop repeated, his voice rising. He had a baby face. His uniform was freshly pressed despite the late hour. A branch snapped behind him, and he started. Willett appeared on the path. "I've got them, sir," the cop said, pointing just to our left. "They went in that way."

We were still concealed by the trees. A barely discernible path behind us led deeper into the forest. I edged toward it, Adam's words echoing in my mind: *Whatever happens, don't let Willett anywhere near you. The Project may have been bad, but it doesn't have anything on Willett and his people.*

Going for the path meant giving up our precarious hiding spot. I leaned in to whisper in Solomon's ear.

"If he keeps coming this way, forget stealth—just go. Run like hell."

She nodded.

Willett glared into the night, his glasses reflecting in the moonlight. Unlike the cop beside him, he showed no fear. I didn't like the set of his jaw or the tension in his spine. Whatever else I thought of Adam Solomon, I was sure he was right about this.

Trent Willett was a dangerous man.

The agent took a breath, rifle clutched in his hand. We had some distance from him—maybe fifty yards. If he turned the other way, we could get away.

Solomon held her breath beside me.

One second hung, suspended, before Willett's eyes found mine in the darkness. Sweat popped on my forehead.

We'd been made.

I grabbed Solomon's hand. "Run!"

Willett charged the brush.

I heard the others coming close on his heels, crashing through the undergrowth. The cover of night and an unfamiliar forest were all that protected us from the agent and his onslaught, the brush thick as we fought our way through.

"Circle back around, goddamn it!" Willett shouted to the others. "Use whatever force you need, kill him if you need to. I want the girl alive."

We continued through the brush, moving fast, my heart pounding. I was damp with sweat. Shaking with fear. Completely lost. Willett and his men were gaining on us. Adam was long gone, I was sure. Solomon ran beside me, her grip tight on Einstein's leash.

We had to make it back to the truck.

"Shit—Diggs," Solomon whispered, breathless. She stopped short.

An instant later, I understood why.

A foot in front of us, the forest just...stopped. In its place was a wall of brambles so thick I couldn't even see a way in, much less a way out. I could hear Willett now, shouting. Moving fast. He sounded like a madman.

Seconds before the agent broke through and found us, trapped, Einstein slipped his collar.

The dog charged through the brush and back toward the agent, barking wildly. I grabbed Solomon's hand before she could run after him. Mass confusion reigned. Through the trees, I caught sight of Willett leading the pack. Sweat ran down his face. Einstein ran straight for him, hackles raised. I held Sol around her middle, my hand clapped over her mouth when Willett raised his rifle. He took aim.

The night shifted to a series of freeze frames: The venom in Willett's eye; the fury of the dog at his feet; the other cops, surrounding them. Willett squeezed off a single shot.

Einstein yelped, his small body skidding across a patch of earth before he found his feet again. Still crying pitifully, he ran for the woods.

Solomon was frozen.

"We have to go," I whispered urgently, pulling her arm.

One of the deputies went for Willett, furious.

With the time Einstein had bought us, we might not be able to get through the brambles, but we could get around them.

"He shot Stein," Solomon whispered to me, her voice just this side of blind panic. "We have to find him."

"We'll come back. Right now we have to get out of here."

There was still no sign of Adam. I dragged Solomon back into the woods, farther from the fight escalating between Willett and the other cops.

This time when we hit the fork in the path, we turned to the right. Within two minutes, the SUV was in sight. Solomon hesitated. I pushed her forward. Willett was in pursuit again. The sound of his angry shouts and forest-rattling footsteps drew closer with every breath. Solomon pulled away angrily, halting on the path. She put her finger to her lips before I could speak. I listened.

Somewhere nearby, I heard a dog whimper.

Somewhere equally nearby, Willett and his entourage closed in.

Solomon ducked past me before I could grab her,

plunging back into the undergrowth toward the dog's cry.

The horizon was just beginning to lighten to a pale gray. I glanced back at the SUV longingly, already seething, and dove into the brush after her.

Five seconds later, if that, I found them.

Solomon knelt beside a thicket of brush, gently luring Einstein out of hiding. His side was bloodied, the fur matted. His tail was curled under his body as he limped toward her. Sol tried to pick him up, but the dog isn't light.

"Erin—"

"I'm not leaving him," she said fiercely.

"I know," I agreed. "But let me get him."

I scooped the dog into my arms. He whined, panting hard, but made no move to get away.

Willett and his men were still behind us. I could hear them arguing again, the voice of the young deputy raised above the others.

"I don't care if they're Al-Qaeda itself, this wasn't part of the plan. You don't just go out shooting after anything that moves in our woods."

Solomon and I kept going, on the right path finally, toward the truck. Behind us, Willett and the others continued to argue. We were almost there—almost safe.

The SUV was no more than five feet away when the first shot rang out. Solomon was behind me, close on my heels. A second shot pierced the dawn. I heard Solomon stumble. Einstein wriggled in my arms, his blood dampening my shirt.

"Keep going," Sol said when I started to turn. "I'm fine—just run."

I ran.

Sixty seconds later, we were at the truck. I unlocked the back door and lay Einstein inside. Solomon scrambled in after him, her shirt stained with his blood. I shut the door behind her and climbed into the front, thanking every god I'd never believed in when the truck roared to life as soon as I turned the key in the ignition. I barreled over rocky terrain, narrowly missing a big old oak tree before I got back on course and found the road again.

We'd made it.

Neither of us spoke for a full twenty minutes, until I'd managed to get out of the woods and back on a rural highway headed away from Willett and his posse. When I was satisfied that we were safe, at least for the moment, I called back over my shoulder.

"How is he?" Einstein whimpered, but a second later I was relieved to find him on his feet, tail wagging, licking my face from the backseat. "Jesus… And they say cats have nine lives. Can you tell where the bullet hit?"

She didn't answer.

"Sol?"

My anxiety ratcheted up again.

I looked back over my shoulder, and nearly swerved off the road.

Sol lay in the back seat with her eyes closed, face deathly pale. The stain I had assumed came from Einstein had grown, blossoming at her side and spilling to the seat beneath her.

"Erin?"

She didn't move.

PART III
FIRE AND RAIN

17
JUAREZ

"I DON'T CARE what your orders were—I got a report that there was an incident involving two suspects out that way this morning. I want to talk to someone about that," Juarez said, his voice rising.

His head throbbed, thanks to a close encounter with the wrong end of Mitch Cameron's gun back on Raven's Ledge. It had been pounding ever since, his blood way past boiling. A call from his assistant about an incident in Tennessee was the first lead he'd had since Erin, Diggs, and Kat had gone missing.

"I'm sorry, sir, but they was pretty clear on this." The deputy on the other end of the line spoke in hushed tones, as though afraid he might be overheard. "We've gotta keep our mouths shut here. Don't matter how I feel about what went on. My ass'll be in a sling if I say anything."

"I got word that there was a shooting," Juarez persisted. "Can you confirm that someone was injured out there this morning?"

There was a pause on the line before the deputy returned, his voice lowered even further. "Look, this is my job on the line. All I can tell you is this fella from the government comes out here claiming to be a patriot, but there's something not right with him, you know what I mean? Like he's gonna get these folks, and it don't matter who lives or dies till he does. Next thing I know he's shootin' at anything that moves in these woods. He hit the dog. I'm pretty sure he might've hit the girl, too, but they took off before I could see for sure."

Fear ran through him in a slow, liquid burn. Jamie was watching from the sidelines, eyebrows raised. Juarez shook his head and let out a slow, cooling breath.

"Is Agent Willett still there?"

"He's on his way out. Guess he's got a lead. Says he wants to try and get to 'em before they get out of the country."

"How do you know they're headed out of the country?" Juarez asked

"He said folks like this are always headed out of the country."

Juarez hung up ready to tear himself inside out, suddenly missing the days when it was possible to actually hang up a phone with some force instead of flipping the stupid thing shut like some child's toy. He resisted the urge to hurl it across the room, seething.

"What happened?" Jamie asked.

"They were spotted in Tennessee. This agent... Willett, apparently opened fire as soon as they were in sight. Shot Einstein; may have wounded Erin."

Jamie looked suitably stricken, though Juarez wasn't sure whether that was on behalf of Erin or the dog. Probably the dog. Before she could comment, he picked up his phone again and punched in Howard Rhodes' home number. Professionally speaking, he knew it wasn't the best move to call the Deputy Director of Homeland Security at home. He just wasn't sure what other options he had at this point.

"What?" Rhodes answered sharply. Though it was only five a.m., there was no trace of sleep in his voice.

"There's been a development in the search for Erin Solomon," Jack began.

"I thought I told you: it's not our concern," Rhodes said. "The second you figured out where J. Enterprises led, this became CIA territory. You're supposed to leave this alone."

"The agent in charge of this isn't going at it in the best way," Jack said. "I've gotten a report that he's recklessly endangering the lives of civilians and other law enforcement... I'm telling you, Director, this is personal for him. I've had the same sense from the moment I talked to him: He doesn't care about the law. All he cares about is taking these people down, and I don't think he's taking them down for the right reasons."

"Jesus Christ, Juarez: The government doesn't give a rat's ass about motivation here. We care about results... and this Agent Willett has a long history of getting results. As for it being personal, that would carry a little more weight if you weren't pleading the case for your goddamn ex-girlfriend. My answer on this is final: I am not approving funds for you to pursue a case that's already been deemed off-limits by the United States government. My advice to you? If you talk to Ms. Solomon, advise her to turn herself in. That's the only way this can possibly end well."

And with that, he hung up.

Loudly.

Which was the benefit of having a real phone.

Jamie waited Juarez out while he paced, hands dug deep in his pockets, headache pounding. *Forget the dark spots.*

"You're a good soldier, Jackie. You'll always be our good soldier." A woman's face, dark and smiling, her hand soft in his hair. The sun is hot on his shoulders, blinding him. The sand is warm and white and soft under his feet. He is a boy, no more than five or six. "Now... show us how you hold the gun."

"Jack?"

He blinked rapidly, jerking back to the present.

Jamie looked at him uncertainly. "You still with us?"

"Yeah," he said. "I'm here."

"I take it you got no help from the powers that be?"

He shook his head. Jamie hesitated. Back on the mainland for two days now, they'd been staying at her business headquarters: a ranch in central Maine with obstacle courses and dog kennels and a proliferation of heavily-tattooed women who seemed to run the place under Jamie's watchful eye.

"What are you going to do?" she asked.

"Order and discipline, Jackie. Rules are there for a reason."

His chest was tight. He massaged the back of his neck, thinking things through. Rhodes wouldn't help. Willett was in this for blood; he didn't care if he brought Erin back alive or dead. He didn't care if he brought *anyone* back alive or dead.

"I have… resources," Jamie said. "A plane, if you need it. A crew—I know Monty and Carl would help out. And I think Cheyenne would like a chance to redeem herself, after what happened."

Jamie touched his arm, looking at him intently. "Jack," she said. He looked at her. Her blue eyes were clear, not a trace of doubt there. "I know it's hard to think about going against your superiors, but something is wrong here. You know that. We can't just leave Erin and Diggs out there to fend for themselves. They're both tough, but I don't know if they can survive this. Whatever they've stumbled into, they'll never make it out of this alive without some help."

He nodded. It was the kind of thing his wife would have said to him, back when she was his world. Before she'd been taken from him, this was the kind of thing Lucia would have insisted on.

"You're right," he agreed, finally. "They were last seen

in Tennessee… I'd like to head down there. Willett thinks they'll be leaving the country, but if Einstein or Erin are hurt, I'm not sure he's right about that."

"Do you have somewhere else in mind?" Jamie asked.

He thought for a minute before finally nodding slowly. "I might. If you don't mind getting the plane ready, I'd like to make a couple of phone calls."

"Of course," she agreed immediately. "Whatever you need to do. If you're ready for it, we can have wheels up by seven o'clock."

His head spun. *Things to remember; things to forget. A woman's scream in the dead of night; footsteps on hardwood; heavy fists pounding on the front door. A gunshot.*

Forget the dark spots.

"That's good," he agreed, aware that Jamie was still watching him closely. "Seven o'clock will be good."

18
SOLOMON

SUNLIGHT.

It bounces off the water, turning everything white and gold. It's a warm day—hot, mid-summer. I stand in a tide pool, the water to my knees. Barnacles cut my bare feet.

"Put your shoes on, Erin," Daddy says. The sun is blinding. He is a hundred feet tall, speaking from the clouds. I hear the cry of sea gulls and the rhythmic crash of the surf.

"I don't need them," I say. "My feet are as tough as yours."

Daddy's feet are as tough as leather. In summer, he never wears shoes. Sometimes, he doesn't even wear them in winter.

"Put your shoes on." I look up. My father is gone; Isaac Payson stands there instead. I feel a shiver of dread. He holds tiny sneakers out to me. His hands are huge, his eyes dark. "Do as I say."

I take the shoes and put them on. He ties them for me, but he doesn't do it right—Daddy sings a song. When he's done, I have loops that look like bunny ears. When Isaac is done, it doesn't look like anything but strings in a knot. He holds out his hand.

I don't want to take it.

"Come," he says. He's angry now. "I need to show you."

I won't give him my hand, so he just takes it. He wraps his big fingers around my wrist and holds on tight. He drags me away from the water and the warmth and the sunlight, into the woods.

I scream and I fight and I try to get away, calling for Daddy.

He doesn't come.

Isaac won't let go.

19
DIGGS

I CROSSED THE BORDER into Kentucky an hour after leaving Willett and his cronies in the dust. Solomon was in the front seat now, tucked into a blanket with her eyes closed. She'd been drifting in and out all morning, her body shaking violently. Heat came off her in waves. Other than incoherent mumbling, she'd said nothing when I moved her to the front seat, checked her pulse and the bullet wound—an ugly through-and-through in her left side. I had enough First Aid training to know how critical it was to stop the bleeding, but the best I managed ultimately was packing bandages around it and puking on the side of the road before we were off again.

At ten-thirty that morning, I pulled onto an empty, heavily wooded road in western Kentucky.

When I reached Sally Woodruff's front gate, I stopped the truck and jumped out, punching Sally's number into my phone as I moved. Before I had a chance to hit send, a pickup pulled up on the other side of the fence. Dogs barked in the distance. Einstein whined frantically in the backseat, effectively recovered from his own trauma.

"Sally?" I called.

An older woman, mid-sixties, lean and leathery, stepped out of the truck. Her grey hair was shorter than it had been when I'd seen her before, just three weeks ago. I waited for her to tell me I should leave; that the police were coming or she wanted nothing to do with any of this... That we were still on our own.

That Solomon would just have to die.

"Hang on, hon. I'll open the gate. Drive on through, and straight to the front door. I got a bed waiting."

I've never been more grateful for southern hospitality.

The yard and driveway were empty at Sally's palatial estate when I drove up. She used the place as an abortion clinic, funded out of her pocket and run with her own blood, sweat, and tears, in a place that definitely did not welcome the service. Three pit bulls barked frantically from a kennel just outside the door.

I went to the passenger's side door and opened it. Solomon almost fell out before I caught her.

She didn't wake when I carried her inside, her body limp in my arms. Sally stood by with her arms folded over her chest, a frown on her face. She wore jeans and a man's flannel shirt, her feet bare. She doled out orders to me with reassuring ease, as though it was a common occurrence for men to show up on her doorstep carrying bleeding, half-dead women.

Given her line of work, I supposed that wasn't unlikely.

"Can you get her upstairs all right?" she asked.

I nodded. "She's—" My voice cracked. I cleared my throat and tried again. "She stopped talking about an hour ago. I can't get her to wake up."

"Just get her up there, hon, and I'll take it from there."

I trudged up the stairs, Solomon still lifeless in my arms. Sally directed me to a door on the left. The room was clean and cream-colored, with black and white photos of pit bulls on the walls.

"Set her on the exam table there," Sally directed.

I did as she said. Another woman—younger, maybe Solomon's age—appeared in the doorway. I had a vague impression of dark hair and brightly colored scrubs, but noticed little else.

"Does she have any allergies?" the woman asked, once Solomon was laid out on the table. Sally went to her immediately, already starting to cut away her shirt and check the wound.

"No allergies," I said, gaze focused on Solomon. "None that I know of, anyway."

"Medical problems?" Sally added. "Chronic illness? Hepatitis? HIV?"

"No," I said again. "She's healthy. I mean…" I hesitated. "It's been a rough year. Last winter she had a miscarriage."

Sally looked at me.

"The baby wasn't mine," I added unnecessarily.

"How long was she hospitalized?"

I thought of the call I'd gotten late one night from Michael—her husband at the time. *You should come—she asked for you. They don't know if she'll make it.*

"I'm not sure," I said. "She lost a lot of blood. And she broke her wrist last summer—she's had a couple of surgeries for that."

"You weren't kidding—that is a rough year," Sally agreed. "Okay. I think that's all we need from you right now. I want you to go on down and make yourself some tea. Keira and I can handle this."

I remained where I was, arms crossed over my stomach. I realized distantly that my shirt was soaked with nearly as much blood as Solomon's. Some of it was Einstein's, but most had come from Sol. "I'd rather stay."

"I know you would, Daniel—but I'm sorry, sugar, that's not an option." She herded me toward the door.

"If she wakes—"

"We'll take care of her," Sally said firmly. "We've got this. I'll come down just as soon as I can to let you know what's happening."

She closed the door.

I stood there for a long few seconds, fighting nausea and fatigue and the kind of heart-crushing fear I've only felt when Erin Solomon is involved.

I went downstairs and out to the car, only just remembering that Einstein was still in the backseat. Willett's bullet had grazed his side, seemingly scaring the mutt more than anything else. Now, he snuffled the grounds, tail tucked between his legs, and followed close behind me once he'd done his business.

The last time I'd been here, vandals had torn the grounds apart. An inverted cross had been burning out front, the same symbol spray painted on every wall. In three weeks, Sally had gotten rid of any trace of the graffiti. She'd patched the holes and replaced the furniture. It was like nothing had ever happened.

I wandered the hallways until I found the kitchen. I made myself a tall cup of coffee and a cheese sandwich, then set myself up at the table with the laptop. After a brief skirmish with the Wifi, I managed to connect to the Internet. The house was quiet apart from an occasional outburst from the dogs. Einstein kept whining at the door—trying to get to Solomon, no doubt. I tried to muster some sympathy. Instead, I felt a slow boil of resentment.

Guilt convinced me to at least scrounge a bowl of kibble for the mutt before I sat back down and pulled up another search on Jonestown. Temporarily sated, Einstein curled around my leg with his chin on my foot. Solomon's face, bloodless and worn, flashed in my mind; the feel of her body limp in my arms when I carried her into the house.

I stabbed at the keyboard, punching in "MK Ultra."

Pages of conspiracy sites came up.

I went back to the search bar and typed in "Project J-932."

It yielded no results.

I went back to MK Ultra. Everyone from Barack Obama to Roseanne Barr had something to say on the subject. I scanned photos and read articles, searching for any sign of Erin's father, Isaac Payson, Mitch Cameron, or any of the other half-dozen players in this global conspiracy. I found none.

It took more than an hour before Sally came downstairs. She cleared her throat. I looked up to find her standing in the doorway, watching me. She was still in scrubs—bloody scrubs now, her eyes shadowed from the early morning and the extended surgery. Her face was a mask, unreadable despite my best effort. I tried to stand, but couldn't make myself; tried to speak, but remained mute.

"She's okay," she said when I remained sitting there, dumb. "She's one lucky girl. Another couple inches to the right and things would've been a hell of a lot more complicated. The bullet went straight through. Missed her organs. It didn't hurt a thing that won't heal."

I was grateful she'd gotten to the good news so quickly, but I sensed a qualifier.

"But…" I prompted.

"But, she lost a lot of blood," she said. "Anyone else would have gone into hypovolemic shock by the time you got here… You did a good job, though, dressing the wounds, keeping the bleeding under control." For the first time, she took note of Einstein, now dancing uncertainly at her feet.

"Is that the dog's blood, or hers?" she asked, indicating his stained fur.

"He's not hurt badly," I said. "He got hit first. If he hadn't…" I stopped. Sally raised an eyebrow, surveying me coolly.

"I guess this is all the dog's fault, then?" she asked. She knelt beside Einstein and checked his side with gentle fingers, murmuring soft words. The dog whimpered.

"That's not what I said."

Sally rose with some difficulty and called into the other room. "Keira, you mind bringing in my kit? I've got another patient to tend to here."

Keira came in with Sally's medical bag, and Sally settled herself on the floor with Einstein half in her lap. The dog made no move to get away, whining as Sally shaved the fur away from the wound in his side.

"So… Erin gets hurt trying to save her dog, and you're pissed off," she said conversationally.

"I didn't say that."

"Well, nothing else I can think of to explain this bug that's crawled up your butt. Funny thing I've found about men over the years is, they lose control of a situation, get a little scared, and their natural reaction seems to be to get PO'd at the world and everything in it."

"I'm not PO'd," I grumbled. It wasn't attractive, I knew. Frankly, I didn't give a rat's ass. "Do you have any idea how many times we've risked our lives because of this goddamn dog?"

Einstein looked up at me with big, wet brown eyes, whining uneasily. I looked away. Sally murmured something to the mutt while I pushed the remains of a cold grilled cheese sandwich around on my plate.

"I'm sorry if that's supposed to make me think less of Erin, and more of you for your lot in life," Sally said. "You're the one who fell ass over teakettle for her. If it makes you feel any better, though, right now she's payin' through the nose for going that extra mile to take care of this dog."

It didn't make me feel any better at all, as a matter of fact. "She'll be all right, though. You said she's okay."

She hedged. Any trace of relief I'd felt slid right out the window. "Like I said: she lost a lot of blood. Then there's the risk of infection… She won't be up for a good few hours yet, so we'll just have to wait and see. But she stands a better chance than not of being just fine."

"But she's not out of the woods yet," I said. I thought of her lying lifeless in the backseat, still clinging to Einstein. Instead of love or loss or any trace of sympathy, I just had the urge to strangle her all over again.

"Not completely, hon," Sally said. "Listen, why don't you go on up and try to get some sleep. I put you two in the same room—we don't really have enough beds to go around these days."

It was a little before noon, bright daylight outside. Irregular sleep patterns and stress and caffeine had turned my natural biorhythms on their head. I knew I should have been exhausted, but, truth be told, I couldn't seem to get far enough beyond pissed off to tell.

"Actually, I think I might take a ride. I could use a little space. Some fresh air."

The humor vanished from her eyes. Sally knows the gory details of my history as an addict intimately. Back in my heyday, she was one of many who saw the road I was headed for long before I did—and one of the few who actually said anything about it.

"You sure that's such a good idea?"

"Probably not," I said shortly. "But it's all I've got the stomach for right now."

She studied me for a minute before she seemed to realize

she wasn't talking me out of anything. Instead, she nodded.

"All right, sugar. Maybe you're right—maybe a little fresh air's the best thing for you right now. But you take my number, all right? And borrow the pickup; it doesn't seem like the best idea for you to take that SUV of yours out again right now. You get tired or you run into trouble, give me a call. Got it?"

I nodded my agreement, irrational anger still burning below the surface. I left without telling her where I was going or when I would be back; without waiting to find out if Solomon was out of the woods, or when she would wake up.

I ran, and I didn't look back.

20
SOLOMON

IT'S DARK.

I hear whispers. The night is so hot that sweat runs down my back. Someone is crying.

"I've got a secret," a boy's voice singsongs in my ear. When I turn my head I see only the glint of yellow eyes before he vanishes.

I can't find my Dad.

"For thine is the power, and the glory…"

Isaac is praying. He always prays so loud—his voice is big and wide; it shuts out the whole forest.

There is a fire, burning bright in the middle of the darkness.

Daddy kneels on the dirt ground. He has no shirt on. His back is bloody.

"Things to remember; things to forget," the little boy sings to me.

"He'll put us in the woods," Allie Tate whispers. She sits beside me. One of her legs is bent backward. It's like she doesn't even notice, staring at me with wide eyes through Coke-bottle lens glasses.

"Are you sorry for your sins?" Isaac asks. He has a snake

in his hands—long and black, hissing and dark-eyed. He stands over my father. Daddy won't look at him.

"We've all got secrets," the boy whispers. He runs again, before I can see his face. His yellow eyes stare out at me from the dark woods. "Keep them buried deep."

"Are you sorry?" Isaac says again. He roars like a lion, and the woods shake under my feet. A lady starts to sing.

Daddy lifts his face. He is bleeding and broken, but he doesn't cry. He looks at Isaac, and I can see that he hates. Hates like he said I never should, and I hate with him.

I want Isaac to die.

"I am always sorry," Daddy says. He says it quietly, like our nightly prayer, except this time all his hate is in the words. "I was born sorry."

Isaac picks up the snake again. Daddy bows his head.

We've got secrets nobody can ever tell.

21
DIGGS

I DROVE THE DIRT ROAD to the Durham farm with my hands clenched tight on the wheel and a burning desire for chemical intervention of any kind. When I reached the house, the hounds were roaming loose. George Durham was on the front porch of his cabin, smoking a cigarette. He shook his head when he saw me stride into view, like he didn't believe his eyes. George has been more of a father than my own from the time I first visited Kentucky at twelve years old, saving my life and my sanity in more ways than one since that time. Recently, he'd lost his son to whatever war Solomon and I had been pulled into. The grief may have aged him, but I could tell by the light still in his eyes that he wasn't letting it beat him.

"Daniel?"

"In the flesh."

He grinned. Got up off his porch swing with some effort and strode toward me, enveloping me in a hug before I could even extend my hand.

"You seen the news, boy?" he asked. "Mae's been worried sick, all the things folks've been saying."

"I'm fine," I assured him.

"It don't look like it—you look like hell, son." He nodded toward the porch. "Come on up, set down before you fall down."

I followed his advice. Two floppy-eared bunnies loped the length of a homemade hutch, staring out at me with twitching noses. The sun was blinding. Sweat trickled down the back of my neck, my shirt clinging to the small of my back. I watched the dogs race around after a couple of hens in the yard, and tried to figure out where to begin.

"Erin okay?" George finally asked, when I didn't volunteer the information.

"Yeah. She's… uh, she's with Sally right now. She's all right," I added, at the concern on his face. When I realized that I didn't actually know if that was true, I fell silent. George dragged the conversation along with small talk for a few minutes before he pulled up short.

"You got something on your mind you want to talk about?"

I nodded, grateful that he'd dispensed with the pleasantries. "I had a couple of questions, actually. About Jesup Barnel." Long before the Kentucky apocalypse Solomon and I had just survived, Reverend Barnel and George Durham had run in the same circles. It wasn't something George liked to talk about, I knew, but in this case it couldn't be helped. "You mind talking a little?"

"I'll tell you what I can."

"You and Barnel grew up together, right? Before he became a lunatic preacher."

"We did."

"Do you remember anyone taking any special interest in him? Or possibly both of you? Any kind of group...or an individual, maybe?"

"Taking a special interest how, exactly? We was just a couple of backwoods boys—not too many folks took an interest in anybody, back this way."

"Okay," I said, nodding as I reframed what I'd been thinking. "Do you remember when Jonestown happened, then? It was 1978—November of that year. You remember Barnel ever mentioning Jim Jones? Or his church?"

"Jim Jones was a little hippie dippie for these parts, you know?" He was genuinely puzzled now, forehead furrowed. "Nobody 'round here was too impressed with the guy, even before he killed all those folks."

"So no one ever came and talked to you about... anything. Jim Jones, or a way to... I don't know, influence people?"

He scratched his head. "What the hell are you talking about, son? I told you—" He stopped suddenly, his eyes clouded. For a second or two, I watched as he worked through some long-forgotten memory.

"What is it?" I prompted.

"When we was young, grade school age, Jesup got recruited for some special group or something... He never talked about it much. When he was real young, he could be uppity about the whole thing—saying he'd been chosen over everybody else. But it kept going over the years, just a couple times a week, and after a while he stopped talking about it and we stopped asking. It just got to be one of those things, a couple afternoons a week when we knew Jesup wouldn't be around."

"But no one ever came to talk to you about anything?" I pressed. "No one ever talked to you about joining this... group?"

"I told you," he insisted. "I reckon I would've remembered something like that, don't you?"

I wasn't so sure, but I didn't tell him that. Instead, I ran through a mental list of the other people involved with the drama that had unfolded in Justice, Kentucky, with Jesup

Barnel. "What about the sheriff—Harvey Jennings? Did you ever hear of him being in a group with Barnel?"

"You mean besides Jesup's cockamamie church? How in Hades would I know that?"

"Forget it—it was just a shot in the dark." I pulled out the page of numbers Solomon and I had decrypted. It was a bad move to have it here. A bad move to pull anyone else into this, when the Durhams had already lost so much.

I scrubbed my hand over my jaw, the exhaustion I'd kept at arm's length for the past seventy-two hours washing over me. There was no one to trust. No way out. George looked at me curiously.

"What've you got there, son?"

I pushed the paper into his hand before I could change my mind. "Do any of these numbers mean anything to you?"

He took a pair of reading glasses from his shirt pocket and leaned back on the porch swing, going through the list entry by entry. Before he'd gotten far, we were interrupted by a shout from across the yard. I looked up to find a short, plump blonde woman striding toward us.

"Thank God," she said at sight of me.

I grabbed the paper from George and stuffed it back in my pocket,   already trying to come up with some kind of plausible story to explain the bullshit the press was putting out about Solomon and me. Mae Durham stepped up onto the porch without breaking stride, ignoring George, and pulled me into her arms.

"You scared the unholy dickens out of me, you fool. What's this about you being one of America's most wanted?"

"It's a long story," was the best I could come up with. Mae nodded seriously. If possible, she looked even more tired now than she had when I'd left Justice—as though the reality of everything she'd gone through was just sinking in. Newly widowed and now raising three kids on her own, it wasn't a reality anyone would envy.

"It's never anything else with you, is it?" she asked. She didn't push for any answers beyond that, moving onto the next topic without so much as a breath in between. "What about Erin? Where is she?"

"She's okay. I mean... she will be. I think." My voice broke. I looked away, mortified when my eyes started to tear.

George and Mae exchanged a look. "George, you mind gettin' us some of that Mississippi mud you call coffee?" she asked.

He looked grateful for an excuse to run, squeezing my shoulder before he went back inside. Mae sat down beside me, but I was grateful that she made no move to touch me. It wouldn't take much to turn me into a blubbering mess—and I couldn't even remember the last time I'd let that happen.

"Where's Erin, Diggs?" she asked.

I stole a cigarette from George's pack and lit it on a long inhale. It was the first one I'd smoked in months. I breathed deep, staying quiet until I felt the nicotine settling my nerves. "She's with Sally," I said. "We were in Tennessee, and these guys—these... cops, I guess, were chasing us. And shooting. She got hit."

Mae's hand tightened on my leg, but otherwise she didn't react. I took one more draw from the cigarette and made myself put it out.

"But she's all right, you said?" she asked.

"I don't know," I said. I focused on a cracked floorboard and breathed through the fear. "She's... Sally took care of her. I didn't know where else to go—the cops are after us, and the... these people, are monitoring everything we do. I couldn't take her to a hospital."

"How do you manage to get yourself into these messes?"

I shook my head with a strangled laugh. "Hell if I know.

I blame Solomon, though."

"Is Sally still working on her?"

"No."

The same image I couldn't seem to shake flashed through my mind again: Solomon in the backseat, lying in a pool of blood—small and broken, and I had no idea how to fix her. I pushed the memory away, trying to summon the rage I'd felt before, that frustration at Solomon for pulling stupid stunts that put her life in danger time after time. It was gone now, though… All I felt was fear. That same sob I'd choked back before welled up again.

This, in a nutshell, is why love is a bad idea: Ultimately, you end up crying like a fucking baby on someone's shoulder while you wait for fate to decide whether life will go on or just… stop. Before any tears could escape, I wiped my eyes with the back of my arm and forced myself to get a grip.

George was standing by with a cup of coffee, which he handed off straightaway, then settled himself in the rocking chair across from us.

"You haven't eaten, I reckon," he said.

I thought of the grapes and potato chips with Solomon at midnight, the sheet twisted around her freckled thigh. "Not today, no. Well—part of a grilled cheese, at Sally's."

"Slept?"

Again, the night before came to mind: Solomon wrapped around me, moving under me, her body pressed to mine. I shook my head. "I got an hour or two last night."

"Well, that's half your problem," Mae said with authority. "You can't run nothin' on no food and no sleep—and you sure as heck can't save the world that way. Let me make up a plate for you. Then, my advice to you is to go on back to Sally's, get some rest, and wait for Erin to wake up."

"And if she doesn't?" I asked. The tears were gone from my voice, but I still hardly sounded like a rock.

"If she doesn't, you'll go on," she said firmly. "But how about we try thinking best-case scenario for a change, huh? Now, come on: we start with the basics 'round here. Food first."

It wasn't until Mae was setting a heaping plate of grits, homemade toast, and a five-egg omelet in front of me that I remembered I'd come here, ostensibly, for a reason. I pulled the list of numbers from my pocket and pushed it across the table.

"I'm trying to find some connection to Jesup Barnel in these numbers," I said. "I don't have a clue what form that might take, but I know you had more to do with Barnel's church than a lot of people, for a while."

I'd barely taken the first bite before she was immersed in the problem.

"These first numbers look like they could maybe be coordinates…"

"That's what Sol and I decided, too," I agreed, impressed that she'd spotted it so quickly.

"I love all them puzzles they have in the Sunday paper: Sudoko and word scrambles, all that silly stuff. Wyatt always used to say I was wasted living around here, raising a bunch of kids."

"You're probably doing more good here than you'd be at some job crunching numbers somewhere," I said. She smiled, nodding her agreement as she continued poring over the list.

"Have you tried looking them up?"

"Yeah," I said. "The coordinates work, but the numbers afterward are what I can't make sense of. Nothing comes up in an Internet search."

I looked over her shoulder, scanning the numbers myself.

"The way I've figured it, if the first part's a location, then this could be Barnel's compound," I said, pausing at an entry toward the end of the first column. "But I don't know what the numbers after that mean."

Mae stopped and pushed her chair back from the table abruptly. "Hang on just a minute."

Before I could argue, she was headed out of the room. I followed hurriedly, clutching my toast in one hand. When I reached her, she was sifting through some paperwork in an antique roll top desk in the parlor.

"I think I have some old files laying around from the church. Jesup didn't know which end was up when it came to managing things, so I helped him out every so often. Just…" She abandoned the desk and dove into a two-drawer filing cabinet beside it. Eventually, she fished out a green folder from the back of the top drawer. "Here we go—I knew I had it here somewhere."

She sat on the sofa and thumbed through the file until she'd found what she was looking for, then looked at me triumphantly. "There you go—that's what I thought. That first bit must be a location, just like you thought. Then this bunch of numbers after it? Those are Jesup's social security number.."

"I thought of that," I said, shaking my head. "They're too long, though. A social's nine numbers, but there are thirteen listed after the coordinates."

"I think that's just to throw you off," she said. "Look here—see the way it's set up? The first five numbers are from the social, then these four numbers after it," she circled the second four numbers in the group, 0313, "They don't belong in here. The four numbers afterward, though… those are the last ones in Jesup's social security number."

"Those four numbers in the middle could be dates," I said immediately. "March, 2013—that was when everything went to hell with Barnel."

The rest of the numbers floated into a coherent, cohesive unit for the first time.

"They're in chronological order," I said, running my index finger down the page, focused now on the four numbers signifying the date in each entry. About ten entries down in the first column, I found the first date I was looking for: 1178. November, 1978: Jonestown.

I searched for August, 1990—when the Payson Church burned—and found it after only a cursory scan. Mae was right: This was what we'd been looking for.

Half an hour later, I pulled into the back entrance of Sally's place. Einstein greeted me at the front door anxiously, tail between his legs. His side was shaved and patched, and one glance at his now-visible ribs and the droop in that usually-wagging tail reminded me that he hadn't had the easiest time of it, either, these last few days. I knelt and ruffled his ears as he whimpered and danced and butted his head against my chest.

"It's all right, buddy," I said under my breath. "No hard feelings, huh?"

He licked my face and continued bumping against my legs as I straightened.

"You two kiss and make up?" Sally asked, descending the staircase.

"Yeah—sorry. I wasn't at my best, exactly, earlier. How is she?" I asked, indicating the stairs with a nod.

"Still asleep. Not unusual—I told you, she won't be up for another couple hours, anyway."

"You mind if I go up now?"

"I'd mind more if you didn't. Second door on the right. Go on." She slapped my ass as I passed her on the stairs. "And take your dog with you—he's been moping all day, trying to figure out what in hell's going on."

"You don't think that's a little… unhygienic?"

"Not any more than you going up there—probably less so. Just don't jostle her too much, and let me know if she wakes up. I'll come check on her shortly."

I went up the stairs, my feet like lead. Einstein pushed past me when I opened the bedroom door Sally had indicated. The room was painted a robin's egg blue, a couple of framed landscapes on the wall. Erin was cocooned in an antique canopy bed beneath a floral comforter. Stein hopped up before I could stop him, curling himself into her side. I knew she wouldn't have it any other way, though, so I didn't try to move him.

Instead, I just stood there for a second or two, trying to make myself move.

Erin's already-fair complexion had gone three shades paler thanks to the blood loss. The circles under her eyes were just this side of purple. I took off my shoes. Forced myself to breathe. She was alive. Sally had said she would be all right.

She was okay.

I laid down on the side Einstein hadn't already claimed, turned to face Solomon, and brushed the hair back from her forehead. My chest felt like it was in a vise grip, that same fear still strangling me. Beneath a flimsy hospital gown, her left side was bandaged. There was an IV in her arm connected to a bag of clear liquid hanging beside the bed. Pain meds, I hoped—though I knew she would be pissed about that. A life with addicts, first her mother and then me, had left Solomon with a deep distrust of any chemical remedy.

For a long time, I just lay on top of the blankets like that, watching her sleep. Her eyelids flickered, eyes moving back and forth through some dreamland where I couldn't follow her. Couldn't keep her safe.

Of course, I hadn't been all that effective at keeping her

safe in the real world, either.

I leaned in and closed my eyes, breathing her in as I pressed my lips to hers.

"Please be okay," was the only thing I could think to say. It felt as much like a prayer as anything I'd uttered since I was a kid.

Eventually, I closed my eyes, and I slept.

22
SOLOMON

YOU KNOW THOSE SCENES on TV where the hero gets shot, he gets wheeled into the ER, and in the next scene you see him creakily getting out of bed and demanding his clothes, so he can sneak out and take down the bad guys?

Yeah… I'm not that hero.

Here's the thing no one ever mentions in those TV shows:

Getting shot hurts like hell.

I woke up with my mouth full of cotton and my head foggy, lying in a strange bed in a strange room. It was dark, the curtains drawn on two windows in the far wall. Einstein was curled up on one side of me, Diggs on the other. I shifted and pain shot through me, so intense that it rocked my bones and rattled my teeth. My first thought—beyond *fucking owwwww*—was that time had passed. And bad things had transpired. And we had missed a pretty goddamn important meeting with the psychopath still hanging onto Kat.

I moved again, intending to try and get up, which of course woke the dog. He got to his feet with an ecstatic little whimper and started licking my face like we'd been apart for weeks.

"Stein—come on, buddy," I croaked. "I'm okay."

He tried to climb into my lap. I swallowed a scream as I sat up, pushing him away as gently as possible.

"Hey," Diggs said sleepily. "Jesus, Einstein—give it a rest, would you?" He got up and set the dog on the floor, then turned on the bedside lamp. "Hang on, let me get Sally. Are you okay?"

He looked horrible—drawn and tired and terrified.

"Don't go yet," I said when he headed for the door. "Just... wait a second. Where are we?"

"Sally Woodruff's," he said after a moment's hesitation. "In Kentucky. I'm sorry—I didn't know what else to do."

"Where's Dad?" No answer was needed for that one—the look on his face was more than enough to tell me something had gone wrong. "What happened?"

"I don't know. He was gone when we woke up. Do you remember that?"

I nodded, thinking back to the cabin in the woods: waking in the dead of night to Einstein barking, darting from room to room, panicked, trying to find my father. Knowing all the while, somehow, that he wouldn't be there. As the memories returned, my stomach got progressively heavier.

"Our stuff—our bag was on the table. Did he...."

"He didn't take anything," Diggs said. "The money was all there. And I had the memory card with me, so we have everything we started with."

I nodded. So, my father might have abandoned us to be killed by some crazy secret agent man, but at least he hadn't robbed us blind.

"Your father hasn't tried to contact us," Diggs continued. "I'm not sure where he is. I just know Willett was there when we left the cabin."

"And he's the jackass who shot Einstein," I said.

"And the jackass who shot you," Diggs said. "Minor point, I know, but worth mentioning."

"What about Jenny?" I asked. "Has she called? We were supposed to meet her. Kat—"

"Slow down," he said. "There's been no word yet. Maybe that's a good thing. Either way, though, there's nothing we can do until we hear from her. How do you feel?"

"Shitty. And sore. And I kept having these dreams…" I stopped, thinking of Allie Tate. Isaac, dragging me into the woods. My father, whispering those words to me. *Things to remember; things to forget.*

"I should get Sally," he said. He brushed the hair back from my forehead. I took his hand.

"Just… wait one more minute. Don't go."

"Okay." His eyes followed mine, a fear there that I had only seen once before—in Black Falls, when we'd both nearly died. When he hadn't been able to protect me.

"Sit with me, please," I said.

"Erin—"

"Please."

He sat on the side of the bed. I lay the back of my hand on his stubbled, stubborn cheek. His eyes sank shut. "Are you okay?" I asked.

"That's supposed to be my line."

The attempt at humor fell flat, and he knew it. I raised my eyebrows, waiting for him to come clean. He took a deep breath and let it out slowly. Painfully. "Now that you're awake, yeah. I'm okay. But don't do that again, huh?" He leaned in and kissed my nose, then rested his forehead against mine. "Please don't do that again, Sol."

Quips and smartass remarks would no doubt come later. For now, I very carefully wrapped my arms around him and we both stayed that way, quiet, for what seemed a very long time. Finally, he pulled away, kissed me again, and stood.

"I'll get Sally. Be right back."

I watched him go with all those dream images still flashing in my mind. Everything was a nonsensical mess—I couldn't make out a timeline, figure out what was real and what I'd just imagined. I had no idea what had actually happened on Payson Isle anymore.

A fresh wave of pain washed over me then, driving that thought out of my mind. Intense pain will do that for you, sometimes: it's hard to focus on much else when your body turns against you.

When I was a kid, I skinned my knee out on the island. My father told me then that pain was all in the mind—it was easy to move past it. *Just breathe. Push it away. Pain can't hurt you… it's not real. Imagine that it's gone and your knee is whole, and it will be gone.*

Had he learned that from J-932? Or was his father the one who taught him his pain wasn't important?

"How's the patient?" Sally asked as she knocked on the door, opening it without waiting for my response. Einstein had resettled by my side on the bed. He thumped his tail at sight of the woman.

"I'm fine," I lied. "It's not that bad." Sally looked at Diggs with a grimace and handed him a ten-dollar bill from her jeans pocket.

"Told you," he said. "She's impossible."

"I'm not—it doesn't hurt that much," I insisted. "I'm all right."

"Sure you are," she said.

"What time is it?" I asked. I'd thought it was the middle of the night, but Sally looked fresh as a daisy, dressed in jeans and a man's flannel shirt.

"Nine," she said. "P.M. You've been out since you got here this morning. Glad to see your idiot boyfriend finally decided to wise up and join you," she noted, looking at

Diggs with clear disapproval.

She checked my vitals and changed my bandage and gave me painkillers that I tried to refuse, but the fire in my side had spread to every nerve ending. It was becoming very, very clear that dear old Dad didn't know shit about pain if he thought something like this was all in my head. I was foggy by the time she said goodnight, and completely out seconds after Diggs crawled back into bed beside me.

At just past midnight that night, when I was lost in a hazy dream world all over again, our cell phone from hell rang. Diggs fumbled for it and eventually answered while I was still trying to pull myself out of my druggy delirium.

"What?" Diggs said into the phone. He usually reserves that kind of greeting for me. Clearly the stress was getting to him, too.

"Speaker," I whispered to him. He pressed the magic button, and Jenny's grating, tinny little voice filled the room.

"…understand you had some excitement last night," she said.

"We're fine," I said. "I want to talk to Kat."

"Wait," Diggs said. "We're not fine. Erin was shot, for Christ's sake. I want this over—just tell us where you want the exchange made, we'll do it, and then we're done."

Silence.

Three seconds passed, then four.

Then five.

"Do I need to remind you of our conversation the other night?" Jenny said coolly. "I'm in charge. This is my show, not yours—you keep forgetting that. I think maybe you could use a demonstration of just how little control you actually have here."

"We don't need a demonstration," I said. The pain meds had worn off, leaving my thoughts blurred and the pain raging. "Trust me, we know who has the control. But Diggs is right: the longer you drag this out, the higher the chance that the whole operation will be discovered."

"Discovered by who?" she said sharply.

"The cops, of course," Diggs said, conveniently leaving Willett and my father out of the conversation. "Since the world's decided we're terrorists, it's made it a little more difficult moving around."

"Well, it's almost over now," she murmured, half to herself. "I trust that if Erin's on the phone now, she survived the bullet."

"I told you, I'm fine," I said. "Where do you want us next?"

"I'll send the coordinates—make sure you're not followed this time."

"Wait," Diggs said immediately. "There's no way Erin can travel yet—"

"Yes there is," I said. "I'm all right. We'll get there."

"Excellent. It's nice to hear we're finally on the same page," Jenny said.

"I want to talk to Kat," I said before she could hang up. "Let me talk to my mother."

There was a brief flurry of whispers and shuffling on the other end of the line, before Kat came on.

"You were hurt," she said, first thing.

"It wasn't bad," I lied.

"Bullshit. Bullets are always bad." Her voice sounded surprisingly clear. I wondered if she'd been sober this whole time. Maybe I should keep Jenny on retainer for the future. This could be her next career: Rapid detox at gunpoint, for the relapsed addict in your life.

"Did you get it out?" Kat persisted.

"The bullet? It was a through-and-through—Mom, I'm okay." There was another long pause on the line. "Kat?" I prompted, when no one said anything.

"Don't come," she said suddenly, in a rush. "It's not worth it—it's not going to work, Erin. There's no happily ever after in this—"

There was a struggle on the other end of the line as Jenny grabbed the phone away. I heard a sharp, solid sound like a palm hitting flesh, and the muffled sound of Kat's cry.

"Don't hurt her, damn it!" I shouted.

"You heard her: she's alive," Jenny said, her voice tight. "But in case you get the idea she's at Club Med out here and you're safe leaving her in our hands, I'll send along a snapshot or two. Your mom's seen better days. That only gets worse if I hear you've been trying to enlist anyone else's help. Sally Woodruff—11 Hillcrest Drive, Justice Kentucky—is one thing, but I don't want to hear anyone else is in on the act."

And with that, she hung up. Seconds later, the text came through with our next meeting spot:

La Iglesia
Coba, Mexico
18:00, Friday April 15

"Shit," I whispered. My stomach rolled. "Do we even have time to get there?"

"If we were going… yeah, we could get there. But there's no way you're up for a jaunt to Mexico right now. For Christ's sake, Solomon—"

"I'm not standing by while they kill Kat. I don't care how much of a pain in the ass she is, I'm not letting her think she doesn't matter."

"Then send me," he said. "Let me go alone. I can do it."

"You know Jenny won't go for that. She wants me there—"

"Which begs the question: Why? If she's not planning to hurt us, why is it so important that you be there for the exchange?"

I didn't have an answer for that, so I chose to ignore it and move onto another pressing concern. There were so many right now, it was hard to keep track.

"How do you think Jenny knew where we are now?"

"They're probably tracking the phone," Diggs said. "It's all right. They may know where we are, but I don't think they have anyone following us. I've already checked for bugs, so I know they're not listening in."

"Then how did she know we ran into trouble last night?"

"I don't know, maybe something on the news. Or maybe she has an in with Willett, and he told her." He set the phone back down and leaned over to touch his lips to my forehead. "You're warm again. Just lie back, okay? If you're dead set on this, you have to get some rest. We can leave tomorrow and still have time to get to Coba by Jenny's deadline. But I won't go if you don't sleep the night."

I didn't fight him. He handed me a couple of pills Sally had left on the bedside table, and I sank back into the pillows. Diggs lay down beside me again with his arm resting carefully on my stomach, his body warm against mine. He kissed my temple.

"We'll figure this out. Things will fall into place, one way or another."

"Since when have you been so damned optimistic?" I asked.

He laughed a little. It was dark, and almost unnaturally peaceful. It occurred to me that somehow I'd gone from fighting like hell to avoid a relationship with Diggs to being pulled smack dab into the middle of one. He ran his finger along the worry wrinkle in my forehead.

"Always look on the bright side of life, right? If it makes

you feel any better," Diggs said, "Sally read me the riot act because I was ready to dump your friggin' dog in the nearest river."

"Why? You love Einstein—"

"No—*you* love Einstein. I like the dog just fine, right up until you start risking your life for him."

My eyelids were getting heavy again, but I fought to keep them open. "You were scared," I said quietly.

He smiled at me, just as quiet, and kissed me on the lips very lightly. "You've got no idea, sweetheart. Now, close your eyes, for Christ's sake. Sleep. Apparently, we're driving to Mexico tomorrow."

"You'll be here when I wake up?" My eyes drifted shut. My tongue was all twisted, my body warm and heavy. "You won't go anywhere."

"I'll be here," he said. Einstein shifted… or Diggs did, maybe. Someone did. I sank deeper under. "I'm not going anywhere, Sol."

"Good," I murmured. And then, I was out.

By ten the next morning, I was almost back to feeling human again. In deep, gut-rocking pain, but human. Sort of. After Sally had checked my bandages and helped me get washed up, I sat at the kitchen table downstairs with Diggs beside me and Einstein curled at my feet. Sally seemed to have a whole staff of wayward pubescent girls at her disposal. One of them set out a huge spread for us before we left town—eggs and homemade toast, bacon and grits and fresh fruit.

Despite everything we'd been through, Diggs looked better than he had since this whole nightmare had begun. Sixteen hours of sleep and a decent meal will do that for a body, I guess. He sat across from me with Cameron's laptop out, nibbling at his food while he continued to work.

"What are you doing?" I asked, when we'd been sitting for half an hour and he still hadn't volunteered the information.

"I'm working on the list," he said after a moment's hesitation. "I think I cracked the code."

"Seriously? When?"

"Yesterday. I wanted to wait until I knew for sure before I mentioned it."

"And you're sure now?"

He pushed the computer toward me and slid his chair to my side of the table so he could sit beside me. On the screen, he had duplicated the entries from the memory card on a spreadsheet, separating them into four columns: LOCATION; DATE; SS#. The fourth column was headed with two question marks in bold, with the initials at the end of each entry listed beneath. About a dozen rows were highlighted in yellow. My heart sped up as I stared at them:

CALIFORNIA – AUGUST 1969 – CHARLES MANSON
GUYANA – NOVEMBER 1978 – JIM JONES
MAINE – AUGUST 1990 – MITCH CAMERON
TEXAS – OCTOBER 1991 – GEORGE HENNARD
OKLAHOMA – APRIL 1995 – TIM MCVEIGH
COLORADO – APRIL 1999 – ERIC HARRIS
KENTUCKY – MARCH 2013 – JESUP BARNEL

"What is this?" I asked when I could speak again.

"I think it's a list of the crimes committed by operatives of J-932," he said. "Once I figured out where the dates are located in each entry, it was easy to put together some of the more significant events…"

"This is crazy, though," I insisted. "George Hennard—that's Luby's Massacre, right? And the Oklahoma City bombing? Columbine? Diggs—"

"Trust me, I know how crazy it is. This whole thing is

nuts. If you look at the numbers, though. Once you break it up, so you have the dates separated and the social security numbers in line...." He ran his finger down the column marked SS#. It only took a second before I understood what he was talking about.

"Several of the entries have the same social security number."

"Because I think the same operative was responsible for whatever those entries represent."

"You don't know Timothy McVeigh's social security number, though," I pointed out. "And the initials at the end of that entry are JL. So how did you make the leap that McVeigh could have anything to do with this? Or Manson? Or any of them, for that matter."

"It's just a hunch," he admitted. "I haven't been able to figure out what the letters at the end of each entry stand for, but I'll get there. But I know the entry dated March 2013 is right—that's definitely Barnel's social security number. And since we know at this point that Cameron was the one who struck the match on Payson Isle, it would make sense that the August 1990 entry would be him."

I glanced down the list again. A dozen entries were marked with the social security number Diggs had assumed belonged to Cameron. Diggs and I had both seen firsthand what the operative was capable of when backed into a corner, but this was a sobering reminder.

The longer I looked at the spreadsheet, the more freaked out I became. Finally, I pushed the laptop away. "We have to get out of here. We have to get to Kat—"

"I know. We will—we already have everything set," Diggs said. Now that he knew I wasn't going to up and die on him today, he'd gotten considerably calmer. "We've got pain pills and clean bandages for you; we've traded the SUV for Sally's truck so Willett won't know what we're driving. As long as we're on the road by noon, we can get where we're going by Jenny's deadline."

"I wish we'd hear something from my dad."

"I know," he agreed. "I'm not sure what happened there—you're sure he wasn't in the cabin when Willett showed up?"

"Positive," I said. I snapped off half a piece of crispy bacon for Einstein and finished the rest myself. "He must have had some reason for leaving without us. I mean, he probably doesn't even know I got hurt. Maybe he found out where the next checkpoint was, and he'll catch up with us then."

There was a flash of something—annoyance, I thought—in Diggs' eyes before he nodded. "Yeah. Maybe."

"What does that mean?"

"Nothing. Forget it, you're probably right. Whatever happened, though, the bottom line is that we're on our own again."

I'd seen that look in his eye enough to know that if I kept pushing, there would be a fight. At this point, I didn't think either of us had it in us to deal with that. Letting things slide isn't exactly in my nature, but in this instance it seemed like the smartest route. Instead of pushing him, I pulled the laptop back toward me. Diggs didn't actually sigh in relief, but he came pretty damned close.

"So—what you're saying, essentially, is that all the lunatic conspiracy theorists in the world have been right all this time, and J-932 is behind it all. Is that what you're telling me?" I asked.

"In a nutshell."

"Good to know.""

"I haven't found Jimmy Hoffa yet, but I'm sure he's in here somewhere," he said.

"Probably buried next to the Lindbergh baby and Amelia Earhart."

"That's my guess," he agreed. He leaned in and kissed me. "You still ready to venture into the belly of the beast?"

"No. But I don't know if we have a choice. I can't just leave Kat out there to die. No matter how many times she tells me I should."

"I know. Believe me, I know." He didn't look happy about it, but I knew this was one thing he wouldn't fight me on. Whatever happened, I had to know beyond a reasonable doubt that I'd done everything I could to save my mother. I couldn't live with myself otherwise.

We were nearly finished with the meal, no one saying much of anything, when the dogs lost their minds and started barking like bandicoots outside. Maybe a minute later, one of Sally's girls came crashing into the kitchen looking completely panicked.

"There's someone at the gate, says he needs to see you," she said, looking at Diggs.

"What? Who?" he demanded. "And how? How the hell did they find us?"

"He says his name is Jack Juarez," Keira said. I looked at Diggs, who looked utterly flabbergasted.

"Maybe we can leave out the back before he gets here," I suggested. "Or just hide. We could take Einstein and take cover in the bedroom until Sally gets rid of him."

To my profound shock, Diggs shook his head. "No."

"I'm sorry—what? No?"

Keira looked at Sally, since neither Diggs nor I were any help. "What do you want me to do?"

Sally looked at us. "Well?"

"Diggs—" I began. He held up his hand, his jaw tightening.

"We can't do this alone. You may be in denial about this, but I'm not. You almost died. They have your mother, your father's vanished without a trace, and…." He looked at me pleadingly. Sally and Keira not-so-subtly vamoosed, leaving us alone. Diggs pulled his chair closer to mine and looked at me intently. "This is what we've been fighting about ever since this whole thing started: you have to trust somebody. And I don't know who else it can be. Jack is already in this, somehow. We know that. Please. Because I can't go through losing you like that again, Sol. I won't."

It took some time before I worked up to a nod. Diggs hurried out to give Sally our decision. I sat at the kitchen table trying not to have a nuclear meltdown over this latest curve ball. Jenny had known about the standoff in Tennessee; she'd known we were at Sally's.

What would happen to Kat, if Jenny found out Juarez was here?

There wasn't even a tiny part of me that wanted to find that out.

Diggs was by my side again by the time Jamie and Juarez reached the front door, holding onto my hand like he was afraid I might run off otherwise.

The man knows me well.

When Sally led them into the kitchen, Juarez just stood at the door for as much as a minute, his eyes locked on us both. He looked like shit.

"Jesus, Jack," Diggs said. "You look like the wolves have been gnawing at your entrails." Diggs got up and went to him, since Juarez seemed to have lost the ability to move. Jack pulled him into a bear hug, almost sagging against him with relief.

"We're okay," I heard Diggs say quietly as he pulled back. Jamie smiled at me, looking a little shy and very much out of place.

"I'm glad you're all right," she said to me. "Sounds like

it was a close call."

"You could say that, yeah. But I'm okay—just a little sore. I'll be good as new before long."

"That's good to hear." She nodded to Juarez, still deep in conversation with Diggs. "It'll be a big relief to him."

I wasn't sure what to say to that, and Jamie didn't have any gems on hand to follow it up with. She busied herself with Einstein, who could have cared less that Juarez was in the building. Jamie was a whole other kettle of fish, though.

The fact that Juarez had crashed our party again was hard enough to take, but I wasn't sure how to take the fact that Jamie was with him. It wasn't like she had anything to do with any of this, beyond a passing interest in Juarez. The thought crossed my mind that she could be a mole sent in by J-932—or maybe Willett.

Juarez refocused on me, thankfully cutting off this train of thought before I went off the rails completely. "I would have gotten here sooner, but the high-ups got wind that I was sniffing around the investigation. I had to assure them I had no interest in the case."

"And then he got suspended," Jamie interjected, still kneeling by Einstein.

I looked at Juarez in surprise. No wonder he looked like shit. "You shouldn't have come. We're all right. You shouldn't be putting your career on the line for this."

"Don't worry about that. It doesn't matter." He eyed my mummified side. "You're hurt."

I attempted a devil-may-care shrug. "I'm okay. It wasn't serious."

"Except for the bucket of blood in our backseat," Diggs said. He's such a drama queen.

"What the hell happened?" Juarez asked.

"You have to answer something first," I said. "Who knows you're here?"

"No one," he said promptly. "Like Jamie said, I'm suspended from the job—so I don't have to check in with them. I made sure I wasn't followed. I'm just here to help, Erin. This has nothing to do with the job. I just want to make sure you two make it out of this alive. Now, what the hell happened?"

"They took Kat," Diggs said before I could stop him. "Cameron showed up that night when we were all on Raven's Ledge."

"I know," Juarez said, pointing to a bruise at his temple. "We had a close encounter—a brief one. I didn't put up much of a fight. I'm sorry about that."

He looked miserable.

"Give yourself a break, huh?" I said. "Cheyenne told you guys she roofie'd us all, I'm assuming? And Diggs and I have already decided Cameron's some kind of genetically engineered robot assassin, so it's not like you didn't have the odds stacked against you. I'm just sorry we couldn't have let you know what happened."

"Where is he now? Cameron, I mean."

"That's where it gets tricky," Diggs said. "He left with Kat, but Jenny caught up with them."

"And now she says she'll only let Kat go if I bring her the memory card Diggs got in Kentucky."

Jamie shook her head. "Jesus. Does this story come with CliffsNotes?"

"Sorry," Juarez said. "It's a little...tangled. This memory card—I assume we're talking about the one you assured me had been destroyed when Kat's house was bombed?" The edge in his voice suggested he'd already figured out I was full of shit on that count.

"I'm sorry," I said. "We weren't sure who to trust. But, yeah—we have the card. And the information that was on it."

Juarez shook his head. He turned and walked away, running a hand through his hair. Jamie straightened and went to him.

"You already knew this," she said, her back to the rest of us. Though her voice was lowered, I had no qualms about eavesdropping. I rarely do. "Brooding might look good on you, but it doesn't help anything. What happens next?"

"All right," he agreed after a minute. He turned to face Diggs and me again. "Jamie's right—let's move on. What's the status now?"

"We're meeting Jenny," I said. "I'll give her the card. She'll let Kat go. Then, she said we can disappear. She'll let us go, as long as we don't go after them."

"And you believe that?" Juarez asked. "Because we didn't break up that long ago... The last I remember, you didn't believe in fairy tales."

"I don't know what choice I have," I said, tensing. "She already warned us about going to the police—and she seems to know every move we make. Which, incidentally, is why I'm not jumping up and down to see you right now," I pointed out. "If Jenny finds out…."

"She won't," Juarez said, without a smidge of self-doubt. It was the kind of confidence I'd admired from him in the past. I couldn't deny it was a relief to see it again now. "I swept for bugs, switched vehicles. If someone finds you, it won't be because I led them here."

He sat down beside me at the table. I glanced at Diggs.

"Would you mind leaving us alone for a couple of minutes?" I asked him, nodding toward Juarez.

"You know, a lesser man might have a problem with you wanting all this time alone with your ex," he said.

"Good thing you're so evolved then, huh?" I said.

He shot me a deadly little grin. "Good thing," he agreed. He turned his attention to Jamie. "What do you say, James?

We could go out back, make out in the barn for a while."

"Or we could take the dog for a walk and you could show me those kennels I noticed out front," she said.

He muttered something about goddamn women and their goddamn dogs, but I didn't miss the glance of concern he sent my way. I caught his arm and pulled him back to me, while Juarez and Jamie did their best to pretend they weren't listening.

"I'm all right, Diggs."

"I'll just be out back."

"Making out with the hot blonde—yeah, I caught that. Just a couple minutes."

He kissed my forehead and left without another word.

"That's why we're not together," Juarez said when they were gone. "Those were the moments we were missing."

"I'm sorry," I said, suddenly uncomfortable. "He's just..."

"Worried," he finished for me. "And head over heels. That's all right—it's the way things should be."

"You and Jamie seem pretty cozy yourselves."

He shook his head. "What is it with you people? Jamie and I are none of your business, is what we are. I assume you had a reason for tossing your boyfriend out on his ear so we could be alone?"

I did. "You asked if I was remembering things, the other day when we were out on Raven's' Ledge," I began, wasting no more time. "Did you ask because things have started coming back to you? Have you remembered something?"

"What kind of something?"

"Cut the shit, Jack. You know what I'm talking about. Something about your childhood."

He hesitated, scrubbing his hand over his face. "Nothing that makes any sense—a lot of fragments, no complete memories."

"How long have you been remembering?"

"A few months."

"A few months, as in…?"

"I had the first one just after Black Falls," he admitted. "They're like dreams most of the time—I'm just awake when I have them. It's like I just…go somewhere else. Something triggers it, usually: a song on the radio, the smell of a woman's perfume…. But then it's just a tangle of images and impressions that make no sense."

"And you were seeing these images when we were dating?"

"Not often. But sometimes, yes."

"Did you know then that they might have something to do with me? Or my father, somehow?"

He looked at me, surprised. "We dated because I care about you. There was no other reason—no ulterior motive, Erin."

I waved him off. "That doesn't matter—forget it, that's the last thing we need to get into right now. But these images you've been seeing: you do think they're related somehow to my father, don't you?"

"I don't know."

"Do you know what J. Enterprises is?" I asked, switching gears.

"Do you?" he asked warily.

I didn't have it in me to play coy anymore. "I know that J was a government-funded operation, short for Project J-932, experimenting on U.S. citizens without their knowledge. And my father was one of those citizens. But you already know that, don't you?"

"I'm sorry," he said, his eyes sliding from mine. That old suspicion crept back again. "I just found out myself. I would have lost my job if I'd said something. I could have been brought up on charges."

"So, why are you here now?" He didn't say anything,

clearly torn. My pain meds were wearing off, my patience stretched thin. "Goddamn it, Jack. The truth, please. Maybe you really are worried about me, or maybe you're just covering your own ass. Whatever the reason might be, you're a shitty liar. What aren't you telling me?"

"I *am* worried about you," he insisted. "I'm worried about both you and Diggs."

"But that isn't the only reason, is it? Tell me what you're remembering. This project: J-932. What do you know about it? What does it have to do with you?"

"I...." He stood there for as much as a minute, a man at the edge of a cliff with no net in sight. Rubbed his eyes, the exhaustion wearing through. "I don't know. But something. When I realized what the project was, the pieces started to come together—everything I can't remember, these flashes I keep getting...."

"Is it possible that you were one of the subjects?" I asked. "That maybe the reason you can't remember is because they don't want you to?"

He sat down—half-collapsed, really, into a chair across the table from me. Hands clenched, jaw tight, eyes distant. Whatever he was seeing just then, it wasn't me. "It's possible. But I don't know what that means—how that changes things. How it's changed me. I need to know that."

"So, you're not just here for my welfare after all, then."

"Not completely," he admitted. "I should have told you sooner, I know, but this is beyond classified. I wasn't lying about that. If they found out I was talking to a civilian—not just a civilian, but a *reporter*—then losing my job would be the least of my worries."

"Then why are you telling me now?" I pressed.

"I checked into Trent Willett—the bastard who shot you. Something's not right there. This is personal for him. I don't understand why he didn't have backup with him in

Tennessee. You said he was just there with a few of the local police."

"I thought of that," I said with a nod. "If this is a huge government operation or whatever, why is he stumbling around the backwoods of Tennessee shooting at my goddamn dog?"

"And you," Juarez pointed out, in much the same way Diggs had. They just couldn't let that go. "He also shot you. But, yeah: I don't have an answer for that. I don't have an answer for any of this, really. I just know that I got word from very high up that I was to leave this alone."

"And yet, here you are."

He frowned, his hands tightening into fists again. I could feel the conflict running through him, something pulling at him that, for whatever reason, he seemed incapable of talking about.

"Jack," I said, as gently as I could.

"I don't care about my job," he finally said, his eyes meeting mine. "I have to find out what all this means. I was thinking about everything that's happened over the years. And I started to wonder if…." He trailed off, looking more haunted than I'd ever seen him.

It clicked, then. The few stories he'd told me about his past: the woman he'd been in love with from the time he was fifteen. The woman he'd married. The woman brutally murdered a few years ago.

Lucia.

"You're wondering about your wife?" I asked.

He ran a shaking hand through his hair. For the first time, I really thought about what this meant for him—A man who had lived most of his life knowing nothing about where he'd come from, who his parents were, what his childhood had been. And now, to find out that he may have sprung from something like J-932….

No wonder he looked like hell.

"I don't know," he said. "But the police never found the men who killed her. It was in Nicaragua, so they just chalked it up to random violence. Closed the case. Refused to let me investigate, saying I was too close to it. I pursued it anyway, for a long time. Then, when it started eating away at everything, when I knew I had to make a choice between her death or my life, I thought maybe they were right. I was too close. There were things that never made sense about the case, though. And now, I can't stop thinking that maybe...."

I reached across the table and took his hand. "We'll figure it out," I said. "We'll figure all this out, Jack. I just have to get Kat back safely first. I can't risk her life, no matter how much I want to finish the puzzle—and make these bastards pay for everything they've done."

The back door opened then and Einstein charged inside, followed closely by Diggs and Jamie. Diggs eyed Juarez's hand clasped in mine with a bit of a raised eyebrow, but otherwise made no comment.

"Everything okay?" he asked, far too casually, as Juarez pulled his hand away. Diggs took a seat beside me, Jamie next to Jack. A dinner party for the psychically scarred. Awesome.

"I want to help," Juarez said firmly. "Whatever you two need."

Diggs looked at me. "I'd rather not go to Mexico on our own. If we could have just a little backup...."

"If Jenny found out—" I began, whistling the same old tune.

"What if we traveled separately?" Jamie asked.

"I thought this was supposed to be a quiet, clean drop," I said. "If we're bringing other people in on this, we need to be clear on what the goal is: Namely, getting Kat and ourselves out of this alive. It's not like we're even remotely equipped to take out the higher-ups with the Project at this point. Especially since we don't know who the hell they are."

"Or how far their reach is," Juarez added. "I agree. Right now, our goal is the same as yours: Get everyone out safely. Once that's done, I'd like to find out…more," he finished lamely, clearly not ready to share the details of our conversation with the others.

"If we meet in Coba…." Diggs began. I tensed, waiting for the phone to ring or the sky to fall; for some indication that Jenny had heard everything, and Kat would pay accordingly.

"At the very least, I could be there to cover you when you make the exchange," Juarez said. "Jamie and I can travel under the radar—I won't tell anyone at the Bureau."

"And as far as my team knows, I'm off having sex with Jack for the week," Jamie said. Juarez's eyebrows shot skyward. She grinned at him, but I noticed just a tinge of pink to her cheeks. "I had to tell them something. That was the most innocuous thing I could think of."

"You couldn't have told them you were helping with a case? I don't know, official business of some kind?" Juarez asked.

"The only business I do is with my dogs, none of whom are with me this time out. Sorry, kitten. Trust me—this was the only way Bear wouldn't be up in my grill demanding details. He's nosy, but the kid thankfully draws the line at my sex life."

"Well," Juarez said, determinedly casual. "If that's the way it has to be played. You better tell them I was good, though."

That endearing pink flush deepened in Jamie's cheeks, but she held Jack's gaze. "Naturally."

I watched the way their eyes caught, tension sparking between them. A tiny, exceedingly petty twinge of jealousy flared.

"Now that you two have your stories straight," Diggs said, "maybe we could move onto strategizing this operation."

"Right," Juarez said abruptly, breaking the smolder between him and the blonde. "Strategy is important."

"You'd think so, but if you two need a little time alone first—" I began. Diggs kicked me under the table, none too gently. I shot him a killing glare; he smiled winningly at me. I moved on. "Right. Strategizing is good."

"There's a place in Mexico where we can meet before the exchange," Diggs said. "I'd like to rendezvous there first, have some time to go into some depth on this."

"No way," I said firmly. "We can meet you and Jamie in Coba, but otherwise we shouldn't be in contact. It's way too risky."

"So you just want them to show up on Friday and hope we're all on the same page?" Diggs asked.

"We'll do whatever you're most comfortable with," Juarez said smoothly. "But I tend to agree with Diggs— with something like this, we should have at least a couple of opportunities to ensure we've coordinated things properly."

"What's to coordinate?" I pressed. "We show up. You show up. Jenny shows up. We give her the memory card; she gives us Kat. We all drive off in separate directions. Sounds pretty straightforward to me."

"Until something goes wrong," Diggs said. "What if Kat isn't there? Or Jenny pulls something? We should know the layout, have some kind of contingency plan in place."

I looked at Jamie, who was following the conversation in silence. "What do you think?"

She considered the question for a second or two before she answered. "I understand your perspective, but the guys are right. Going into something like this blind is a recipe for disaster. You've already got things working against you. You said you're doing this exchange in Coba? That's a red flag right there, if you ask me. Have you been there?"

Diggs nodded. "It's got some great sites if you want to play tourist," Jamie continued, "but otherwise it's not exactly a hot spot. And it's remote enough that if something happened, no one would come running."

"But we're not doing it at midnight," I argued. "This is six o'clock on a Friday night, at the ruins. The place will be packed. Or at least well traveled."

"All the more reason to make sure we have things well-coordinated," Juarez said. "Otherwise, we run the risk of some sightseeing couple from Cleveland getting caught in the crossfire."

"I'm not fighting about this," Diggs said. He was focused on me now, the rest of the room falling away. "There's a hotel in Tampico. We meet there Thursday night, then we catch a commuter plane into Valladolid on Friday. End of story."

Before I could tear into Diggs about the innumerable ways his whole 'end of story/end of discussion/my word is law' routine drives me sideways, Sally burst into the kitchen. Her face was flushed, her eyes wild.

"We have a problem," she said. "There are some guys in town asking about you. Keira ran into them when she was running some errands."

I looked accusingly at Juarez, who shook his head. "You know better than that—I didn't bring them here."

"Well, someone did," I said.

"It doesn't matter whose fault it is," Diggs interrupted. "We need to get out of here. You've got the back gate open?" he asked Sally.

"Gate's open, truck's ready to go," she confirmed.

"How much time do we have?" I asked.

"Ten minutes if you're lucky—she said she saw 'em headed out this way. Got directions from goddamn Curt Mires up to the Quicky Mart."

"We're already packed," Diggs said over his shoulder, headed for the stairs. "I'll grab the bags and we'll get you in the truck."

Einstein ran after him, got halfway out the door, and headed back for me. His side was shaved and bandaged. He'd lost weight in the past few days, and he got panicky now whenever I was out of sight for more than two minutes. I called him back and crouched to meet him, ignoring the agony in my side, dimly aware that Juarez and Jamie were debating their next move. Meanwhile, Diggs had grabbed our bags and was barreling back through the kitchen door.

"What the hell are you doing?" he asked. "Get him in the truck—we need to move."

Einstein whimpered uneasily, tail wagging, head lowered to butt against my chest.

We were going to Mexico. I didn't even know how Diggs and I would cross the border, forget getting the dog over there. And Diggs was right: One of us could have died yesterday. If it had been Einstein, I wasn't sure how I could live with myself. If it had been Diggs, I knew I never could.

"You need to go," Juarez said. Out of the corner of my eye, I saw Diggs shake his head warningly once he realized something was up.

"She knows. Give her a second."

I hugged Einstein tightly. He licked my face, pawing at my chest.

"We can't take him," I said numbly. "There's no way. Sally...."

She nodded without making me finish. "No problem. He'll be in good hands until you get back."

If we got back. The dogs started barking out front. Willett was here. Einstein shook pitifully against me, sensing the worst. Diggs laid his hand on my shoulder.

"We have to go, Sol," he said quietly.

"I know," I said, nodding. I hugged Einstein one more time and whispered into his fur. "I'll be back before you know it, Stein. I promise."

Diggs offered his hand, pulling me up gently. A door slammed out front. Stein knew something was up—he didn't even bark, totally focused on me instead.

"Erin—" Diggs said.

"I know," I said, stuffing down the anvil in my throat. "I'm ready."

We went out the back, Diggs supporting me as I gimped along. Every move I made sent pain rocketing straight through me. Stein barked after us—a couple of sharp, high-pitched yelps before the barks gave way to a desperate howl.

"You made the right decision," Diggs whispered as he helped me into the truck carefully. "Jack will handle Willett, and Sally will take good care of Einstein."

I nodded through tears, and kept my eyes locked straight ahead. Diggs started the truck. The last thing I heard before we drove off was the sound of my dog barking and men's voices, raised in pure, unadulterated rage.

23
KAT

"YOU'RE GOOD AT THIS, YOU KNOW," Adam said. Kat had been on Payson Isle for a week, watching over her patient around the clock most of that time.

Her patient.

The truth was, Adam Solomon was more than a patient—she knew that, even then.

"Just got lucky," she said with a shrug. He tried to sit up in bed, but fell back with a groan. "But luck will run out fast if you don't take it easy. You have a long recovery ahead."

And not just from the shooting, either.

Adam's blue eyes were intense, mournful, his body nearly emaciated. He'd been shot twice: once in the thigh, once just above his kidney. The idiots on the island had been praying over him, but otherwise they hadn't done a damn thing to try and help him. Kat wanted to call her father in, but Isaac Payson wouldn't hear of it.

And so, at seventeen, Kat had operated in a makeshift OR inside the massive Payson boarding home, on her own. She removed the bullets, stitched the wounds. And only then, when Adam was resting and there was nothing more to be done, did she settle in and do what everyone else had been doing all along: She prayed like hell.

And now here he was—alive. Recovering.

"How long do you think it'll be before I can get out of here?" he asked. "I'd like to be useful, at least."

"Not for a while," she said firmly. "You'll be useful down the road. Right now, you're at my mercy."

She actually felt herself blushing when he smiled at her, his eyes lingering on hers.

"Well, I guess there are worse things in the world," Adam said.

A sharp slap on the cheek brought Kat back to the present: Hands behind her back, trussed like a Christmas goose in a twin-engine plane flying high. Cameron was beside her, also tied.

"Don't go too far, Katie," Jenny said. She was smiling, but Kat noticed how the girl avoided looking at Cameron. She barely spoke to him; certainly took no pleasure in having him there. "I don't want you to miss any of this. We're gonna have some fun."

Frustration rode dangerously close to the surface. Kat's temper had always been a problem. If she ever got free again, she planned to take full advantage of it.

"Look, you stupid bitch, I don't know what you think any of this accomplishes—"

Jenny backhanded her, her knuckles grazing Kat's mouth. She tasted blood and blinked back tears. It wasn't the worst blow she'd ever taken, but it wasn't pleasant.

"You don't want to test me," Jenny said. The words were tight, and deadly serious. "I've got orders not to kill you, but there's a lot that can be done before the heart gives out. Trust me, there's no one I'd rather test that on than you."

"Why?" Kat asked. She leaned to her left and spat blood onto a rubber mat at her feet, testing her teeth with her tongue. Everything was still intact. "What, exactly, did I ever do to you? The way I see it, I have a lot more right to hold a grudge."

Light came to Jenny's eyes, a slow smile to her lush lips. "Daddy didn't tell you, then? Well, this will be fun."

"Jenny," Cameron said. A warning.

"Dear old Dad broke up our happy home over you and your little girl. You didn't know that, did you?"

"I don't know what the hell you're talking about," Kat said.

"He never had the gumption to say it to your face," Jenny continued. "But you were always the woman he wanted. 'A woman with some fight,' he always used to say. Someone who stood up for what she believed in. 'No one would ever push Katherine Everett around.' Isn't that what you used to say, Daddy?" She smiled sweetly at Cameron, the expression in direct contrast to the bile in her eyes. "It turns out, all it took was a threat to your little girl and my father switched sides. He's been betraying us for years, all thanks to you."

"Well, I sure as hell didn't ask him to," Kat said, temper flaring again. "Look, you little bitch, I never—"

"Stop!" Cameron said. His voice was quiet. Deadly. The blood had turned to a deep brown on his shirt, his nose swollen—no doubt broken, Kat thought. "Katherine didn't have anything to do with turning me. I saw what I was doing—I woke up after the fire on Payson Isle, and everything had changed. It wasn't Katherine; it wasn't Erin or Adam or a single life I'd taken. It was all of it together."

"Spare me," Jenny said. She turned on him, looking her father in the eye for the first time since she'd taken him. "You left us. You left Mom. You left *me*. You know what that did to her. Don't paint yourself a victim here. You killed those people. You chose it, everyday—the same way I choose it. The same way Mom chose it. We work so the Project works."

"We work because we've been drugged and conditioned and...dehumanized," Cameron said calmly. Kat recalled the way Adam had told her this story, tearful and broken, so many years ago. *They took our lives. They made us monsters.*

Cameron had no tears, though. His voice stayed strong, steady, as he continued. "They did it to me; they did it to you. They've done this for years, and now they'll continue to murder more innocent people if someone doesn't stop them—"

"No one is innocent," Jenny said coolly. "It's one of the first things you taught me. People will die, yes—weak people. There are too many of them, anyway. It's time to let the strong stand. We're paving the way for a new country... A new world. And you're here sniveling over a few lives, semantics that don't matter. That never mattered."

"You realize that they would say the same about you," Cameron said calmly. "That your life isn't worth sniveling over to them, either."

"The good of the many versus the good of the few," she returned. "You've obviously forgotten that. They would be right in thinking that. My life doesn't matter, in the grand scheme."

"I disagree," he said. "I think your life matters a great deal." Kat watched the way his eyes changed, reminded of their conversation the night before. His dream of retirement, grandchildren, a corner bookstore.

The briefest flicker of doubt, maybe even confusion, crossed Jenny's face before it vanished. She turned her back on them both. "We'll reach our destination in a few hours. I suggest getting some sleep. This will all be over soon."

She strode back to the front of the plane. Kat leaned in toward Cameron.

"Way to go—now she's psychotic *and* conflicted. That's so much better than what we had to work with before."

"Give her time," he said, his eyes lingering on the spot where his daughter had stood. "I know who she is—who she was, growing up. If I could get away from the Project, I know she can."

Kat looked at him doubtfully. It was a nice thought, but she sure as hell wasn't ready to bet Erin and Diggs' lives on Cameron's daughter suddenly growing a conscience.

There had to be another way.

24
DIGGS

SOLOMON AND I HIT TEXAS at seven o'clock Tuesday night. Sally's truck didn't have much in the way of shocks and no air conditioning to speak of—which was unfortunate, given the direction we were headed. And while I was sorry we weren't traveling in Jamie Flint's handy commuter plane, in this particular instance, I was fairly sure Solomon was right: Jenny and her people might not know every detail of what we were doing, but at this point she was coming pretty damned close. If she found out Jamie was flying us out, Kat was as good as dead.

We caught a few hours of sleep at a rest stop not far beyond the Texas border, but I had a destination in mind and a deadline to make. We didn't linger.

Understandably, it wasn't one of our best road trips. Between the pain and the blood loss and the dog loss and the fact that her abusive mother was being held captive by a psycho, Solomon was bordering on catatonia. Usually, we're both pretty good at pulling each other out of a funk when the need arises, but this one was beyond me. For the most part, she slept and I drove, and the miles slowly passed beneath us.

Thanks to Cameron's IDs, an inside tip from Juarez about when and where to cross the Mexican border, and a very healthy bribe, we managed to get out of the country with almost shocking ease. By the time we reached Tampico, it was two o'clock Wednesday afternoon. The meeting spot Jenny had chosen was another thousand miles south, but I didn't care. Clearly, Solomon needed a break.

She came back around when I pulled up in front of a massive white resort, consisting of block upon block of beachfront stucco.

"What are you doing?"

"Getting us a room," I said. "Hang tight, I'll be right back."

"We don't have the money to stay here."

"Actually, we do. And I have no idea what will happen in Coba, but for all we know this will be the last night we can do something like this for a while. And so... I'm getting us a room."

A distant, barely-there smile touched her eyes when she took in the stretch of sand and surf. "Okay. Maybe that's not a terrible idea."

Considering her state, I took that as progress.

Our room had a king-sized bed, Jacuzzi tub, balcony overlooking the beach, and access to all the resort amenities: golf course, health club, restaurant and bar, hotel masseuse, and about half a dozen different pools of varying shapes, sizes, and operating hours. Bedraggled as we were, Solomon and I were hardly the ideal patrons, but I managed to get a room on the first floor reasonably isolated from other guests without causing too much of a stir.

That afternoon, we cranked the air conditioning, Sol popped a couple of pain pills, and we laid down together. She was out within minutes, but sleep was hard to come by for me. I lay beside her, listless and uneasy, going over our options for the coming days, weeks, and months. There were too many variables, too many ways this could all go to hell. When it was clear that Solomon wasn't waking anytime soon and I sure as hell wasn't sleeping, I gave in and got up.

I showered, ordered some food up to the room, and then focused my attention on deconstructing the rest of the coded numbers from the memory card. I was sure Mae had been right about how the numbers were arranged and what they were; what I wasn't sure of was what each entry in the list represented. The entries with significant dates in history were simple enough to figure out. What worried me was the fact that nearly half of the dates listed extended as far as five years into the future.

From what I could gather, Solomon and I were now officially in possession of a list predicting a long series of atrocities I had no clue how to stop.

As this nightmare had unfolded over the past few months, I'd been powerless to stop the reporter side of my brain from writing this story, if only in my own head. The narrative was staggering: the men and women involved; the government cover up; the hundreds—thousands—of victims who had fallen prey to J-932 over the years….

The problem, however, was getting any proof about all of it.

Not that I should be thinking that way, I reminded myself. Because telling the story, after all, was not what this was about. Regardless, I couldn't imagine Sol just letting this go—not when she knew the body count we were talking about. Not when she knew they would just keep doing this, keep killing, keep moving toward whatever diabolical endgame they had in mind, unless someone stopped them.

And then there was Jack Juarez's role in this whole thing. On the trek from Kentucky, Solomon had filled me in on her conversation with Juarez at Sally's place. I wasn't surprised that he had suspicions about being another subject of J-932; I'd been thinking the same thing myself. What worried me now was whether or not there was a possibility that he was still under J's control. And if he wasn't, how had he escaped from them at thirteen years old? Who had helped him? And did the higher-ups at J know who he was now?

I drew a timeline, tracing the most significant events referenced in the list of numbers—from Jonestown to Charles Manson to Columbine to Kentucky, and everything in between. Over the roar of the air conditioning, I could hear laughter and music outside. Nice to know someone out there was still having a good time. I shut out the noise and kept working. By the time Sol woke at nine that night, I'd created a color-coded timeline using post-its I'd begged from hotel management, stuck to the bedroom wall.

"What are you doing?" she asked, rubbing her eyes as she sat up. I saw the flash of pain on her face at the move, though she didn't acknowledge it.

"Nothing—just killing time."

"By writing down every bad thing that's ever happened in the past fifty years?" she asked, studying the dates. The pain meds were slowing her down, but she caught on after a minute. "These are all from the memory card? J-932 was behind all these?"

"I think so."

"This is nuts. I mean—you know that, right? How do we even begin to prove something like this?"

I squelched a smile at the knowledge that, despite everything, Solomon was still thinking like a reporter, too. "We're not supposed to be proving anything," I pointed out. "We're supposed to be saving Kat. And running away."

"Right," she said dryly. "How could I forget?"

Her hair was tangled, her complexion still a shade paler

than usual. The bandage at her side made her look oddly lopsided.

"How are you feeling?" I asked.

"I got shot. So, you know. Not awesome." Still, she managed to get out of bed with some effort. "I need to change the bandage. I'm just gonna…." She nodded toward the bathroom.

"Sure," I agreed. "Let's do it."

"You? No, thanks. In my state, it would be way too hard to catch you when you pass out."

"Seriously," I said, losing the smile in a vain attempt to convey my gravity. "You can't change that thing alone. I'm all right—I don't mind."

"I'm fine, Diggs. I've got this."

As is usually the case with Solomon, I decided pushing the issue was pointless. Eventually, she'd realize she couldn't change her own fucking bandage, and I would help. Would it save time and agony if she'd just listen to me to begin with? Undoubtedly. But then that wouldn't really be Solomon, would it?

Five minutes later, I was immersed in my list again when, sure enough, there was a crash and a string of fairly inspired curses from the bathroom.

"Sol?" I called through the door. "You okay?"

"I'm fine," she spit out. "I just…. Leave me alone, I've got it."

Seriously, the woman is maddening. I tried the door. It was locked. "Let me in, damn it. I promise to stay upright if you promise not to bleed to death."

Ten seconds passed before she opened up. She'd tamed her hair, and ditched her clothes in favor of one of my shirts. Half a dozen hotel-sized shampoo bottles had been hurled against the wall in her frustration. One of them had exploded, leaving a streak of yellow glop that ran all the way to the floor.

"That'll teach 'em to cross you," I said mildly. "Relax. You can talk me through this. Here—come on up." I patted the marble vanity.

I helped her up carefully, then eyed her shirt. It had slipped sideways during our maneuvers, now showing creamy thigh and the swell of her breast. I shifted my focus.

"So... How do we do this?" I asked.

I'd never seen her more uncomfortable. "It's just... I can do it myself, Diggs. It's not exactly pretty."

"Because gunshot wounds are usually so attractive. Give me a break. How about if we start by losing the shirt."

"Fine." Her lips pressed in a thin line and her cheeks flaming, she avoided my eye as she unbuttoned her shirt and pushed it aside. That left her in cotton panties and matching bra, a flush burning from her chest up to her cheeks. At her left side, gauze was taped from her hip to her ribs.

"Now what?" I asked.

"I just need to change the bandage, clean it, and check that everything's draining okay. I couldn't get hold of the bandage, though."

"Which is why you have me," I said. "I'm not as delicate as I look, sweetheart."

Tough talk for a man dangerously close to swooning. Nevertheless, I peeled back the bandage carefully and tried to keep my face impassive at sight of the viscous yellow fluid seeping from an ugly black hole at her side. Despite Solomon's insistence that she could take care of this herself, Sally had already briefed me on what I could expect, and the steps I'd need to take to help ensure she healed all right. There were no stitches, since Sally said closing the wound sites increased the chance of infection. I felt like stitches would be easier to handle, somehow.

With shaking fingers and churning stomach, I cleaned

the wound and the area around it.

"So, how much does this hurt right now?" I asked, trying to be casual. One look at her face told me she was in agony, but she shook her head.

"Not much," she said. It came out strangled and small.

I found myself thinking again of her lying bleeding and unconscious on the way to Sally's—and what easily could have happened, if Willett had been even a slightly better shot.

"I'm okay, Diggs," she said.

"Sure you are. You're great."

I handed her a compact mirror so she could check both entry and exit wounds for signs of infection. That bought me a few seconds to get my nausea and shaking hands back under control. When she was satisfied with whatever she'd been looking for, she handed the mirror back to me and nodded to a fresh pack of bandages Sally had provided. I set to work. Solomon got down to business.

"So," she began, "if we were going to try and stop these people, or at least prove what they're doing—hypothetically, I mean…. Where would we start?"

"Well—we know some of the people involved," I said, putting the first layer of bandages over the wound. "But I'm guessing Cameron isn't willing to do a one-on-one interview."

"My father probably wouldn't be up for it, either," she said.

"Probably not," I agreed. "Has Juarez told you anything about what he's remembering?"

"He says just flashes—Ow, what the hell are you doing?" She twisted around to survey my handiwork, now that I'd almost finished dressing the wound.

"You're so dramatic. Would you hold still?"

"Sorry—I've been *shot*, so that 'ow' was actually justified."

She returned to her starting position and waited for me to continue. "Where was I?"

"Just flashes."

"Right. He said he just has flashes of events from his past, but I have a feeling those flashes have left him pretty shaken."

"Do you know when his wife was killed?"

"A few years ago, but I'm not sure of the exact date. Why?"

I taped the last side of the bandage and stepped back. "You said she was killed in Nicaragua? One of the entries has those coordinates."

"When?"

October, 2008."

"That has to be it, then," she said. She twisted her head and checked out the bandage. "That's actually not bad."

"Oh, ye of little faith. I told you I could handle this. Now... If you're up for it, Juarez and company should be here soon. You okay with hosting here?"

Her eyes widened. "Wait—what? I thought we were meeting them in Coba."

"Nope. I called while you were asleep during the drive, let them know where we'd be. We need to have some time together to figure out what the hell we're doing here. How we plan to run things when we're making the switch for Kat."

"It isn't safe—"

"None of this is safe," I interrupted. "You almost got killed. We're going to meet a psychopath in the middle of Mexico, to give her a super-secret code of atrocities her employer is responsible for committing."

"If we're seeing Juarez, you know he's going to ask about the memory card again," she said. "Do we tell him that his wife's murder was definitely part of the project?"

I shook my head without a second thought. "We can't

risk him going off the rails right now. All we want is to get out of here alive. Then, we can tell him what we've found."

She thought about that for a moment before she nodded with a frown. "I wish my father would show up. I feel like he'd know what to do."

"Right," I said, the word wrought with tension.

"You have something you want to say about my father?"

I knew this was one of those times when it was best to shut up. I've been married three times, after all: I know when a topic is worth fighting over and when it's an IED just waiting to explode in your hands. And yet, I kept right on talking.

"I think you might be deluding yourself about just what a spectacular human being he is, that's all. He was gone when Willett got to the cabin—you said it yourself. Which means he took off on both of us, without a word. If someone had come in for him before that, Einstein would have barked his head off—that's the only way we knew Willett was coming in the first place. Let's face facts here: Your father left you. Again."

"Well—yeah, I know he left." She grabbed my shirt from the vanity beside her again and managed to get both arms sleeved while she was sitting there, every move stiff and painful. "We don't know what was going on with him, though. Maybe he was trying to protect me."

"By running away, leaving us exposed when Willett and his posse came for us? Jesus, Sol. I don't know what this guy needs to do before you realize that your father isn't the man you've convinced yourself he is. You've got a blind spot the size of a black hole where he's concerned. You almost died yesterday. Where the hell was he?"

"Taking care of something else," she said, her voice rising. Her efforts to get the damned shirt on were driving me nuts; finally, I moved in to button it myself. She pushed my hands away and continued fumbling the job on her own. "I told you," she continued. "We can't possibly know what's going on inside his head. What he's been through."

"So how about we stop thinking about what *he's* been through, and start thinking about what he's put the rest of his family through. His sister; his parents; his wife. You. Things go wrong, and he checks out—he started doing it the day he ran away and left his little sister to die alone in the woods, and it's just been more of the same ever since."

She hopped off the vanity, stifling a cry of pain when her feet hit the ground. She stood there in her underwear and my shirt, buttoned halfway with most of the buttons misaligned.

"You don't know what you're talking about," she bit out. "Everything he's done has been to protect Kat and me."

"Well, he's done a hell of a job, hasn't he?" She glared at me, her eyes brimming with anger and, worse, hurt. Nice, Diggins: Kick the shit out of the woman with the bullet holes in her side. "Look, I don't want to fight about this," I said, willing myself to tone it down. "Whatever goes on between you and your father is your business, not mine."

"Damned right it is," she said. When I moved to touch her cheek, she tried to step away. I didn't let her. "You seriously want to do that right now?"

"You're sexy when you're angry."

"I'm homicidal when I'm angry, you jackass."

I ran my hands along her arms, then lifted her carefully back onto the vanity. When she was safely up there, eying me with clear distrust, I set to work unbuttoning her shirt again.

"What the hell are you doing?"

"You buttoned it wrong. I'm helping."

She tried batting me away, but I caught her hands.

"You're going to hurt yourself," I said quietly, serious

now. "Let me do this."

She sat in silence as I buttoned her back up and then took a pair of folded yoga pants from the counter beside her.

"I can do that myself," she said. "My arms still work. My legs still work. I'm not crippled, Diggs."

"I know," I said. When she tried to push me away again, I stopped. Leveled a look at her, forcing her eyes to mine. "You almost died, Sol. You have a hole in your belly. You have a hole in your back." I leaned in and kissed her, my lips lingering on hers. "Let me take care of you. Please."

When I pulled back this time, there was something raw, naked, in the way she looked at me. She shifted her gaze. Crossed her arms over her chest. "Fine," she said roughly. "I've never had a guy give me so much grief about getting my fucking pants *on*."

Solomon was back in the bedroom ten minutes later,when there was a knock at the door: three raps in quick succession, two more five seconds later. I don't care what anyone says: Secret knocks aren't just for ten-year-old boys.

When I opened the door, Jamie and Juarez stood in the hallway. Juarez still looked like hell, but I assumed based on the spring in her step that Jamie must have gotten some rest during their trek. She wore shorts and a tank top, her long hair pulled back. Juarez eyed the hotel room uneasily when he walked through the door, as though checking for exits and rogue points of entry.

"Erin's in the other room," I said when they came in. "She'll be out shortly."

They nodded.

"How did it go back in Kentucky?" I asked Juarez. "Were you able to get anything from Willett?"

"Other than the promise that my career was over?" he said. "No—not much. He was furious, though; said finding you two is his number one priority right now."

I glanced back at the bedroom door, still closed, and lowered my voice. "Did he mention anything about Erin's father?"

"Not a word. But when I asked, he said they had that under control."

I frowned, not sure what that meant. Was Adam in their sights, or was he actually working with them? Either seemed plausible, though I didn't understand why he would have led us on a wild goose chase instead of just handing us over at the Harrisburg rest stop when Willett first showed up.

Rather than dwelling on it, I offered drinks and nodded to the sitting area. "We should get started. If we can make this an early night, that's probably for the best. Everyone should try and get a little shut eye tonight."

Juarez produced a map of the ruins of Coba and spread it on the coffee table. Solomon joined us a few minutes later. She was barefoot, her hair up and my shirt hanging to her knees. For someone teetering on the brink of death two days ago, she looked surprisingly good.

Between the four of us, we spent the evening going over entry points surrounding the ruins, searching for the best areas for cover and the best for ambush; where Jenny's people would most likely be positioned, and how we would handle things if they weren't.

By the time ten o'clock rolled around, Solomon's eyes were drifting shut every few minutes and the conversation had gone from stilted to nonexistent.

"We should wrap this up," Jamie finally said, mercifully. "Like you said: a good night's sleep is in everyone's best interest."

"That's probably not a bad idea," I agreed. Solomon sat beside me on the sofa, her eyes glassy as she stared at the map. Despite the warm night, she'd been shivering until I offered my jacket about an hour before. Now, she wore that over her shoulders like a cape, her mind clearly not on our guests.

Jamie stood, but Juarez hesitated. I already knew the question he wanted to ask. The same question I'd be asking in his place: Did we know who killed his wife?

"Why don't I meet you downstairs," Jamie said smoothly, sensing there was something he was holding back. Her hand lingered on his arm as he nodded. I tried to decide whether they were actually sleeping together yet. I didn't think so, but Juarez kept those kinds of things pretty close to the vest.

"Thanks," Juarez said. "I won't be long."

I was sure he would have preferred to have this conversation alone with Solomon, but I had no intention of leaving. She looked too shaky sitting there, side bandaged and eyes glazed. If she was about to get the third degree, I planned to stick around to take the worst of the heat.

"Diggs…" Juarez began, looking meaningfully at the door. To my relief, Solomon shook her head.

"He can stay. You can trust him with whatever you have to say."

He hesitated, clearly unhappy with the arrangement. After a turn or two pacing around the room, he finally stopped and turned to look at Solomon again. "Do you have the memory card here?"

She hesitated.

"We do," I said. "We're still trying to crack the encryption, though."

"I'd like to give it a shot, if you don't mind," he said. "I've had a little training in this area."

"I don't know if that's such a great idea right now," I said. "When it's over…."

He looked at Solomon, a vulnerability in his eyes that I'd never seen before. Sol looked away.

"I'm sorry, Jack—" she said.

"You know, don't you?" he said. He took a step toward her, ignoring me. "I could tell as soon as I walked in the room tonight. You have the proof I've been looking for on that card—whether you'll admit to it or not. They murdered my wife."

"We don't know," Solomon insisted. She stood with some difficulty and started for the front door. She'd never been less believable. "We're all tired right now, Jack. Go back to your room. Get some sleep."

Juarez's jaw tightened. In the space of a single cold second, before I had anticipated what he was about to do, he strode toward her.

"Stop lying to me, damn it! I need to know—did they kill Lucia?" He grabbed her arm before I could get to her, and she gasped at the pain. I was across the room in a blur half a second later, Juarez with his back against the wall and my elbow at his throat.

"She's right, Jack. Go back to your room. Get some sleep," I ground out.

Juarez didn't struggle—which was good, since I was sure he had enough hand-to-hand training to wipe the floor with me.

"I'm fine," Solomon said. Her face had paled with the pain, but now a flush of color returned to her cheeks. "Damn it, Diggs, let him go."

"I'm sorry," Juarez said. He looked worlds more shaken by what he'd done than she did. "I just…. Please, Erin."

She turned her back on both of us and went into the other bedroom. When she returned, she held a copy of the page we'd deciphered. Before she handed it to the Fed, she looked at him intently.

"We have to get Kat back tomorrow. You have to promise me that you won't put that goal in jeopardy."

He didn't say anything, his attention fixed on the paper still in her hand. She reached up and touched his face, forcing his gaze to hers.

"Jack? Please—I don't want to lose her."

He nodded. "I promise: We'll get Kat back before I make a move. I'll make sure everyone is safe."

"Thank you."

Against my better judgment, I watched as Solomon handed him the numbers. He took the paper and sat, poring over each entry. It was easy to see when he found the code for Nicaragua, his fingers tightening convulsively on the page.

He studied it for another minute or more, pulling himself together—gathering his resolve.

"They're not done," he said, indicating the paper. "Some of these entries here are dated years from now."

"I know," Solomon said.

"We have to stop them."

"We will."

I shifted uncomfortably, half wishing I had just left them alone. Juarez turned back to me.

"Thank you for trusting me," he said. "I won't make you regret it. We'll get Kat back. And then, we'll make them pay."

After Juarez had gone, Solomon sank back on the couch and closed her eyes.

"How can I be tired again? All I've done is sleep for the past three days."

"Apparently getting shot is exhausting business. Who knew," I said coolly.

She looked at me, one eyebrow arched. "You think giving him the codes was a mistake."

"I don't know. It seems like he's in control now, but that may change once he actually has Jenny in his sights. You saw the way he lost it tonight. Don't get me wrong—it's not like I don't sympathize with him. If anyone ever did something like that to you…." I trailed off, the thought a toxic burn in my stomach.

She studied me for a second before she held out her hand. "Come sit with me."

"Are you pissed at me for going after him?"

"I'm too tired to be pissed. I think it's a first."

I sat at the end of the couch and wrapped her in my arms as carefully as possible.

"What are you thinking?" I asked after a few minutes of silence.

"I was thinking you looked pretty hot when you pulled that Ninja move on Juarez." She looked at me slyly. I wasn't ready to let it go, though.

"He had no right going after you like that."

"He wouldn't have hurt me."

"He *did* hurt you," I corrected her, thinking of the look in her eye; the gasp of pain. "I don't care what he's going through. He had no right to do that."

"You've always been too protective of me." She pulled back to study me, running a cool, small hand along my cheek. "I'm not as breakable as you think, Diggs."

"I don't think you're breakable. I know you can take whatever gets dealt to you. But given the choice, I'd rather see you avoid it. A crazy concept, I know."

"Yeah, well. You can't protect me this time. Whatever happens with Kat, I have to deal with it. There's no avoiding that."

"She's a tough woman," I said. I touched her knee, running my hand along her thigh. "She'll be okay. She's strong. Like her pain-in-the-ass daughter."

"I've never been as strong as her. Nothing gets to her." A minute, then two, passed before she spoke again. "I need her to be okay, Diggs."

"I know." I pulled her back into my arms, brushing my lips against her temple. Breathing her in. "I know you do."

I wanted to reassure her—to tell her that everything would be fine. We would all come out of this unscathed. But the closer it got to showtime, the more we learned about Jenny and Cameron and the project that had destroyed so many lives, the more convinced I became: It wouldn't be that easy.

This time, no one was coming out unscathed.

25
JUAREZ

JUAREZ WALKED THE BEACH outside the hotel after he left Diggs and Erin, pushing himself to remember something other than jumbled fragments of his past. They had killed Lucia. It wasn't God who took her away, it wasn't random violence or some desperate guerrillas in a third-world country… It was the Project.

But why?

It made no sense—why kill her? What could that possibly accomplish, besides bringing him to his knees?

And then, there were those other flashes from his childhood: the woman teaching him how to hold a gun; the words he kept hearing. *Forget the dark spots, Jackie.*

He had no idea what any of it meant.

After an hour, when he found he couldn't handle the chaos inside his own head any longer, Juarez finally returned to the room. It was after midnight, but Jamie was still awake, head bowed as she worked at her laptop in the living room. She looked up when he came in.

"I ordered up some room service if you want," she said, nodding to several dishes on the table. "It might be a little cool, but it's probably still edible."

"Thank you."

He sat and checked the dishes: tortillas, refried beans, chicken. His stomach rumbled.

Jamie remained where she was, continuing to work.

"What are you doing?" he asked.

"Just budget stuff. I may be able to justify a few days of imaginary sex, but it doesn't mean I can ditch work altogether."

"I guess not."

He stopped eating after the first few bites and studied the veritable stranger now sharing a suite with him. Her hair was up, her legs tucked gracefully beneath her on the sofa. She'd changed from shorts to light cotton pajama pants and a thin-strapped top that highlighted sculpted shoulders and a slim, graceful neck. When his gaze fell to her breasts, small and pert beneath the thin fabric, his blood warmed. He looked away an instant before she looked up, but he had the sense she knew full well that he'd been staring.

"If you want to talk, I can put this away," she said. "I just figured I'd give you the option."

"It feels weird, sitting here watching you work while I eat."

"No one said you had to watch," she said. Her smile was light, but her blue eyes smoldered when they met his. "Unless that's your thing, of course."

"No—I've never been a fan of the sidelines." When it became clear she wasn't going to make this easy for him, he nodded to the table. "Put the work away and come sit with me."

She obliged without comment, putting the laptop back in its case before she chose a seat across from him at the table.

"You have everything set for tomorrow?" she asked.

The question brought the weight back to his shoulders.

"As much as possible."

"Good. We'll meet up with Monty and Carl in the morning. I'll be glad to know we have a little extra muscle behind us."

He nodded his agreement. "It's good that Diggs insisted on meeting here first. We might as well try to make sure we're all on the same page."

"You don't think tomorrow will go according to plan, then?"

He looked at her frankly, eyebrows raised. "Do you?"

"I don't know anything about these people," she said with a shrug. "Maybe they're all honorable, upstanding citizens."

"Right. Honorable, upstanding citizens who kidnap, lie, kill…."

"Or maybe not," she conceded. She watched him as he picked at his food, tearing off a piece of cooled tortilla and dipping it idly in the refried beans. "I have my reservations."

"That brings up an interesting point," he said, meeting her eye once more. He set the tortilla down on his plate without taking a bite. The room got quiet. As much as he'd enjoyed having Jamie on this trip—and there was no denying that he had enjoyed it, more than he cared to admit—he had been avoiding some fairly serious questions since they'd left Maine.

"Jack?" she pressed, when he didn't say anything.

"Why are you here?"

"Here in this room, here in this country… Here on the planet?" Despite her smile and the lightness in her tone, he saw a shade of unease in her eyes. "Sorry, you'll need to be more specific."

"You know what I mean. Why are you here with me? We barely know each other. You're not getting paid. You don't know Erin or her mother or Diggs well enough to justify sticking your neck out this far."

She shrugged. He liked the fact that she didn't break eye contact. Her slender throat moved when she swallowed. She wet her lips. "I didn't see anyone else lining up to help you."

"That wouldn't matter to most people."

"I'm not most people."

"No," he said, a residual heat still warming his blood. "You're not."

Their eyes locked, the heat intensifying. It was clear that she felt it, too—he could tell by the flush of color in her cheeks, the intensity of her blue eyes. After a moment, she dropped her gaze and nodded toward the dishes still between them.

"Are you going to eat all that?"

"You didn't eat earlier?"

"I did," she said. She pulled the tortillas toward her. "I'm still hungry. Late nights and deadly missions do that to me."

26
KAT

KAT HAD NO IDEA how long they traveled before she heard Jenny talking to the pilot about setting down. She'd dozed occasionally, her chin on her chest or else resting on Cameron's shoulder. Her hands had been bound so long that her arms ached and back screamed with tension—both physical and mental. Her lip was bloodied and her face bruised from close encounters with Jenny's temper. Which, it turned out, was formidable.

"When we set down, don't fight," Cameron whispered to her when they were alone, both Jenny and Lee up front with the pilot. "They'll blindfold us next. Probably gag us. If you fight, it will be worse for you."

He remained calm beside her. His mouth had stopped bleeding, but his lips and nose were crusted with dried blood.

"It doesn't feel like it could get much worse. When we land, I say we make a run for it while they're trying to move us."

He twisted his head to look at her with the faintest of smiles. "I don't recommend that. I know it's not your strong suit, but right now we need to be patient."

"Hey!" Lee lumbered back from the co-pilot's seat.

Cameron's bullet had merely grazed him back in the hotel room. At this point, he didn't show even a trace of pain. "No whispering. If you have something to say, you share it with the whole class."

"Apologies," Cameron said stiffly. He looked the man in the eye. "I was just talking about how pleased I'll be when I slit your throat."

The response caught Kat off guard—and Cameron, based on his gasp before he contained himself. Lee struck him twice, hard and fast, once in the kidney and once in the face. Cam's head snapped back. Blood hit Kat's cheek, warm and wet.

"What the hell is wrong with you?" Jenny roared from the front. She came back and knocked Lee soundly upside the head.

"He said he was going to slit my throat."

"Yeah, well—Keep that up and I'll do it for him," Jenny said. "Now, go on up front. Jesus. I have to do everything myself around here."

Jenny reclaimed the seat facing them and leaned forward, studying her father. "I know what you're doing, you know."

His nose was bleeding again, his face pale from the unexpected body blow. Still, somehow he managed to keep his tone even.

"Oh? And what's that, sweetheart?"

She shook her head, her jaw set. "You're trying to make me feel bad for you." The girl took a bottle of water and dumped a small amount on a handkerchief she produced from her bag. She slid forward in her seat and wiped the blood from her father's face. Kat caught the tenderness there, the flash of conflict, before Jenny could hide it. "It won't work, you know," she said.

Cameron nodded, holding his daughter's eye. "I know. Sorry."

She wiped his nose and mouth, her lips pressed in a thin line. "There's nothing I could do," she whispered. "Even if I wanted to. You chose this—not me. You made your bed."

Kat resisted the urge to speak, knowing it would break the fragile spell Cameron was weaving. She remained silent, hands bound, thinking of parents and children and the complicated bond between them.

She hadn't been prepared for it, giving birth to Erin at eighteen years old. Her father had cut her out of his life as soon as she told him she was staying on the island. When Kat told him she wasn't coming home—over the phone, too afraid of his reaction to do so in person—there had been a long silence on the other end of the line. He hung up without another word. When she tried to call back, he hung up again the moment he heard her voice. It was nine years before he even found out she'd had a child.

So, no, she hadn't been prepared to give birth. She sure as hell wasn't ready to be a mother—didn't even know what that meant, really. Her own mother died having her. Kat was raised on military bases, while her father played surgeon to soldiers at home and abroad. All she had been was terrified, when she realized she was pregnant. That terror grew teeth once she understood who Isaac Payson was; the way he controlled everyone around him.

Maddie, the best friend who had once invited trouble at every turn, was so deep under Isaac's spell that Kat couldn't imagine ever getting her back. The preacher treated her like crap, like some whore continually putting temptation in his path...and Maddie couldn't get enough of him. She wasn't the only one, either: Kat saw other women pass through his doors and follow him to the greenhouse late at night. Saw the way his wife just pretended she didn't notice. She saw how intent Isaac was on keeping other men away.

"We have to leave here," she'd whispered to Adam, lying together in his room one early morning. It was a month, maybe less, before her due date. Adam looked at her like she was the crazy one.

"I can't leave here, Katie—I've told you that from the start. I promise you, we are safe here."

"You're nuts if you believe that. You've seen what he does... How he treats people."

"He has problems, I know. We all do. But he's created a place for these people out here—that isn't easy. Everyone has their weaknesses."

Like they were talking about Isaac having a goddamn sweet tooth, instead of screwing every girl who crossed his path. Adam saw the look in her eye, how furious he'd made her, and immediately looked contrite.

"I know it's hard for you. I know this isn't what you would have chosen for your life," he said. "You'd rather be headed to college right now, instead of being stuck with someone like me."

And of course she'd fallen for it, assuring him that she wouldn't want to be anywhere else on the planet. That he was the only one for her. Their voices had been soft, whispering in the sanctity of the bedroom they had shared since the wedding ceremony Isaac had performed six months earlier. Adam kissed her enormous belly, her tender breasts.

"I promise you, Katie: I'll keep you safe here. I'll never survive off the island, but I can control Isaac for you and the baby. We'll be all right."

It took only a few months before they both learned how wrong he was.

●

After Jenny tended to her father, she pulled out a roll of duct tape and tore off two short strips. She looked nearly apologetic when she stuck one across Cameron's mouth, but she was downright gleeful when she gagged Kat. The fear built in Kat's chest. When Lee handed Jenny two black hoods, that fear turned to panic.

Jenny saw it in her eyes before Kat could hide it. The girl smiled at her, her full lips twisting into a sneer. "Don't worry, Kat. This will be over before you know it."

She pulled the hood down over Kat's face. For a few seconds, Kat fought against it—reduced to grunts and whimpers, trying to escape a darkness that seemed all-consuming; a black that came from within and spread. Cameron pressed his arm against hers, reminding her of his presence. She forced herself to calm down. Take shallow breaths. Go somewhere else. She could watch all of it from above, from a place where the pain and the fear couldn't touch her. God knew she'd done it before, in circumstances every bit as bad as these.

She would survive this.

When the plane landed, she and Cameron were manhandled down the stairs and over uneven ground, to a waiting car. Bound and gagged, the hood still over their faces, they were pushed roughly into the backseat. Kat had no idea where they were, but within a few minutes they were on the move again.

When they reached their destination hours later, Kat felt the car slowly come to a stop. In the distance, she could hear kids shouting—in play, not anger, based on the bursts of laughter accompanying those shouts. The air inside the hood was stifling, her throat parched from too many hours with her mouth duct taped shut. Cameron was still beside her, equally silent, the warmth of his arm against hers one of the only things keeping her grounded.

Once they were stopped, her car door opened and someone took her arm roughly. Jenny—she could tell by the nails digging into her skin; the sickly sweet smell of her perfume.

"Time for a little walk," she said, holding tight to Kat's arm. Kat felt the barrel of a gun jammed into her side. There was the dense, ripe smell of verdant jungle all around them, the world alive with night sounds: the high-pitched scream of monkeys; the rustle of something moving through the brush nearby; a thousand unidentifiable screeches, calls, and cries.

As they walked along a rough path, Jenny pointed out obstructions for Kat to step over or walk around. Kat could hear people behind them—she assumed Cameron, though he didn't speak.

After they'd walked long enough for her lungs to burn, her tongue swollen and bone dry in her mouth, Jenny came to an abrupt halt.

"He wants them alive," Kat heard Lee whisper, somewhere to her left. "That means they need water. And you can't keep a hood on them this whole time—not in this heat. They'll suffocate."

"I don't want to spend the next sixteen hours staring at them," Jenny bit out. Kat thought again of how uncomfortable the girl had been in the plane, looking her father in the eye.

"I'll handle watching them, then," Lee said. "You should get some rest, anyway. He wouldn't be happy knowing you've been up this long."

Kat had no idea who 'he' was. She had never known all the players in this game—she'd never wanted to. She learned enough to ensure her and Erin's survival, and then she let it go. Now, though, she found herself going back over all those names: Isaac and Jonah; Jim Jones himself; Cameron and his wife, Susan; a man named Mandrake, whom she had never met; Adam. Other factions had been revealed in the past year, but Kat had never known about any of that. Adam had assured her years ago that the killing was over after Jonestown. Stupidly, she had believed him.

There was a brief silence before Jenny spoke again, reluctance plain in the tone. "Yeah—okay, fine. But if you need anything…."

"I'll call," Lee assured her.

Kat heard footsteps retreating. A moment later, a hand tugged at the hood over her head. It was dark outside, but that darkness was nothing compared with the pure black she'd been immersed in. Lee eyed her dispassionately. She realized quickly that this hadn't been a show of mercy on his part. He really was just keeping them alive under orders from above.

Well, that didn't matter. She would take what she could get, and make the most of it.

Cameron stood a few feet apart from her, the hood still over his head. Lee pulled the tape from Kat's mouth roughly, unconcerned at her cry of pain. The duct tape had been on long enough to bind with her skin—one pull and the sensitive flesh at her cheeks and jaw tore like paper. Tears sprang to her eyes. She pushed them far, far down.

Cameron received the same treatment, though he made no sound when the tape was removed. They were both given water, then led to a stucco block of a building at the end of the trail. Lee kept a gun on them both as he gestured them up a single, high step and inside.

It was black inside, the darkness broken only by moonlight streaming in through a single narrow window high off the ground.

"We'll come for you tomorrow," Lee said when they were both inside. "If you scream, no one will hear you—and I'll be forced to come in and put the tape back on."

Her cheek still wept blood from the first round. Kat shook her head. "You won't need to. I won't scream."

Lee looked pleased, a flicker of sadistic pleasure in his eyes at the power he obviously wielded over them both. Kat fought to keep any sign of anger from her eyes, knowing that kind of thing only fueled men like this.

When they were alone in the room, seated on a hard concrete floor facing the only entrance, she turned to look at Cameron. Her eyes had adjusted to the darkness now, reading the light and shadow in a way she couldn't ever remember doing before. Not that what she saw inspired much hope: one barred, narrow window high up; concrete floor with a hand woven rug at its center; single exit, no doubt guarded. She noticed, however, that Cameron seemed strangely at peace.

"You look pretty goddamn cheery for a man beaten half to death."

"That's because we're leaving."

"Because in addition to being a heartless brainwashed assassin, you're also Harry Houdini?"

"Not at all." He smiled at her. "Just be patient."

It wasn't her strong suit, but she gave it a shot, watching as Cameron squirmed himself back against the wall and then used it to leverage himself to a standing position. Then, he moved with his back to the wall, patting down the stucco with his bound hands as he went. Kat watched in silence, convinced he'd finally lost his mind. After sixty years, J had finally pushed him too far.

Halfway across the room, he stopped. He smiled at her, using his bound hands to work something set into the wall. A piece of stucco clattered to the floor, echoing in the closed space. He paused a second, both of them holding their breath.

No one came.

Another thirty seconds was all it took for Cameron to free himself and return to her side, a knife gleaming in his hand. It took another minute for him to cut through the rope that bound her wrists. Gratefully, Kat stretched her arms in front of her, shaking her wrists out to restore circulation.

"You mind telling me what the hell is going on?"

"In time. Right now, go to the door and see if you can hear them."

She did as directed, pressing her ear to the wood. Outside, Lee was arguing with another of their captors—a male voice, so clearly not Jenny. She gave Cameron the report and he nodded, his face once more a mask of focus and impenetrable calm.

He flipped up the rug at the center of the room. In all the years she had known him, Kat had never seen the man smile wider.

"What the hell are you doing?"

"I told you: we're leaving."

A small trapdoor was concealed beneath the rug. Cameron pulled it up with a deafening creak that, Kat was sure, had been heard all the way across the jungle.

"What is this?" she hissed at him.

"I'll explain soon. Just stay quiet—we'll be traveling directly beneath them for a couple of minutes before we're done."

The darkness in the room was nothing compared to the black tunnel below. Kat watched as Cameron climbed down a wooden ladder and, moments later, was swallowed in the depths.

She followed without a word or a backward glance.

●

The tunnel was damp and dark and Kat could hear things crawling along the walls, skittering at their feet. Her body ached. The skin around her mouth was still raw. Cameron retrieved a pistol and a lantern hanging on the cave wall once they reached the bottom of the ladder, but Kat wasn't sure being able to see the creepy crawlies around them was an improvement.

"Where do we go now?" she whispered. "We need to reach Erin and let her know what happened."

"I'm not sure we'll be able to. We can try, but finding a way to communicate with them out here will be difficult."

"How do you know about this place, anyway?" she asked. "What is it?"

"Drug runners used to stay here. Mandrake knew about it, somehow or other. Susan and I used to bring Jenny here."

"So Jenny knew about the escape route?"

A flash of life, maybe even hope, crossed Cameron's face. "She did," he said. "Her putting us there was no accident."

"She let us go," Kat said, not believing it for a second. "Why the hell would she let us go? Why the hell would she let *me* go?"

"She knew I wouldn't go without you," he said simply. "I told you she wouldn't be able to go through with it. Susan did what she could to make her hard, but you can't erase everything."

"No," Kat said. She studied the man before her, this strange mix of integrity and brutality. "I guess you can't."

They continued in silence. The tunnel wasn't elaborate, and got smaller the deeper they got. Before long, they were both forced to their hands and knees to continue, Kat following behind Cameron in an inch or more of water the whole way. He stopped at one point, signaling her to do the same. She could hear voices nearby—above them, she thought, though the acoustics in the closed space made them hard to pinpoint. Something skittered across her hand, then crawled up her arm. Kat willed herself to stay silent until the voices faded. As soon as they were gone, she brushed at her arms and clothing, then raked her hands through her hair in search of mite-sized monsters.

"Are there scorpions down here?" she whispered to Cameron.

"Probably. Just don't think about it."

"Right. What an idiot—why didn't I think of that?"

"The great Doctor Everett isn't really afraid of bugs, is she?" he asked over his shoulder.

"The great Doctor Everett is afraid of anything that can kill her with a touch of its tail. I don't think that's unreasonable."

"We'll be out soon, Katherine."

Not soon enough, she thought.

Still, Kat managed to keep it together until the end, when that inch of water they'd been crawling through became at least a foot deep as the tunnel opened up. The moon shone through a hole at the top of the cave, a pale white slice of light illuminating a world brimming with life.

"What is this?" she asked Cameron. He stood, the water to his knees now, and helped Kat to her feet.

"A cenote. There's a way out just ahead."

Just ahead, across an expanse of murky blue-green water. Above them, she heard the flap and flutter of bats either returning from, or leaving for, their nightly hunt.

"How do we get over there?" she asked, already dreading the answer.

"Swim, of course. It's not far—and it's perfectly safe.

People swim down here all the time."

"I know that. But they don't do it in the middle of the night."

"Maybe not. But the same things are in the water now as would be here at two in the afternoon. You'll be all right."

"What do we do when we get to the other side?" she asked. That was the harder question, she realized. They had no way to contact Erin. No map. No clothes, other than the ones on their backs.

"I've got everything under control. Take off your shoes," Cameron said. "And whatever else you want to keep dry."

"Why? Are you planning on levitating them across?"

He shined the light in her eyes, an impatient grimace on his thin lips. "You're impossible, you know. Just do it."

Since she would rather keep every damn stitch of clothing she had as dry as possible, she stripped to nothing without batting an eyelash. She'd half expected Cameron to get flustered, maybe blush and turn away—honestly, shocking him was half the reason she'd done it in the first place. Instead, she noted with some interest the even way that he watched her; the way his eyes roamed her body, the faintest flicker of heat in them when their gazes met. He stripped to boxer briefs, his own body sinewy and lean, the muscles defined in his legs and arms. His chest was broader than she had expected.

He caught her staring and smiled, holding her gaze for another moment before he nodded toward the water. "We should go. We don't have much time before Lee figures out what happened."

"What happens to Jenny then?"

A shadow crossed his face. "Nothing good, but she can take care of herself. She'll have to. I'll go back for her as soon as I can. Now, stop stalling and get in there already. Please."

Holding her breath, Kat eased into the water. It was

warm and it was wet, but those were really the best things she could say about it. Something below the surface brushed against her foot. She pushed herself to get across quickly.

You're the most fearless woman I've ever met, she remembered Adam telling her once, years before. She hadn't told him then how wrong he was; that she was only fearless because that's what he needed. She was strong because he was terrified most of the time—of the past and the future, the dark and the light, the ghosts that haunted him and the people he swore would torture him, kill him, if he was ever found.

Kat had always been strong, but she became indestructible, hard as steel, when she was with Adam. She'd never had the luxury of weakness, where he was concerned.

"We're almost there," Cameron said. He floated on his back, their clothes held above him in one hand.

Kat dove under without a word, eyes open, and stared down the darkness. She brushed past eyeless white fish and other cave dwellers, ignored the memories that haunted her, and finally reached the other side. Once there, she pulled herself onto a rock slick with bat guano. She took the bundle from Cameron when he reached her and watched as he climbed out himself, his body dripping.

"And now," she prompted as soon as he was back on dryish land. "You said you had a plan?"

"I do. You'll want to get dressed first, though."

The air was cooler now, a humid breeze blowing in from the opening above. Bats continued to fly in and out in droves, occasionally diving low enough to make her consider jumping back in the water. Cameron was right: clothes were a good idea.

When they were both fully dressed again, Kat's clothes damp but certainly more comfortable than standing there stark naked, she indicated the cave exit above with a wave of her hand.

"All right, now what? We have no vehicle, no way to communicate, no money..."

"True," he agreed. "But we're free. And unhurt." He stepped forward, taking her by surprise. His hand rose to touch the raw skin around her mouth with infinite care. "Relatively, anyway. I'm sorry about that—Jenny's angry. Hurt. Susan spent a lot of time convincing her that you and Erin were to blame when I walked away from the marriage." The color rose in his cheeks. "Which was absurd, of course."

"Of course," she agreed, ignoring the sudden, inexplicable up-tick in her own heartbeat. "It doesn't matter, anyway. I'm fine. I just want to find Erin, let her know that I'm all right, and get us all the hell out of here."

"Jenny won't let anything go until she has the information Erin is holding. That's going to make disappearing considerably more difficult. I wish I'd known about that before I left her at Raven's Ledge."

"Do you have any idea what it might be?" she asked. "This information she says she has?"

He hesitated. "There was someone at Smithfield College, down in Kentucky—Professor Munjoy. He'd started work investigating Jim Jones a few years ago. That ultimately led him to a number of other...concerns, related to the Project."

"And so the information on that card was what he pieced together?"

Cameron shook his head, a flicker of remorse touching his eyes before it vanished. "No. Munjoy was never meant to see the information on that card. He had a source who had been supplying him with details about the Project. He stole the card from that source."

"That source being?" Kat prompted.

Cameron wet his lips, his jaw hardening. "Me," he said shortly. "I was the source. I'd been feeding Munjoy information, trying to plant a seed that could ultimately expose the Project in a way that law enforcement and mainstream media could not, since both are too easily manipulated by those in power."

"So, they killed Munjoy," Kat finished for him. "Using Reverend Barnel and his church to do it. Did J know you were the one supplying him with information?"

"Not until Erin got involved. At least, I don't believe they knew. But now…."

"Now, they know," Kat said. "And now Jenny's supposed to get that information from Erin, no matter what it takes."

"Which is why we need to get to Erin and Diggs, before that happens."

Kat nodded, setting her jaw with grim determination. Ignoring fatigue and the pervasive ache of tired, admittedly aging bones, she squared her shoulders and eyed the exit.

"All right," she said with a humorless smile. "Let's go find my kid, before your kid tears her eyes out."

27
SOLOMON

SLEEPING BESIDE DIGGS that night in Mexico, I dreamed of Allie Tate and Payson Isle again. This time, though, she didn't come to me in flashes. Instead, she appeared as clearly as anything I'd ever seen, her brown hair pulled back in a ponytail, her thick glasses reflecting the sun. She held out her hand.

"Isaac says you can see now. He wants you to come to the woods, too."

I stayed rooted to the spot, frozen. Terrified.

"You said you want to see," Allie said.

She pulled me down the path, limping, occasionally looking back at me with a kind of childish glee. The night got darker. I couldn't hear anything—the world silent in a way I'd never experienced before. And then, rising from the ground, I heard it: a low, animal moan. Isaac's raised voice. *These are the secrets we can never tell*, I heard my father say.

Suddenly, I wasn't holding Allie's hand anymore—I was holding my dad's.

We walked farther into the woods. When we reached the clearing, Allie was on the ground. Her glasses were broken, her leg bent backward beneath her.

Isaac stood over her, his eyes blood red: Vengeance personified. I screamed when he knelt beside her, forcing her down. His hands pinned her shoulders, his body over hers. My father pushed me toward them. I fought him, trying to get away, screaming for Allie. I could hear her crying. Could hear Isaac's breath, low and rasping. I could feel his eyes on me.

"He won't hurt you, Erin," my father said. "You can trust him. I wouldn't stay if you weren't safe. You can trust us."

But when I looked at my father, his eyes were as red as Isaac's. His hands were covered with blood.

"These are the secrets we can never tell, baby."

I fought as my father got closer, trying to wake up—trying to pull myself out of those woods.

"Erin—you're safe, it's okay. Come back to me. It was just a dream."

I woke to Diggs' voice, soft in my ear. I scrambled up and away from him, my heart thudding in my ears, pain piercing my side at the sudden movement. When he touched me, I flinched.

"No one will hurt you here," he said softly, as though soothing some feral beast. "It was just a dream, Sol."

"Easy for you to say," I mumbled when I finally found my voice. My hands were shaking when I ran them through my hair. Fear ran through me like shards of glass coursing through my veins. We sat there quietly for a few minutes. Diggs made no move to touch me again.

"You want to talk about it?" he asked, finally.

I shook my head, still unable to reach for him. The pain burned in my side, only slightly more potent than the fire in my gut.

"I remember," I said hollowly, when I could finally speak.

"The island?" A shadow crossed his face at my nod. It hit home for the first time just how long he'd been dreading this moment. "How much?"

"I don't know. I mean…not everything. It's still blurry. But I know Isaac wasn't a good man. I know what happened to people who disobeyed him. What happened to my father. My best friend there…." It felt like someone was sitting on my chest. I slowed. Tried to get my breath. Diggs sat back, giving me time. "She was this girl. This skinny little kid with glasses. And I saw them… There was a place in the woods where he would take sinners, to punish them. I saw him with Allie. She broke her leg, trying to get away… But he wouldn't let her go."

My voice shook, but my eyes were dry. Diggs raked his hand over his hair, still eying me as I shivered. The clock by the bed read five a.m. I thought of Einstein, and a lump lodged in my throat. In the real world, my everyday former life, I would have my bed and my things and my dog… Everything I needed to soothe myself, keep me on an even plane. I had Diggs now, but it felt too naked to lean on him right now. Too raw.

"He hurt her," I said, finally. My stomach rolled. I forced myself to stay with the memory, trying to sort through it. "I think… I think he might have killed her, Diggs."

Silence fell. I sat on the bed shaking. Sick. And suddenly, I knew. It wasn't memory so much as knowledge:

Isaac had killed Allie.

He'd murdered her, in the woods that day.

I closed my eyes. Ground the heel of my hands into them. I don't know if I was trying to force the images up, or erase them completely. I felt Diggs' hand on my back, rubbing in small, soothing circles. I was going crazy. All those memories I had of Allie: The two of us playing together. Her limping along beside me. Rooting through the house, looking through Isaac's stuff….

Were they even real?

Why had I really been sent from Payson Isle?

"Sol?" Diggs whispered. When he pulled me to him this time, I didn't fight him. I leaned against his chest, my ear pressed to his heart.

"I don't even know what's real anymore," I said. "Those memories of me with my father.... The people I loved out there.... How safe I felt.... It was all just some psychotic mind fuck."

"This is real," he said. He pulled back and kissed my forehead. My nose. Looked me in the eye. "We'll figure out the rest, Erin. Whatever happened out there, you can handle it."

I laughed. Sort of. "Yeah, right. You're not the one whose childhood turns out to have been some kind of psychedelic fairy tale."

"True," he said. He smiled. Again—sort of. "But it could be worse, right?"

I arched an eyebrow, waiting for the punchline. "How's that, exactly?"

"I don't know. It was the '80s. You could have been raised by Rick Astley fans."

This time, I really did laugh. It hurt like hell.

Diggs held me for a few minutes, the two of us quiet on the bed, before he pulled away and kissed my forehead. Then, he got up. His boxers rode low on his hips—low enough to distract me momentarily, despite everything. Sensing the shift, he managed a slip of a grin.

"Not too traumatized to ogle; I guess that's a good sign. Come on. Get dressed."

"We're not meeting the others until ten."

"I'm aware of that."

"Then why do I need to get dressed now?"

"Because I'm asking you to."

"But why? It's still dark out."

"Is it?" he asked, rolling his eyes. "I hadn't realized.

Come on, sweetheart. Up and at 'em. Just because you've got a couple bullet holes and a childhood of nightmarish repressed memories doesn't mean you should waste a sunset in Mexico."

I groaned, but I did as he asked. I figured considering all he'd given up and gone through for me in the past several months, it was the least I could do. When I started to put on yoga pants, he told me I needed shorts instead. And he still wouldn't tell me why.

I put on shorts.

Love is hell.

The air was cool when we left the hotel, the beach out front empty. We'd packed everything, and I felt a twinge of fear at the thought that Diggs had probably been right the day before: This would likely be the last chance we'd have to stay somewhere like this. Wherever we were going next, we weren't headed for the lap of luxury. Without Kat or with her, whether Jenny lived or died, whether my father showed up or remained lost, anyway you sliced it, Diggs and I would be fugitives when the day was done.

And in all likelihood, we would be fugitives for a good, long while.

We got in the truck and drove north along the coast. I didn't point out that we were headed in the wrong direction, figuring Diggs was well aware. He took a very badly paved road about half an hour from the hotel, and parked in a small dirt parking lot not too far in.

"We don't have much time."

"Much time for what?" He didn't answer. Instead, he came around to my side of the truck and opened the door, helping me out. The sky was just beginning to lighten. I could smell salt and sand and the sweet tang of pot in the air.

"No questions," he said before I could ask. "Here—just lean on me."

"Lean on you for what?"

"What part of no questions do you not understand, woman?"

I got out of the truck.

Pride kept me from taking his help, but he kept a watchful eye as I limped along beside him. We broke through a short, densely forested trail to find ourselves on the beach. A big beach. A beautiful beach. A few clusters of people—surfers mostly—rode gentle swells along the shore, but otherwise things were quiet. Diggs told me to wait, then jogged over to a group around a bonfire just beginning to die out. They talked for a few minutes before he dug out some pesos for them. A minute later, he returned to me.

"What are you doing?" I asked.

"I rented a board from them. Come on."

"Did you forget the part where I have a couple of extra holes in me, or are we just ignoring that now?"

"Just trust me."

Right.

I followed reluctantly behind as he said something else to the surfers, then helped himself to one of their boards. It wasn't a surfboard, though—not by a long shot. Instead, the board Diggs carried was twice the width and a couple of feet longer than your standard long board.

"You're taking me paddle boarding? Because, again... Bullet holes."

"Would you just trust me for once? Enjoy the morning. Don't ask questions—which, I know, is completely contrary to your nature."

"All thanks to your stellar tutelage, Diggins."

He dropped his shoes and his t-shirt in the sand. On the horizon, the sun was just beginning to rise, the sky burning deep gold above the pale blue sea. Diggs waded to his knees, floating the paddle board behind him.

"Hop on."

I looked at him blankly. "What do you mean?"

"I thought it was pretty clear: Hop. On. Get on the board, ace."

"I'm not supposed to get my bandages wet."

"Which is why I'm telling you to get *on* the board, not under it. You trust me?"

"It depends on the circumstances."

He grinned at that. "Bullshit—you trust me. You know I'm not going to do anything to put you in danger. Now, hop on."

I waded out to him. The water was warmer than the air, instantly soothing frazzled muscles and frayed nerves. Gentle swells lapped at my calves. He helped me onto the board with minimal pain and very little rocking, then Diggs instructed me to settle in toward the front of the board.

"Now what?" I asked, once I was seated.

He hopped aboard easily, showing nary a tremble in his strong calves as he positioned himself toward the back and began to paddle us out.

A light sea spray wet my face as we moved farther and farther from shore. Diggs was right: I trusted him. If I ever needed proof, this was it. I sat calmly breathing in the sweet ocean air, no doubt in my mind that I was safe with him. The shore was still in sight but far off when Diggs stopped. He laid the paddle down and sat behind me, his hands at my sides, his legs spread so that his body cradled mine.

"What are we doing?" I asked.

He pointed over my shoulder, where the sunrise had turned from gold to deep pink. Something broke the surface of the water: A dorsal fin; the gentle curve of a dolphin's body. My breath caught.

"How did you know they'd be here?"

"Lucky guess. Sunrise is one of their favorite times,

and I've been here once or twice. I knew if we came out far enough, we'd find them."

For the next half hour, we sat in silence, watching the sun rise while a pod of dolphins leapt and dove, sometimes coming as close as a few feet away. The air got warmer. The sun rose higher. Diggs never moved from his spot behind me, rock steady. I could feel his heartbeat, combining with the movement of the waves beneath us to create a rhythm that was sensual and soothing by turns.

By the time the sun was up, I'd forgotten the pain in my side and the fear of what was to come.

When the last of the dolphins were gone and the sun was up, I forced myself to shake the spell. "We should probably get back," I said.

"Yeah," Diggs agreed. He hesitated. Diggs isn't usually the kind of man to monitor his words, but it was clear he was doing that now.

I leaned back against him, loving the power and warmth of his chest and arms. "You have something you want to say, clearly. How about you spill it now, before we drift any farther out to sea?"

He thought for another minute or two, then brushed his lips along my neck before he spoke. His arms tightened around me.

"I was thinking, last night—about the before and the after. That line in life, when everything changes."

I twisted to look at him, ignoring the twinge in my side. I didn't speak, letting him continue in his own time. He wet his lips, brow furrowed. Still thinking it through.

"It's that moment that you never see coming until it's already passed. For me, there's the day my brother died—before that day and after it are two different animals. The day I got clean... The day I met you. The night we made love for the first time."

"The fire on Payson Isle," I said. I took his hand, stroking his long fingers absently as the memories washed over me. "The day I went to live with Kat. The first time you and I kissed."

"The before and the after," Diggs repeated. "You can never predict how things will change when you're still living in the before, you know?"

"And you think right now we're living in the before?" I asked.

I could feel him nodding behind me, his head brushing lightly against mine. "I do."

"And after today, everything changes," I said. I tightened my hands on his thighs, fear building in my chest.

"Not everything," he said. His certainty grounded me. "Some things won't change. The way I feel about you—what we have. Wherever we are, whatever happens... that will stay the same."

"You don't know that. You just said we're living in the before. And you can't predict what happens in the after when you're living in the before."

I could feel his smile against my neck. "God, you're a pain in the ass. It won't change, okay? Before, after, or in between, no matter how hard I try to fight it, I'm in love with you."

"And we're in this together."

The smile broadened to a grin. He kissed my ear. "And we're in this together," he agreed. "But I just want to take a few minutes to enjoy this... What we have now. Before it changes."

For a few minutes, I focused on doing what he'd asked—on marking the moment, staying with him without a thought of what had come before or what would come next.

The waves rocked us gently, the water lapped at the board, and Diggs held me close as the sun beat down and the air heated and time passed.

Too much time.

Finally, I squeezed his leg and took a deep breath.

"Okay. I'm with you. Now what?"

I could almost feel him gearing up for the shift we both knew was coming. "Now, we move forward. Whatever comes next."

He stood, got the paddle, and pointed us back to shore. As we got closer, I was surprised to find peace give way to a sense of focus I'd been lacking until then. Whatever was about to come, it would happen whether I was prepared or not. Better to meet it head on with Diggs by my side than to fight it any longer.

●

A cluster of miscreants were waiting for us when we got back to shore: Jamie, Juarez, Monty, and Carl. I was shaky on my feet and already in pain despite our reprieve, but Diggs provided a supportive arm when I stumbled. Beyond that, though, I felt clearer than I had in months.

"We thought you'd left us," Monty said when we were within hearing range. They all remained seated, lounging in the sand. "Figured Diggs was just gonna run you out to sea with him somewhere."

"I was tempted," Diggs said, then nodded to the paddle board under his arm. "Let me just return this. I'll be right back."

When he was gone, I lowered myself carefully into the sand with the others. "Thank you for coming," I said. "I really appreciate this. I know you didn't have to."

"And miss out on recon in sunny Me-Hico?" Monty asked. "Forget it. It beats freezing my balls off in Maine. Now… what's the plan, senorita?"

I looked at Juarez, surprised. "You haven't gone over it yet?"

"We have," he assured me. "But we want to make sure everyone is on the same page."

"Right." I agreed. "Okay, well… Diggs and I are booked for a commuter flight to Valladolid at noon. We'll rent a car and drive to Coba from there. The meeting time is six o'clock. Then—"

My cell phone rang before I could finish my itinerary. The steadiness I'd felt seconds before took a serious hit.

"Did you get a good night's sleep?" Jenny asked as soon as I'd said hello. The words were no surprise, but there was something about her tone—a tension I was sure I hadn't heard before.

"I've had better," I said. "Why are you calling? Did something happen?"

"Not at all," she said, too fast. Something was wrong. I could feel it; could hear it in her voice. "There's just been a little change in plan, that's all. New meeting time. Same location, but we're pushing it back. Ten o'clock tonight."

"What?" I said, just shy of shouting the word. "You agreed on six—"

"And now I'm changing it. Use your friend's plane and you can get here in plenty of time for a little sightseeing before we meet."

I hesitated. It was a good move on her part: I was instantly on the defensive, Jenny fully in control. "My friend?"

"You think I don't know you're with Juarez and that cute blonde friend of his? Give me a break. I told you—I know every move you make. It doesn't matter, as long as you don't try to bring the cops into this. I'll see you in Coba."

"Wait! What the hell is going on? I want to talk to Kat—"

"Forget it," Jenny said abruptly. "I'm done playing games. Be there at ten, or Kat dies. And I'll send her back to you piece by piece. Capiche?"

She hung up.

Diggs returned just after we had disconnected, the phone still in my hand. I couldn't figure out whether I was pissed off or just plain terrified.

"Was that Jenny?" Diggs asked.

"She changed the time. The exchange is at ten now... And she said we could use Jamie's plane."

"How does she know about Jamie?" Juarez asked.

"No idea. She's got to have someone following us. Or… I don't know," I finished lamely, thinking of spy satellites and hidden cameras, microscopic listening devices and the rise of Big Brother. Or, the more disturbing answer: Someone in our group was leaking information.

"Why is she changing it at the last minute?" Diggs asked, directing the question to Juarez.

"To shake you up, I would assume," Juarez said. "Re-establish the fact that she's in control."

"There was something different about her today, though," I said. "Like she *wasn't* in control." I paused, forcing myself to consider what that could mean. "I think something happened."

"You don't know that," Diggs said. "Juarez is right: She's had us by the shorthairs from the start. This is just another power play—she gets off on this shit."

"What did she say when you asked to talk to Kat?" Juarez asked.

"She just cut me off—said we needed to be there at ten or she'd start sending Kat back to me piece by piece. That's a quote, incidentally."

"She's trying to psych you out," Diggs said.

"Well, she's doing a damn good job," I said. "I'm so sick of waiting for this freaking thing. I just want it over."

"If she's shifting things around, she's doing it for a reason," Juarez said. "Even if that reason is just to prove she has the control. I don't like the idea that she's calling all the shots here. It's not as though you aren't bringing something to the table."

"What do you suggest? That I send up a smoke signal with my counter-offer and hope she gets the picture? Forget it—I'm not risking Kat's life by playing games."

"You're risking *everyone's* life by following her rules," Juarez insisted. "There's no way you can call her back?"

"None. This has always been on her terms. The only other option is to sit here and wait for her to call when I don't show up tonight." Juarez looked like he didn't think that was the worst idea in the world. I shook my head. "No. I'm not sitting around anymore. You guys can hang out here waiting for a call, but I'll do whatever Jenny wants if it means I get Kat back safely and end this thing."

"You're not going alone," Diggs said. "I'm in."

Juarez didn't look surprised by his decision. He didn't look especially happy, either. He looked at Monty and Carl.

"I didn't come all this way to sit around jerking off in the sand," Monty said. "I'm ready to have a little fun."

"I'm in," Carl agreed.

Jamie retrieved her backpack and stood, dusting the sand from her butt. "All right, then. Let's do this."

Diggs helped me up, but I told him to go on without me. As the others were walking away, I caught Jamie's elbow. "Can you hang on a second?"

She let the others go ahead.

"What's up?"

"Do you have a dollar?"

She looked confused, but she pulled a change purse from her bag anyway. I stuffed the worn buck she gave me in my pocket, and handed her a folded piece of paper I'd been carrying around for the past day. Diggs was right: We needed to be ready for whatever was coming next.

"What is this?"

"A bill of sale," I said. "You need a new base of operations, right? I just happen to own an island. It's in Penobscot Bay—plenty of acreage, maybe slightly haunted, but it has a couple of outbuildings and a huge house, great land... It's all yours."

"What? You can't give me your island." She tried to push the paper back in my hand. I wouldn't take it.

"The taxes are paid up. No zoning, no problems with noise or neighbors."

"Erin, you don't have to—"

"Yes, actually," I interrupted. "I do. Whatever happens today, Diggs and I won't be back for a while. The island might as well be doing something useful. I just have one request."

She didn't say anything, waiting for me to continue. Which I happily would have done, if I could have swallowed past the lump in my throat. Finally, I pulled myself together enough to speak.

"I'd like you to go back to Sally's and get Einstein. Keep him with you until I get back. I think he'd be better off with you—happier."

She didn't argue. Apparently, even an outsider could tell there was no way life was going back to normal when this day was over. "It's done," she said seriously.

"Thank you."

Before I could break away and try to catch up to Diggs, Jamie touched my wrist—carefully, as though she knew it was already a sore spot. When I looked at her, her eyes had gone dark.

"I know we don't know each other," she said. "Not really. What you're doing is important, though."

"Thanks," I said awkwardly. She still wouldn't let me go.

"The next year will be hard," she continued. "You'll lose more than you can imagine, in this fight. You just need to know what you're doing isn't for nothing."

The reporter side of my brain kicked in, pushing aside my discomfort. "How do you know that? Do you have some connection to this that Jack doesn't know about?"

She lowered her eyes. Let go of my arm. The darkness disappeared. "No," she said. "I don't have any connection to this. I just…" She looked embarrassed.

"You just what?" I pressed.

"You ladies coming or what?" Diggs called to us.

"We're coming," Jamie called back. When she met my eye again, a wall had gone up. There was something oddly vulnerable about her now. "Sorry. I didn't mean to freak you out. Don't worry about Einstein. He'll be in good hands, I promise."

And then, she walked off without another word.

My arm was still warm where she'd touched it. I thought of the dolphins. The feel of Diggs' arms around me. The sight of my father, coming toward me after a decade away… The Before and the After.

You'll lose more than you can imagine.

"Sol?" Diggs said, walking back toward me. "You all right?"

"Yeah," I said. I stepped up the pace, shaking off whatever the hell had just happened. "I'm okay." I took a breath. Diggs eyed me with eyebrows raised. I didn't need another heart-to-heart, though—I just needed this to be over.

"Let's go get Kat," I said. "And then, let's get the hell out of town."

28
KAT

DESPITE THEIR BEST INTENTIONS, ultimately Kat and Cameron spent the rest of the night and most of the next morning lost and running. Kat was covered with bites and scrapes and scratches, her body aching with hunger and fatigue. Cam didn't look much better, though he held up well. Every hour or so, he would stop, shimmy up the nearest palm tree, and select the greenest coconut he could find. He used his Swiss army knife to drill into one of the coconut 'eyes,' then promptly handed it to Kat. The first time, she'd looked at him like he was insane. By the time the night was out, she accepted the gifts without question and drank deeply.

It was eleven o'clock before they finally found any semblance of civilization. By that time, the sun was up. The air sizzled. A cluster of grass-roofed huts lined a dusty road. Goats and chickens roamed free, a couple of mangy dogs slinking from yard to yard. Kids shouted, kicking a partially-deflated soccer ball in the dust.

All shouts came to a stop when the two limping, bloodied Gringos came into view, however. Cameron approached a stout, wary-eyed woman in a white dress as she primed an old fashioned water pump, chickens pecking the ground at her feet. Cam spoke to her in rapid Spanish, using a regional dialect Kat wasn't familiar with.

The woman shook her head, responding to Cameron in a rapidf-ire, near-identical dialect. Kat was fluent in Spanish, but she could barely follow their conversation.

The woman gestured to the water pump, picking up half an emptied coconut shell. She mimed drinking, then dumped the empty shell over her head, scrubbing at her arms. Kat nodded gratefully. A drink of contaminated water and a sponge bath in the wide open spaces sounded heavenly at the moment.

Cameron smiled and nodded, then promptly grabbed Kat the moment the woman's back was turned. A full half-shell of water was already in Kat's hand.

"Unless you want to add dysentery to our growing list of problems, I suggest you put that down," he said. "You've had enough fluid to keep you hydrated so far. We'll find something else soon."

"What kind of idiot do you think I am?" she snapped. "I've done Doctors Without Borders for years... I think I know enough not to drink the water."

"Sorry," he said. He let her go. "I just didn't want to run the risk..."

"I know." She eyed the water pump and the old plastic bucket beside it, the chickens and the goats and the mangy dogs. She shook her head with a sigh, and began to undress. "You know, half my stints with Doctors seem glamorous compared to the past twenty-four hours."

"You lived on Payson Isle, though," he said conversationally. He pulled up a patch of dirt and sat painfully. Despite the fact that Kat was down to bra and underwear, he showed no inclination to give her any privacy. "You must have gotten used to roughing it there."

No running water and a lack of flush toilets was hardly a match for what they'd been through in the past twelve hours, but she knew what he was fishing for. "You have something you want to ask me, Cam?"

"No," he said. He removed his shoes, then spared an inquiring glance up at her. His feet were bloody, she noted, with blisters big enough to make a grown man cry. He'd never said a word. "I just... I always understood how Adam got sucked into Isaac's insanity. I could never quite see you with the Payson Church, though."

"I was only there for a year," she reminded him. "And I wouldn't have been there that long if I hadn't gotten knocked up."

She finished washing herself as best she could, then reluctantly pulled her jeans back on. They were filthy, torn, and considerably looser than they'd been when she and Cameron first set out. When she was dressed again—more or less—she sat on a wooden crate beside Cam and reached for his left foot.

An unexpected flicker of vulnerability touched his eyes.

"Your feet are a mess," she said. "Let me see if there's anything I can do."

"It's all right."

"Not if they get infected, it's not," she said firmly.

Reluctantly, he surrendered. Kat filled the coconut shell and dumped water over his long toes, scrubbing at the soles of his feet with her bare hand.

"You think they have a First Aid kit here anywhere?" she asked. "Or, better yet, a medical clinic?"

"Doubtful." He closed his eyes when she swept her thumb across the tendon at the back of his right foot. She felt scar tissue there, alongside a blister the size of her knuckle.

"How did you, anyway?" he asked. He looked uncomfortable. Not in pain, necessarily, but acutely uneasy at her touch.

"How did I what?"

"Get pregnant. Out on Payson Isle."

She raised her eyebrows at him. "The usual way."

He laughed—actually laughed. She found herself fascinated that such a thing was even possible. "No. I mean, I know you were young, but I imagine you knew about the birds and the bees. You weren't *that* young."

Oh, but she had been. She almost rolled her eyes at the memory.

"Adam told me he couldn't get anyone pregnant—that they'd done something to him. He was sterile."

"He lied, then," Cameron said.

"He said my getting pregnant was a gift from God. A miracle."

"He lied, then," he repeated, more firmly. Their eyes caught, and held.

"Yes," she agreed. "He lied. And I was stupid enough to believe him."

She found herself caught in a barrage of memories—the best and worst scenes from her brief time with Adam on Payson Isle. First kisses and first sex; the day Erin was born; sunshine and darkness and long cold nights on Payson Isle. The day she realized Isaac Payson's interest in Maddie had faded, shortly after Maddie had given birth to a bouncing baby girl of her own.

The day Kat realized his interest lay elsewhere now.

"Are you all right?" Cameron asked.

She saw Isaac's eyes on her, at church service after church service after Erin was born. The way he'd followed her. Sent Adam away from her, whenever he could.

"Katherine?"

Isaac, waiting for her in the greenhouse. The full moon overhead.

You have no right to deny this… No right to deny me. Adam doesn't decide this. You don't decide this. God has decided.

She started when Cameron reached for her, his hand cool on her arm.

"Kat?" he said again. "Are you okay?"

She pulled away abruptly. Stuffed the memory of those days on Payson Isle back down, as far as humanly possible. Past was passed—that's what her father always used to say.

Lately, though, it seemed like the past had become brutally present.

She lowered Cameron's now-clean feet to the ground.

"Fine," she said briskly. "I'm fine. We should find some antiseptic for those blisters, though."

She could tell he hadn't missed her change in tone. He pulled his feet back and stood to take his turn at the water pump. His eyes lingered on hers, softer now. The change didn't please her.

"That will wait," he said. To her relief, he sounded just as brisk. They were back to business, then. Good. She could handle business. "We need to get moving. Find some food, to start with." He pulled off his shirt. In the light, Kat noted half a dozen long, pale white scars on his back. "Then we'll need to find a vehicle."

She looked around. A single, rusted-out pickup was parked in a yard farther along the road. "And then?" she asked.

"Then?" He shrugged. "Then, we find Erin, get her, Diggs, and you the hell out of here, and put this thing to bed."

"You make it sound so easy."

"It won't be. We'll do it anyway."

He leaned forward and dumped a shell-full of cool water over his head, splashing Kat in the process. She stepped back as he scrubbed the dirt from his scalp. When he looked at her, it was with an impish grin she wouldn't have imagined possible a few days ago.

"Unless you want to wash my back, maybe you could give me some room."

"Tempting, but I'll pass," she said dryly. "You finish up. I'll see if I can scrounge some food."

The woman who had loaned them the use of her water pump was named Maria. She had at least four kids as far as Kat could tell, along with mother and father, husband, and two brothers—all of whom appeared to sleep under the same grass-thatched roof. Kat tried an awkward, mostly-mimed introduction at the open entrance to the family's palapa, but the woman was way ahead of her. Before Kat had even asked, plates were set on a wobbly wooden table inside. Maria put out steaming tortillas, scrambled eggs, and refried beans, gesturing to the food enthusiastically.

Humbled and grateful, Kat went back out for Cameron. He was dressed again, his graying hair already drying in the sun.

"Think you could eat?" she asked. "Maria has one hell of a spread in there for us."

He nodded, but she could tell he was distracted. His head was up, his eyes sharp. "I'll be in in a minute."

"Is something wrong?"

"Just being careful," he said. "Go on in—eat. Give me a couple of minutes."

Nearly ten minutes later, Cam came in and sat beside her. Maria hovered over them, her aging parents seated in stony silence across the table. The floor was dirt; daylight provided the only illumination. Cameron asked the family a few questions while Maria bounced a toddler on her hip. A group of dark-eyed, smiling children played outside.

They were in the middle of a conversation, the toddler babbling happily, Maria's parents finally drawn out of their silence, when Kat saw Cameron's head come up.

"What is it?" she asked immediately.

He held up his hand. Then, he shot off a question to Maria in rapid-fire Spanish. Fear crossed the woman's face. She shook her head. Cameron said something more, his voice suddenly laden with tension.

Maria's eyes went wide. Outside, the sound of the children's laughter gave way to an eerie stillness.

Cameron got up from the table so suddenly the chair toppled behind him. The toddler bouncing on Maria's hip started at the noise. Once he'd recovered, he started to howl.

"We have to go," Cam said. Kat was already on her feet.

There was an entrance at the front and back of the primitive structure, both of them open. Cameron herded Kat toward the back. A dog barked nearby. The toddler wailed, his voice amplified in the small space. Maria continued talking to them... Pleading with them, Kat was sure by the tone alone. With Cameron on her heels, practically pushing her forward, Kat flew out the back door.

Straight into the business end of Lee's AK-47.

29
DIGGS

COBA IS A MAYAN VILLAGE of about thirteen hundred people on the Yucatan Peninsula. Despite a long day of travel, we still managed to pull into the dusty parking lot outside the ancient Mayan pyramid known as La Iglesia by six that night. Jamie was behind the wheel, driving a van Juarez had rented at the air strip in Valladolid. Solomon had gone monosyllabic again. The sun was still up, producing a damp, smothering heat that easily outmatched the van's shaky A/C.

There were a few tourists with floppy hats and elaborate cameras still roaming, but otherwise it seemed the place was empty. Two cars and another van were the only vehicles in the lot, which was ringed by grass-roofed booths and sleepy-eyed vendors. I didn't see any sign of Jenny or her cohorts.

Carl was the only one missing from the party, as he'd rented a second car. That car would be the getaway vehicle for Solomon, Kat, and me when the moment arrived. Our plan was in place, then: We would do the exchange with Jenny, handing over the memory card and a copy of the list we'd decrypted from the card. As soon as we had Kat, Solomon and I would take her with us in our getaway car, bound for the Cancun airport. Meanwhile, Juarez's team would return to Jamie's plane and head back stateside.

Assuming, of course, that nothing went wrong.

Right now, that didn't feel like a very realistic assumption.

"So much for meeting in a public place," Juarez said once we were parked. He eyed the dusty parking lot critically.

"The place will be deserted by ten," I said.

"At least we're here early enough to do some recon," Monty said. "I want to check the place out. No sense sitting around here waiting for an ambush—I say we make use of the time we've got."

Beside me, Solomon nodded seriously. "He's right. We should scope the place out, see if we can make sure we have an edge."

"I didn't mean you, sweet cheeks," Monty said firmly. "I was talking more to the people in the van who didn't almost die a couple days ago."

"I'm doing a lot better," she said.

"A lot better than what?" I said. "Forget it, ace."

"I wasn't talking to you either, actually," Monty said. "Sorry, Diggs. You keep your girl entertained, and stay the hell out of the way."

I tried not to be offended. It wasn't easy. Solomon looked at me knowingly. "Sorry, slick. Guess you're not the Great American Hero we always thought you were."

"It's not that," Juarez said. He twisted around to look at us. He and Jamie were up front. Monty had claimed the bench seat in the middle, relegating Solomon and me to the far back. "But I don't want anyone to be alone while we're doing this. There's safety in numbers."

"Relatively speaking," I said.

"Relatively speaking," he agreed.

"Sucks for you," Solomon said. "If you're stuck with me, that's definitely going to cut into your sightseeing time."

"I think I'll live." Though, having said that, it was hard not to get swept up in the lure of Coba, even under the circumstances. I wouldn't have minded taking a stroll around.

"Yeah, right," she said knowingly. "You're getting that look in your eye."

"What look is that?"

"The reporter-y, history nerd look."

"I'm not a history nerd," I insisted. "Though if I was, I might mention that the network of ruins in Coba extends nearly fifty square miles—many of those ruins still under the cover of jungle. Or that the remote location and subsequent lack of excavation lend a mystery to these ruins that's hard to come by in the overexposed, heavily-trod-upon world we live in today... Or that Nohoch Mul, one of the central pyramids in this complex, is the tallest on the Yucatan Peninsula. Or—"

"Or, it's creepy as fuck out there," Monty interrupted.

"Or that," Solomon agreed. Sol patted my hand. "If we don't die today, I promise I'll listen to you ramble ad nauseam about all that crap. You should probably let it go for now, though."

"I just want to get out there already," Monty said impatiently. I took Solomon's point: No one gave a rat's ass about the complexities of ancient Mayan civilization right now. "We need to find some higher ground, so I can figure out where I'm gonna watch this whole thing go down."

"I don't see what the point in hiding is," I said. "Jenny knows we'll be here. She knows we have back up."

"She won't know where that back up is, though," Juarez pointed out. "I know she'll have people here, as well, but I want to make sure if she has any big ideas about ambushing you to get the memory card, we're there to stop her."

There was a pounding on the side of the door that nearly

sent the whole crew into orbit seconds later. Carl peered at us through the window, grinning widely. Monty slid the door open for him and he climbed aboard.

"Does anyone else feel like we're in a lost episode of the A Team?" Solomon piped up.

"Not enough explosives," Monty said. "But I could probably fix that with a little lead time."

"We'll pass on that," I said. I was a little sensitive about explosives by then. "But thanks."

"What did I miss?" Carl asked. He was looking uncharacteristically chipper. I eyed him suspiciously. "Is something wrong?" he asked.

"He's just concerned about how upbeat you seem, considering we're facing an imminent showdown with a psycho killer. Qu'est ce que c'est?" Solomon said.

The reference went right over Carl's head. "I know it is serious," he assured her. "But it's better to enjoy one's work, don't you agree?"

None of us could find fault with that logic. It didn't make his apparent gleeful anticipation any less creepy, though.

"We're just figuring out the layout," Monty said. "You want to give us the grand tour?"

Carl nodded, looking more eager than I'd seen him since the card game on Raven's Ledge. "I have some ideas, actually."

He reached for the door. The others followed suit, while I sat like a lump beside Solomon. Juarez paused before he abandoned us completely, lingering at the open door.

"This really is where we need you both most right now," he said. "I know it doesn't seem that way."

"You can go if you want," Solomon said to me. "I'll be fine here. It's not like I'm not armed... You don't need to babysit me."

Juarez looked at me expectantly. Time for me to man

up, clearly.

"You heard what they said," I said. "We stay out of the way. Not just you. It's not babysitting... At this point, it's just being smart."

"Exactly," Juarez agreed. "Shout if you need something, though—we won't be far. And someone will be back soon to check on you. I don't expect we'll be long."

"Go," I said. "Once you've scoped the place out, we'll make sure we have everything else in place before Jenny gets here."

I watched him go with some regret—partly because being stuck in an overheated van for the next few hours wasn't incredibly appealing; partly because I was honestly terrified at how exposed Solomon and I were out here.

"Looks like it's just you and me, kid," Solomon said. Her hair was damp on her forehead, her eyes bright.

"Looks like," I agreed. I put the back of my hand against her forehead. It came away hot and damp.

"It's hotter than hell out there," she reminded me before I said anything.

"Or, your fever's back." I grabbed a spare t-shirt, rolled it, and set it on one end of the seat. Then, I got up and carefully helped her lie back. "You should sleep."

"All I do is sleep now," she grumbled.

"Tell me about it. Now, be a good girl and close your eyes."

She glared at me. "Once I'm healed, you'll pay for that."

"I look forward to it." I kissed her forehead, and left her to rest.

It was close to seven o'clock when I got out of the van to stretch my legs. I took in the jungle and the limestone road, the nearly-deserted parking lot and the setting sun on the horizon. There was a warm breeze blowing in. Compared to the heat of the day, it was heavenly. A couple of tourists, sweaty and spent, eyed me curiously before they climbed into their car. A year ago, I wouldn't have hesitated to start a conversation with them. Now, I hung back with my chest tight until they drove away.

How the mighty had fallen.

30
KAT

THERE WAS NO TRAPDOOR in the room Lee put them in this time. No secret escape hatch. There was a dirt floor and solid walls and barely any light. Hell, there was barely any air. And the room was not unoccupied.

In the corner, her face bruised and bloodied, sat Cameron's daughter. She kept her eyes locked on the floor when they came in. Cam spared barely a glance at his surroundings before he went to her.

"Jenny?"

She looked up. Somehow, she managed to look resentful even with the state she was in. Cam sat down beside her, touching her chin gently to guide her gaze to his. Her eyes remained hard.

"Lee did this?" he asked.

"I betrayed the Project," Jenny said evenly. "You knew as well as I did there would be a price."

"I didn't expect this. I thought..." He shook his head. "I don't know what I thought. Where else are you hurt?"

"I'm fine. Lee knows how to inflict pain without doing real damage. It looks worse than it is."

"They make mistakes," Cam said. "You should know

that by now. Let Katherine look at you."

Jenny sneered at them both. "Not on your life. I told you: I'm fine."

Cameron looked over his shoulder at Kat. She was still standing at the door, watching curiously. The father-daughter business held no interest; the fact that Jenny clearly needed medical attention was hard to ignore, though. Kat walked the three steps it took to cross the room and knelt beside the girl. Jenny scrambled backward like a caged thing.

"Stay the hell away from me."

"Jenny—" Cameron said.

"Relax," Kat said smoothly before he could intervene. She shot Cam a look. He got the message: Back off. He fell silent and took a step back.

"You can murder me in your sleep the first chance you get," Kat said. "I promise. But in the meantime, how about we make use of all that cash my father shelled out for medical school, huh?"

Jenny's shoulders relaxed slightly. Kat moved in closer, going as gently as possible when she palpated the girl's swollen cheek, ran her hand along her bruised jaw. She was right: It looked bad, but there were no broken bones. Her right eye was bruised and swollen, but there was no orbital fracture.

"Congratulations," Kat said dryly. "Your friend beats women like a champ. Your face will be fine—maybe a couple of scars, but nothing disfiguring. What about the rest of you? Any body blows?"

"A couple," Jenny said. "Nothing bad."

"Did he rape you?" Kat kept her focus on her hands as she continued searching for injuries, her voice notably casual. The room fell silent. She could almost feel the tension radiating from Cameron, though he stood behind her now.

"No," Jenny said after a second.

"You sure about that?" Kat asked, still casual. She looked Jenny in the eye.

"I think I would have remembered," Jenny said flatly.

"Probably," Kat agreed. "But maybe you don't want to say something with dear old Dad with us. He's a big boy, though—he can handle it. I need to know if there are injuries I'm not seeing here."

"There aren't," Jenny said.

The women's gazes remained locked for another few seconds, while Kat tried to figure out whether or not Jenny was lying. She didn't think so. It was hard to be certain when you were dealing with someone trained in the art of deception since birth, of course, but, in this case, Kat was reasonably sure she was getting the truth.

"Good, then," Kat said. She straightened. Jenny's posture relaxed a little more. "Looks like you're right: You'll live to fight another day. Or get the snot beaten out of you, as the case may be."

Cameron lowered himself to the floor again, close to his daughter. Jenny may have relaxed for a minute or two, but her tension was back in spades the second Cam came near.

"I'm sorry about this," he said. "But it's a good lesson. This is what they do, Jenny. This is who they are. It doesn't change."

"This happened because I tried to help you," she said. Her voice remained flat. "I was fine… I've been fine, for a long time with them. You were, too. You just chose to forget."

"I didn't forget."

She looked at him. "You sure about that?"

"I loved my life with you and your mother," Cameron said. "I didn't love what they did to you both. What they did to me. The price we paid whenever we disagreed. They took too much from us… From you."

"They gave me everything," she said. Her voice got tighter, her body taut as wire. "What did you give me? Everything started with them: the roof over our heads, the food on our plates. I've lived my life for them. So have you. They clothed us. Fed us. Trained us. Gave us something to work toward; something to believe in."

"They gave us lies," Cameron said roughly. "They gave us shit. They gave us nightmares and murderous impulses and a sense of right and wrong so skewed I didn't know for years what all the blood on my hands meant. How the hell is that a gift? You wanted me to stay with them, for that? To thank them for it?"

"And now you think you can just put the white hat on, and all that blood on your hands won't matter anymore?" she said. "You're an idiot. You're blind."

"I know there's no redemption for me. I accept that. That's not why I'm doing this. But you..."

"I didn't ask for redemption!" Jenny screamed the words, her body tightening with fury and a pain so deep Kat could feel it in the air around them. Tears spilled now. Jenny seemed unaware. "I just want them. I want my life. I want J. You forced me to choose—"

"I didn't ask you to let us go," Cameron reminded her.

"No—I could have stood by and watched them torture you. Peel everything away until I didn't even recognize you anymore—until all you were was a mass of exposed nerves. They know how to do that, remember? We know how to do that."

"Jenny—" he tried again.

"No," she said, shaking her head violently. "It doesn't matter. He said I have one more chance. That's it. Get the information tonight... Don't interfere with whatever they have in store for you, and I can go back. I'll be safe."

"You know you're never safe with them," Cam said

quietly. He reached out and ran a gentling hand along her cheek. "We can make this right. If you work with us, we can make it right."

When she met his eye this time, Kat was certain she'd never seen anyone harder. Anyone colder.

"Get away from me," Jenny whispered. "I don't need you to make this right. I don't need you at all."

Cameron removed his hand.

He didn't reach out to her again.

31
DIGGS

AT 9:15 THAT NIGHT, things started happening. With the six of us crowded in the van with a tropical rain pouring buckets outside, we went over the last of the plan before we set everything in motion.

"It won't be easy out here," Monty said. "This is a whole lot of land, and the biggest structures are those goddamn ruins. It's not like we can find higher ground to watch what's going down."

Carl nodded as Juarez continued. "You'll need to be far enough up that you'll have a good view of everything happening below. Jamie will be at the head of the road—"

"You don't need to keep me out of the way," Jamie protested. "I can handle myself."

"I'm sure you can," Juarez said evenly. "But I need someone I can trust who'll let us know when Jenny arrives, and whether Willett shows up."

"You think he will?" I asked.

"He seemed pretty determined when we met in Kentucky," Juarez said. "I have a feeling he'll find his way here. If he does, he can't know I'm here this time or I'm out of a job… and probably facing charges."

"All right, fine," Jamie said. "I'll play lookout. Monty, you have some brilliant way we can all stay in touch?"

"As a matter of fact," he said with a grin, "I've got that covered."

He retrieved a large duffel bag from under his seat and rooted through until he came out with a cardboard box. From it, he removed five small plastic cases containing an earbud and a microphone the size and shape of a tie clip. He handed out cases to Juarez, Jamie, Carl, and me, keeping the last for himself.

"This isn't the kind of equipment you typically see on the open market," Juarez said, eying the earwig he'd been given. I couldn't tell whether that was admiration or angst in his voice. Probably a healthy dose of both.

"A man's got to have his hobbies," Monty said. "If Uncle Sam's gonna keep his eyeballs on everything I do, I'm damned sure gonna have the equipment to eyeball him right back. Anyway, these'll keep us all connected."

"We should have a code word, in case anything goes wrong," I said. "Right? If someone says that word, we'll know things have gone to hell."

"Dragons," Solomon said absently. She watched the path to the ruins, barely acknowledging the rest of us. "For a password, I mean."

"It should be something we can work into casual conversation," Juarez said.

"I can work 'dragons' into any conversation," she said readily.

"Right," Juarez said with a faint smile. "Of course you can. So… 'dragons' it is."

Monty took another minute to explain the details of our equipment, but time was winding down fast; we were all anxious to move. He and Carl got out first, wearing camouflage plastic ponchos that hid a seriously intimidating arsenal. If the cops happened to make their way out here tonight, we would all be facing time in a Mexican prison. I've already done that once; I'm not anxious to repeat the experience.

The rest of the group piled out of the van next, shoulders slouched miserably in the rain. Juarez went to the driver's side window, where Jamie waited.

"Remember the code word," Juarez said seriously.

"I don't think that will be a problem. I'll be fine, Jack. Just worry about yourself, hmm?" She leaned out and kissed him on the cheek. Solomon turned and looked at me, one eyebrow arched, but remained quiet. "See you on the other side, Agent Juarez," Jamie said.

She drove away, leaving us alone in the muddy, dark parking lot.

"Told you she was sweet on you," I said to Juarez when she was gone. Solomon just sent him a knowing smile.

"Shut up, both of you," Juarez grumbled. "Let's get on with this, or I'll unleash the dragons myself."

Before he left, he scooped Sol up in a careful hug. I realized suddenly that this was the only goodbye we would get—once we had Kat, we would be headed in opposite directions. I had no idea when we would see Jack Juarez again.

"Be careful," he said.

When he let go and pulled back, Sol's eyes were wet. I was reasonably sure it wasn't just from the rain. "I'll see you again soon," she said. "We'll figure out... everything. All those things we've forgotten—we'll figure out what they were. Why they took those memories."

"I know," he said. "You can count on it."

I was next. He wrapped his arms around me and held on. I thought suddenly of the brother I'd lost so many years ago.

"Be good to yourselves," he said to me. "You know how to reach me if you need anything."

"We do," I agreed. We parted, and I clapped him on the back in as manly a gesture as I could muster at the moment. "We'll be back, man. Don't worry. Now, let's move—they'll be here soon."

After Juarez had disappeared into the jungle, leaving Sol and me to travel the muddy path to the pyramid on our own, I took a slug of water and handed the bottle to Solomon. We started out in silence, rain still pouring down, the trees a canopy of deepest black over our heads. Monkeys and tropical birds screeched above us. At least the rain kept the bugs at bay.

Solomon's face was flushed, the rain plastering her hair to her forehead. The fever was back, and then some: 101.6 when she'd taken her temperature back at the van. I didn't harp on it, knowing that right now nothing could be done. It didn't make any of this easier, though.

To our right, I pointed out a Mayan ball court recently excavated, but otherwise untouched by modern hands.

"We should come back here sometime," Solomon said. "When we're not running for our lives, I mean. It would be nice to explore out here."

"I'd like that. I'll even try to steer clear of my reporter-y history nerd zone."

She bumped up against me, slipping her arm through mine. "I don't know. To be honest, I kind of like it. It's very Indiana Jones."

"Does that mean I can start talking about the wonders of Mayan civilization now?"

"Don't push it."

Our destination was just up ahead, a hulking mass of stone, mystery, and power that had stood in this spot for fifteen hundred years: La Iglesia. Another five steps and the trail opened up to a large clearing. Carl was already halfway up the pyramid, moving steadily up the narrow steps. Among the trees around us, I spotted a stout stone figure not far from the pyramid. Another stood farther in the jungle, barely visible from our spot. By the time I'd gotten a good look around, I had the uneasy feeling that we were surrounded by vengeful stone gods.

"This is creepy," Solomon said, echoing my thoughts.

"I'm in position," Juarez said in my ear. I looked around, but saw no sign of him.

The pyramid rose above us, its rough-hewn limestone blocks stacked to the sky. Despite the rain, we sat on one of the narrow steps at the bottom and waited. Solomon leaned against me, her arm still through mine. "You've been here before," she said. Not a question.

"I have. You?"

"Once, with Michael." I felt the gentle weight of her head on my shoulder. Several seconds passed before she spoke again.

"She saved Einstein once, you know."

It took a second for my mind to follow the notable lack of a segue. "Kat, you mean?"

She nodded. "He was dying when I first got him... He had Parvo. Was the only one in his litter to survive. Just this tiny scruff ball who wanted to be in my arms constantly."

"Not so different from today, then."

"He's a little bigger," she said. I could hear the smile in her voice. "But... no, not really. Anyway, Kat was spending the night at the apartment in Boston one night—Michael's idea, not mine," she added unnecessarily. "And Stein's fever spikes. I wake to him in mid-seizure. I knew the only decent thing to do at that point was call the vet and have him put down. So, I'm sitting on the kitchen floor with this puppy in my arms and the phone in my hand, ready to make the call."

Her head was still on my shoulder, but I got the sense that she was far, far away. I turned and kissed her warm forehead.

"And Kat came to the rescue?" I asked.

"She just swooped in, you know? Took Einstein from me, made up god-knows-what from the crap I had in the refrigerator, got him warmed up and stabilized and..."

"And he made it."

"The next morning, I wake up and Stein is sleeping beside me. Kat's already gone—she had a conference that day, I think. She left a note with instructions on what I needed to do. Nothing special—nothing remotely personal." She paused. Wiped her eyes. "That was the only thing she ever gave me that she signed 'Mom.' I still have it... It's stupid, I know. But I can't throw it away. She never sent letters or care packages when I was in college. Even birthday cards, she signs 'Kat.' But that stupid note..."

"She loves you," I said. "It's a complicated thing for her, I think, but I know she does."

Silence fell as she considered that.

The minutes wore on.

Finally, after what seemed an inordinately long time, Solomon sat up with a heavy sigh. She looked around the clearing.

"How much longer do you think it will be?"

It was only nine-thirty. "I don't think they'll make us wait long."

She nodded. After a second, she forced herself back to her feet. I didn't care for the glassy shine to her eyes. She rocked where she stood before she began walking, circling the ruins.

"Does Jack see any sign of them?" she asked me.

I got up and followed her. "Any sign?" I asked Juarez.

"None so far," he said in my ear. "I have a good view of the trail in, and Carl will be able to see anyone in the area. There's no movement."

"No sign yet," I said to Solomon. She frowned, turning her back on me to scowl into the trees.

"Something's wrong," she repeated.

"At least wait until the meet time comes and goes before you start panicking. You're freaking me out."

"Sorry," she murmured. She began to pace, every step clearly painful as hell. The rain slowed. The heat got thicker.

Another five minutes passed with no sign of anyone.

And then, there was a crackling in my ear.

"We've got movement at the trailhead," Juarez said in my ear.

"Can you tell who?" I asked. Solomon looked at me.

"One person—male," Juarez said.

"Any sign of Jenny? Or Kat?" I asked.

"Not yet."

"What's happening?" Solomon demanded.

"Someone's here," I said. "Juarez isn't sure if they're with J or just out for a midnight stroll."

"Not likely in this weather," she said. I'd been thinking the same thing.

"He's headed your way, Diggs," Juarez said.

"Can I get a description?" I asked.

"Tall. Fit. Older—fifties or sixties, maybe."

At Juarez's description, the tension I'd barely been holding at bay spiked. Shit. It wasn't much to go by, but I had a sinking feeling I knew exactly who was coming our way.

"Sol?" I said. At the anxiety in my voice, she turned.

"You know him?" Juarez asked. "What do you want us to do?"

"What is it?" Solomon asked me.

"Don't shoot," I said to Juarez. "But be on alert. Ten to one, I know exactly who's about to crash the party."

Solomon looked at me in confusion.

Thirty seconds later, sure enough, Adam Solomon stepped out of the jungle and back into our lives.

32
KAT

IT WAS POURING by the time Lee came to get them from their hot, humid prison. Kat had been dozing fitfully, while Cameron and Jenny maintained their stony silence. At sight of Lee at the door, however, everyone in the room came immediately to attention. Lee looked at Jenny intently, silently assessing the girl.

"You still with us?" he asked her.

Jenny nodded without hesitation. "I am."

"Did they say something?" he asked. "Any big plans to escape again?"

"No," she said. "He tried to get me to join them. I said no."

"Good girl," Lee said. He held out his hand. Jenny hesitated only a moment before she took it. "You're either for us or against us, Jen. You know that."

"I do," she agreed.

"Did you miss what they did to Jonah?" Cameron asked, out of the blue. Lee very nearly growled at him.

"Shut up, Cam," Kat said.

"Yes," Lee echoed. "Shut up, Cam. Don't start getting chatty on us now."

"You saw them, Jenny," Cam continued, heeding neither warning. "You saw the children who died. Left there to rot, like garbage."

"We didn't do that," Jenny said. "That wasn't us. Jonah did that to them. He took them out there; he fed them that poison."

"Because he couldn't bear knowing what the Project would do to them, if he didn't. That's what you're part of—an operation that men would rather murder their grandchildren over than let them join."

Lee advanced on Cameron. Outside, Kat could see two of the other men with the Project waiting, rifles at the ready.

"We're done talking, old man," Lee said. He pulled a gun from the back of his pants, focused on Jenny again. "I can't keep you on if you're not loyal. If he keeps feeding this shit to you, screwing with your head..."

"He'll stop," Jenny said. She cast a nearly-desperate look at her father. Cameron looked away. "If he cares about my life at all, he'll shut up. I'm with you. I'm with the Project. You won't have a problem with me again."

Lee continued to study her, gun still at the ready. Kat found she was holding her breath. Cameron didn't move.

"I hope that's true," Lee said finally. He turned the gun away, opened the chamber, and removed the clip before he handed it to Jenny. "You earn your ammo. Same as when you were first coming up the ranks."

"Thank you," Jenny said, eyes lowered. "I will."

"Solomon will be expecting you tonight," Lee continued. "Stay cool. Follow the plan. Make sure that's all she's expecting."

"I will," she said, still nodding. Kat waited for him to say something else—to give some clue about whatever he had in store, but he offered nothing. He signalled them out into the rain. The other men were on high alert.

Outside, Lee herded them into a waiting Humvee, the engine already running. Kat looked at Cameron. He lowered his eyes.

"I'm sorry," he said quietly, as Lee loaded them roughly into the vehicle. "I did everything I could."

33
SOLOMON

"WHAT THE HELL DO YOU WANT?" I asked my father. He stood in front of me like some apparition, dripping rain, his familiar eyes searching mine. "What are you doing here?"

"I'm here to help," he said. He hesitated. "I'm here to take your place."

I blinked a couple of times, sure when I opened my eyes he would have vanished again.

"Where were you when Willett was hunting us like dogs?" Diggs demanded. Diggs usually keeps his temper on a short leash. At the moment, that leash was nowhere in sight. He was on his feet and headed for my father before I could stop him. "When she was bleeding to death in my arms? You show up now—"

"Diggs," I interrupted. I stopped him with my hand on his shoulder, before he ended up actually killing my dad then and there. "It's all right. I've got this."

"We don't have much time," he said to me quietly. Like I hadn't been watching the clock for the past twenty-four hours.

"I know," I agreed. "Just... Let me handle my father. I'll take care of it."

Diggs backed off, though he didn't go far—a couple of steps was the most space he would give me. In this instance, I didn't mind a bit.

I leveled a cool, killing glare at my father. Or as close as I could get while delirious and dripping wet. "We don't have time for this. Jenny will be here any second. I don't care what you have or haven't done... I don't know whether you're a good man or a friggin' monster... It doesn't matter. You're still my father. Which means I don't want them to get their hands on you. So, go. Run."

"I'm not leaving," he said, intractable. "Give me the memory card. Let me stay here and wait for Jenny and the others. I'll make sure your mother gets away safely. You don't have to worry anymore."

"Well, that's comforting," I said bitterly. "No, thank you. We can handle it."

He closed the distance between us. "You don't need to handle it anymore—that's what I'm trying to tell you, Erin. Let me take care of you. Let me protect you, the way I should have years ago. Please."

"I can't keep her safe anymore, Katie. She doesn't listen to me. She's too much like you that way. You have to take her...I can't protect her out here. Not anymore."

I shook my head, trying to clear it. Colors swam and blurred around me. I struggled to focus. Dad came closer. He looked worried.

"Baby, you're hurt. You shouldn't be here."

"She's hurt because you took off the first time," Diggs said. He sounded more wary than actively furious now.

"I know that," my father said. "So, let me make it right. Give me the card. Get her away from here."

"And you'll make sure Kat gets away," Diggs said. I could tell he was tempted.

"If I give you the card, I don't want you to just disappear

again," I said. I kept my back to Diggs and focused on my father. Everything had happened too fast—he'd come out of nowhere. I tried to make sense of it; tried to re-establish the connection I'd felt just a few days ago. "Before you go, I want to understand. I want you to tell me the truth about Payson Isle. Nothing makes sense to me."

He reached out to me. I couldn't figure out how he'd gotten so close. My brain wasn't tracking things right. His hand was cool on my cheek, his eyes sad when he looked at me. "I know it doesn't make sense. But I promise, you'll know everything in time."

"You'll understand when you're older, baby. Right now, listen to my voice. There's light and there's dark in your life." My father sits beside me on my bed, brushing my hair back. "I want you to live in the light. Remember everything we love about it here. Take the dark spots... Let them go."

I blinked hard, shaking my head again. Dad was close now. He was right there.

"Erin?" Diggs said, behind me.

"They'll take you," I said again. "Jenny said before that there was no deal for you. If they catch you, they'll kill you."

"I won't let them," he said.

"But how? Damn it, Dad, explain this to me. How is me giving you the card now any better than me ignoring Jenny's demands for Kat, and taking off to leave her to die? Why would I abandon you, when I wouldn't her?"

He didn't answer for a few seconds. The rain had stopped. Heat and darkness lay heavy over the scene, while an unholy host of nocturnals screamed bloody murder above. I wondered where Juarez was, suddenly; if he was whispering in Diggs' ear right now. I tried to imagine what he might be saying.

A wash of fear, slow and creeping, burned through me.

"If we are going, we need to leave now," Diggs said. "We

don't have time to debate this."

"*Your father has his own secrets,*" Isaac Payson said. *His eyes were blood red. He stood over me, dark and angry.* "*He's too busy running from them to protect you all the time.*"

"*Forget the dark spots, Erin.*"

"*I can't protect her.*"

I ground the heels of my hands into my eyes, trying to stop their burning. I could feel him waiting for me to say something. Waiting for me to decide.

There was light, on Payson Isle. Not all of it was a lie. Those light spots I remembered hadn't been planted there... My father had taken care of me. He had loved me. That much had to be true, didn't it? *Something* had to be true.

I shook my head. "No," I said. My throat was parched. The word came out small in the wide open spaces. Mayan gods watched me from the trees. My head wasn't right— too hot. Life and death decisions shouldn't be left to people with bullet wounds and temperatures topping the hundred-degree mark.

"We'll take care of it," I said, forcing strength into my voice. My father still stood in front of me, his hand on my cheek. I could feel the tension in his body, just from that single point of contact. "I have everything under control."

"You don't have *anything* under control, where they're concerned," Dad said. "The only way you or me or any of us will ever be free, is if you give me that memory card."

He held his hand out, waiting for me to comply. The way he used to do when I took something that didn't belong to me. Expecting me to obey.

"Leave while you can, Erin," he said. "Run away. Forget everything you ever knew about the Project."

I twisted around to look at Diggs. He seemed too far away. I backed away from my father.

"I told you: No," I said. "I'm not forgetting anything.

When this is over, Diggs and I will drop out of sight. We'll lay low. But that doesn't mean we're giving up. I'm not letting this go. Whoever these people are, whoever the operatives on this memory card might have been, they need to answer for the things they've done."

Fear sparked in my father's eyes.

"Your father has his own secrets."

Why was he afraid? Was it because of what was about to happen?

Or was it something else?

"Your father has his own secrets, darker than anything I could do," Isaac whispered to me.

When understanding finally hit me, it struck like lightning. I wet my lips. Backed away. Dad reached for me. His fingers curled around my arm.

"That's why you want the card, isn't it?" I asked. I couldn't get a full breath. "Not to save Kat... It doesn't have anything to do with her. Or me. You're on that card, aren't you? All those entries... All those horrible things these people have done. You were one of them. You didn't just stand by. You didn't just run."

My father's eyes went cold. His fingers tightened on my arm.

"You killed for them," I said.

If I hadn't been hurt, I like to think I would have seen the shift before my father made it. Maybe I'm just kidding myself, though. Maybe I was always doomed to blindness, where he was concerned.

In a flash, before anyone in any direction could react, Dad pulled me to him. His hand snaked around my middle, coming to rest directly on top of my bandages. Blinding pain shot through me. I barely swallowed a scream, my knees buckling.

"You're hurting her, damn it!" Diggs shouted. He started

toward us. When he stopped, barely a second later, it took me a second before I could figure out why.

Until I felt cold steel at my temple.

And like that, in a flash of light, I was back on Payson Isle.

"Forget the dark spots."

I'm in the greenhouse with Isaac. Afraid. He's watching me. I remember Allie—even though I'm not supposed to. I know what he did. He takes a step toward me.

"Your father has his own secrets, darker than anything I could do. Given the choice between protecting you or those secrets, he'll always choose his secrets. He'll take care of you when he can... He'll let me beat him. He'll hate me for it. But given the choice between his life and yours, his past or your future, he will choose himself. It's the way he was made."

My father tightened his grip on me, forcing me back to the present. The world blurred grey at the edges.

"Let her go, Adam," Diggs said. Dad took a step back, jerking me with him.

"It doesn't have to go this way," my father said. His voice shook. I could feel him trembling against me. "Just give me the goddamn card. Then you can leave."

"And you'll run," I said. I swallowed bile. Tried to keep my head above the pain. "You never meant to save Kat. That's not why you're here."

"I can't let them get to me. You have no idea what they would do—What they've done. If you'd just given me the damned card while we were on the road, it wouldn't have come to this. And then Willett showed up before I could just take it."

I watched Diggs, trying to figure out what was happening. Was Juarez talking to him? Was Jenny here yet? Did anyone have any clue where Kat was?

"Just get me the memory card, Diggs," my father said.

His voice was cold now. Calculating. I tried to remember that part of him from my childhood. I couldn't. "It's in the bag, right?" He nodded in the direction of my backpack, now a sodden lump at the base of the pyramid. "Bring it to me."

"I don't think so," I heard Juarez say. I searched the clearing, trying to figure out where he was. He stepped out of the trees with a rifle held high, aimed straight for my father's head. The fury in his eyes was terrifying. I was looking at a different man. "We keep the card. You let her go. There's no other deal."

"I hope you'll reconsider, Jackie," Dad said. Juarez stiffened, tensing at the name.

"And if I don't?" he asked.

"Then I'll hurt her," Dad said. I struggled against him, trying to get away. Every move I made just meant he held me tighter. "I'm sorry," my father said. And he sounded it, this time. "It's not what she deserves... You know that."

He dug his fingers in just below the entry wound in my side. Someone screamed, loud and long. It took a second before I realized it came from me. I fought to stay conscious. When my knees went out from under me this time, my father tightened his hold around my stomach. The pain became white light, pulsing through me in a blinding, endless fire.

"Put the gun down, goddamn it," Diggs shouted at Juarez. "Give him the card. What the hell does it matter now?" He went to the backpack and rooted through until he came up with the card. Juarez didn't lower his rifle, though. And my father didn't loosen his grip.

When Diggs turned around, he'd gone deathly pale. "Please, Jack," he said to Juarez.

"Where were you in October, 2008?" Juarez asked my father. Dad was shaking hard against me, sweating. His gun hand stayed steady. He dug the barrel into my temple.

"That wasn't me, Jack," Dad said. "I'm not the one you're looking for. I can give them to you, though. I can lead you to the men who killed your wife. I can take you to the man who made it happen." For the first time, Juarez wavered. "Just let me have the memory card."

Juarez looked at Diggs. He held up the memory card. "Please," Diggs said. I'd never seen him so pale. So scared. "Let me give it to him. Whatever Adam did, Erin shouldn't pay for it."

"I'm still right here," I said. My voice didn't sound like my own. The grey closed in. "Don't talk about me like I'm already gone, for Christ's sake." I shifted, trying to force some strength into my legs. It didn't work.

Diggs took a cautious step toward us. He held the memory card like an offering. Juarez lowered his rifle, but his eyes remained hard, his body taut.

When Diggs was no more than a couple of feet away, he paused. "You let her go—then you get the card," he said to my father.

"No," Dad said. "Even exchange, on the count of three. One."

Diggs came closer. Dad loosened the hand at my side, getting ready to grab the card. The gun stayed at my temple, though.

"Two," Diggs said. He held out the card.

My father held out his hand.

Something rustled in the trees.

I heard a voice, tinny and close.

My father heard it, too:

Someone shouting into the earwig in Diggs' ear.

Before we ever got to three, the rustling of trees got wilder, the tinny voices closer. My father froze.

Diggs froze.

Juarez lifted his rifle again.

Dad's hand came back around my middle, pulling me snug against him. He was warm and damp, his fingers stretched to my side all over again. It didn't matter how much he hurt me this time, though.

When Jenny stepped into the clearing, I could tell she didn't give a rat's ass about my pain.

●

"Drop the gun, Adam," Jenny said. Her face was purple, one eye swollen shut. She sounded calmer than anyone else in the whole damned place, though. Beside her was a man I didn't know—a giant with a gun pointed at Juarez. Kat stood by the tree line. Cameron was beside her, two other men I didn't know holding guns on them both.

My father wavered, but he kept the gun to my head. I thought of holidays when I was little, on the island. Hikes along the shoreline, my hand in his.

"I don't care if I have to shoot through her to get to you," Jenny said. "You know that. So, just let her go. And you, blondie—" She nodded to Diggs. "Take a step back. Put the memory card on the ground."

"You have to let Kat go," I said.

"I'll let her go just as soon as I've sorted out this clusterfuck you've got going here," Jenny said shortly. She came closer, her gun up. Pointed at my father. I heard a soft *snick* as she released the safety. "I'm not going to say it again, Adam. Back off. Let her go."

My father continued to hold onto me, pulling me tighter. I didn't think he even knew he was doing it anymore. Pain roared. Grew teeth. Jenny took a step closer.

"Now, Adam."

Dad's hand relaxed just slightly around me. The pain

remained, like it had been carved into the bone.

He lowered his gun.

Let me go.

Without someone to hold me up, I fell to my knees. Diggs started to come toward me, but Jenny waved him off.

"She'll be fine," she said shortly. "Stay where you are. Adam, put your gun on the ground. Slide it toward me."

This time, he didn't hesitate. He crouched and set the gun in the mud. The memory card was there, too, in a little plastic baggy. I focused on that. Forced myself to my feet. I had the vague notion that I might somehow rally and grab the gun. And the memory card. And develop mad fighting skills and the healing powers of one of the X-Men, and take everyone down then and there.

I got as far as standing up.

Jenny got the gun and the memory card. I didn't know where Monty and Carl were. Or Jamie. Juarez had lowered his rifle at sight of the Giant with the gun trained on him, but he looked pissed as hell. Poised to attack.

But then, pretty much everyone did.

"So, how do we run this?" Diggs asked Jenny. "You take the card. You take Adam. You kill Kat. Are you killing us, too?"

Jenny frowned. She looked honestly annoyed. "I told you: We had a deal. The memory card for your lives. You lived up to your end of the bargain."

The Giant shifted. I caught Kat's eye. She looked... not scared, really. Resigned. Her hands were tied behind her back, one of the men beside her holding tight to her arm.

"Jenny," the Giant said.

"I know," she said. Quiet. He was in charge, not her. She went to him with the memory card. I saw her look at Cameron—just a sideways glance. Between the pain and my vantage point, I couldn't see much, but it seemed like something passed between them.

I tensed.

Jenny took another step. Diggs looked at me. "Wait," he mouthed to me. I nodded. I didn't see a lot of alternatives.

The Giant held out his giant hand.

Jenny set the memory card in it. Waited until his fingers closed over it.

Then, faster than my mind could even follow in the dim light, her gun came up.

She fired without taking the time to aim.

Without hesitation.

The air exploded in a hail of pink mist as the Giant hit the ground. Maybe a milli-second after, Cameron threw his elbow into his own captor's gut. His hands, bound as far as I'd known, were suddenly around the man's throat. Someone fired again. The man holding onto Kat went down. She backed away fast, headed for me. My father turned and started to run.

"Stop!" Juarez shouted. He fired a warning shot that barely missed Dad's head. My entire body went tight.

My father stopped, hands up.

Meanwhile, Jenny pried the memory card from the Giant's clenched fist. She still had her gun up. No one else was fighting, though—both men who'd been holding Kat and Cameron were now dead on the ground. Our entire party was still intact.

Relatively speaking.

I sank back to my knees, those grey edges closing in. Obliterating the picture around me.

Kat was the one who caught me. "Just relax," she said. "You're all right."

"I know. I'm fine," I agreed. When I put my hand to my stomach, it was wet. It wasn't from the rain, I knew. Somewhere far off I saw Cameron say something to Jenny. She nodded. I expected her to leave. Instead, she stayed where she was. Cameron came close.

"Is she all right?" he asked Kat.

"She will be," I said. All the third-person was starting to grate. Kat pushed my sopping hair back from my sopping head. "I'm glad you're all right," I said to her.

"You too," she said. She wiped at her eyes. Her hands were shaking. "Don't pull this shit again."

"No problem. This is the last time I save your life. You've got my word."

Cameron looked back at Jenny. She stayed rooted where she was.

"Katherine... Are you coming?" he asked.

Kat looked at me again, then focused on Diggs. "Infection's setting in. There's a doctor in Melbourne—Reggie Bergen. He'll take care of her. He won't ask questions. Find him, and tell him I sent you."

Kat got up. Diggs pulled her into a hug before she could resist. "Take care of yourselves," I heard her say.

"You too," Diggs said.

She pushed him away and wiped her eyes again. Cameron raised his eyebrows at her. She nodded.

When they ran away, disappearing into the jungle without a trace, no one tried to stop them. I just laid there, on the ground with Diggs beside me, staring at the sky. Everything sounded like it came from inside a tunnel.

Kat and Cameron had barely left the scene when Monty raced down the path toward us, shouting something. When he saw me lying on the ground, he faltered.

"What is it?" Juarez asked. He still had the gun on my father. I struggled to sit up and catch up to the rest of the scene, shifting my focus.

"Willett—he's on his way," Monty said. "And it looks like this Project may have reinforcements, too. We need to move."

When I looked around, I saw my father watching me. I

thought of Allie Tate. Had she known I was there, when she died? Had I tried to save her? I swallowed a fresh surge of fear. When I looked at my father, I saw something long past repair in his eyes.

"You're everything I ever wanted, baby. God saved me, when you came."

"We'll try to buy you some time," Juarez said to Diggs. "The plan's still the same: You run. You're not safe otherwise."

Using Diggs as a crutch, I forced myself to my feet. "And my father? What happens to him?"

"I'm taking him," Juarez said. His eyes were hard. Dad looked at me again. In the greenhouse on Payson Isle, he'd taught me about evergreens. Photosynthesis. The name of every constellation.

Now, he smiled at me. I realized he was crying.

"I'm sorry," he whispered.

"How much time do we have?" Juarez asked Monty.

"Not much," he said firmly. "They're headed our way. Maybe five, ten minutes. That's best case."

No one was even paying attention to my father, too busy mobilizing to get out of here. I couldn't take my eyes off him, though. The way he watched me. The way he wept.

Diggs took my arm, careful not to touch my side. "We have to go. Can you walk?"

My father took something from his pocket—something small.

It gleamed, silver in the moonlight. He took a step away from Juarez.

The world slowed. The grey receded. Everything came into crystal-clear focus, suddenly: the overhang of jungle above; the smell of soil and trees, life and death; the feel of Diggs' hand on my arm. The gun my father lifted to his head.

I pushed myself forward, forcing Diggs away from me.

Forcing everyone away.

"No!" I shouted. The word came out raw.

"Nothing happens the way we want it to, baby. Forget the dark spots. Live in the light."

I watched Dad swallow. Saw the way his face changed. He didn't say a word. The gun came up. I watched him turn his back.

I screamed.

The gun went off.

EPILOGUE
DIGGS

THE BEACH STRETCHED ON for miles in both directions: golden sand, strong surf, the sun just coming up on the horizon. A brunette, her hair pulled back in a ponytail, ran flat out across the sand—arms pumping, legs strong. She was lean, her body lithe and corded with muscle, her eyes focused straight ahead.

I felt a familiar pull, an ache that blew me sideways with its unexpected power. Nine months after her father shot himself in a remote Mexican jungle, the Solomon who shared my life and my bed seemed a different animal than the one I'd mentored in Littlehope more than a dozen years ago. She still smiled, she still laughed, she still drove me mad...

But now, there was a piece of her that I couldn't reach—a sorrow that she held locked up tight, refusing to let anyone near it. As though acknowledging that pain would make it bigger than she could manage.

When she was finished trying to outrun her demons, Solomon flopped down on the sand and stared out at the sea. I waited a few minutes, then went to her. I sat down just behind her. She leaned back against me, her back damp with sweat.

"Couldn't sleep?" I asked.

She shrugged.

It was two days till Christmas. We were living in a ramshackle cabin on the shore of northern Australia, though, so it was tough to tell.

"Maybe we could give Jamie a call," I said. "You're overdue for a chat with Einstein."

"We shouldn't risk it," she said. "Last time..."

Last time was three months ago. A day after our call, we got word from a friend that two suspicious-looking men were asking about us at the local airport. We were on the move again within the hour.

"If we're more careful, it might be okay," I said.

She shook her head. "No. It's all right. I thought we might try to reach Kat, though."

"Okay," I said, surprised. "Sure."

We didn't know where Kat was, but Cameron had left us with instructions for how to reach her when we hit Australia. It was an intricate process involving Craigslist and code words, and we'd only used it twice. The first time was when we'd first arrived here, when Solomon was still healing. Still so deeply in shock over what had happened to her father, I wasn't sure I'd ever get her back again. I was the one who reached out to Kat that time.

One phone call, which quickly escalated to a shouting match between the two women, was all it took to pull Solomon back from the edge.

The second time had been Sol's idea: A birthday call, for no other reason than to say hello. Kat had seemed as baffled as I was. Not displeased, necessarily... just baffled. During the call, she couldn't—or wouldn't—tell us if Cameron was with her, or why Jenny had suddenly turned on the Project that night in Mexico and saved us. That whole turn of events remained a mystery. She and her daughter talked about the weather, and Solomon's rapidly-healing wounds, and not much else.

Neither of them mentioned Adam.

Of course, Solomon never mentioned Adam, so that wasn't a huge surprise.

As far as I knew, she had only cried for her father once since his death—the night he pulled the trigger, grief spilling from her like life blood as she breathed air into his lungs, pumped his chest, desperate to save a man long past salvation. If she cried about her father after that black night in Mexico, she kept those tears to herself.

On the other hand, she welled up over her damned dog every day. Every puppy we passed, every stray, every hound on a greeting card or a magazine ad, earned a second glance. The other day she'd gotten teary about a fucking dingo.

I kissed her neck, tasting the salt of the sea and the sweetness of her skin. Wrapped my arms around her.

"I think it's time," she said.

I knew she could feel me tense against her. She waited for my response, letting me come to it on my own. Over the years, Solomon and I have had some legendary battles. In the past nine months, however, we'd gotten along remarkably well for being together twenty-four/seven. This was the only thing we fought about now.

"I never said I was doing this forever," she said. She twined her hand with mine, resting on her flat stomach. "I needed to regroup. But you agreed—we're not letting them get away with what they did. I can't."

I could tell she was expecting a repeat of the same argument we'd been having since Mexico. Instead, I nodded, ignoring the fear rising in my chest.

"Just tell me when and where. I'll make the arrangements."

She twisted in my arms. "Thank you," she said. She pressed her lips to mine. "When this is over..."

I didn't say anything, waiting for her to finish the thought. We hadn't talked much about the future since leaving Mexico. We hadn't talked much about the past, either. In fact, for two people rarely at a loss for words in the real world, Solomon and I had been damned quiet for the past nine months. We kept to ourselves, avoiding the locals, living off the money Cameron had provided and the occasional odd job wherever we landed. I taught her to surf. We caught up on our reading. We made love with an intensity I'd never experienced before—as though infusing every kiss, every caress, with all the love and fear and pain neither of us could voice.

The reprieve was what we'd both needed, while we healed from the hell of that first year pursuing her father's secrets. But now, she was right: It was time to go back. I would never get back the woman I'd fallen in love with, if we didn't.

"When this is over...?" I prompted, when she didn't finish the thought.

"I don't know," she admitted. "I don't think I'll know anything, I don't think I'll start believing in tomorrow, until we put them down, though."

I turned her around fully and pulled her down with me into the sand. Her body was warm, strong, whole on top of mine. We both still had scars, but they were healing. Some faster than others.

I twined my fingers in her ponytail and pulled her to me, touching my lips to hers again.

"Well, then let's put them down," I said. "I'd like to start believing in tomorrow, for a change."

Looking for more Erin Solomon?

Turn the page for a free excerpt from
the next novel in the critically acclaimed series,

THE BOOK OF J.

1

WITH ONLY SLIGHT VARIATIONS, the dream remains the same: A Maine forest deep in the night, rain pouring down. I stand in the shadow of a pyramid that shouldn't be here—an ancient ruin that dwarfs the tall evergreens around me.

My father stands at the foot of the pyramid. His lips are moving, but I can't hear a word he says. He has a gun in his hand. Around him, there are bodies—dozens of them. People I knew from the Payson Church, burned but still recognizable. A woman who used to do the baking for the church sits on the ground, crying. Half the flesh of her face is burned away, one eye socket empty. Joe Ashmont is there. Matt Perkins, wailing like a lunatic. Max Richards. Bonnie Saucier, a bloody J. carved into her pale, naked breast. Everyone is dead—there's no question of that, but they are more real, more animated, than any live thing I've ever seen.

"Is this what you wanted?" my father asks me. He's younger than he was in that jungle in Coba—about the age I remember him from my childhood. The age I am now. "You did this. Is it what you wanted?"

My father raises the gun. I try to get up, but those masses—the writhing, rotting dead—are coming for me. I'm frozen. Terrified. My father points the gun.

The barrel touches his temple.

An instant before the gun went off, something shattered beside me. I sat bolt upright in bed, my heart galloping. A gust of icy wind blew into the dark room and sent the curtains flying. I tried to figure out where my father was. Where the bodies were...

Where the hell I was.

I reached for Diggs beside me. His spot was empty.

A wriggling mass of fuzzy curls tried to escape my grasp. Einstein.

"Easy, buddy," I said. The sound of my own voice eased me back toward the real world.

I was in the Payson boarding home, I reminded myself. Shards of glass, strewn across the floor from a broken window behind me, sparkled in the moonlight. I could make out peeling wallpaper and ancient furniture. Einstein whined, still trying to get away from me. After nine months without him, I wasn't keen to let the mutt go—forget the fact that his paws would be cut to ribbons if I did. As would mine.

"Diggs!" I shouted. No answer.

I reached for a battery-powered lantern on the nightstand, and turned it on. It did little but cast eerie shadows. I hung my legs over the side of the bed, mindful of the evil dead that could be lurking underneath, waiting to grab my ankles and devour my toes. While I searched for my slippers with one hand, I held tight to Einstein's collar with the other.

My first coherent thought was that J.—the organization that Diggs and I had been running from for the past several months—had found us. We'd been stateside for twenty-four hours, maybe less, though, and we'd been careful. Unless they were psychic, I couldn't see how the hell they could have found us.

Jesus, I really hoped they weren't psychic.

I finally found my slippers, shoved my feet inside, and sat up. I was gradually getting acclimated to the real world again—the one without ghosts and zombies and my father, all casting blame.

My eyes settled on the rotting doorframe, my heart still pounding too hard...

In an instant, reality fell away all over again.

A dark-haired girl, no more than nine, stood at the door. She wore glasses. The left lens was broken.

"How many lies do you believe?" she said in a whisper—the tone Allie Tate, my childhood best friend, had always used when we were talking about something important.

The problem was that Allie Tate, like so many others from Payson Isle, had been dead for twenty-five years. My mind blurred. Was I still dreaming? The wind howled and the curtains blew; Diggs remained missing. My father was nowhere to be seen.

Allie stayed where she was.

Which meant she was either a ghost, or I was losing my mind. I voted for the latter. Panic rose and bloomed in my chest. Outside the room, something crashed into the door. Allie didn't budge.

"You're dead," I whispered back.

She didn't say anything. Behind the broken eyeglass lens, blood ran from her left eyebrow. She wore a pink dress that was torn in the front.

"How many lies?" she said again.

The door burst open. Einstein flew from my arms and scooted out of the room. Allie vanished.

Diggs stood in the doorway in jeans and a jersey, breathing hard. He looked as terrified as I felt. "Are you all right? What the hell happened?"

●

Fifteen minutes later, I sat at a picnic table in the old Payson meeting room. A fire was raging in the fireplace, but it didn't do much to warm the cavernous room. The walls had been stripped of the artwork members of the Payson Church had done—no more satin crosses or faded paintings of Jesus and his flock; no sign of the terrifying artwork Reverend Isaac Payson himself had done of Christ, crucifixions, and burning Romans. Nothing had been put up in their place, however.

I'd signed Payson Isle over to Jamie Flint before Diggs and I left the States nine months before, and Jamie had definitely left her mark on a good part of the island since relocating her business there. She trained search-and-rescue dogs—reputedly some of the best in the world—and ran a search-and-rescue business of her own, which meant the island was now home to kennels and training grounds, dog runs and dog trails. She may have been using the rest of the land well, but I got the sense Jamie didn't know what the hell to do with the Payson House.

Diggs returned bearing antiseptic and cotton balls, interrupting my thoughts. He still looked freaked out. Personally, I had yet to stop shaking.

"You okay?" he asked for the tenth time.

"Yeah. I think so."

He dabbed at a cut at my temple I hadn't even realized I'd gotten. "It was probably just a gust that tore a tree limb off. Jamie said the wind's been bad out here this winter. I'm sure it was nothing."

"Probably so," I agreed. I stared into the flames. *How many lies do you believe?*

"Hey," Diggs said after a second or two. He tipped my chin up so I looked him in the eye. "We can leave if you want. Catch the first plane out, and go back where women glow and men plunder. Just say the word."

We'd been over this before—a few times, actually. "No," I said. "We're here for a reason. I'm not going back now, just because of a little wind and a ghostly apparition."

He raised his eyebrows at me. It seemed impossible that seventy-two hours ago we'd been in Australia, both of us sun-kissed and moderately relaxed. What the hell had I been thinking?

"I'm sorry, a what?" he said.

"Forget it. It was a joke." He frowned. "Okay, not my best material. I'm bleeding from the head here—cut me some slack. Are Monty and Carl checking the island? What the hell time is it, anyway? Our first night here, and I'm already getting people out of bed in the middle of the deep dark."

He smiled at me inexplicably. "I think they'll get over it. It's not really that deep dark."

"What do you mean? What the hell time is it?'

"Six." I stared at him, still confused. "At night."

We'd taken off from the Albany Airport in Western Australia at ten till seven p.m. on December 26, and from there were scheduled to get into Portland, Maine, at just past eleven p.m. on the 27th. Four layovers and three flight delays later, we landed in Portland at seven a.m. this morning—the 28th. By the time we got a rental and drove the two hours to Littlehope, then hopped a boat for the hour-long ride out to Payson Isle, it was almost noon. We had barely managed a coherent hello to Jamie before Diggs and I both passed out in the room she had waiting for us.

"I thought it was later," I said. "Or earlier."

"It'll take a day or two to get re-acclimated," Diggs said. "You'll get there."

Diggs didn't look like he needed any time at all to get re-acclimated; the man thrives on long hours in planes, trains, and lobster boats. He'd trimmed his hair and shaved his beard in order to fit the fake ID Cameron had given us, but he still looked good. I'd had to dye my hair brown again—which I'm not a fan of. All things considered, he'd definitely fared the trip better than me so far.

"Right. You never answered my question—where are Monty and Carl?"

"They're just taking a look around, to make sure we've got nothing to worry about. They'll be back shortly." The idea of the two men out there alone didn't sit well with me, even if it was only six at night. And the window had broken because of the wind. And the creepy ghost girl was all in my head—obviously. I saw the look on Diggs' face at my uneasiness.

"I'm fine," I said before he could press it.

"You're shaking and white and you look like you're about to toss your cookies on my favorite t-shirt. You're not fine. What's going on?"

"You mean besides the bedroom window exploding all over me while I was dead asleep?"

I could tell he knew I was deflecting, but a second later Monty burst through the door, and that put an end to the conversation for the moment.

"No one on the island but us," he said. "Must've been the wind, princess. It blows like a whore at Mardi Gras out here most nights."

"So I've heard," I said. "About the wind...not the Mardi Gras whores."

"Strictly going by word of mouth, you understand," he said. He winked at me.

Monty worked for Jamie Flint. He was southern, about five foot eight, with dark, burnished skin and the body of a man who clearly knew his way around the gym. The first time we'd met was during that whole horrific chain of events that led to my father's death in Coba the winter before. Despite the circumstances, I'd liked him immediately. Diggs wasn't quite so keen on him, but I think that mostly had to do with how quick Monty was with a double entendre—and the fact that many of those double entendres seemed to revolve around me. Personally, I thought it was kind of cute.

Carl came through the door next, closing it quickly behind him to shut out the elements. Carl was taller, thinner, darker, and much, much quieter than Monty. Originally from Nigeria, he had enough of an accent that I had to focus to understand him, but there was something about his wide, dark eyes that made me think of that phrase, 'Still waters run deep.' Right now, that stillness was reassuring.

"We didn't see anything, but it appears the winds are quite still, for now," he said, his words clipped and precise. "Seas will be high and the winds gusting for the next two days, until the storm hits. But I don't believe we're seeing that effect yet."

"All it would've taken was a good stiff wind, though," Monty said. "Half the trees out here have dead wood we'll need to trim once spring comes. I'm sure that's all it was."

"Right," I said. "Thanks for checking, though."

"Do they know yet when the storm's supposed to get here?" Diggs said.

"Too early to say," Monty said. "It's been a cold goddamn winter, but this'll be the first major snow. Whole state is on the alert. I thought you Mainers were supposed to be tougher than this."

"It's just because it's the first one of the season," I said. "Give it another couple of storms, and nobody will think twice. They're still saying New Year's Eve?"

"That's when it should be worst," Monty agreed.

Of course.

Jamie came down the stairs next, a graying German shepherd by her side. Jamie was blond and lean, with a dancer's body, a pierced nose, and a faint Georgian accent that just added to the charm. As usual, she seemed totally Zen about the mayhem I'd brought to her door.

"It's all set up there," she said. She joined us at the table. Einstein greeted the shepherd—Phantom was her name—with enthusiasm that Phantom didn't really return before both dogs settled in front of the fire. "If you want to switch bedrooms, though, it's no problem. There's another one made up farther down the hall."

I did some mental calculations. The room Diggs and I had been sleeping in was my old bedroom—the room the other young girls in the Payson Church had shared when I was a kid. Which made the room Jamie was talking about most likely the one where my father used to lay his weary head.

"That's all right," I said. Like my father didn't already haunt me enough these days. "The one we're in is fine. I think I'm done with sleep for now, anyway." I looked at Diggs for confirmation, not sure whether our plans had changed while I'd been in Dreamland. "You still want to head for Littlehope before it gets any later?"

"You two are still fugitives, right?" Monty asked. "I mean, that hasn't changed in the last few minutes. You really think heading out into the world is the best idea right now?"

"That's why we waited till dark," I said. Diggs and I had been on the run from both the FBI and the fine folks with Project J. ever since we'd left on a wing and a prayer last April. The Feds wanted us for questioning, ostensibly on suspicion of consorting with terrorists since shit tended to blow up at an alarming rate around us. J. just wanted us dead. "We'll go into town, do what needs doing, and be back later tonight."

"That actually brings up a good point," Jamie said. "I know this is your island, so obviously you're free to come and go as you please, but I'd love to know just exactly what brought you two back now."

"A, it's your island now—I gave it to you," I began. "And B… Diggs and I aren't ready to share B with you yet. We just need a place to rest our heads that's out of sight—otherwise, you're out of this."

"But—" Monty began.

"That's nonnegotiable," Diggs said. "We're just gathering information. If we have any reason to think things will get dangerous, we'll let you know."

Monty put up a little more of a stink, but Jamie and Carl seemed content with our lack of an explanation. Jamie's son, Bear, came in a minute later and effectively ended the whole debate. He had a white pit bull with him. Phantom couldn't have cared less who was around as long as Jamie was there, but the pit bull greeted Einstein like they'd been separated for years instead of just a few hours.

"I got the dogs in for the night," Bear said. He was seventeen, with short dark hair and a big, sturdy build.

He didn't talk much, but there was something about Bear that made me think he knew things—Deep Things. Dark Things. The kind of kid who probably got a lot of shit from the guys in his class, while the girls were lined up ten deep. "Is everything straightened out here?"

"It is," I said. "The consensus is that it was just the wind. Sorry if I disrupted the routine."

"No disruption," he said. He looked at me strangely, a little too intent. When he realized I'd caught on, he shifted his gaze. "We would've been wrapping up soon anyway. Dinner almost up?" He directed the question at Carl, who nodded.

"I was waiting for everything to settle," Carl said. "It won't be long. Urenna is in the kitchen, if you would like to help her." He said the name like he was saying a prayer—Er-Renna, a smile coming to his lips with the name.

I saw a hint of a blush before Bear nodded and excused himself. Whoever Urenna was, my guess was that she'd inspired those pink cheeks. The kid headed for the kitchen with both my mutt and the pit bull on his heels. Phantom didn't move from her place by the fire.

"You will stay for dinner?" Carl said. "You must be hungry."

I was starved, actually. As much as I wanted to get started on the nightmare Diggs and I were about to take on in Littlehope, I figured sustenance before the fact would be a good idea. Sustenance, and a shower, not necessarily in that order. Then we could set out to save the world. Even superheroes have to keep their priorities straight.

"That sounds good," I said. "Thanks. Though before I break bread, if there's any chance I could scrub some of this travel dirt off me, I think we'd all be a little happier."

"Diggs knows where the showers are," Jamie said. She and Diggs shared a secret smile I wasn't crazy about. "He can show you."

Diggs grinned back at her. Cute. "I'll tell you now though, kid," he said to me. "You're not gonna like it."

Sun showers are open air showers using rainwater warmed by the sun. In Australia, Diggs and I used to take them all the time. They're great: good for the environment and the wallet, they're the perfect way to wash the salt off or cool down after a long day. As I said—they're great in Australia. Taking a sun shower in Maine in December is the kind of thing they'd come up with at Guantanamo Bay.

A half-moon hung overhead, the stars still not quite visible in the early evening sky. A wooden partition staked into the frozen ground was the only thing that protected me from the prying eyes of the world around. I stripped naked, pulled a string, and screamed when ice-cold water rained down on me.

"Told you it was cold," Diggs said from the other side of the partition. I let loose with an impressive litany of expletives while I lathered up and rinsed off, my teeth chattering, nipples tighter than pebbles, goose bumps on my goose bumps.

He came round the wooden partition with a fluffy towel and wrapped it around me while I shivered. "Refreshing, right?" he said.

"Fuck you," I said. "Why would anyone do that to themselves?"

He rubbed the towel up and down my arms while I pulled a clean pair of underpants, long johns, and jeans up my still-damp legs. Diggs eyed my frozen, naked breasts for just a second before I shot him a withering glare and grabbed a clean sweatshirt—one of his, of course—from the pile.

"Sex in the freezing cold isn't sexy," I said.

"I'm not arguing," he said. "It's not great for the ego, either. Shrinkage is too much of a factor."

He took the sweatshirt from me and pulled it over my head. He kept hold of the fabric afterward and pulled me closer. I looked up at him.

"We should go in," I said.

"We will."

Instead, he leaned down and kissed me. His mouth tasted like cinnamon and ice water—in a good way—but my hair was literally freezing and I was still shivering. I kissed him back anyway. It's easy to forget the elements when you lock lips with a man like Diggs.

"I don't like this business where I can't just ravage you whenever I feel like it," he said when we parted. I tried to come up with a pithy response, but my brain was partially frozen. He laughed. "All right, come on. Back inside. You want me to carry you?"

"I think I'll make it." We started back to the house. With Diggs' hand in mine, I scanned the night in search of Allie Tate or Mitch Cameron or any of the nameless, faceless monsters who wanted Diggs and me dead. All I saw were trees, frozen ground, and darkness.

"Have you heard anything from Juarez yet?" Diggs asked me when we were almost to the front doorstep.

"No. He's still MIA. I asked Jamie earlier—she hasn't heard any word, either."

Diggs squeezed my hand. "I don't like it. If we're doing this, I'd feel a lot better about it if he was with us."

"I'll keep trying," I said.

We hadn't heard from Jack Juarez for about four months, when we risked a phone call from Tasmania because we'd heard through the grapevine that he wasn't doing so well. According to our sources, he'd been suspended from the FBI after the whole shit-storm in Mexico, and was getting more and more obsessed with unlocking memories of his childhood that he was convinced would lead him to the men who'd murdered his wife six years ago.

The fact that Jack had fallen completely off the radar since then had been keeping both Diggs and me up at night, worrying about what could have happened.

Diggs stopped walking a few feet from the front door. The walk and the six layers of clothes were starting to work their magic, and I'd warmed up marginally; I could even feel my toes. I looked at Diggs.

"Why are we not moving?"

"I just want to make sure you're sure," he said. "Because if we start doing this tonight…"

"I know," I said. "J. could find out. They could find us. But I can't sit back anymore—we've talked about this."

"We talked about it when we were ten thousand miles from all this shit. It's different when we're just a boat ride away from possible catastrophe."

"I told you, I can do it alone." That earned a glare. Diggs isn't a big fan of that argument. "I'm not saying that to guilt you into something—you know that. But I can't let any more time pass, knowing J. is out there. That they're continuing to kill, and I'm not doing a damned thing about it."

The number of times we'd had the exact same argument must have been approaching triple digits. Diggs looked as tired of it as I was. He nodded.

"Yeah, I know. I just wanted to make sure you hadn't

changed your mind. If that's the case, let's grab some grub and get to work." He draped his arm around my shoulders and drew me closer. "You'll give me a shout if you come to your senses?"

"You'll be the first to know."

Having dinner with Jamie and her clan, I couldn't shake the feeling that we were suiting up for some kind of cable reality show. In addition to Monty, Carl, Jamie, Bear, and the dogs, we had Urenna—Carl's daughter, a gorgeous, dark-skinned teen probably close to Bear's age, with a quick smile and intelligent eyes,—Diggs and me, and three heavily tattooed women who worked with the dogs. I recognized one of them—Cheyenne—from the year before, but the others weren't familiar.

We sat around the picnic tables with the fire roaring, the smell of Indian spices thick in the air as Carl and Urenna served up some kind of potato vegetarian thing and a thick lamb stew that tasted better than pretty much anything I'd tasted in the past nine months. The dogs sprawled in front of the fire while the crew debriefed their day. There was a lot of laughter mixed in with talk of the business and the dogs and the dog business. Before long, I found myself drifting.

I thought of Allie again, and tried to remember community dinners with my father and other members of the Payson Church. We would have sat right here for a lot of those dinners. There would have been a prayer to kick things off—Isaac Payson at the head of the table, our heads bowed. *Close your eyes,* Allie hissed at me. *He'll catch you otherwise.* I jerked my head up sharply at the voice—one real enough that it could have come from anyone seated at the table around me. Allie was nowhere to be found, though.

I realized Bear was watching me with the intensity of a serial creeper. He looked away when our eyes met.

I tried to get back to my memories of the Payson Church. Everything surrounding my childhood was hazy—especially anything having to do with Allie. We'd been best friends growing up. It was only last year that I'd remembered the truth about her death, or at least flashes of it. Allie had died a couple of years before the Payson fire, killed by Isaac himself. Or at least that's what I thought had happened—the whole incident was fractured, coming to me in fits and starts that sometimes made no sense at all. The only things I knew for sure were that Allie hadn't died in the fire, Isaac had been responsible for her death, and my father had used some kind of J.-created psychological warfare to erase the memory from my mind—the way he'd apparently erased anything else that might have been deemed disturbing about Isaac Payson and the congregation he led out here.

"Solomon," Diggs said.

I looked up, snapping back to reality again. "Yeah— sorry. Daydreaming…"

"We should probably get going."

"Right." Only Jamie, Bear, Carl, and Urenna remained at the table with Diggs and me. "Do you need help with cleanup?" I asked them. "Diggs slings a dishcloth like a pro."

"That's all right," Urenna said. Unlike her father, she had no accent. "Bear and I can do it." She looked at Bear. "Right?"

"Sure, no problem," he agreed. I got the feeling she could have suggested they dip themselves in honey and roll in a nest of fire ants and he would have had the same response. They got up. Urenna took a few dishes; Bear took a few more. On his way into the kitchen, though, I sensed him watching me again.

When he came back for the last of the dishes a minute later, Carl, Jamie, and Diggs were talking. Bear came round to my side of the table. I handed him my plate. He hesitated before he took it.

"She won't hurt you, you know," he said.

That cold chill I'd felt earlier came gusting back. "Who won't?"

He just smiled at that. "You don't have to worry about her. Whoever blew out that window, it wasn't the girl."

The others at the table had fallen silent. Diggs looked at me curiously.

"Go on in and help Urenna, please," Jamie said to Bear. I wasn't sure whether there was a warning in her voice or I was hearing things. And seeing things—apparently, things that Bear also heard and saw. This just got better and better.

Diggs continued to watch me after Bear was gone. "What was that about?"

"Uh…nothing, really," I said. I shook my head and forced some certainty into my quaking voice. "Seriously, it was nothing." I got up from the table. "We should really get going before it gets any later."

"Right," Diggs said, still watching. Still wary. I went upstairs to grab my gear and hoped to God I didn't run into any other ghostly visions along the way.

More Erin Solomon Mysteries

In Between Days
Diggs & Solomon Shorts
1990 - 2000

Midnight Lullaby
Prequel to
The Erin Solomon Mysteries

The Payson Pentalogy
The Critically Acclaimed 5-Book Set
Readers Can't Put Down!

Book I: All the Blue-Eyed Angels
Book II: Sins of the Father
Book III: BEFORE THE AFTER
Book IV: Before the After
Book V: The Book of J

And the First Novel in the Jamie Flint K-9 Search and Rescue Series

The Darkest Thread

ABOUT THE AUTHOR

Jen Blood is a freelance journalist and author of the bestselling Erin Solomon mystery series. She is also owner of Adian Editing, providing expert editing of plot-driven fiction for authors around the world. Jen holds an MFA in Creative Writing/Popular Fiction, with influences ranging from Emily Bronte to Joss Whedon and the whole spectrum in between. Today, Jen lives in Maine with her dog Killian, where the two are busy conquering snowbanks and penning the next mystery.

Made in the USA
Middletown, DE
14 January 2018